UNRIVALED

UNRIVALED

a novel

SIRI MITCHELL

BETHANYHOUSE

a division of Baker Publishing Group
Minneapolis, Minnesota

© 2013 by Siri L. Mitchell

Published by Bethany House Publishers
11400 Hampshire Avenue South
Bloomington, Minnesota 55438
www.bethanyhouse.com

Bethany House Publishers is a division of
Baker Publishing Group, Grand Rapids, Michigan

Printed in the United States of America

Library of Congress Cataloging-in-Publication Data
Mitchell, Siri L.
    Unrivaled / Siri Mitchell.
      pages cm
    ISBN 978-0-7642-0797-6 (pbk.)
      1. Candy industry—Fiction. 2. Saint Louis (Mo.)—History—20th century—
Fiction. 3. Christian fiction. 4. Love stories. I. Title.
PS3613.I866U57 2013
813'.6—dc23   201204035

This is a work of historical reconstruction; the appearances of certain historical figures
are therefore inevitable. All other characters, however, are products of the author's
imagination, and any resemblance to actual persons, living or dead, is coincidental.

The internet addresses, email addresses, and phone numbers in this book are accurate
at the time of publication. They are provided as a resource. Baker Publishing Group
does not endorse them or vouch for their content or permanence.

Cover design by Jennifer Parker

Photography by Mike Habermann Photography, LLC

13 14 15 16 17 18 19   7 6 5 4 3 2 1

To my sweet.

1  *Lucy*

Soon, soon, soon. My thoughts kept tempo with the horses' hooves. It was all I could do not to stare as the carriage passed the sites of my beloved St. Louis: the brown brick Cave Ballroom; the tall Morgens Brothers Building with its deep bay windows; Ford Motor Company. And all the shoe and boot stores lining the district. If I looked out the other side of the carriage, I knew I would see the St. Louis Club.

An advertisement for Royal Taffy candy caught my attention. *Give the Queen of Your Heart a Royal Gift.* The brazen red of its oblong wrapper was echoed in the border of the poster. It was the third of its kind that I had seen on our journey down Olive Street. I wondered how many more of them had been put up around the city. And I wondered, too, why I hadn't seen any for my father's candy, Fancy Crunch.

The carriage lurched to a stop again. My, but there were

7

so many more automobiles on the streets than there had been when I'd left for Europe. And it had only been a little over a year! Such a bother they were.

And it was so hot! I'd forgotten about Missouri's humidity. Though it had been made in the new open style, my white silk collar was sticking to my neck, and I suspected my Denmark blue blouse-waist was already damp at the back. I shifted forward on the seat as the streetcars and automobiles sailed past us, reminding me of all the ships I had seen on the Mediterranean.

Awnings shaded shop windows while men and women hurried up and down the street. I noted how tall all the buildings were. Pride bloomed in my breast: Even Europe with all her splendors had nothing to rival my native city.

I had worried that I would find my home too dull and provincial, that it would be diminished by the grandeur of all the things I had seen and the places I had visited on the Continent. To the contrary! Dear, sweet home. I wanted to embrace it all, every piece of it. There were dozens of things I couldn't wait to do. And there were a hundred things I wanted to tell of: eating linzer torte in Austria; viewing glaciers in Switzerland; drinking coffee at the cafés in Italy.

Soon, soon, soon.

I'd voyaged halfway around the world, but this last journey from Union Station to my house was interminable.

Glancing down at the newspaper I'd twisted between my hands, I determined to at least look as if I were patiently waiting. It was a discarded copy of the *Chicago Tribune* someone had left on the train. A headline in bold type declared *Suspect in South Side Murder Arrested*. The article went on to explain beneath: *A twenty-two-year-old member of one of the South Side's notorious athletic clubs was arrested for the murder of Micky Callahan*. How gruesome! My eyes strayed from the article to the face of the hardened criminal, which stared back at me with beady eyes. It was enough to make me shudder. I hoped they kept him in that jail for a very long time! I folded it up and laid my hands atop it.

Seated on the bench across from me, my aunt and uncle exchanged a glance. I'd grown used to such glances on the Continent. But more than that, I had grown used to their exchange of tender gestures. I could only hope that I would someday find myself in a marriage as loving as theirs.

Four blocks more.

Three blocks more.

Oh!—there it was. The gracefully curving, columned gate that guarded Vandeventer Place from the world outside it. I knew every twist of the metal flowers that scrolled up the ironwork. The carriage left off its jarring bounce as it glided onto the smooth granite flagstones that lined the threshold of the gate. My heart thrilled to hear the splash of the fountain beyond, and tears pricked my eyes at the sight of the statue that topped it. Leda and her swan. And—look! Old Mr. Carleton was still sitting in that same wicker chair on his porch, supervising the pruning of his roses. I could not help but grin and wave my handkerchief at him.

"Perhaps you should settle yourself more fully on the seat, my dear." Though her words were corrective, my aunt smiled as she said them. She had often helped to guide my behavior while we were in Europe. But she was right. Perhaps I should sit back. I wouldn't want Father and Mother to think that my manners had suffered in Europe while I was gone.

I could not wait to see them!

Though . . . the thought of my father brought with it a pang of guilt. I'd been allowed to accompany my aunt and uncle on their tour in the hopes that it would turn me into a lady. A lady didn't succumb to enthusiasms, and she didn't go about waving handkerchiefs, and most of all, she did not join her father in his business.

Not even when the best and happiest parts of her childhood had been spent with him by a stove, as they created new candies, anticipating the glorious success of his efforts.

How long we'd been waiting for that success.

But now I'd been to Europe. I'd seen her delights. And I had also tasted of her many sweets. In doing so, my resolve to join him in the business had only hardened, and I'd concocted a plan. I was going to share with him all that I had discovered. I'd collected labels from candy boxes and wrappers to paste into my scrapbook to show him. And I'd saved some samples for him as well. Perhaps that's what I would do first: Let him taste my treasures. And then I'd talk to him about adding a new line of candies to City Confectionery's offerings: Premium European Sweets. "How many new candies do you think Father created while I was gone?"

"Well . . ." My aunt's glance veered away from mine and a frown tugged at the corners of her mouth. "I don't know . . . but . . . Lucy, dear? There's something I think you should know." She looked again at my uncle.

There it was at the end of the street: my own dear house. The one Grandfather had built, with its gabled roofline and porticoed entry. It took all the strength I had to restrain myself from leaping out and dashing up the steps.

"Lucy!"

I wrenched my shoulders back and put up a hand to adjust my new straw picture hat. I felt the mound of white ostrich feathers atop it sway as I looked down and folded my gloved hands once more atop my lap. "Yes, Auntie?"

"There's something that . . . well . . ."

My uncle cleared his throat. "Something's happened to your father."

That last block took an eternity to travel. The coachman must have helped me down from the carriage because all of a sudden I was inside, back in my own front hall, and I was being enfolded in my mother's arms. "Papa——?"

"He's resting."

"Can I see him?"

"Not right now. Let him sleep. Perhaps tomorrow . . ."

I could see the old, familiar hallstand and smell the yeasty scent of Mrs. Hughes' dinner rolls. But I could neither hear my father's quick steps, nor was I enveloped by the warmth of his embrace. Though my palms had been sweating in my new kid gloves just a moment before, my hands were now as chill as ice. I gathered my skirt and put a foot to the front stair. "I would only look in on him. He wouldn't hear me; I wouldn't wake him."

My aunt put an arm to my shoulders and drew me away with her to the parlor. "Be assured your father's making progress. His condition is stable."

Why wasn't anyone doing anything? How could they be so calm? "But——what happened?"

"He had an attack. Of the heart."

I slipped from my aunt and accepted my mother's embrace once again. She ducked beneath the brim of my hat and kissed my cheek. "He hasn't grown any worse. And we must remember: It's only been three months."

Three months! But that meant . . . I thought back to where I had been in June. I'd been sketching the Bernese Alps and floating in a boat on Lake Thun in Switzerland. "Someone should have told me!"

Mother adjusted my hat. "We didn't want to worry you. And besides, there's nothing you could have done."

Aunt Margaret patted my arm and then took me by the hand and drew me further into the room.

I gasped in astonishment. It had been redone. Gone were the gleaming molasses-brown woodwork and the cherry-red wallpaper. The trim was now creamy white and the walls . . . they were the most peculiar shade of light green. It looked so . . . plain. And pale. "Why did you paint it?"

Mother blinked and glanced around the room. "I find it rather pretty. And painted trim doesn't have to be polished. It's saved so much time I was able to dismiss one of the maids."

She'd dismissed one of the maids? "Who?"

My aunt had continued speaking. "And don't you remember, Lucy? Just then we were in Interlaken. We would have had to go back into France and try to book passage. It would have been much too tedious to attempt."

They hadn't told me because it would have been an inconvenience?

She gave my arm a squeeze. "It would have spoiled the trip for you. It would have diverted your energies for no good purpose."

Spoiled the trip? Diverted my energies? For no good purpose? "I am not a child!" I blinked back the tears that had begun to blur my vision at the edges. "I am not a child, and I would have appreciated knowing."

"Come, now." Mother pulled me to the divan, and we sat upon it, springs protesting, as Mrs. Hughes came in with a tea tray. My mother poured, handing cups to my aunt and uncle and then to me. After she poured her own cup, she left it on the saucer. "Tell me about your trip. I've been longing to hear. Tell me everything."

My mother might have intended the words to be encouraging, but they belied the anxiety in her eyes. I couldn't reconcile the mother I'd left behind with the woman who sat before me, with the gray that had spread like a stain through her hair or the disheveled apron she wore over her shirtwaist and skirt. She looked embattled, weary, and worn.

Aunt Margaret and Uncle Fred sat in matching armchairs across from us. Everyone was looking at me, as if they couldn't wait to hear what I would say, but all of the excitement and the joy of the trip had gone. How could I have toured countless art museums? How could I have laughed at the antics of the guignol puppets in the Tuileries Gardens? How could I have enjoyed myself at all when Papa's heart had failed him?

I took a sip of tea, then set the cup back down on its saucer. "I don't—I'm not quite sure . . . where to start . . ."

My aunt put her own teacup down and smiled, brow lifted, the way she had done when I had ordered squid in a restaurant in Athens. I hadn't known it would come with all those legs and tiny tentacles attached. "Perhaps I can begin and give you a chance to collect your thoughts."

Yes. That's what I needed. A chance to collect my thoughts.

She told Mother about Munich and Florence. And about the new mountain railway up the Jungfrau. And then they talked about when exactly she and Uncle would continue their journey on to their own home in Denver.

Aunt broke off suddenly and smiled at me. "You must be feeling tired, my dear, but why don't you tell your mother about our visit to the dressmaker's in Paris."

My mother.

Suddenly the whole trip seemed so misguided, so cruel. How had my mother felt when Father had his heart attack, knowing I was halfway across the world, traipsing around in blissful ignorance? What right had I to enjoy myself while she was here, facing my father's illness alone? "I'm sorry. I think—I'm going to need just one more moment." I rose and left the room. It took all my effort not to run from it. I went upstairs, one step at a time, never once breaking my pace.

In my room, I took off my hat. Not being able to find my hatpin holder, I pushed the pins back into the brim. I drew off my gloves, one at a time, folding them up just like the glover in Florence had shown me. And then I threw myself upon my bed and wept like the child I had just about managed to convince myself I no longer was.

2 — Charlie

"Charlie Clarke!" I could hear the jail guard banging his billy club against the bars of cell doors as he walked down the long hall. His footsteps echoed as they struck the floor.

I fisted my hand around a bar. "Here. I'm right here." Least I was last time I checked: sitting in a cell on the South Side of Chicago. I wished I could say it wasn't a familiar place.

The footsteps came to a halt as the guard peered through the bars at me. He fished a key from his pocket and fumbled with the lock. "You're wanted."

I already knew that. It's why I'd been arrested. I'd been wanted for Micky Callahan's murder, which is something I had taken no part in. But the cops didn't care. I belonged to the same athletic club as Manny White, who *had* taken part in it, who had planned it even, and that was good enough for them. I knew they wouldn't be able to prove I'd done it and eventually Manny would get me out. I just hadn't figured it would be this soon.

I pulled my suspenders up over my shoulders and put my derby on. Taking up my coat, I pulled my rubber collar from the pocket and buttoned it into place.

The cop swung the door open and beat against it with his club. "You coming? Or would you rather stay?"

"I'm coming." Manny was particular as to grooming. It wouldn't do to show up with my collar undone. My shoes could use a shine, but hopefully he'd understand. After all, I'd done him a favor. I'd let myself get caught so he could escape.

I whistled "Bill Bailey" as I followed the cop. But my good cheer withered the moment the guard opened the door at the end of the hall. That's when I saw Honest Andy.

His enormous frame was folded into one of those wobbly jailhouse chairs, and he was staring across the long, scarred wooden table at me. He sent a glance beyond me to the guard. "I'll take care of him now, Gordy."

The guard nodded and left. I had half a mind to chase him down and beg him to put me back in the cell, but I was twenty-two and long past the age for begging. A flash of my dimpled smile usually got me what I wanted. That, or a well-placed fist.

Honest Andy gestured toward the chair that sat empty across the table from him.

"I'll stand."

"Suit yourself."

He was twenty years older than I was, but he was a good ten inches taller too. And he was built like a prizefighter. Which was what he'd been before he'd found religion. Now he talked softly and carried a big billy stick around with him as he walked the streets. Honest Andy was the one cop that Manny White couldn't buy.

He looked at me with eyes that seemed to peer down into my soul. "Care to tell me what happened?"

"No." Manny had gone with some of the boys to Micky Callahan's. They'd taken him out into an alley and beat on him, and then Manny jumped on him with his spiked boots. That's when I'd come upon them. I'd been making my rounds, minding my own business, putting up advertisement posters for a prizefight when I'd cut through that alley. There was nothing I wanted to tell Honest Andy about a man who had died so terribly. It made me sick to even think about it. Sicker still to think I'd grown up with Micky.

Andy chewed on his mustache as he looked me over. Then he folded his hands atop the table. "You're a fine boy, Charlie—"

"I'm not a boy anymore, Andy."

"You're better than this."

"I am what I am." I'd only joined the club because I had to. In order to do business on the South Side, you did whatever it took. If that meant paying a commission to Manny for the poster orders I took, then I figured it was just the cost of doing business. At least it guaranteed that what had happened to Micky wouldn't happen to me.

"Your past is not as important as your future. Did you know that? Can't change anything about what you've been, but you can change who you'll become."

I'd heard him say that before. Many times. Too many times. So many times that it set my teeth on edge to hear it.

"Did you know that God—"

"I can't imagine God would want much to do with somebody like me."

"Ah!" A gleam came into his eyes as he leaned forward. "But that's where you'd be wrong. Even with all the things you've done, you're just as worthy of His love as—"

"If all you came here for was to preach me a sermon, I'd rather go back and sit in that cell."

He sighed. "Fine. But I need to tell you that your mother's worried about you."

He had to bring her up, hadn't he? "I do fine by her. I've never heard her complain."

"It's not that she doesn't appreciate what you've provided."

"I've kept a roof over her head, haven't I?" That's all I'd ever wanted to do. And I'd done it for all of us: my sisters, my mother, and me.

"I think it's more the how of it that pains her."

"Do you just want to rub my nose in it, Andy? Is that why you came?"

"I came because I'm tired of all of this. You don't belong here. So . . . I've signed for you. They've made me your ward."

What! "I'm long past the age of needing a ward." And I hardly needed *him* to vouch for me.

"Consider me a sort of interested party in your whereabouts, then."

"They're releasing me to you?"

"They are."

"Don't I have any say in it?" I couldn't imagine anything worse than being indebted to Andy.

"Sure. You can stay right here and break your mother's heart. Is that what you'd rather do?"

"No." My mother's heart had already been broken. Over and over again. Trust him to find my soft spot and then beat on it.

"Then if you'll agree to my conditions, I'll get you out."

"What conditions?"

He smiled. Then he clapped his cap on his head and stood. "The ones I'm going to tell you about after they release you. If we hurry, we can make it home to your place and join your mother for dinner. We'll talk about them there."

I couldn't say that home wasn't better than jail. But I could complain about the company. We'd been doing just fine, my mother and I, until Andy had set his cap for her. It might not have been so bad if she hadn't shared his feelings. She'd been tired and faded until Andy had happened along, and then she'd bloomed like a flower to his sun.

I had nothing against the man . . . except his habit of being in places where he didn't belong. And his other habit of making a note of things he shouldn't have.

"It's like this." He took my mother's hand in his as we sat together at the table.

She sent a glance his way as a blush colored her cheeks.

"I've become rather fond of your mother, son."

Son. I didn't like the sound of that. I'd gotten used to not having a father around, and I didn't see the point in getting one now. But it seemed my mother had become rather fond of Andy as well. In the interest of keeping peace—and staying out of jail—I put on my best smile. "I suppose I don't have to worry about your intentions."

"I'll tell you nothing but the truth: They're the most honorable kind."

I would have expected nothing less from him. He was one of Chicago's finest and most bothersome cops. Always ready to inquire about your business and never failing to interrupt anything he found that wasn't part of his.

"But there's something we want to talk to you about."

We?

Mother was nibbling at her lip.

The policeman cleared his throat.

I hoped he wasn't going to say what I thought he was. I can't say I hadn't been expecting him to propose marriage, but I wasn't very happy about it. And that fact only made me more unhappy. But if my mother's happiness depended upon my blessing, then I would do everything I could to seem pleased. I smiled again, putting my dimples into it. "If you're asking can you marry her, you'll hear no objections from me." No one's idea of happy would have included us living on the slippery edge of poverty in a house that threatened to fall in on our heads. I'd had bigger plans—and dreams enough for all of us. Especially for me. But it took money to make something of yourself in the world, and money was the one thing we'd never had.

Mother blushed fiercely, but then she leaned over and kissed me on the cheek. "God bless you, Charlie. I hope he does. But that's not what we wanted to talk about."

Honest Andy cleared his throat again. "You know that I'm a policeman, son."

"Yes." Everyone knew he was a policeman, and I was tormented about it unmercifully every blessed day.

"I'm thinking that might make things a bit complicated."

I stopped smiling. "Complicated for you. Is that what you mean?"

"And for you as well."

I looked from my mother toward him as I considered his reply. I hadn't thought about it from that direction before, but I supposed it could. Andy couldn't be bought. And if he couldn't be bought, he might eventually suffer the consequences. If I were ever placed in a situation where I was asked to betray him . . . I looked over at my mother.

She looked me straight in the eye, something she usually avoided whenever I, or anyone else, brought up my membership in the club. "I'm grateful for all you've done for me, Charlie. I can't tell you I haven't appreciated the money you bring home, the way you looked after your sisters, or the way you've kept this house in repair. But I think it's time now to consider . . ."

"Let's be honest, son. You need to find some different friends."

As a condition of my club membership, Manny had asked me to do a little business for him on the side. I was supposed to keep his old friends happy and help him make new ones. I was good at making friends. I was also good at collecting and delivering money. And spending a night or two in jail in order to keep the others out of it. No matter what most people thought, I had nothing to do with guns or breaking kneecaps. Manny had other people for that. "So . . . what are you asking me to do?" I wasn't in the habit of kidding myself. I knew I only had two talents: my easy manner and my winning smile. I didn't have any other skills. Besides poker. I also had an ear for ragtime, and I wasn't too shabby on the dance floor either. Which helped me make friends, which in turn helped with advertisement sales and with Manny's money collection and delivery.

"We're asking you to consider a different kind of work." Mother clutched Andy's hand. "I want you to make something of yourself, Charlie."

"Something respectable." Honest Andy leveled a look at me that let me know he'd seen more than I thought he had. "That's one of my conditions."

"You want me to . . . do what? Be . . . an office clerk?" I secretly envied all those honest men I regularly mocked. Those who sat in a chair for nine hours and then went home to supper with a clear conscience. I'd never found a way to be proud of Manny's methods of doing business. Personal opinion and public confession were two different things, though. I didn't thank either my mother or Andy for making me feel like some two-penny thug.

"I've taken the liberty of writing to your father, and it seems he has a position for you."

"You—wait—what?" My father? My father, who left us all when I was seven? My father, who walked away from his wife and all of his children? Who'd not only abandoned my mother but then let her suffer the shame of divorcing him as well?

He was a man who had dragged us from city to city, determined to make a success of whatever fool thing he happened to be selling at the time. We may not have had any bread or any milk when I was a boy, but we'd had shoelaces and watch fobs and bottles of hair tonic by the dozens.

I'd wanted to drop school, but Mother wouldn't hear of it. She made sure I stayed . . . and I made sure that I left the school yard after class let out just as quickly as I could. I sold newspapers for a few years as a newsie, then I became a delivery boy for a printer. I had worked my way up to taking orders for advertising and pasting posters across the South Side for the customers.

My mother's lips hardened. "Your father's offered you a position."

"Doing what? Selling pen wipes?"

"He's done well for himself. He owns a company now. A whole factory."

A company? He owned a whole company while we were still holding on to every penny we could find? "Good for him."

Andy squeezed her hand. "And we want you to take him up on his offer. That's the other of my conditions."

"Where is it? Here?"

"It's in St. Louis." The blush had faded from Mother's cheeks, and her blue eyes looked worn and sad again.

Andy leaned back in his chair. "It's an opportunity I think you should take."

Of course he'd think that. Then he could have my mother to himself. "Is it . . . in his factory?"

My mother shrugged. "It's a position. A respectable one . . . and you were always your father's son."

I'd spent my life hating my father, but I couldn't deny that my brown eyes and dark hair had nothing to do with her soft, blond beauty.

"You have a gift, Charlie. A rare and special gift. You move people; they respond to you. You can talk them into anything. But you should be using your gift to help others, not to harm them."

"I've never hurt anyone." Some of the others had done things that would make me ashamed to set foot in a church, but I never had. Not that I had time to waste sitting around in church pews.

"But have you ever helped anyone? Besides me? Anyone that was worth helping?"

There weren't a lot of choices on the South Side. I doubted I would ever be offered anything more respectable than the job my father was proposing. Even if it was factory work. "If I'm going to be working, at least I can do it honestly. Is that what you're after?"

She just watched me, eyes fastened on my face.

I shrugged, trying to not to care too much that they wanted to be rid of me. "Might as well give it a try. How bad could it be?"

She smiled, then put a hand to her mouth as tears sprung from her eyes. "Thank you."

3

Lucy

I woke to the soft, gentle hand of my mother stroking my hair. I moved my arm from my eyes and turned so that I could see her. "Is he going to be all right?"

She stopped stroking for a moment. "I don't know. No one really knows."

"Why did it happen?"

She took her hand from my head and pressed it to her throat. I sat up. "Mother?"

She sighed and shook her head. "It was the candy foolishness. He has so much talent. He could have used it to accomplish so much. He could have made . . . ointments. Or face creams. Or even pastries. Why couldn't he have gone into the bakery business?"

In spite of my mother's fondest wishes to the contrary, my father couldn't have done anything other than make candy. He wasn't suited for anything else. Royal Taffy, his ultimate triumph, had been his whole life . . . until the company and the right to produce the candy had been taken from him. Though he'd started a new confectionery and created new candies, he'd never quite been able to match the success of Royal Taffy.

Mother reached out a hand and stopped my fingers from picking at the stitches on my matelassé cover.

"Standard started a new advertising promotion for Royal Taffy. You know how he flies into those rages."

I knew.

"The doctor says his heart just can't handle it anymore. He wants your father to make some changes."

"What changes?"

She didn't reply.

"Mother?"

She looked over at me. "We've been advised to sell the business."

"But—he can't!" How could my father sell the company? And what would he do without it?

She grasped my hand. "The most important thing for his recovery is that he stay calm. He can't do that if he's in the confectionery kitchen experimenting with candies, or if he's trying to figure out how to out-advertise Royal Taffy."

"But—"

"There's nothing to worry about. I've been speaking with a lawyer."

"A lawyer!" City Confectionery wasn't a company; it was our life. And even if our Fancy Crunch couldn't outsell Royal Taffy, there was always hope that one day Papa could create a candy that would. I didn't understand how he could just let it all go. As I looked at Mama, a suspicion crept over me. She no longer seemed so old and tired. She looked devious and conniving. "You haven't told him, have you!"

She looked at me with such great disappointment that I almost blushed. "There's really no need. If he knew—"

"If he knew, he would never let you! It's not your company, it's his."

As she stood, her lips compressed into a thin, straight line. "It might as well be mine. It was my own father's money that started the company, and it's this house I grew up in that's borne the brunt of all your father's schemes." I watched her look sadly about the room and realized that half of my bedroom suite was gone. The pitcher and basin that used to sit on my washstand were now perched on my dresser. And the large French beveled mirror that had once hung above them was nowhere to be seen. My eyes began to register other changes as I peered through the afternoon light that had filtered in through the lace curtains. "My rug!" And my silk upholstered chair.

Her shoulders dipped. "I sold it."

"But—!"

"And it's not just this house, Lucy. It's my—my *own* dreams that have been sacrificed to those candies, along with his. If I'd known just how far he would go in his pigheadedness . . ."

"Some people call his pigheadedness passion."

"Not those with any business sense."

I couldn't blame her. Not really. She wasn't a Kendall; she was a Clary. She didn't understand candy like my father and I did. At least that's what Papa had always whispered to me through the sugar-scented steam that lifted from our copper pots. She'd come from a family of bankers and merchants. So when Papa had fought with his accounts clerk over raising the price of Royal Taffy and when he'd insisted on treating his workers like family, my mother had told him he was being a fool. She'd urged him to leave the candy business altogether and go into another profession; I suspected she'd been hoping he would join her father at the bank.

Mother had always wanted Papa to be something other than what he was, Papa had always wanted more than what he'd had, and I'd always wanted to be something I never could. I didn't want to be a daughter. I wanted to be a partner in the business.

I wanted to make candy in the confectionery alongside my father. But my mother insisted that the kitchen was no place for a lady, and my father forbid me even to enter the confectionery's doors once I'd graduated from high school. *"Child's play is well and good for children, but candy making is a serious business,"* he'd become quite fond of saying.

None of us had gotten what we'd wanted. The Kendall family, it seemed, was doomed to failure. "Is there a buyer?"

"I have one in mind. And I hope to conclude the sale well before Christmas."

I looked toward the window. I'd longed for my room as we'd traveled about Europe like gypsies. I'd missed the familiar squeak of my bedsprings and the passion flowers that twined across my papered walls. The comforting smells of lemon soap . . . and even the slight odor of camphor, left over from my grandfather's time when he had used the room just down the hall. But now that I was here, I could hardly bear it. "Do we have to sell?"

"Since your father got sick, the company's been losing money. I thought we could manage until he got well, but . . . I don't know what else to do now. Your father isn't able to do much of anything anymore."

The image of the Royal Taffy advertisement unfurled, like a medieval battle standard, in my mind. Mother was right: If Father had been able, he wouldn't have let those posters sit unanswered. He would have pasted one of his own up beside them. "I could manage things."

"Lucy, no!" She seemed as shocked as Papa had been when I told him I had planned on joining him in the confectionery kitchen following graduation.

"I can." As I said it, my heart thrilled to the challenge. It was the chance I'd been looking for! I could prove to Papa that he was wrong. That, given the opportunity, a girl could be a help to a business rather than a hindrance. "I brought back so many candies from Europe. If you give me a few weeks, I'm sure I can come up with something divine! Something no one has ever tasted before."

"Your father would never—"

"What he doesn't know won't worry him. And what if I succeed?" I *would* succeed. All I needed was a chance.

"No."

"Please!"

"No. I won't discuss this further. And in any case, I came up here to tell you something." She took an envelope from my dresser top and presented it to me with a flourish. "You've been named the Queen of the Veiled Prophet Ball!"

How could she think of balls at a time like this?

"It wouldn't do for a member of the court to take part in commerce. It's your debutante year, Lucy." She grimaced. "It's actually a year behind your debutante year. The rest of your friends have come out already, and most of them have married. Perhaps this has been fated all along, your coming out into society at a time when your father and I need you. A good marriage would help us all."

Marriage? I hadn't realized I had recoiled from her until she sought my hand and said, "I'm only trying to think of your future."

"And I'm trying to think of all of our futures. If you would just let me—"

"The business needs to be sold." She spoke the words slowly as if I hadn't understood them the first time.

"I can't believe you'd just give it up without—without even trying to save it! That's not what Father would want."

"Your father has done exactly as he wants for years now, and all it's given him is a heart attack. Isn't it about time we tried something else? Found some other way to manage?"

I pushed from my bed and stalked to the door. "I'm going to tell him. I'm going to tell him exactly what it is you're trying to do."

Something flashed in her eyes. Fear? Guilt? "Don't."

"If you give me a chance to save the company, if you give me time to create a new candy, then I won't."

She gave me a long, steady look, then seemed to deflate before my eyes. "Fine. I'll give you one month. But promise me one thing: You *must* take part in the Veiled Prophet Ball. And you have to put your heart into it, Lucy. It's an opportunity you can't afford to miss."

I thought it over for a moment before nodding. If I could come up with a new candy, then the ball would be the perfect place to introduce it. Standard Candy Manufacturing would never be able to top that. "I wouldn't think of missing it."

The next morning I was permitted to see my father.

He was awake when my mother ushered me through the door, though the curtains were still drawn against the day.

"Lucy. My Sugar Plum." His skin was ashen, his eyes were sunken. Even his voice seemed somehow diminished. I had been alarmed when I had been told of his heart problems. Now I was truly frightened.

"Papa." I had come home, hoping to mend the rift I'd made between us. Hoping to prove to him my worth. Now I was afraid even to touch him, for fear of causing more harm.

He reached an arm out toward me. "You've come home. At last."

I'd never seen him in his nightshirt before. It made him seem . . . different. Weakened. Less. "I have." I stood at his bedside, hands clasped in front of me.

"Sit down. Stay awhile. Did you bring me any candy?"

Mother helped him to a sitting position, plumped his pillows, and then eased him back onto them. "No candy. Doctor's orders."

"Have you ever considered that just one little piece might give me the strength I need to recover? You can't make a Fancy without the crunch." He tried to smile at me.

Mother pulled a handkerchief from her cuff and dabbed at the sweat that had broken out upon his forehead. "It's not worth getting upset about."

"There's got to be something worth getting upset about. Something more than the lukewarm soup and dry bread you keep forcing me eat."

Mother smoothed his hair back from his forehead and left the room. But not before giving me a stern glance of warning.

"She refuses to let me eat butter either. Or cream." He winced for a moment, and then his features relaxed. "Tell me about your travels."

"They were nice."

He raised a brow. "Nice? You went halfway around the world, and the only thing you have to say is that it was nice?"

I felt my lips curl into a smile. I hadn't realized until then that I'd been holding my breath. "It was so . . . amazing. So different. And there were so many things to do and to see."

I told him about the ballrooms of Vienna and the cathedrals of France. I described how it felt to stand on the Jungfrau and see the world spread out at my feet. I told him about eating mussels and eels and snails.

"And they were all so delicious! But they were nothing compared to all the sweets. It seemed there were at least a dozen confectionaries in every village. I can't count the number of candies I tasted. In Florence, there was even a—"

A raspy snore lifted from the bed.

"Papa?" I could see now that he had fallen asleep, chin resting on his chest.

I rearranged the blanket, pushed his head back onto the pillows, and left him to his dreams. Then I went down the hall to my room and unpacked all my candy treasures, plucking one of my favorites, a Salzburg *Mozartkugel*, from the pile. I peeled away the foil wrapper and bit into it, admiring the multitude of layers hidden beneath the dark chocolate coating. How had they managed to make it so perfectly round? My tongue separated and identified the flavors: pistachio, marzipan, and chocolate. My mouth exulted in the contrasting textures. Creamy and crunchy, chewy with just the right amount of graininess. I sighed as the last of it melted away and wondered if there would ever be anyone to share candy with again.

I reached into the trunk and brought out the gifts I'd collected. The lace tablecloth for Mother. A Bavarian pipe for Papa. And an assortment of embroidered pillow tops and lace doilies for my girlfriends. Really, I ought to transfer them to my hope chest and store them properly, wrapping them in paper instead of my underclothes.

I asked a maid to bring up some old newspapers, and then I wandered downstairs, looking for Mother. I found her in the sitting room she used as an office, talking to my aunt. They looked up as I entered. "I'd like to go see Annie Farrell. I bought something for her on the trip."

Aunt Margaret excused herself. "I'll go see what your uncle is doing."

"Annie Farrell . . . ?" Mother's brow creased. "Oh! Annie Wagner. She married while you were gone."

"She . . . what? But whom? Whom did she marry?"

"Roy Wagner."

"Who is Roy Wagner? I don't think I—"

"He's a third cousin. On her mother's side, from Kansas City. They moved there last spring."

I gave a quick gasp. "Away? From here?"

"Well, of course! His business wasn't here. It was out there."

Annie was gone? I'd never gotten the chance to say good-bye. "Is there . . . anyone else? Who got married?"

"Oh my, yes! Harriett Marcus did. And Julia Shaw." She paused as if debating with herself about something. When she spoke, it was in a whisper. "Julia . . . eloped."

The horror! I groped for the chair and sat in it, feeling rather disoriented. Annie and Julia had been my closest friends. They'd married—eloped, even!—and I hadn't known it. "Did anyone *not* get married?" Wasn't there anyone who was still like me?

"Cora Taylor went away to college. To Vassar . . . or was it Swarthmore? I can never keep them straight. And Stella Lawrence went off to the Orient to be a missionary, if you can believe it. I don't know what's gotten into young girls these days."

Suddenly, St. Louis felt dismal and friendless.

The maid presented herself and passed me the stack of newspapers I'd asked for. That dreadful murderer glared out at me from the top page. I turned it over so I wouldn't have to look at him.

"I'm sure Harriett Marcus would be happy to see you, although she's Harriett Patterson now. She's at-home for calls on Tuesday afternoons."

I didn't want to call on her, I wanted to *see* her. To go up to her room and dance while we listened to phonograph records. I didn't want to sit in some strange parlor and talk about . . . whatever married people talked about. "Whom did she marry?"

"She married Archie Patterson." Mother said it with a bend to her brow as if daring me to disapprove.

I'd never liked Archie Patterson. And now Harriett was living with him in some new house, taking calls on Tuesdays, and . . . sitting with him at church on Sundays! All of my girlfriends were gone.

"But Winnie Compton is still here. And she's not married." Mother reached across the table and patted my hand. "We can post your gift to Annie in Kansas City. I'm sure she'd love to hear from you."

She'd probably forgotten all about me . . . the same way I'd forgotten about her. I thought I'd returned to a city that was just the same, but everything had changed while I was gone.

4

Charlie

I slept most of the way to St. Louis as the train swayed along the tracks. The previous day I witnessed my mother's marriage and visited the grave of my little sister who'd died several years before. I hadn't told anybody I was leaving. I figured it was better if no one knew where I was headed.

I'd decided to give my father's company a try. He owed me that at least. If it didn't suit me—and why should it?—then I'd skip town and head out to Seattle. Or San Francisco, maybe.

As the gaps between towns narrowed and the landscape outside my window lost its wheat fields and gained more roads and smokestacks, I sat up straighter. Spitting into my hand, I smoothed it over my hair and then I used my reflection in the window to straighten my tie.

I set my derby back on at a tilt, barely pushing it down on my head, and regarded my reflection. A club man stared back at me. I grasped the hat by the brim and set it straight. Then I took hold of my rubber collar and stretched my neck, adjusting the way it lay. That was better. Now I was just plain old Charlie Clarke, who could be anything he wanted. I glanced around the train at the men riding in the car with me.

There wasn't anyone with Manny's style. No one who wore his hat with the same tilt he had or held himself with quite the same flair. But then again, none of them had probably ever beaten a man to a pulp in an alley. I put a hand to my tie and tried to make the knot smaller. Tighter. The way everyone else was wearing theirs.

I wished I could have traded my blue shirt for a white one. That's what all these respectable folks were wearing. Slumping into the seat, I stared at myself while the world rushed past.

I hadn't seen my father in fifteen years. Maybe this wasn't a good idea. Had Mother told him about Manny? She couldn't have. If she had, he never would have asked me to come. I wondered if it were really true that he had asked for me. That he wanted me.

He hadn't before. Why should anything have changed?

As I sat there, staring out the window, I thought of everything I'd done in the past fifteen years. There wasn't one thing I was proud of. A familiar wave of fear lapped at my stomach. That old sense of doom. The thought that I could do nothing that would please my father. I pulled my flask from my pocket and downed a swig of whiskey, reminding myself that I was headed toward a new start, a new chance. Telling myself this time I wasn't going to make a mess of it.

He wasn't there. After the crowd meeting the train had melted away, I'd found myself alone. But what had I expected? That he'd be there waiting to greet me like some long-lost son when he hadn't even bothered to say good-bye all those years ago?

A wiry old man wearing a suit festooned with shiny brass buttons came over and squinted up at me. Then he reached for the satchel I held in my hand. "With looks like yours, you'll be Mr. Clarke's son. I'm to take you on up home."

I followed him out to a touring car that had the top pulled up. The dark green chassis had been polished to a shine. I squinted from the sunlight's glare off the white tires. It was the kind of car I had only ever dreamed of riding in. The mayor of Chicago himself had nothing half so fine.

The man opened the door for me. I stepped up inside. The black leather seat was so long and so comfortable, I could have laid down on it and gone to sleep. And it smelled . . . it smelled just like money.

Though I spent the ride through the city staring out the window, I couldn't have told anyone what I'd seen. Eventually the driver slowed the car to turn onto a street lined with some of the biggest houses I'd ever seen. And then, down at the end of the long block, he stopped the car entirely.

"*This* is my father's house?" It was too big, with too many columns, too many steps and . . . too many windows. I couldn't live here.

"Fifty-four Portland Place. Guess it's your house now too."

My house.

No. It wouldn't be my house. It would never be my house. My house was back in Chicago on the South Side. People like me didn't live in places like this.

The driver hopped out, then came back to open the door for me.

I didn't want to get out.

"Are you coming, sir?"

Of course I was. I wasn't some seven-year-old kid anymore. What did I have to be afraid of? What more could my father do to me than he had already done? If anyone was leaving, this time it would be me. Maybe I should have done it right then, because as the driver was reaching past me for my satchel, the door to the mansion opened and my father walked out.

He'd hardly changed since the night I'd last seen him fifteen years before. But I knew now what I would look like when my dark hair turned gray and my already thick eyebrows got tangled up with hair. The mouth that had been so swift to make promises, the eyes that had been so quick to wink, had left lines in his cheeks.

He paused. And then he smiled.

It was that same smile I used to see in my sleep when I was younger. The smile that had always made me feel as if everything would be all right. The smile that used to make me cry when I'd wake up and realize I would never see it again.

He jogged down the walkway and came up to me, arms extended.

I stuck out my hand.

He took it between both of his and pumped it up and down. "It's good to see you again."

I bit back the first reply that came to mind: *It's good to see you again too*. I'd been right there where he'd left us for all those years. He could have seen me anytime he'd wanted to. Apparently he hadn't.

Some sort of fancy-smelling oil had finally managed to tame the hair that had always fallen forward, onto his brow. "You look good." He clapped me on the forearm. "Come on inside. We're leaving for the theater in just a few minutes, but that'll give you a chance to get settled." He propelled me up the walkway with a hand to my back.

I walked a few steps ahead of him in order to be rid of it, but that meant I was first through the front door. Once I was inside,

I didn't know what to do. I'd stepped into a cavern framed by shiny wood panels that stretched two stories above my head.

My father stopped to talk to the man who had opened the door. Then he joined me, hand extending toward my satchel.

I gripped it tighter.

"Is that all you brought?" He glanced at it with a frown. "I'll have the butler take you upstairs and make sure you have everything you need. The kitchen will have supper ready for you whenever you want it." He pulled a watch from his pocket. "I was thinking of having a drink and smoking a cigar before I go. If you care to join me, I'll be in the library, just there." He nodded down the hall.

I didn't care to, so I followed the butler up a long, curving flight of stairs and then took my time putting my few things away. And I didn't go back downstairs until I was sure he'd left.

I woke to the sound of . . . nothing at all, to find I'd slept straight through the night. There'd been no fights on the streets outside. No sounds of an argument in the apartment next door. Indeed, there was no apartment next door. And this morning there were no wheeled carts tumbling through the streets. No clatter of horses' hooves. No cows mooing in their pens as they waited to be taken to the South Side slaughterhouses.

Maybe this is what wealth bought: silence.

My stomach began to rumble, and I decided I should find out what rich people ate for breakfast. I walked around the room opening doors before I remembered which one led into a bathroom. I turned a spigot and water came gushing out into a sink that was attached to the wall. Imagine that! I splashed some onto my face and shaved. After cleaning my rubber collar with a cloth, I fastened it to my blue shirt and dressed. Finally, after brushing off my coat, I took it from the stand where one of those servants had placed it. Then I fastened the hook on my already-knotted teck tie.

All was quiet downstairs too—there seemed to be no one about.

The previous evening I had eaten supper alone, served in a dining room that had sparkled with china plates and fancy glasses. All of that had been put away somewhere. But a few covered silver bowls were sitting on a sideboard. I lifted one of the lids.

Eggs.

I lifted another.

Bacon.

I looked beneath a third.

Toast.

So rich people ate what poor people did. They only served it from fancier dishes.

"May I help you, sir?"

I turned to see a girl standing at the entrance of the dining room. "I just . . . well . . . I wanted . . . breakfast?"

She took a plate from a glass-fronted cupboard and filled it from the silver bowls. I moved to take it from her, but she stepped past me and placed it on the table. "Please, sir." She gestured toward the chair.

I sat.

She brought me a cup and a silver pot filled with something. "Is that . . . ?"

"Coffee. Would you like anything else, sir?"

I might have, but I didn't know what else there was. "No. Thank you."

She moved toward the door, but there was one thing I wanted to make plain. "I'm Charlie."

She nodded.

"And you are . . . ?"

"Sir?" For the first time, her quiet confidence seemed to desert her.

"Your name."

"It's Jennie, sir." And she whispered it so quietly I hardly knew if I understood her.

"How long have you worked here?"

"Five years."

I was just about to speak to her again when a woman walked into the room. She was wearing the kind of dress my sisters had always admired. And her blond hair had been piled on top of her head in a bunch of curls.

I stood.

Jennie, if that really was her name, bobbed her head and left.

The woman smiled at me as she sat at the foot of the table, several places away. "Charles. I must tell you how delighted we are to have you."

If she was, she was hiding it well. I tried on a smile of my own. "I'm delighted to be here . . . but you've got the better of me. I don't think we've met."

"I'm Augusta." She said it as if it should mean something.

"It's nice to meet you, Augusta." I sat down.

"I'm your stepmother."

Stepmother? "I hadn't realized . . ." My father had remarried. I don't know why it should have surprised me. My parents had divorced long ago. And I'd just watched my mother get married to Andy two days before.

She frowned. "Your father said you hadn't communicated with each other, but I didn't really think that . . ." She tipped her head to one side as if considering something. "I should have made further inquiries, but Warren is always so busy. . . ." She sighed. "This must be awkward for you. But what you probably don't realize is how awkward this is for me too, Charles."

"Charlie. Please call me Charlie."

Her frown deepened. "I'm sure Charles will do. In any case, we're going to have to decide how to explain your presence."

"How about: My father abandoned his family fifteen years ago, and now he's decided to make up for lost time?" I picked up a piece of bacon that had been draped across my eggs.

"I don't think you understand. People are bound to talk. Scandals of this nature—"

"Listen, I don't have anything against you, Augusta. You seem like a nice lady. But if you're expecting sympathy, you'll have to look somewhere else. While you've been living here in this—this *mansion*, I've been trying to keep the roof of my house from falling in on top of your husband's first wife and his daughters. I hope you'll understand when I say I can't bring myself to care much about what people will say."

She looked at me for a long moment, and then she nodded. "I think I do. I'm sorry for the pain he caused you. It wasn't right. If I'd known about you sooner I would have . . . I would have done something."

Easy for her to say.

"I hope we can become friends. In the meantime, your father asked me to tell you that he'll see you as soon as you've finished."

He'd been waiting for me? I used the bacon to push some eggs onto my fork. As I bent to eat them, I looked up from my plate.

She was watching me, brows drawn together. She wasn't much younger than my mother, and she wasn't really any prettier. She was just more . . . proper. "We hold a certain position in society, your father and I. We've worked very hard to obtain it. It would be most unfortunate if he were driven from it."

For her, maybe. I stood, folded my napkin, then placed it on the table the way my mother had taught me. "Please excuse me from the table."

She nodded. "The driver will meet you out front."

I had the same driver I'd had the day before. I'd been busy staring out the window then, but now I held out my hand as I approached. "Charlie. Thanks for the ride yesterday."

He glanced up from the crank as if startled, then stood and offered his own. "The name's Nelson, sir."

"I've never driven a car before. Is it hard?"

"Nothing to it. Just turn the steering wheel the way you want it to go."

"Better than a horse, then."

"Now, I didn't say that!" He patted a head lamp and then, after leaning close to squint at it, pulled the tail of his shirt out, spit onto the brass and gave it a shine. "You still got to feed her and give her a washing off. Polish her up and talk nice to her. She's got more tack than the boss's horses ever had. And she'll throw fits every now and then too." He tucked his shirttail back in and then took his brass-buttoned coat off and hung it from one of the head lamps. Then he bent to the crank.

"So tell me about this place, Nelson. You been with them long?"

"Since they been here."

"How long have they been married?"

He gave me a long look over his shoulder before he answered. "'Bout ten years now. But surely you know that."

I shrugged. "Do they have any children?"

"No, sir."

"Augusta must not have been very happy to hear about me."

"The missus? Oh . . . I don't know about that. More surprised, I'd say, than anything else."

Once the car sputtered to life, he moved around to open the door for me. I stepped up, ducked inside, and settled into the corner of the tufted bench. I looked at the houses we passed by. All that luxury, all that wealth . . . it should have been my mother's. And mine. But my father had gone on without us. If he'd remembered us just once, if he'd given us even a tenth of what he'd managed to make since he'd left, so many things might have turned out differently.

Soon the large lawns and houses with towers at their corners gave way to smaller, though still tidy, houses and yards. But then they, too, left off for row houses. Nelson turned to look at me. "We're headed down to South St. Louis."

I couldn't seem to escape my fate. I'd left one South Side only to find myself headed toward another.

"That's where the factory is. You can see the smokestack just ahead."

I bent to get a clear view through the front glass, cocking my head, and saw *Standard Manufacturing* painted in white up the side of a red smokestack.

Nelson stopped the car by the front steps of a large smoke-spewing building. He got out and opened the door for me.

"Ever been inside this place?"

"Yes, sir."

"Know where I should go?"

"Why, just walk up those front steps and keep on going. Up to the top. That's where the boss's office is. I'll stay right here and wait for you."

I tipped my hat at him, then walked up the steps and through the door.

My father was sitting in a chair behind a large desk when I was shown into his office. Gleaming wood bookcases lined the walls, and dark patterned rugs carpeted the floor. "Sit down, Charles."

"It's Charlie."

He studied me for a moment. "Charlie's a boy's name. But you're a man now. Charles has a nice ring to it, don't you think?" He pointed with his cigar toward the chair that sat across from his. "Your mother said you'd gotten yourself into a bit of trouble."

I sat, resting my ankle on top of my knee, and gripped the arms of the chair. "I wouldn't call it trouble." Necessarily.

"Why don't you tell me about it."

I might have made the sort of excuses that had satisfied my mother, but something about the look in his eyes warned me from it. So I did something I wasn't in the habit of doing: I told the truth. "After you left, things got bad."

He glanced down.

"I worked at what I could. A couple years ago, I got a promotion. To sales."

He looked up with a grin. "Sales! Like father, like son. Have to say it does me proud to see you carried on the family tradition."

I ignored him. "But working on the South Side, I had to have connections. So I joined a club."

His eyes narrowed as he took a puff on his cigar.

"A man got killed, and I got arrested up for it. By accident. I never hurt anyone, if that's what you're worried about."

"I'm not worried about some man who's dead. I'm worried about you."

It was a little late for that.

44

"And I have nothing against loyalty. I require it from all of my personal staff. *Especially* from my personal staff."

Personal staff?

"You know what I deal in, Charles, don't you?"

I nodded. Now I did. Seemed like everyone in the country must know.

"I deal in money. Lots of it, just so we're clear. From what I've been told, you used to deal in it too."

Exactly how much had my mother told him?

"I need someone I can count on because I plan on making quite a bit more. My business isn't child's play. I take it very seriously."

He seemed to expect a reply. "Of course."

"My wife has no children, and family is important."

Since when?

"I can't tell you how happy I am that you're here." He sat back in his chair and grinned at me.

I didn't smile back.

He pulled out a drawer, took a card from it, then pushed it across his desk toward me. I leaned forward and took it.

"That's the best clothier in town. Go see him. Can't have my son going around looking like a two-bit salesman. Have Dreffs set you straight and place the charges on my account."

I could have reacted to that insult, but I decided not to. Deciding not to be offended had saved my life on more than one occasion back on the South Side. And besides, my father couldn't hurt me any more than he already had.

I found the shop. Dreffs Fine Clothing. But I was wearing my best clothes: my gray checked suit and my fancy blue percale shirt, topped by my one and only hat. I asked for Mr. Dreffs, and a man appeared from behind a curtain a moment later. He took one look and me and then turned as if he were going to go right back to wherever it was that he'd been.

I stepped forward. "Mr. Clarke sent me here. Told me you could set me straight. He said to charge everything to his account."

He turned back around. "Mr. . . . Stephen Clark?"

"Mr. Warren Clarke."

His brow lifted at that. "Mr. Warren Clarke of Standard Manufacturing?"

"That's him."

The man pursed his lips and then excused himself. I saw him pick up a telephone at the end of a counter. "Standard Manufacturing, please." He said nothing for a good long while, though he stared at me from across the store the whole time. "Yes. This is Mr. Dreffs of Dreffs Fine Clothing. I've a young man here that—yes, of course. It's just that I have a young man here inquiring about a wardrobe, and he's insisting that it be charged to Mr. Clarke's account." Another pause. "Oh. Yes. I see." A longer pause. "Of course. Yes, of course. Thank you very much."

He put the telephone back down, came around from behind the counter, and made a short, smart bow. "I didn't realize Mr. Clarke had a son in town."

If St. Louis was anything like Chicago, everyone would soon be realizing it.

"I hope you'll forgive me . . ."

I smiled and held out my hand. "No hard feelings."

He shook it. "That's very gracious of you, sir." From a drawer he took out a measure. He motioned an assistant forward. "If you will kindly divest yourself of that . . . *that*."

I let the assistant help me from my coat. As Dreffs took my measurements, the assistant wrote them down in a little book, as if they were secrets, holding it close to his chest. Dreffs took out a different measure and held it up to my shoulders from several different directions. "Right shoulder one-half inch shorter than the left."

The assistant scribbled in the book.

"Are you sure? Because I've never noticed that before." Wouldn't I have noticed something like that?

He addressed me over the rims of his glasses. "And neither did the tailor who made your previous suit."

"That would be Sears, Roebuck and Company." I winked at the assistant.

He didn't even crack a smile.

"There will be no more talk of Sears. Or of Roebuck. They might do fine for the common man, but there is nothing common about Mr. Clarke. And the fact that he sent you here means that you, young man, have just come up in the world."

He put away his measures, then began to flip through a book of fabric samples.

"You'll have three sack suits. Single-breasted. Three-button. One in a dark gray worsted, one in a black and gray club check, and one in a worsted twill stripe. One tuxedo-style suit faced with silk. One full dress suit with a swallowtail coat faced with silk. One wool tweed suit for leisure. One long single-breasted overcoat. Two pairs of woolen knickerbockers and two pairs of tweed trousers." He took in a deep breath. "That should do for autumn and winter. In the spring we'll have a top coat made in gray, order you some seasonal suits, and ask you to come in for a fitting." He took another breath before continuing. "He'll need seven shirts with long bosoms, five plain, two plaited."

"Could you make me one in blue and another one in red?" I wasn't counting on wearing fancy clothes all the time.

"I could not." He kept dictating to the assistant. "He'll need two pairs of black blucher oxfords, a pair of black patent leather shoes, and a pair of cap toe spat boots."

"I've got some shoes already."

"Is there anything to recommend them? Like the presence of genuine calf's leather? *Any*where on them?"

I shrugged.

"He'll need the shoes. All of them. As well as a pair for playing tennis."

"I don't play."

"You will. Everyone at the club plays."

I might have told him I wasn't a member of any club here in this city, but he hadn't listened to me yet, and I doubted he would start anytime soon.

He took some belts and suspenders from beneath the counter top and had me try on some hats. He handed my already-tied teck tie to his assistant and then addressed himself to me. "There will be no more teck ties. From now on, you will wear *neck*-ties. A refined gentleman always ties his own knot." He pulled an assortment of neckties and pocket squares from a case and had the assistant wrap them up. He chose a silk top hat, two homburgs, and a flat cap. Then he disappeared into a back room, returning with a suit that he handed to me. "It won't fit perfectly, but at least it will do until I can get the others made. If you change in there—" he gestured toward a curtain that had been drawn across the back corner of the room— "I'll take care of your old one." He had already taken my rubber collar and my derby and thrown them into a trash bin. "I'll have the rest of the items delivered to Mr. Clarke's residence."

It took a moment in that dressing room, as I looked into the mirror, to get used to myself. The person looking at me wasn't the old Charlie Clarke of Chicago's South Side. And it wasn't the new Charlie from the train either. In the mirror, staring back at me, was a man. Old Charlie was gone forever; all his rough edges had been rubbed off. In his place was a quite proper and rather stuffy-looking Charles.

Dreffs pushed aside the curtain and gave me a look-over. "Excellent. Now, I am going to tell you something that I expect you to remember." He tapped at each of my coat's buttons with his finger. "Always. Sometimes. Never."

Always, sometimes, never . . . what?

"You must *always* button the top button of your coats. You may *sometimes* choose to button the middle buttons, but you must *never*, under *any circumstances*, button the bottom one."

Well, then why was the fool thing there in the first place?

Mr. Dreffs added socks and handkerchiefs and several caps. He instructed me on what to wear to work, to the opera, to a dinner party, and to golf outings.

I hoped he didn't expect me to remember.

He also chose three sweaters with a rolled neck style that I had always publicly scorned but secretly admired. "You're to wear these with a pair of tweed trousers or knickerbockers. Never underneath a suit. And *never* with worsted." He leveled a look at me over his glasses and then commanded me to repeat all of his advice. Next, he selected a plain though heavy pocket watch and three pairs of gloves.

An hour later, I was walking down Olive Street feeling as if St. Louis was paradise itself. Where else could a man be given a chance at a new life? I'd left Manny White and the past behind. I might have to work for my father, but that was all right. He owed me. And once I was able to put some money aside, once I figured we were even, then I planned to walk away. Just once, I wanted to leave him the same way he'd left me.

5

Lucy

"Oh!" My handbag slipped from my wrist as I walked right into a man on Olive Street. The wide brim of my new mushroom-style hat had hidden him from my view.

His hand at my elbow was the only thing that kept me from falling.

"I am so sorry!" I looked up into the most delicious eyes I'd ever seen. They were like pools of the best milk chocolate . . . with caramel swirls at their center.

He lifted his hat. "A girl as pretty as you could never be at fault." He flashed a dimpled smile as he stooped to pick up my handbag.

"I—"

"Lucy?" My aunt had continued on down the sidewalk without me, but now she was turning back. "Lucy?"

As I took the handbag from him, I smiled my thanks. Looking up into his eyes, there was something about the man that seemed familiar. I hadn't met him before, had I? Surely I would have remembered. I could never have forgotten those dimples or his eyes. I felt a blush warm my cheeks.

"May I help you?" My aunt stood before us, glowering, as if she were shooing away street urchins at the ancient forum in Rome.

The man retreated. "No. I'm sorry. I was just—"

I slipped my handbag back over my wrist, then put a hand to my aunt's arm. "He was kind enough to help me after I walked into him. It was all my fault."

He was already walking away.

"Thank you!" I nearly shouted as I said the words, but I wondered if he even heard me.

"I'm sorry, Lucy." My aunt linked her arm with mine. "At first glance . . . well, I know we're not in Europe anymore, but I find myself erring on the side of caution, nonetheless. Though, considering the way he was dressed, I ought to have known it was harmless."

I tried to glance back over my shoulder, but the brim of my hat blocked the view. "It just . . . it seemed like I ought to know him. As if I'd met him somewhere before."

"If you haven't, and he belongs here, then I'm sure you will. We'll have to ask your mother if any eligible bachelors moved to the city while you were gone."

I felt like rolling my eyes. Eligible bachelors had been a frequent topic of conversation on our travels. And now that I was back home, I had hoped not to hear about them anymore. Besides, I had no time to think of bachelors. I had to come up with a new candy. And soon!

My aunt and uncle were staying for a week's visit before continuing to their home in Denver. We all went to church together on Sunday, and then on Monday my mother, my aunt, and I went to Vandervoort's so I could be fitted for my Veiled Prophet Ball gown. My mother had ordered it several months before, when she had received the news, but only now was it ready for a fitting.

"What kind of dress is it?" I knew my aunt was only making idle conversation, but it brought to mind our fitting sessions at the couturier in Paris.

"It's a semi-princess." Mother seemed to answer with a strain in her voice.

"Of course." Aunt Margaret's reply was dismissive, but I don't think she meant it to sound so rude. Everything was a semi-princess these days, with the long, sleek lines of traditional fitted gowns broken only by a seaming of the bodice and skirt together at the waist.

"With a square neck. And mousquetaire sleeves." Mother seemed very proud of herself.

"Short sleeves?" Aunt asked with a quirked brow.

"Long."

My aunt frowned.

"But the ball is in October—at night." Mother seemed to send me a plea as she spoke. "There's a fichu drapery at the waist. They said it was the very latest in modes." The words came out as an appeal. As if she hoped I wouldn't be disappointed.

I smiled, and that seemed to reassure her. I'd noticed, though, since I'd been back, that the very latest modes in America seemed slightly behind the latest modes in Europe. I wondered . . . "Is it . . . white?"

Mother looked at me as if I had suddenly lost all sense. "Of course it's white!"

I'd traveled so far and seen so much in the past year . . . wearing a white gown seemed like a denial of all that I had experienced and everywhere that I had been. As I walked into the store with them it seemed such a bother to have to concentrate on dresses and balls when there were more important things to be accomplished.

The dressmaker brought the gown out from behind a curtain with a flourish. "Only the finest for the Queen of Love and Beauty!"

Mother hushed him. "No one's supposed to know!"

He leaned forward, reducing his voice to a whisper. "And no one does . . . except for me."

"Is that marquisette?" My aunt was craning forward in her chair, evaluating the gown, which had been draped over the counter.

"It's net. Over satin."

"Oh. But wouldn't a marquisette have worked better? It would be much more distinctive."

The dressmaker's brows had risen to dizzying heights. "Better for what? A summer gown?"

"A princess style in marquisette would have been much better suited to the occasion."

Mother broke in to their discussion. "Perhaps in France, but we're living in St. Louis, if you had not noticed."

I let my thoughts wander as my mother and aunt exchanged opinions. Sitting in one of the glass counter cases was a sample of watered silk in a delicious shade of green. It reminded me of the pistachios we had tasted in Vienna. Maybe the new candy I created could have a base of pistachios. But what flavoring would go best with them?

Orange flower syrup!

My mouth began to water. Yet . . . maybe that was too exotic. What about . . . honey? I could make a pistachio chew with honey and nougat. But . . . I'd never even seen a pistachio before

I'd been to Europe. How expensive were they? Whatever else this new candy turned out to be, it needed to be inexpensive to make and easy to sell.

It couldn't entail extra fuss and care. Which meant no chocolate.

But I could make a nougat. And so could the confectionery. Nougats were easy. Only water, sugar, and egg whites were needed. And honey and possibly pistachios as well. But . . . nougats weren't very exciting. And my candy had to be something different. Something special.

My mother placed a hand on my arm. "Which do *you* prefer?"

They were all looking at me as if in expectation of a response. "Pardon me, I'm sorry. I didn't hear the choices."

"Next Monday or Tuesday?"

"For . . . what?"

"Your next fitting."

It didn't matter. None of this mattered. The important thing was the candy. I needed a candy that would truly stand out. One that would be noticed and remarked upon. It couldn't be just another white dress worn to another debutante ball. I needed something no one had ever seen, or tasted, before.

My mother would have had me devote all of my time to practicing dances and to going about the city making calls had I not reminded her, nearly constantly, of her promise.

"But you are not to neglect your duties. This is a chance not to be missed, nor to be despised."

"I don't intend to miss it." I was, however, beginning to despise it. But everything depended upon my attending . . . and upon the successful debut of the new candy.

I hurried up to my room after the morning's calls and exchanged my dress for a shirtwaist and skirt. Then I went down into the kitchen and helped Mrs. Hughes stir up the fire. I slipped on an apron and fastened it about my waist. "I'll need the big copper pot today, Mrs. Hughes. We're making candy."

Our family's cook had always been a willing participant in candy-making endeavors and our first tester of new sweets. But today she swatted my hand away when I reached for the pot. "Not until I've boiled my potatoes."

"Please?"

"If you're wanting to make candy, then maybe you should go down to the confectionery." A hint of regret in her eyes softened the frown on her face.

The confectionery . . . where everyone had witnessed that final argument with my father. Better, perhaps, to wait. I sat on a stool and buttered a tray in preparation, then helped Mrs. Hughes peel the potatoes.

I wanted to try out my idea for a nougat to learn what it would taste like with a flavoring. The trick of it would be to have the egg whites whipped at the same time the syrup was ready. While I was waiting for the potatoes to boil, I found some rose water at the back of a cabinet that I'd once used with my father. It wouldn't taste like orange flowers, but at least I'd find out if the texture was right. Next, I measured out a small amount of butter and set it on a saucer, sliding it onto the windowsill where it could soften in the sun. Then I separated eggs, collecting the whites into a bowl.

After Mrs. Hughes had drained the potatoes and washed out the pot, I put it back on the range and added sugar, water, and honey, stirring until the sugar dissolved and being careful to wipe away the forming crystals with a damp cloth.

I heard the screen door at the back of the kitchen yawn open and then slap shut. "Someone told me Lucy's back."

I felt my face break into a smile. "Sam!" I turned from my stirring.

"Lucy." He tipped his cap up as he winked at me.

Of all the people I'd missed during my time on the Continent, Sam topped the list. The son of my father's foreman, he had spent nearly as much time in the confectionery's kitchen as I had. He delivered candy around the city for the company and did odd jobs around the house. Tall and rangy, he still moved with steady deliberation. And his pockets still bulged with packages of Fancy Crunch. At least his wrists no longer stuck out from his cuffs as if stranded there at the end of his sleeves. Or if they did, I couldn't tell. He'd rolled his sleeves up, exposing muscled forearms I hadn't known he possessed.

I took another look at him. Where had all the sharp angles and gangly limbs gone? He seemed to have grown into himself somehow. As he approached, I felt shy and rather . . . small. He'd turned into a man while I'd been gone.

I swallowed.

He smiled and that grin made up for all the uncertainty and awkwardness I'd felt at his approach.

"I'm making a new candy. Want to help me?"

"I don't know, Lucy. Maybe I should come back some other time." He was backing toward the door.

"Please?"

"How long is this going to take?"

"Not long. Not as long as toffee would."

I gave him charge of the pot of syrup as I took up a whisk and began to beat the egg whites. My time on the Continent had done me no good at all. Though I changed hands, my arms quickly grew tired, and I had to ask Sam to trade with me.

As I lifted the spoon from the pot, syrup trickled from it in a thick thread. Almost ready. Taking the spoon out of the pot, I let a few drops of syrup fall into a clear glass filled with water. Scooping out the ball that formed, I pressed it between my thumb and finger. It was getting hard, but I could still feel it give a little as I squeezed: time for the egg whites. "Can you bring that bowl over here, Sam? Quickly?"

He came over, holding the bowl against his chest in the crook of his elbow.

I grabbed a ladle from a drawer and dribbled a bit of syrup into his bowl. "Keep beating those. Don't let up."

"My arm is going to fall off! I thought you'd have given up candy making by now."

Why had everyone assumed that my affection for candy was something I'd grow out of? "Just keep going." I dribbled a little more.

"Are we done yet?"

"Not yet." I took the bowl from him and beat the egg whites until they'd become stiff once more. I thrust the bowl into his arms and went to look at the still-boiling syrup. It needed to reach the hard-crack stage before I could add it to the egg whites.

I waited for the color to change, then dipped a spoon in and dripped some syrup into my glass of water. This time, when the syrup hit the water, it formed spindly threads. As I fished one out, it snapped in two. Perfect!

Wrapping a cloth around the handle, I elbowed Sam. "Set your bowl down for a minute but keep beating. I'm going to dribble this syrup into it."

He obliged while I dribbled. Then I discarded the pot and set about beating the mixture in the bowl myself. After a while, it began to separate into ribbons as I pulled the whisk through it. "Can you do exactly what I say, when I say it?"

"Haven't I always?" Though he mumbled the words, I heard them.

"I need you to add a few drops of that rose water to this. S*lowly*. And then follow it up with that butter that's on the windowsill. And after that, I'll need a couple dashes of salt too."

He complied well enough with the rose water and the butter as I beat them into my mixture. But I pulled the bowl from him when he took up the salt cellar and dipped into it with a teaspoon. "A couple of *dashes!*"

He set the salt down and took the bowl from me along with the whisk. "If you're going to be so persnickety about it, then you do it."

I added a couple pinches and grabbed the bowl back. Once it began to ribbon again, I poured it out onto the tray. After rubbing the saucer that had held the butter across my fingers to grease them, I pressed the nougat into a thin, flat layer. "There! Now we can let it rest the night."

"The whole night? You mean I can't have *any*? After I worked so hard?"

Good grief. "Can you butter a knife for me, then?"

Sam rummaged through a drawer, found a knife, then opened the icebox and plunged it into a bowl of butter.

Mrs. Hughes let out a cry.

"Sorry. Just doing what Lucy said."

It wasn't near being set, but I pried out a piece and handed it to Sam. "Try this and tell me what you think." I gave one to Mrs. Hughes as well.

He took the piece I offered. Chewed for a moment and then stopped. Swallowed. Once. Twice.

"Well?"

"It tastes fine."

"Fine?"

He shrugged. "It's fine."

"I don't want fine, Sam. I want wonderful. Delicious!"

"It tastes like . . . roses."

"I know. I used rose water."

He dug furiously in his pocket for something and came out with a handkerchief. Then he stuck his tongue out and scrubbed at it. "If I wanted to eat roses, I'd have picked some of Mr. Carleton's when I walked by."

"So . . . you wouldn't buy this sort of thing?"

"If I were going to take a lady flowers, don't you think she'd appreciate the normal kind?"

"You wouldn't buy *any* of this ever for yourself?"

"And have everyone down at the confectionery laugh at me? For eating roses?" He sniffed at his fingers. Scowled. Wiped them off on his shirt.

"I think it tastes just fine, Miss Lucy." Mrs. Hughes put another piece into her mouth. "And it smells divine. My mother would devour a tray of these." She gave Sam a long look as she spoke.

"Here." I passed the tray to her. "You can take these home to her, then." I wasn't interested in creating a candy for old ladies. I wanted to make a candy that everyone wanted to eat. Something unrivaled. Something like Royal Taffy, the candy I wasn't supposed to mention, let alone eat.

But it was a candy that haunted me, the same way it haunted my father. He had spent the last ten years of his life trying to create a candy that could top its chewy sweetness, match its glossy sheen, and surpass its creamy texture. And I had lived those same years wanting to help him. Even when I had tasted the finest confections Europe had to offer, Royal Taffy lurked in my thoughts.

Everyone loved it. Standard claimed it was the bestselling candy in America. Though I didn't trust them for one minute, I had to believe they weren't lying about that. Certainly, it had the broadest appeal. Newsboys spent their hard-earned money to buy it. Schoolgirls saved their pennies for it. I'd even seen men eat it without any apparent embarrassment.

I needed a candy that could compete with creamy, chewy, melt-in-your-mouth Royal Taffy. Not even our sweet, colorful, candy-coated nuts could do that. And rose-water nougat wasn't going to be able to do it either. I nibbled at a piece and closed my eyes as I analyzed the texture. It was light and chewy, dense and airy, just as I'd hoped.

It was perfect.

But it didn't compare to Royal Taffy. I'd have to come up with something else.

6

Charlie

I wished that girl would run into me again. The one down on Olive Street. She was the best thing I'd seen since I'd been in the city. And when I'd smiled at her, it was the first time I'd felt like myself in a long time.

And then that woman had accused me of being some thief.

Not in so many words, of course. She'd been much too polite for that. Those fancy people always were. And God knew I'd done worse. Still, I wished I'd gotten the girl's name. Then I'd know who it was I'd been daydreaming about.

I sighed.

Better not to think about her at all. When that girl had gone on down the sidewalk without me, it was all for the best.

I looked over at Mr. Mundt, my father's secretary, but he was trying hard to ignore me. I crossed my legs at the ankles and folded my arms across my chest as I sucked on a piece of candy.

It was already Tuesday, and though my father had mentioned placing me on his personal staff, I had no idea whether he intended that I work for him at the house or from his office. I'd never yet overslept, but I hadn't woken early enough to join him at breakfast either. And aside from some winks and a pat or two on the back as he and Augusta went out in the evenings, I hadn't really seen him. I asked Augusta if there was something I should be doing, but she only told me that I would be sent for the moment he wanted me.

I might have wandered the city, but my new clothes didn't fit the places I normally would have gone, and I didn't know where rich people spent their time. Besides, I didn't want to stray too far from my father. After another day spent waiting, I asked Nelson to take me to the factory.

I couldn't say for sure that I surprised Mr. Mundt. Truth be known, I don't think anything ever surprised him. Pale to a fault, he might have been thirty or sixty or anywhere in between. He only blinked as I walked in, then held up a box filled with candy. After taking a couple pieces, I'd sat in an uncomfortably stiff leather chair reading the newspaper and examining the company's brochures. But my father never came out of his office, and he never rang the secretary. I'd been waiting my entire life for him, in one way or another, and I was tired of it. If I was going to work for him, then I needed to learn about his business. I finished off the candy, balled up the wrapper, and pitched it toward the dustbin. "Mr. Mundt?"

After marking his place in a ledger with a finger, he looked up at me. "Yes, sir?"

"I wonder if I could have a look around. Over in the factory, maybe?"

He blinked, offering blessed relief from his pale blue eyes. "Now, sir?"

I shrugged. "I don't see why not."

He frowned. "The boss never goes over there."

I winked at him. "The boss brought me here to help him, so I figure I should know how things work around here."

After a moment, he nodded. "I'll telephone the superintendent and have him come up to escort you."

The superintendent appeared not five minutes later. He came in through the door, red-faced and panting. "The boss wants me?"

Mr. Mundt shook his head. "Not the boss. The boss's son. Mr. Clarke."

"Oh! Well, that's a relief." He fanned his face with the hem of his apron, then used it to dab at the sweat that had broken out on his brow.

I put a hand out once he'd finished. "I'm Charli—es. Charles. I'm Charles Clarke."

He brushed his hand off on his apron before extending it to me. "John Gillespie, sir."

"Mr. Gillespie, I hear you're just the man to show me what it takes to be successful in this business."

"The business? You mean . . . you want to go down to the *factory?*"

"Why not?"

"The boss won't mind?" He asked the question of Mr. Mundt.

Mundt gave Mr. Gillespie the smallest of shrugs.

Mr. Gillespie sighed. "All right. Fine." He untied the apron and pulled it off over his head, handing it to me. His sleeves and trousers had gone gray where the apron had not covered them. "Might not help much, but you'll not want to dirty that fancy suit of yours."

I put it on and followed him out the door and down a staircase at the back of the long, dark hall. We went through a maze of halls and up and down stairs before emerging into the sunlight alongside several sets of railroad tracks. He nodded across them to a long bay of doors in the building on the opposite side. "That's where the supplies come into the factory."

"From . . . ?"

"Just about everywhere. New Orleans, Chicago, Cincinnati."

I looked up and down the track. "What railroad is this?"

"It's a private spur. Boss had it built. It connects with the main railway back toward Union Station. Once the supplies are taken off, then we load the cars up and ship our crates out."

"Where to?"

"Pretty much everywhere. Royal Taffy's the bestselling candy in the whole United States." There was a note of pride and satisfaction in his words.

I ate Royal Taffy all the time, but I hadn't realized everyone else in the country did too. "So . . . the supplies come in and then what happens to them?"

"Well, now, that's when it starts to get interesting." We crossed the tracks to the factory building that stood on the other side. He motioned to a loading dock that jutted from the wall. Trying to forget that I'd ever met Mr. Dreffs, I took a step backward and then leaped forward to vault up onto the platform.

The superintendent climbed a ladder I hadn't seen on the other side of the dock.

That would have been handy to know about. "I just thought . . ." Now my hands were dirty, and there was no other place to wipe them than on the apron.

The superintendent sent a questioning look my way. "Might have thought you'd worked on a dock a time or two yourself—if I hadn't known you were the boss's son."

I hadn't really ever worked *on* a loading dock, though I'd seen my share of them, delivering messages on the South Side. I cleared my throat. "After the supplies are delivered?"

Gillespie took me across the bay and through a door that opened into an enormous room. It was filled with light and sound and motion. "It depends on what part of the process they're for," he shouted over the clatter of machinery.

I leaned close to him. "Give me a for instance."

"Well . . . over here are the melting pots. That's for the sugars—brown and white, vinegar, and water. Butter gets added later." He walked toward a raised concrete grid work. Huge kettles hung from metal bars. Beneath the kettles, fires danced, throwing off a scorching heat. Between the kettles, men walked on a precarious treadway peering into the huge pots.

A trickle of sweat slid past my collar and down between my shoulder blades.

"For the melting, we use men. Boys aren't tall enough. And girls can't take the heat. After a couple hours, once it gets hot enough, we pour the syrup off into those buckets." He gestured toward a line of wheelbarrows that were filled with pails. As we watched, two men wearing masks and padded mitts tipped a kettle, pouring off some of the contents into the pails in one of the wheelbarrows. A boy wheeled it away, head turned from the steam, as another one came to take his place. "The boys take the pails over there, to the mixer where the flavoring gets added."

"Over there" was halfway across the room, where several men on ladders were shaking the contents of jugs into huge vats. At least . . . that's where the procession of boys steering the wheel barrows was headed. But they had to dodge a parade of carts that were being pushed along some sort of track that had been set into the floor.

The traffic inside this building was the worst I'd seen since I'd arrived in St. Louis. With the open flames beneath the kettles and the dusty powder that covered the room, the place was a firetrap.

Gillespie gestured past the mixer to a different machine. "And then, once everything's been mixed in, the boys bring over trays, and the men pull that plug there at the bottom of the mixer. The taffy pours out, and then it's wheeled over there to cool." He was pointing away from the mixer to one of the corners of the room. Trays that had been placed on what looked like tea carts were being pushed in that direction. "It's got to cool for a while, but not for too long. Then those trays get wheeled over to the pulling machines."

He didn't have to point those out. The mechanical arms were waving like madmen.

"After it's been pulled, we throw it back into the wheelbarrows and take it to the tables. Couple of the men size out the ropes, then cutters take over. They dump their pieces back onto the trays, and they get wheeled off to be packed." He pointed to the fourth corner, where I could see a dozen white-capped women plucking the log-shaped pieces from the trays, folding red waxed wrappers around them, and pushing the rectangular candies farther down the tables. At the end, a small army of girls swept the pieces into boxes, then placed the boxes into crates.

"From there?"

"Got some boys who load the crates onto carts." He nodded in the direction of one of those track-bound carts that rolled past us. "Then they push the crates out to the docks, where I've got some fellows who put them onto a pallet."

I looked at the far corners of the building where Royal Taffy made its way through a number of steps in its dizzying path around the factory. "Wouldn't it make more sense to have the packers near the docks? And the mixer next to the melting pots?"

He shrugged. "But then where would you put this?" He gestured to an enormous funnel that was pierced with all kinds of pipes that hadn't had anything at all to do with the process I'd just watched.

"What's that?"

"It's a grinder."

"What does it have to do with Royal Taffy?"

"Nothing. It's for something different. Something new. But the powder has to be pushed out and taken next door."

This was one of the largest buildings I'd ever seen, and there was another one next door? "If it has to go next door, then why isn't this grinder next door too?"

The superintendent shrugged. "This was the only space available."

We parted the procession of children pushing wheelbarrows and walked past packers, out the door, down a few steps, and into the next building. It looked newer than the previous one and just as big. It should have been brighter, too, but a murky haze hung like a cloud over the room.

The superintendent handed me a gauze mask.

I tied it on. "Why is it like this?" It wasn't as noisy in this building, but there was a thumping vibration that seemed to pound my words back into my chest. I had to make an effort to force them out.

"It's the pulverizer."

I could tell this was the domain of children, though the powder-coated ragamuffins looked more like phantoms. "Are there any other buildings?"

"No. It all takes place here. And back where we were." He pointed the way we'd come, and we walked in the direction of that first building. "Let me show you out."

With the haze and the strange sight of children marching through the gloom, I might have wandered there for hours before finding the door I'd come in through.

As we approached the railroad dock, a train puffed up. We pressed ourselves against the wall while men rushed forward to

unload it. They swarmed the cars, pulling off boxes and carrying them into the building. Once the train left, I gave the apron
back to Mr. Gillespie, walked across the tracks, and eventually
found my way to the front of the office building.

I could do a lot worse for myself than work for my father.
But from what I'd just seen, I knew he could do a lot better.

7

My aunt and uncle left the day after my second fitting at Vander-voort's, so I worked the rest of the week on the new candy, soliciting Sam's help with my efforts.

He came into the kitchen on Friday afternoon, face glum. "A peck of pistachios costs more than a peck of peanuts *and* walnuts put together."

I felt my hopes plummet to my toes. I had been experimenting with honey-flavored nougat in hopes that I could mix pistachios in with it. "You haven't told your father what I'm working on, have you?" I didn't want word getting back to my father, or anyone else, until I had a chance to unveil the candy at the ball.

"No . . . but it's been hard, trying to use the telephone down at the confectionery without him knowing. But he's going to find about all those calls I made when the bill comes in."

"I need to keep it a secret."

"It will be. For two more weeks. I promise."

"No one can know, except for you and me." I had to stand on my toes in order to whisper the words into his ear, magnifying the impression that he'd grown.

"No one but you and I and Mrs. Hughes, you mean?" As he whispered back to me, he gestured with his chin toward the cook, who had been watching our work during the course of the week and making suggestions; she was, even now, party to our conversation, leaning just as close to Sam as I was.

I put a wrist to my forehead to push away the damp tendrils that had escaped from the cap I'd donned for candy making. "Yes, of course." I didn't bother to whisper this time, and I really couldn't think why I had in the first place. The cook knew everything that went on in City Confectionery. She always had. "And Mrs. Hughes."

She smiled and carried on with the drying of a pan, turning from us to place it into the cupboard.

"Do you think . . ." Honey was such a mild flavor. It wasn't very remarkable. "Could I interest you in something made with violets? A violet cream, maybe?"

"No!" His eyes were wide with horror.

"But—"

"I mean it: No flowers. I'm begging you." He pantomimed going down on bended knee.

"But you haven't—wait!" I'd been hit with an inspiration. "Stir this and just wait here for a minute." I fled the kitchen for the back stairs.

"And where else would I go, I'd like to know?" His voice floated up the stairs behind me.

I went to my room, being careful to avoid the squeaky floorboards in the hall so as not to wake Papa. Once there, I knelt before my chest and gathered a selection of the candies I'd brought back from Europe. I heaped them onto a handkerchief and drew the corners together into a knot. And then I retrieved the gift that I'd bought for Sam in Germany. I'd meant to keep it for Christmas, but he'd been so helpful in the kitchen I couldn't think of any good reason to save it.

Back in the kitchen, I offered up my treasures to him.

He took his gaze from the pot and eyed them. Then he looked over at me. "Are they any good?"

"They're the best of all that I tried while I was there."

"What's this one?" He was pointing at a small cube that had been wrapped in waxed paper.

"A caramel. Want to try it?"

He glanced down at the pot he was stirring and then at me. "I suppose."

I picked it up, unwrapped it and put it in his mouth.

As he bit down, his face changed.

"It's a caramel with pine nuts."

He looked as if he were going to spit it out, but then he drew his jaw back together and chewed. A look of something close to relief swept across his face as he swallowed. "It's not half bad."

I handed him a hard candy.

He took it with his free hand, popped it into his mouth, and sucked on it. Raised his brows. "I like this one. It tastes . . . different."

"I know! There's a pinch of pepper in it. Chile pepper, they called it."

He made a face. "In a boiled candy?" He crunched it up and then swallowed.

"Try this one. Open up your hand." I took a packet from the handkerchief, tore the flap and poured some of the powder from it into his palm.

He looked down at me. "What am I supposed to do with it?"

"Eat it, you ninny!"

He shook it into his mouth, eyes soon widening with surprise. He opened his mouth just enough to speak. "What is it?"

"Sherbet powder. It's—"

"Fizzy! What do you think of this, Mrs. Hughes?" He turned toward the cook, letting some of it foam from his lips as if he were a rabid dog.

I pulled him back. "Stop teasing, Sam. This is serious business." I took the spoon from him and set it down.

He slurped the foam back and swallowed it. "I don't think you should make a—what did you call it?"

"Sherbet. Try that other one." I nodded toward my handkerchief. "The square one. I don't want to do a chocolate, it would take too much time, but I want you to try it."

He took a block of what the English had called a *Scottish tablet.*

"It looks like fudge."

I nodded.

He put it to his mouth and bit off a corner. "It doesn't feel right. It's . . ."

"The sugar's been crystallized. So it's crunchy."

"Who wants crunchy fudge?"

"You don't like it?"

The glance he gave me was apologetic. "Not much."

He didn't like any of them? Not one of my carefully collected treasures? He'd spurned all of the best candies Europe had to offer. "I don't suppose you'd want to try a jelly drop flavored with geraniums?"

"*No flowers.* I'm serious. If you make me eat flowers again, I'm not helping you anymore."

I picked up another hard candy. "How about a sour plum?"

"*Sour* plum? Are you trying to poison me? It's called candy for a reason. It's supposed to be sweet!"

72

I sighed as I popped it into my own mouth. My taste buds tingled with an explosion of saliva. It was followed by a pleasing tightening of the inside of my cheeks and a prickling at the sides of my tongue.

"Is this all you brought? I mean, they were fine and all, but I was just hoping . . . I was hoping for something new. Something . . . *grand*."

I sighed. I was too. I liked the novel tastes and textures of the candies I had brought back, but there was nothing among them that was truly magnificent.

"There's *nothing* else?"

"Well . . ." There had been, in fact. "There was a box of hazelnut chews . . . but I ate them all." I'd devoured the entire box that first night back, alone in my bedroom in the dark as I worried over my father's health.

"Were they any good?"

"Oh! I can't even tell you! They were like . . . nothing I've ever tasted before."

"Then that's what you should make. Forget about all these others. Make the one you'd most want to eat."

"Do you think so?"

He gave me a look at me I recognized from the days when he had decided that boys were superior, in every way, to girls. "You had your choice of all of these and which one did you choose?"

Hazelnut chews. That's what I would make. As long as hazelnuts weren't too expensive and I could make the candies using the equipment the confectionery already had, then my dream might just be within reach. "Sam? Do you think you could—"

"Find some hazelnuts?"

I nodded as I moved to embrace him.

"Guess I'll have to make some more telephone calls."

"Before you go . . ." I took the present I'd brought back for him from my pocket.

He undid the string and opened up the box. After lifting the paper, he drew out the gift, cupping it in the palm of his hand. It was a whistle in the shape of a cuckoo bird. I'd thought it was the cleverest thing when I'd seen it in a village in the Black Forest. But now that he was holding it, I realized how silly and childish a toy it was. "I saw it . . . and thought of you. I'm sorry, Sam . . ."

"This is perfect. I know just what to do with it."

"Lucy?" I heard my mother's footsteps coming down the hall.

Sam took the packet of sherbet from the handkerchief. "You mind if I use some of this?"

I didn't mind at all. He liked my gift! Perhaps I could trust my instincts after all.

"Lucy—there you are!" Somehow my mother managed to simultaneously frown at Sam and smile at me, while she leaned over to sniff Mrs. Hughes' apple pie. "Have you forgotten about the Gilbertsons' tea?"

I had.

"Our agreement involved your participation in society."

"But I'm not done yet! I need another half an hour." At least.

"You don't have another half an hour. What you have is fifteen minutes to clean yourself up and change before we depart."

"But—"

"I don't wish to hear any excuses. Candy is not my primary concern. It's not going to propose marriage to you or ensure we have food to put on our table."

Sam wiggled his eyebrows at me.

I smothered a laugh with my palm. Maybe he hadn't changed so much after all.

Mrs. Hughes was untying my apron as Mother spoke. As I pulled it from my head, my cap came off along with it.

"Upstairs." Mother preceded me into the hall. "Now!" The word rang out like the slap of a ruler at Mary Institute, where I'd gone to school.

I brushed against Mrs. Hughes as I passed. "If you pull the syrup off now, you can probably use it for pancakes."

She patted my arm.

Mother was waiting for me at the bottom of the stairs. "I'd like you to consider that Samuel Blakely is not a suitable companion for a girl in your position."

He'd been just fine before I'd left for the Continent.

"And I don't expect that you were ever late to any of your appointments in Europe."

We hadn't been. In fact, most of the time, we were so anxious to see the sights we'd been early. "No."

"Then please allow those of us who stayed behind the same courtesy."

8

The telephone rang on Monday morning, and I heard Augusta answer. A minute later, the butler found me in the parlor, where I'd been working on a better plan for the factory. I'd been at it for over a week now, and I thought I'd almost got it.

He bowed. "You are wanted on the telephone."

Augusta was in the hall standing beside it. "It's your father. He's asked to speak to you."

I'd never, in fact, used one of the contraptions.

She gestured to what looked like a horn.

I picked it up, not knowing what to do with it.

She sighed and then guided it to my ear.

"Hello?" Funny. There was a buzzing sound, but no one was there. "Hello?"

She tapped my on the shoulder and then gestured to a candlestick-looking piece.

Oh. Maybe . . . I leaned over and spoke toward it. "Hello?"

"Mr. Clarke?" I jumped as the voice came to me, not from

the candlestick, but from the horn that was pressed to my ear. "This is Mr. Mundt. The boss would like to see you at the office. Immediately."

"Oh. Well—" I was speaking into the horn. Augusta picked up the candlestick and held it in front of my mouth. I leaned toward it, pressing the horn back against my ear. "Fine. Fine, then. Thank you."

There was a click from the horn, and the annoying buzz stopped. I held it out toward Augusta. She took it from me and set it on the hook that projected from the stand. "If you're needed at the factory, Nelson can take you."

Though I'd been told my father had wanted to see me immediately, I waited at the office for nearly an hour before Mr. Mundt waved me toward his door. Apparently, some things never changed.

My father pointed toward a chair with his cigar.

I sat.

"I was hoping you could help me."

And I'd been hoping he would ask. "I've been working on a new plan for—"

"You see, I find myself in a bit of a bind. I owe someone a favor, and it's time to pay it back. But it involves putting an end to a competitor."

Putting an end to someone back in Chicago had meant breaking their kneecaps or throwing them off a bridge. I was almost sure it didn't mean anything quite so drastic down here. At least . . . I hoped it didn't.

He looked at me over the tip of his cigar. "To start with, I've ordered up an advertising campaign. New posters, since the old ones are getting faded. That sort of thing. I don't want to do anything messy. Quick and tidy. If I can just take away all their business, that's best for us and for them. I need you to make sure the posters get put up in prominent places across the city. Atop my rival's would be a good start."

All of St. Louis was much bigger than Chicago's South Side, but I could do it. I'd figure out exactly how later. "I wanted to talk to you about the factory."

He turned his attentions to a sheaf of papers that was sitting before him. "Factory concerns should be taken up with Gillespie."

"I did take them up with him. Or mentioned them at least."

"And?"

"The factory isn't very well organized. I think you might be able to increase production if your machines were placed closer together. That way the workers wouldn't have to waste their time—"

"Haven't had any complaints about production. We sell more candy than anyone."

Sales. It had always been about the sale for my father. But life was more than money. "You're wearing out the workers for no good reason. If you'd go down and take a look—"

"Waste of time. Gillespie gets paid to take care of all of that. Sales is where the money's to be made."

"But he could make more candy for you to sell if you'd just—"

"You always were a stubborn one. Once you got something stuck in that head of yours, you wouldn't let it go. Not for anything." He smiled and winked, then picked up one of the papers sitting in front of him.

"Why did you leave?"

His brows peaked.

I'd startled myself with the question just as much as I must have startled him.

As he pushed the cigar into his mouth, his hand was shaking. He took a long draw on it before exhaling a billowing cloud of smoke. "Water under the bridge."

"But I want to know. I have a right to know."

"Does it matter? You turned out fine, didn't you? And you looked after them all just like I knew you would."

What kind of a man would leave the responsibility for his family in the hands of a seven-year-old?

"And you probably did a better job of it than I'd been doing."

"But *why?*"

He ground his cigar into an ashtray. "Why?" He shrugged. "Why should I have stayed?" He tried to smile. "I doubt you even missed me."

"Miss you? You were never there anyway!"

"Do you think I didn't want to be? Do you think I liked knowing I couldn't provide for my own family? No matter how hard I tried? No matter how much I managed to sell? Every time I walked in the door, my failure slapped me in the face. All I did . . . all I tried to do . . . it was never enough."

"So you just . . . gave up? Is that what you're saying?"

"What good was I to you anyway?"

"You gave all of us up . . . and then you walked away and fell into this." It didn't seem like he'd suffered much. Not the way we had. It sounded like he'd abandoned us and never looked back.

"Can we . . . forget about all of that? It's not really worth remembering, is it? Besides, you're here now."

But being here had required a lot of years of being back there, in Chicago.

"Sometimes you have to leave the past behind and start again," Father continued.

"But what about us? Because you left, we never had that chance."

"I won't say it was the right thing to do. . . ."

"Why didn't you come back for us?" Why hadn't we mattered?

"And say what? What would you have wanted me to say?"

"I'm sorry?" That would have worked as a start.

My father's shoulders dropped. "I am. I've always been sorry. But sorry wouldn't have done you any good back then. So . . . why don't we concentrate on what I can offer you now?" He stood and held out his hand.

When I didn't extend mine, he jammed it into his pocket. "I know I don't deserve a second chance, but I'm hoping you'll give me one anyway."

A second chance.

He only wanted me to offer him what he was giving me, but it didn't seem fair. What had he ever done to deserve it? I owed him nothing. He owed me everything. So it was much easier to ignore his request and think instead about what he'd asked me to do. It didn't sound too difficult until Mr. Mundt had told me there were a thousand posters waiting to be hung.

One thousand posters.

To be put in prominent places.

Were there even a thousand places to hang posters in the city?

That afternoon, I rode a streetcar downtown and walked through the city. I battled shoppers on Olive Street. I pushed through vendors on Washington Street, counting all the Royal Taffy posters I could find and looking for new places to hang them. It was hot, thirsty work, so I took a break to listen to some ragtime in a place called Chestnut Valley. It wasn't much of a valley. Wasn't much of anything I could see, but as soon as I heard the music, it felt like home.

I walked into the middle of a cutting contest and joined the crowd in cheering as two pianists played up and down a pair of pianos, each trying to leave the other behind by changing keys and tunes. Eventually one outplayed the other. The loser left his piano and collected a beer from the bar before joining the rest of us in hailing the victor.

As I walked the streets, I didn't see many posters for other companies' candies, and those I did see had been pasted up alongside signs for prizefights or election notices. They were mostly in alleys and on the sides of buildings. I planned to cover them all with Standard posters—it wouldn't take too much work—but I needed to find someplace better to put our advertisements. Someplace that people couldn't help but see.

Where did people gather?

They went to and came from Union Station by the hundreds, but where else did they go? I asked Nelson that evening. "Where do you go when you get time off?" I was watching him polish the brass headlights of the car I'd learned he called Louise.

"Well . . . Sunday afternoons, what I like to do is go to Forest Park. They got some bears there and that big birdcage you can walk through. The one leftover from the Exposition. There are boats you can rent. Usually someone playing music at that bandstand. Always something going on at Forest Park."

"What would you say most people here like to do? Where do they go on Saturdays or on Sunday afternoons?"

"It depends. There's that swimming pool over on Delmar with its dancing pavilion." He straightened for a moment and put a hand to his back. "Some go over to Chestnut Valley to listen to that ragtime music." He shrugged. "Folks go all over, I suppose."

So how could I make sure they saw Standard advertisements everywhere they went?

Augusta was having some club of women over for tea the next day, so I hightailed it out of the way and found myself once more on a streetcar headed into the city. We passed houses and schools and churches. At each stop we picked up mothers and their children. Soon the streetcar was crammed with them. One of the little boys beside me was sucking on a log of Royal Taffy.

He clutched it tighter when he saw me looking at him.

At a nickel a stick, Royals weren't cheap. They were a treat to be saved up for. A prize to dream of. Across from me, I saw a child counting her pennies as she eyed the boy and his candy.

If I had to put up posters, it should be in places children could see them.

I knew what it was to be a child, hoping against hope for something good to happen. I knew the victory that came with each carefully collected penny and the triumph that swelled the chest on the walk to the store. But best of all was the satisfaction that came from having a Royal Taffy taste exactly like you'd dreamed it would. A gooey, chewy, creamy piece of heaven. I'd always been able to count on a Royal Taffy in a way I was never able to count on my father. The candy had never disappointed me. Not the way he had.

If hanging up those posters would give some boy like I'd once been something to hope for, something to believe in, then to my way of thinking, it was a job worth doing.

9 ——————————————— — *Lucy* —

The Veiled Prophet parade that preceded the ball was inter-minable. I just wanted the whole thing over and done with. I'd been making and packaging my new candy for two weeks now, hiding the cube-shaped, cellophane-wrapped pieces down in the cellar. There were ten thousand people expected at the ball. Tonight, I would finally have the chance to introduce my hazelnut chews to the city!

I smiled and waved along with the other members of the court as the horses drew us down Olive Street. Firecrackers exploded; confetti filled the air.

I caught a glimpse of Sam. I waved and tossed a flower in his direction. He didn't see me. He seemed taken with the girl who was standing by his side. I might have said she was just a child, she was that short; only she wasn't looking at him in the way a girl would. And her figure filled out her dress in a way that I could only hope mine would one day do.

"Wave! Smile!" One of the other girls reached over and poked at me with her bouquet.

The wind gusted, blowing the skirts of our matching white dresses about and teasing our hair from our flowered coronets. It made conversation nearly impossible, unless we wanted to scream our words. I didn't have much to say to them in any case. I contented myself with watching the crowds, and I assumed the others had too . . . until the wind subsided for a moment and I could hear what they had been saying.

" . . . only reason was because she went abroad . . . or maybe they felt sorry for her father . . ."

" . . . thinks she's too good for us . . . gown in Paris . . ."

"Why? Isn't Vandervoort's good enough?"

My face flushed as I wove together the snatches of conversation. I'd had nothing to do with being chosen as queen! And I hadn't gotten my gown in Paris. I'd gotten it at Vandervoort's, the same as they probably had. Did they think I couldn't hear them?

One of them looked back over her shoulder at me and smirked.

They knew I could hear them?

Well. Just . . . *well*! My chin began to tremble. I raised my arm and waved it vigorously. Too vigorously, perhaps. After a while I felt perspiration bead up on my brow and when I licked my lips, I could taste salt. But with my arm in front of my head and sweat trickling down my face, at least no one was able to see my tears.

At last the parade ended, and one of the city patrolmen drove me home in an automobile. Glad to be rid of my court, I put their ill-spirited comments aside as I turned my thoughts toward the evening.

If I hurried, I thought I just might have enough time to help Sam with the candy before I had to leave for the ball. By the time I'd washed my face, fixed my hair, and exchanged one white dress for another, more elaborate one, he was already more than half done.

"Remember, Sam, you're to bring them out—"

"As people are gathering, before the court is presented. I know."

"Do you think . . . no one should notice you, should they?"

"No. Unless you force them to because you're so worried about it and they wonder what on earth you keep staring at." His voice was piqued. His tone, annoyed.

"Do you think a Veiled Prophet Queen has ever fallen away in a dead faint before?"

He slanted a look down at me. "Do you really want me to answer you?"

"No."

He smiled. "You'll be the prettiest one up there. Don't worry."

"I'm not worried about *that*. I'm worried about *this*." I gestured toward the boxes of candy that he'd stowed in the delivery wagon.

"Everything will be fine."

Everything had to be fine. I gave the candy one last look before turning away. It was up to Sam now. I took up his hand in mine. "Thank you for being a true friend."

The hitch in his brows caused my heart to plummet to my stomach.

"What?" Something must have gone wrong.

"Do you think your hair is supposed to be falling down?"

I put a hand up to my hair only to discover one whole side had slipped its pins and was sliding down the back of my head. "No!" Not after I'd just re-pinned it. "Can you—can you help me?" I couldn't ask Mother. She'd want to know how I'd come to be in such a state. Last time she'd seen me, I'd assured her I was almost ready for the ball. Though she'd become used to seeing me in the kitchen, I doubted she would ever expect—let alone condone—what I planned on doing tonight. She would never approve of my using the ball as the venue for my candy's debut.

Sam scowled for a moment, and then his face suddenly brightened. "Just a minute." He ducked back into the kitchen, screen door flapping behind him, but soon returned. He fiddled with my hair, poking here and there, before pronouncing it done.

"Do you think it will stay?"

"It should. I used caramel sauce."

"What!"

"Mrs. Hughes was making some, and it hadn't cooled yet. Should hold like glue."

"The Queen of Love and Beauty can't go around with candy on her head!"

"It's the same color as your hair. I don't see why anyone should notice."

Why anyone should notice? Why wouldn't they! I took a deep breath. There was nothing I could do about it now. Even if I washed it out, my hair would take too long to dry. "Forget about my hair. Think about tonight. Let's rehearse it again. Once people start exclaiming over how good the chews are, you're going to say . . . ?"

He threw back his shoulders and pushed out his chest. "I'll say, 'I've heard it's City Confectionery's new premium candy.'"

"Right. And you have the recipe?"

He patted his coat pocket. "I've got it here. The minute I get home, I'll hand it to my father."

"And . . . ?"

"And tell him to start production first thing tomorrow morning."

People would go home from the ball talking about the candy. With luck, maybe the newspaper would even mention it. By tomorrow evening, people across the city would be clamoring for my chews. The company's future was all but assured!

"There's no need to be nervous."

I wouldn't have been if my mother hadn't kept telling me there was no need to be nervous. And if the car we were riding in wasn't being escorted down Olive Street by a pair of policemen on motorcycles who kept tooting their horns at every person they happened to see.

Mother smoothed the train of the gown that was looped over my arm, then stroked the ermine that lined my cape. "I don't think you've seen him since your return, but the Minard boy has quite improved since you left."

Not so much, I expected, as to overcome his unfortunate tendency to bray like a donkey. Though if he liked my candy, he could certainly proclaim its virtues to everyone with that piercingly loud voice of his.

At the Coliseum, we were escorted up the steps by the policemen. I didn't know what they thought might happen to me on the way from the car to the building, but I arrived quite safely. Inside, my old dancing school instructor, Mr. Mahler, met us. His hair was slick with oil, and he was in his accustomed knee breeches, although this night he was not wearing his black velvet ballet slippers. And in spite of all his efforts to the contrary, chaos reigned.

The girls in the court crowded close, exclaiming over my dress and paying compliments I now knew they could not mean. One of them commented on the scent of my delicious perfume. I resisted the temptation to check if my hair was still holding and told her it had come from an exclusive shop in Paris.

Mr. Mahler made us all bow and curtsy several times before finally approving of our efforts. Then he drilled us on the steps to the Veiled Prophet lanciers and to his own dance, the Ostend. I hadn't performed the steps in months, but my schoolgirl training took charge of my feet. Thankfully, the intricacies of the dance were hidden by my trailing skirts. By the time he sent me up to the box of honor to wait for the ceremony, I was more than ready.

Up there, I had a bird's-eye view of floor. As the attendees began to appear, some of them gave a surreptitious look around the room and then edged toward the table filled with refreshments. I could see Sam down there. He was standing behind the tables and—oh! He'd already put my candies on display. They were mounded on a silver tray, their cellophane wrappers gleaming in the electric lights.

I held my breath as a man, resplendent in full dress with a swallowtail coat, snuck two chews from the tray. He placed one into his mouth and handed the other to the woman standing beside him. I could have clapped my hands in delight. Perhaps by the time I was crowned queen, word of my candies would already have spread through the room. Tonight could be nothing but a triumph!

10 — *Charlie*

Tuesday, October fourth, marked my entrance into St. Louis society. I'd spent the week before pasting posters onto telegraph poles outside schools. My neck still had a crick in it from all the time I'd spent peering up at walls and telegraph poles. My hand had callouses where I'd gripped the handle of a pail of paste. But I'd coaxed streetcar operators into letting me put posters on the outside and inside of their cars, and convinced my father that several dozen posters placed in prominent locations around South St. Louis weren't a waste of my time or his posters. If Royal Taffy were a treat, then even the newsies and factory workers should be allowed to dream of them. One thousand posters were now up across the city.

That night after supper I dressed in my new swallowtail coat. I took extra care with my razor, guiding it over the scar on my jaw, and I buffed my shoes to a first-class shine. It took three tries to get my white bow tie to sit straight, and by then it was already eight o'clock.

I spat into my hand and then pressed it to the cowlick at my temple. It lay flat for a moment, then sprang back into place. I frowned at Charles-in-the-mirror, wondering if he were in danger of becoming as dull and stuffy as he looked.

After taking my top hat from its box, I left my bedroom. I did a quick two-step before pulling my gloves on and walking down the stairs in what I hoped was a respectable manner. Someday, when no one was around, I planned to slide down the long curving banister.

But not tonight.

Not with my father and Augusta watching.

My father clamped his cigar between his teeth, then grinned and nodded. I shoved down the pride that began to warm my chest at my father's approval. Pretending I belonged, I followed them out the door.

We were driven downtown to the Coliseum by Nelson. The buildings were still draped with bunting from the parade that had passed through town earlier in the day, and confetti still littered the streets. We'd watched, the three of us, from the safety of a private room at a hotel. But there were no processions now. No floats or dirigibles. We were one of many in a long line of cars waiting to pull up at the front steps of the building. As we sat there breathing in fumes, Augusta leaned around my father to look at me.

"All the best families will be here, so we need to make sure you meet them. It's best to just make the introductions now and get them over with. I wouldn't want anyone to think we have anything to hide."

She'd already said that twice this evening.

"The Veiled Prophet Ball is one of the most important events of the year."

I knew that too. "Who is he, by the way?"

She frowned. "Whom do you mean?"

"The Veiled . . . person."

"Prophet. And no one knows. It's a secret." She put a hand to her head and adjusted the feathers that swirled out from her hair. "You do know how to dance a lanciers . . . ?"

I assured her that I did. Dancing was as good a way as any to stay warm during long winter nights. So was drinking. I forced my thoughts away from saloons. I needed to figure out how to be more like Charles, to become the person I looked like. And fast.

We walked into a room that evening that was even larger than the Standard factory buildings. Up around the ceiling it was ringed with a bunting-draped balcony. At the far end of the room was a platform. It was covered with fancy carpets. Potted plants and clusters of tall feathers surrounded a throne that had been placed in the middle. As I stood there, feeling as far from home as I'd ever felt, my father began introducing me around as his son who had finally come home to live with them. As if my absence had been my doing instead of his.

"This is Mr. Gray, Mr. Campbell, and Mr. Perry."

They were Important People. I could tell by the way they carried themselves, as if dressing up in swallowtail coats and attending balls were things they did every night of their lives. As I shook hands with them, another man, younger and taller, joined them.

"And this is Mr. Alfred Arthur."

I smiled and shook his hand too.

Mr. Perry shot Father a look from beneath his shaggy eyebrows. "Your son? I'd heard something about that." He looked at me, lips pursed. "You should bring him out to the club, Warren."

Mr. Gray turned to me. "You can play a round of golf, can't you?"

Golf? I'd never done it before. Never had the chance to. "Sure. Sure, I can. I can swing a . . ." What did they call those things? " . . . a bat along with the best of them."

They broke into laughter. All but the Arthur fellow. He sent me a wink. "Clarke's got the right idea. Who hasn't wished he could take a bat to one of those balls and hit a home run right down the fairway?" He clapped a hand to my shoulder, then nodded and walked away.

I stood there for a while with my hands behind my back, listening to them talk about taxes and telephones and gas works. Eventually, when my collar began to itch and my feet had swelled, I excused myself and left the room. Out near the entrance, I found a staircase. It was quiet and it was dark, so I decided to see where it led. Soon I found myself stepping into the balcony.

From up there, the ball was manageable. The air wasn't as stuffy, and I didn't have to worry so much about being Charles.

I slipped a finger between my bow tie and my collar and gave a good tug. Turning my head from side to side, I cracked my neck.

I wondered if this was how I was going to feel for the rest of my life: desperate to fit in with all these rich people and scared to death that I wouldn't. When my mother had told me I had a gift, it wasn't new information. I'd always been able to get people to like me. But that was back on the South Side.

I didn't know if it would work here.

The crowd swelled and the rumble of conversation began to rival the noise at the factory. But then the band played the kind of music that signaled a change in events, and everyone fell silent. Someone stepped onto the stage and announced the Veiled Prophet himself. I propped my elbows against the railing and folded my hands atop it as I watched. I just needed a

couple more minutes, and then I was sure I'd would feel like . . .
my new self again.

Charles Clarke. Son of Standard Manufacturing's Warren
Clarke.

If only Manny White could see me now!

I smiled at the thought.

A man walked out onto the platform. His head was wrapped
in a cloth, and a veil had been draped over it. He was dressed
in a long robe that had all kinds of tassels and things dangling
from it. He marched around the room, up and down, back and
forth. Three girls dressed in white gowns followed him. Eventually, he led them back to the platform. The girls were escorted
up onto it, then they turned to face the crowd as a fourth girl
began walking toward them down the center of the room.

The Queen of Love and Beauty.

It had to be her. The long trailing end of her gown was carried
by a pair of boys, and she held herself stiffly. But as I looked at
her, it seemed to me she didn't want to be there.

She looked the way I felt.

But who could blame her? Who could blame me? It was a
silly business, dressing up in turbans and robes.

She was given a crown, and then the veiled man said something I couldn't hear. The queen was presented with a sash.
And then she smiled.

Was that . . . ? I squinted, trying to get a good look at her
as she stood beneath the bright electric lights. Was she the girl
who'd walked into me on Olive Street? Before I had a chance
to decide, the band began to play again and the Veiled Prophet
swept her into a dance.

A lanciers.

If she were my partner, I would have asked for a waltz. A
waltz allowed you to take a girl into your arms and let her know

you liked her being there. A lanciers meant a whole lot of bowing and shuffling and trading partners. It was for people who couldn't decide who they wanted to dance with and were too dull to have a good time. It was probably impolite to think so, but I didn't care.

I went back to the ballroom after the ceremony. There were people to meet, and as Augusta had said, this was *Important*. I put on my best Charles face: that slightly bored, impatient look that all those rich fellows seemed to wear. I shook hands for a while as she made introductions, signing the dance cards of the girls she told me to.

"I'd like you to meet Winnie Compton, Charles." She indicated a girl with a mass of straw-colored hair and a very large smile. "She's from the Compton Consolidated Company Comptons. You ought to try to get on her card."

I let Augusta make the introduction and then tried to use the words *pleasure, delighted,* and *happy* in the same sentence as I asked if she had a dance available.

She took a look at her card. "I do. I have a two-step left if you'd like it."

I didn't really. I didn't want to dance with anyone, but I figured I shouldn't say that. I smiled instead as she handed me her pencil.

"It must be very trying to be the talk of the ballroom."

I glanced over and saw that she was smiling. I smiled back; I didn't know what else to do. "I . . . didn't realize that I was."

"Everyone's talking about you! But don't worry. When they ask, I'll tell them all that you were a perfect gentleman."

Was she implying that I wasn't? Was I supposed to thank her?

Eventually, people started to come up and introduce themselves to me. "I hear you're Warren's boy." They said it as if they didn't quite know what to think of me. I'd smile, they'd smile. "It's a good thing, what your father's done for you." That was one way of looking at it. I knew they were only trying to be polite, but I was starting to feel the same way I had when I'd been Manny's message boy. As if I owed my father a debt for something I wasn't quite sure I wanted . . . and that I could never hope to repay.

11 — *Lucy*

The crowning ceremony was performed with quite a lot of fanfare. I did Mr. Mahler proud, bowing low before the Veiled Prophet and standing supremely straight while the previous year's queen transferred her crown to my head. Once I'd danced the Veiled Prophet lanciers, the ball was officially declared open.

After that first dance, I pulled away from well-wishers and friends just as politely as I could. I saw people at the refreshments table trying my candy and wanted to make my way over, but my progress was blocked by my mother. She had a gentleman in tow. I thought . . . he seemed familiar, but I couldn't quite put a name to his face.

"Look who's here, Lucy!" She was smiling brightly. "It's Mr. Alfred Arthur."

I bit the inside of my lip to keep from giggling. We had always joked, my girlfriends and I, about which of those two names was his first and which was his last. He was a good ten years older than I, and his father owned the city's electricity company.

Often present at the social events in the city, he seemed to prefer to watch and hang about the fringes rather than participate. He was not unhandsome. *Pleasant* was the word I would have used to describe him, rather than attractive or even stylish.

He nodded at me. "I'd heard of your return, Miss Kendall, and I'm delighted to see you crowned our queen."

"Thank you." In spite of his years, I was flattered that he would take the trouble to tell me that himself.

The mother of one of my school friends approached us, clasping my gloved hand in hers and kissing my cheek. As she left, another woman came to take her place, clucking about my father's illness. As I greeted her, Mr. Alfred . . . Arthur . . . stepped back and disappeared into the crowd.

Walter Minard joined us, boldly taking up my gloved hand and planting a kiss atop it.

I vowed to throw the glove away once I got home.

"I don't see how they could have chosen anyone else. You're first in the city. A veritable model of pristine beauty."

The Alps were pristine; I didn't see how the word could be applied to a person. But then, he had never been especially bright. Just terrifically loud.

He flashed his large, yellow teeth at me in a grin.

I'd forgotten how obsequious he could be. "You're too kind, Walter. But you mustn't say things like that. The rest of the court would consider your compliments a snub." I struggled to see over his shoulder. If only I could reach Sam! I wanted to know what people were saying.

"A word to the wise." He stepped close enough that I could smell the stench of his breath. "I'd stay away from the refreshments if I were you. There's some sort of funny-tasting candy on the tray in the center."

I felt as if someone had pinched me. Quite hard. My breath

hitched for just a moment. "It's not nice to tease, Walter. Someone must have gone to a great deal of trouble to make it."

"Of course." He flashed those horrid teeth again in a semblance of apology. "Be glad it wasn't City Confectionery! And please give my regards to your father." He saluted and moved away.

Funny-tasting? Well! No one had ever accused Walter Minard of having any taste at all. "I need some punch." I left Mother before she could stop me and pushed through the crowds toward Sam.

Or tried to.

With every step someone stopped to congratulate me. Or welcome me back to the city. Or commiserate about my father. Sam bobbed in and out of view, but he never looked in my direction.

"Lucy!" A woman seized me by the shoulders and embraced me.

Did I know her?

"Don't you remember me?"

"Of course I do." I smiled, hoping that I would, and soon, before I embarrassed myself.

"Alice Fulton."

"Fulton . . . ?" The Alice I knew had been a Bingham. And she'd still been a gangly girl when I left, not a full-figured woman.

"I'm ever so glad you're back."

Her voice sounded right. And her eyes were that appealing shade of brown that I remembered. It had to be her . . . didn't it?

"Look at you! The Queen of Love and Beauty. I might have made the court last year, but I was already married by then."

"Married?" The Alice Bingham I'd known hadn't been able to talk to any boy without bursting into giggles.

"Hadn't you heard? To Peter Fulton."

A vision of a towheaded boy chasing her down a street with a frog danced in my head.

"You have to come over. Sometime this week. We can—or maybe . . . no. I forgot that Georgie has the colic. Maybe next week. He should be over it by then. I'll let you know. I'll send a note." She kissed me on the cheek and moved away, leaving me standing there watching her.

Who was Georgie?

A fluttering hand caught my eye. "Yoo-hoo!"

I had no trouble recognizing that wave. Or that voice: Winnie Compton. I grabbed the hand of the woman standing next to me and shook it. "So pleased to see you here tonight."

Her eyes registered surprise and then her brows drew together in consternation. "Have we . . . met?"

No. We hadn't met. But talking to a stranger was better than talking to Winnie Compton. I was hoping the woman would feel compelled to say something—anything!—but she only gathered up the skirts of her gown and turned her shoulder to me.

I felt a tap on my arm. "Lucy Kendall. It *is* you, isn't it?"

What could I say? Of course it was me! Who else would it be? Talking to Winnie always made me feel so irritated. And surly.

"So you're back." She was smiling at me. She was always smiling. I used to think that if someone threatened to murder her, the only thing she'd do in reply would be to smile and thank him.

"Yes."

"And you're the queen this year."

Yes. I was.

"We're the only two from our class that haven't married yet. Or gone off to the Orient as missionaries. Or gone to college. Or . . ." She leaned closer. "Eloped. I guess it's just the pair of us."

I felt a desperate longing to be engaged. "It was so nice talking to you, Winnie, but I really need to go now."

Her smile wobbled. "Oh. All right, then. That's fine." Another reason I felt like throttling Winnie: She always made me feel as if I'd somehow disappointed her. And she *was* awfully nice. She'd never done anything to anyone except smile. I was a bad person.

"When are your at-home days, Winnie?"

"This week?"

I already regretted the words I was going to say, but I nodded anyway.

"Thursdays. From two o'clock until four."

"I'll come for a visit."

"You will?" Her smile grew even larger, her eyes even wider.

I nodded. "I promise."

She squealed and kissed me on the cheek, then darted away toward the dance floor.

At last I reached the refreshments. As I surveyed the table, my spirits lifted. There wasn't one piece of candy left. I clasped my hands to my chest as I looked at Sam. "It's a success, then? It looks like every piece has been eaten!" As I spoke, a server whisked away one of the empty trays.

"No, Lucy, it's—"

Mistaking him for a fellow server, the man turned to Sam. "Now that those awful candies are gone, go back into the kitchen and get something else to take their place."

Had he said . . . ? "Did you say—?"

The server bowed. "Yes, miss. Someone delivered us candies that weren't worth eating, but we've thrown them all away. You're not to worry."

"Weren't worth—? But . . ."

Sam drew me away by the elbow.

"Weren't worth eating?" I looked up at him. "What was wrong with them?"

"Lucy . . ."

"No one liked them?"

"It wasn't the candy exactly. It's just that nobody liked the way they tasted. Maybe if—"

"No one?" No one had liked my candy? My father had been right. There was no place for me in his business. And it wasn't because I was a girl. He must have been trying to spare my feelings all this time. The truth of it was that I had no taste. I was just like that awful Walter Minard . . . and that's what hurt most of all. I took a step back from Sam.

"Lucy, wait—"

I couldn't. I didn't want to. I turned from him, gathered up my trailing skirt, and ran.

12

Charlie

I looked beyond the man who had introduced himself to me. The Queen of Love and Beauty was over by the food tables, talking to one of the servers. I'd been trying to get a good look at her face, but so far, I hadn't been able to. After I'd come down from the balcony, I'd almost talked myself into going up to her and introducing myself. After all, I'd probably never look more presentable than I did right now. But as I stood there, she put a hand to her mouth and spun away from the server. Then she gathered up her long skirt and ran from the room.

I watched to see who would go after her.

No one did. No one even seemed to notice. It's as if they'd all been put to sleep by the band's version of a waltz.

Putting my hand out to the man, an owner of some kind of store or other, I smiled. "It was nice meeting you. Please excuse me." I could have walked around the edge of the room, but the fastest way to reach the door was across the dance floor. Taking up the rhythm of the waltz, I slid between dancing couples, ducking once when I saw the girl I was supposed to dance with next.

I'd expected to see the queen out in the hall, but the only people there were drivers, waiting for the ball to end. Where would she have gone? Where would I have gone if I'd wanted to get away from everyone?

※⟨ↄ

I had already circled the balcony once before I found her. She had pressed herself into a corner, back against the wall, far from the reach of the ballroom's lights. She was crying the way my little sister had the year my mother told her Santa Claus wasn't coming.

As I walked up, I pulled my handkerchief from my pocket. "Those don't sound like tears of joy."

She turned her head from me.

I pressed the handkerchief into her hand. "Take it. I only carry one because that's what someone told me gentlemen should do."

She tried to give it back.

"Please, don't tell me he was lying."

Though she still wouldn't look at me, her fingers curled around it, and she lifted it to her cheeks.

I thought . . . if she would just look at me . . . I thought it might be *her*. That girl from Olive Street.

"Most girls would be over the moon, being named queen."

"I'm not like the others." She said it fiercely, eyes glaring at me above the handkerchief as if I should know better.

"So . . . if you're not crying about being queen, then what are you crying about?"

Her chin trembled as she dabbed at an eye. "No one liked my candy." She'd barely finished speaking before she began to howl as if I'd just declared the sun would never rise again. I probably shouldn't have done it, but I put an arm around her shoulder. I knew what it was like to have people disappoint you.

She clung to me, sobbing into my shiny silk lapels, burrowing into my shoulder, and tickling my nose with all the hair she'd piled on top of her head. But I didn't mind. She smelled delicious, just like caramel. It was a scent that matched the color of her hair. For one sweet moment, she stayed within the curve of my arm, but then she pushed away from me, turning once more, as if to hide her tears.

"*No one* liked it?" Didn't everyone like candy? What was wrong with the people in St. Louis?

Her chin dipped. "They threw it all away."

Something wasn't making any sense. "You mean you made candy and you brought it *here*? To the ball?"

She cupped the handkerchief over her mouth and held it to her nose, nodding.

Making candy seemed like a strange thing for a queen to have to do. "*I* never had the chance to try it. And I consider myself an expert in candy."

"You do? You like candy?"

"*Like* candy? You could say it's become my profession."

"Would you—would you like to try some?" The glow of the ballroom reflected off the tears that had made a path down her cheek. If she would just turn her head a little bit more . . . maybe I would recognize her.

"I would love to try some."

Her chin tipped up as a trembling smile crept up her face. She drew in a deep, shuddering breath and for the first time that evening, she looked up into my eyes.

It was her.

As she looked at me, her eyes widened. "But—I know you, don't I?"

I flashed her a grin and bowed. "I believe we've met before."

"You're—you're the man from the street! The one I bumped into." Her smile disappeared as she glanced toward the floor. She took a step from the shadows, moving toward the stairs. "And now I've inconvenienced you again. You must think me so rude."

I stepped forward and caught her hand in mine. "Don't go. Not yet. You promised me a taste of your candy."

For one long moment, she looked as if she might leave, but then she held up a fancy bag that dangled from her arm and fished inside it. When she brought out her hand, her fist was closed.

I held out my own hand, palm up.

She dropped something into it.

My fingers closed around it, but not fast enough to trap hers. I put it to my mouth and took a bite. Chewed. "Hmm."

She'd been watching me. At my comment, a silvery tear spilled from the corner of an eye. "You don't like it either."

"I didn't say that. What I said was . . . hmm. It's just that I've never tasted anything like it before." And I didn't particularly want to again.

"They're hazelnuts."

I nodded.

"And nougat."

I swallowed the rest whole before I'd have to chew it again. It had a strange, musty taste to it. "Have you ever thought of trying peanuts?"

Her chin trembled. But then it lifted. "Everyone's tried peanuts. I wanted to do something different."

She was so pretty with that hair around her forehead and those large blue eyes. "Then I have to say you succeeded."

Her eyes darkened for a moment, but then she broke into a smile. That dazzling, breathtaking smile. "That's the nicest thing anyone's said to me all night."

I smiled back. "The texture's very . . . different."

"I know! The chewiness of the nuts and the creaminess of the nougat. I tried something like it once before and I wanted to see if I could match it."

"And did you?"

She seemed to give my question some thought. Then she looked me right in the eye. "I think—I *had* thought—that mine was even better."

"Then does it really matter if no one else liked it?"

"That was the whole point. The *only* point. To make something I thought everyone else would like." The corners of her mouth had dipped again.

"Do you do this often? Just . . . make things up?" Usually people seemed so set on doing the same things the same way they always had.

"All the time! When my father was still . . ." A shadow seemed to pass over her face. Something about her glow dimmed. "I used to do it all the time when my father was well. Back when I was a child."

"I don't have the first idea about how to make candy." At least not without a factory and an army of workers. "But I do like to eat it."

The beginnings of a smile pulled at her lips. "Then you're my favorite kind of person."

"You really like it, don't you? Making candy?"

"It's all I've ever wanted to do: help my father make candy."

"Then it would be a shame if everyone down there talked you out of doing it."

Her shoulders sagged. "But why should I even try anymore if I'm not good at it?"

"Aren't you? Even the best candymakers must sometimes make mistakes."

She smiled again, but this time it didn't seem to reach her eyes. "You're very kind." She handed my handkerchief back. And then she glanced around the balcony. "Did you . . . follow me up here?"

I shrugged. "Someone had to. Besides, I don't belong down there, with all those fancy folks."

She gave me a look, from the tips of my bow tie to the tops of my shoes. "Why not?"

"I'm not like them. Not really. You can pretend to be anyone if you wear the right clothes." I turned back toward the railing and looked out at the people who were dancing down in the ballroom.

She put a hand to my arm.

I wanted to take it up and press a kiss to it, but I didn't. It was something I was sure Charles would never do.

"You should go back. They need you down there. *I* need you down there. You're different."

I flashed her a smile. I knew all about being different. "Different isn't always better."

"You're the only one tonight who truly saw me. I meant it, what I said before. You're very kind."

That's the second time she'd said it. And tonight was the only time anyone had ever accused me of that. Except for my mother. But mothers didn't count. They were always saying things like that.

She squeezed my arm, then drew her hand away before I could reach over to grab it. "Besides, who cares what they think? Isn't that what you just told me?"

I straightened and looked at her. "Easy for you to say. I'll bet you grew up here with all of them."

"I did." She looked away. "But everything's different now. I don't really belong either."

Then that made two of us.

I glanced over at her. She wasn't crying anymore. And soon, someone was bound to notice their queen was missing. Even old Charlie knew enough to understand that Charles couldn't be the man she was found alone with in a dark balcony. I held an arm out toward the door, where a pale light shone from the staircase. "Shall we?"

I let her leave first, then I waited a few minutes before I followed. I knew what happened to girls who ruined their reputations. Though I didn't know how those things were handled in polite society, I couldn't imagine anyone looking on them more kindly than folks from the South Side would have.

Unfortunately, my father met me at the bottom step. "I'm not sure what's considered proper in Chicago, but here in St. Louis, the only kind of girl you'd be alone with in the dark is a whore. Or your fiancée." He frowned. "The rules are different here, and I'm taking a lot of risks trying to make sure you're accepted. You need to act like a gentleman as long as you're here in the city with me."

"I wasn't—"

He waved off my protests with the hand that held his cigar. "And stay away from that girl, in particular."

"But—"

"Here's something I've learned since I've been here: A gentleman is as a gentleman does. All these people here are happy to treat you like one just as long as you don't give them any reason not to. This city can give you a second chance at life, just the way it gave me one. You can be anything you want here."

"And I appreciate that, but I was only—"

He leaned close. "I know what I'm talking about. I've left the past behind. Finished and done. You can do it, too, just as long as you don't mess up." He turned and walked back into the hall, leaving a cloud of pungent smoke hanging in the air behind him.

13

Lucy

"Are you all right, Lucy?" Sam had seen me walk back into the ballroom. Unfortunately, so had my mother.

I looked back over my shoulder, hoping to catch a glimpse of that man I'd been talking to. As I watched, he stepped through the door and acknowledged me with a touch of his hand to his forehead. And then he flashed me that dimpled smile.

I smiled in return before I could remember not to. Being up there alone with him in the balcony probably hadn't been wise.

"Lucy?" My mother reached my side and took hold of my arm. "You have responsibilities to uphold tonight as queen. Everybody knows you've only just got back from Europe. You need to show them that you're more refined, not less."

"I am." Of course I was. I looked back once more as my mother steered me through the crowds, but the man had gone.

Mother and I rode home later through gaslit streets as automobiles buzzed up to and then swung out around the carriage to pass us. I dug into the tufting of the bench with my finger.

Neither of us spoke. At the house, the coachman handed us down from the carriage. As we went up the walk, Mother gestured to Father's room. The light was on. "He hasn't been sleeping well. At least, not at night. Why don't you go tell him about the evening."

He might have predicted the outcome himself. No good could come from a girl meddling in business.

Mother pushed me toward the stairs with a firm, though gentle, hand. "Go on."

I knocked on the door, softly enough not to startle him if he were sleeping, but loudly enough for him to hear, should he be awake.

He answered and so I entered.

A smile lit his face. "Sugar Plum! My Queen of Love and Beauty." The smile was the only sign of vitality. Everything else about him—his hair, his eyes, his face—was gray. "How was it?"

Terrible. Wretched. Humiliating. "It was fine." At least my mother hadn't known of my candy's debut.

"I wish I could have been there. I wish I could have seen it when they announced you as the queen. I'm sure you were a complete success."

I was an abysmal failure.

But still the man's words echoed in my thoughts. *"Does it really matter if no one else liked it?"*

It did . . . and it didn't. If I hadn't created the candy in order to save the company, then I would have exulted in the fact that I'd made a chew even better than the one from Europe. But it was poor solace, given the fact that nobody else wanted to eat it. What good was a candymaker if she couldn't create anything anyone liked?

"What is it, Sugar Plum? You look as if someone's stolen all your candy."

I had a sudden, wild urge to laugh. Someone had stolen it. They'd taken it and thrown it all away.

"Tell me about it."

I bent and kissed him on the cheek. "There's nothing to tell. I'd been holding on to a dream for a while, and tonight I realized that it will never come true."

He sighed. "I'm sorry. Can't save spun sugar once it starts to melt, but you can turn it into something else."

Something else. I didn't want anything else. I patted his hand, then turned off the lamp.

Mother was right. She'd always been right. A lady didn't belong in the kitchen . . . and Father was right too. She didn't belong in business either. I hadn't had to go to Europe at all in order to learn those lessons. I'd learned them right here. I'd have to tell my mother that I'd failed. There was no point in trying to delay the sale of the company any longer.

Only I didn't know how to tell her.

Admitting to myself that I'd failed was hard enough. I couldn't yet bring myself to admit it to anyone else. Except Sam. He already knew, though he was hardly sympathetic.

He paused in sweeping the back porch the next morning. "You have to admit it's hard to top Royal Taffy. And your father's been trying for ten years now."

"I don't have to admit anything. And I'd have thought you'd be just a little more understanding." He *had* changed while I'd been gone. And it hadn't been for the better. It really was just me against everyone else. I felt a tear slide down my cheek and for one mad moment wished for the comforting arms of that man from the ball. What an odd thought! And why hadn't I asked for his name? "I just . . . don't you have a handkerchief?"

He looked up from the broom at me, startled. "I, uh, sure. Of course I do."

"Can I have it?"

"I was saving it."

"Sam!"

He looked chastised and stuck a hand into his pocket. But when he brought it out, a red wrapper fluttered from it and drifted to the ground.

"Is that a—"

He snatched it up and shoved it back into his trousers.

"Is that a—a—" I stepped forward so I could whisper. "Is that a *Royal Taffy* wrapper?"

"Uh . . ." His gaze darted about the room. "It's not mine."

"Not—! Then why is it in your pocket?"

"It's . . . because . . . I'd rather not say."

"A Royal Taffy? Sam!" There could no worse form of betrayal.

"I have to . . . uh . . . be going. Now. See you later." He shoved the broom into the corner and headed out toward the stable.

"Sam!"

His only reply was the slap of the screen door.

I used his handkerchief to wipe at my tears. When I went to refold it I saw that it had been embroidered. The initials *SHB* had been worked into the cambric with brown floss.

SHB?

Sam had a middle name? Of course he must have a middle name. But I had never known it. With his mother having died when he was a baby, and with the material being so crisp and shiny, it could not have been she who had done it. So who knew Sam's middle name? And why had she embroidered a handkerchief for him?

I could think of several answers to my questions, and I didn't like any of them.

I also didn't like the fact that I had promised Winnie I'd come calling. Specifically because she had told her mother, and her mother had told my mother, and so the next afternoon I found myself sitting beside her on a yellow silk divan in her parlor. I'd been seated next to a green parakeet that harmonized with the color scheme. He swung from a squeaky trapeze when he wasn't tossing seeds at me.

"Is he bothering you?"

Yes. "No."

"I've always liked birds. Did you know parakeets can live nearly twenty years?"

Perish the thought.

Winnie smiled. Did she *ever* stop smiling?

She'd smiled when she'd greeted me. She'd smiled when we'd sat down. She'd smiled as we were served tea. And if it were possible, as she turned to look at me, she smiled even wider still. "I wonder, Lucy, did you hear? You must have. I'm sure you must have."

I waited for her to continue, but she didn't. Did I hear what? "I . . . don't believe so."

"Because it was such a surprise!"

"What was?"

"That there even *is* such a thing!"

Was anyone ever as maddening as Winnie Compton? "Such a thing as *what*!" I felt like I had missed an entire part of the conversation.

"As another Mr. Clarke, of course."

"There's a . . . *another* Mr. Clarke?" Mr. Clarke of Standard

Manufacturing? I contemplated that riddle for a moment, but
then quickly conceded defeat. I set my teacup down on the table
beside me. "Winnie, I have no idea what you're talking about."

"Mr. Clarke's son."

"He has a *son*?"

"He was at the ball. Surely you must have met him."

"No." A spawn of the devil would have been highly memo-
rable. I would not have forgotten someone like that.

"Charles was his name."

Charles. That sounded dreadfully dull and stuffy.

"He was being introduced to practically everybody." She sent
a glance my way as her smile dimmed for a moment. "But I'm
sure you weren't meant to have been overlooked. There were so
many people there that night. You have to admit that it would
have been easy to forget one or two."

Yes. Especially me with that enormous crown atop my head.

"I'm sure there was nothing meant by it. But such a shame
you didn't get to meet him. He was enormously handsome.
Although no one seemed to know that Mr. Clarke even had a
son. Don't you think that's odd?"

Everything about that man was odd. Worse than odd!

"I don't understand how you could have a son and then forget
you had him and then remember and . . ." She put a hand to
her head as if she had suddenly come down with a headache.
"It's just all so confusing. But he was very nice."

As Mr. Clarke had been. Before he'd stolen our candy from
us. Like father, like son! "There was probably a scandalous
divorce, and the son was raised in some slum somewhere in a
rat-infested house and fell in with the wrong group and went
to jail for some terrifically abominable crime from which he's
just been released. *That's* why we haven't heard about him."
I clapped my hand over my mouth. What had I just said? All

those novels I'd read on the voyages to and from Europe must have corrupted me.

Winnie's eyes widened for a moment, and then she broke into that tinkling laugh she had. "Oh! You're just teasing, Lucy. For a moment, I thought you were actually telling the truth!" She touched me on the hand as her laughter died. "I'm so glad you came to call. I didn't used to like you at all, but now I can see that I was mistaken. You aren't at all mean and bossy and selfish. Isn't it funny how long I've been suffering under that impression?"

She didn't used to like me? Winnie Compton hadn't liked *me*? I climbed into the carriage.

I hadn't liked *her*.

How could she have the gall not to like *me*?

Mean and bossy and selfish. Was I truly like that?

Who could I ask? Sam?

No. He would probably agree with Winnie.

Mother laid a hand atop mine. I hadn't even realized I'd been picking at the tufting again. "I was very pleased with the way things went this afternoon."

I wasn't.

"I think it's nice that you'll have a companion to see you through the season."

I didn't. Not if it that companion was Winnie Compton.

After an eternity of sitting in a parlor on such a fine, bright day, my fingers itched to do something. Make something. So once my mother disappeared into her sitting room, I wandered into the kitchen. Mrs. Hughes had just pulled a roast from the oven. It was sitting on the counter, steaming.

"Lucy, love, could you get me a ladle?"

I handed one to her.

As she took it, she peered up at me. Then she put a hand to her waist. "I know that look. You've got candy on your mind. I suppose it's best just to get out of the way and leave the place to you."

"I don't want to run you off. I could just work around you."

"No, no." She tilted the pan and ladled the juices from the meat into a jar.

"If you don't need this pot . . . ?" I took it from its hook, then ducked my head as I tugged an apron down over it.

I wanted something . . . something that reminded me of how I felt when I looked into that man's eyes, back at the ball. Back when he'd made me feel like everything would be all right. But I also wanted something that would satisfy the urge I had to snap the head off Winnie Compton. Something magical and airy . . . and brittle at the same time.

A meringue!

Perfect. I'd have to beat egg whites again, but it would be worth it. I gathered several eggs, some sugar, and a bottle of vanilla extract. Then I pulled out the breadboards and wet them down with a washrag.

"Mrs. Hughes? Do you know where the paper is?"

"The paper . . . ? And *what* are you doing with my cutting boards!"

"I was hoping to make some meringues." Meringues were one of Mrs. Hughes' favorites. I pressed a kiss to her cheek. "I promise to set some aside for you."

"And for Mother?"

"*And* for your mother."

She smiled. "I suppose that's fine, then. What was it you were asking for?"

"Paper."

"The brown paper? It's in the pantry somewhere . . ."

"Somewhere" turned out to be on the floor beneath one of the shelves. I pulled it out and dusted it off, then cut several lengths and laid them out on top of the boards.

After separating the eggs, I took up a whisk and started whipping them. As my arm churned, my thoughts wandered to the man from the ball. To the dizzying sensation I'd felt as I stared into his eyes.

Good heavens—I hoped I hadn't stared too long! What must he think of me?

He'd been perfectly respectable in every way, but the feelings he'd raised in me were . . . alarming. Alarming? Maybe not alarming. That wasn't quite the right word.

I stopped to check the consistency of the egg whites. They slid right off the whisk, so I kept whipping.

Alarming wasn't the right word—it's not as if he were some criminal. My feelings were . . . different. But different wasn't bad. Strong. Maybe that was the word. I'd had a *strong* reaction to him.

Just like I'd had to sherbet powder. Such a strange, fizzy effervescence that had been . . . delightful. Dizzying. Delectable. Delicious.

I felt myself blush. He was a man, not a piece of candy!

Telling myself to concentrate on my work, I whipped the whites stiff, added most of the sugar, then whipped some more. Once the mixture stopped collapsing on itself, I added the vanilla and the rest of the sugar, whipping it until it rose into glossy peaks.

The oven was still hot from the roast, so I left the door open to cool. Since I had the time, I spooned the meringue into a bag and then piped it onto the boards in fancy shapes.

Kisses.

I felt myself flush again. Taking up a saucer, I used it to fan my face. I wished I'd thought to ask that man his name.

Bending, I slid the boards into the oven and closed the door. Then I took up a towel and dried dishes for Mrs. Hughes.

At least I hadn't had to meet the new Mr. Clarke—even though he was nice and very handsome according to Winnie, who probably thought everyone was very nice and handsome. Except for me, who was mean and bossy and selfish.

Half an hour later, the meringues were done. And half an hour after that, they had cooled enough to eat. I bit into one with a satisfying crunch. And as the meringue dissolved in my mouth, so did my anger at Winnie. Who cared about Mr. Clarke's son? The man I wanted to meet was the one from the balcony. The one I'd run into on Olive Street.

There was just something about his eyes.

I took another meringue and then a third, stuffing them into the apron's pockets. Tiptoeing up the back stairs, I went to see my father.

"God bless you, Sugar Plum!" He popped the meringue into his mouth, chewed and swallowed it in one bite, closing his eyes as he savored it. "I've always thought a meringue is a thing like hope, buoyed as they are with plenty of hot air. A bit pretentious at the start, don't you think?" He settled his hands on his chest. "But let that hope wait, let that resolve harden for a while . . . Leave the oven door closed, and something wonderful happens. You just have to be willing to wait for it." He smiled. "And speaking of hope, I find myself hoping . . . you don't happen to have another, do you?"

The only thing I found myself hoping for that week was a chance to see that man again. And the next time I did—*if* I did—I was going to ask him his name.

Even in church, I couldn't seem to keep my thoughts on the

119

eternal. They were too filled with balls and dancing. Wondering who the man was, and which family he belonged to. So distracted was I, that I almost glanced in the direction of the Clarkes as we passed their pew. But at the last moment I remembered to turn my head. Father had been adamant about not changing churches after Mr. Clarke had taken the company. It was bad enough that they'd stolen his livelihood; Father vowed they wouldn't steal our church from us too.

I tried to peer around the edges of my hat during the service to see if the man might serendipitously be there, but the brim was too wide. By the time the minister announced the Prayer of Confession, I was all but nibbling on my nails. Though I dutifully bowed my head and clasped my hands, I'd always wondered about the utility of confessing. If God knew every-thing, then there oughtn't be a need to confess to the things we'd done wrong. So I sent up a prayer—a wish, really—about the man instead. Although . . . that was just as ridiculous. But there was no one else to talk to about the ball, and I didn't know who the man was.

Please, God, could I see him again?

As the prayer ended and the organ played an introduction to the next hymn, I felt guilty and more than a little foolish for using confession time, which I didn't believe in, in order to beg a favor from a God I wasn't really sure was listening.

14 ———————————— *Charlie*

On Monday afternoon I stood back to look at the advertisement that had just been painted on a building along Grand Avenue. Now there was no trace left in the city of anyone's candy but ours. It hadn't been all that different from Chicago: Find where the other fellow had put up his advertisements, and cover it over with yours. And since it was a free country, I knew if I wasn't careful, the other fellow could just as easily put up *his* advertisements over mine.

Nelson drove me back to the factory. I waited with Mr. Mundt for half an hour before my father invited me into his office. He was standing in front of the window, looking out at the factory across the railroad tracks. "When crates of Royal Taffy leave the factory, they go to all four corners of the country." He turned around, strode to his desk, and crushed his cigar violently into an ashtray. He took another cigar from his drawer and sliced the end off with a cutter. "Standard used to have another owner. Did you know that?"

I didn't know anything at all about my father's time in St. Louis.

"He hadn't a thought in his head about business. He had the recipe, he's the one who came up with Royal Taffy, but he couldn't have given it away to a beggar. No sense at all. I don't even know if he realized what he'd created. But he gave me my first job in this city." He struck a match and put it to the cigar, then took a long drag on it, exhaling with a big sigh. "Hired me to sell his candy for him and set his books straight." He took another puff on his cigar. "One thing I always knew how to do: Focus on the bottom line. But he always seemed to spend himself right back into trouble. Always experimenting, always ordering new ingredients for this or that."

"I'd think experimenting could only make a candy better." I thought of the Queen of Love and Beauty and her candy.

My father scowled. "Why should things always have to be better? Why can't people just leave well enough alone and figure out how to sell what they've already got?"

"Wouldn't things sell better if they were, in fact, better?"

He shook his head as if I'd just spouted nonsense. "Royal Taffy sold just fine. Even back then. I was getting paid in commissions, and I couldn't seem to stop making money. And then, when an opportunity came up, I took it. I loaned money to him in exchange for a share of the ownership. When he needed more money, I got more shares. And that's how I got the recipe too. Didn't take long before he was working for me. That's how it's done, Charles. You wait, you watch, and when someone presents you with an opportunity, you take it!"

"What did you do with him?"

"I fired him. Part of the agreement."

I couldn't keep my mouth from dropping open. "He agreed to that? Being fired from his own company?"

"He deserved it, really. He might have come up with the recipe, but everything he'd done since had nearly brought the company to ruin. He was a complete incompetent."

"But if the recipe was his to begin with . . . ? You didn't . . . I mean . . . you must have at least *bought* the recipe from him."

He shook his head. "No. But I own everything outright. We made sure of it."

We? "Who—I mean—"

"You'll have to learn that sentiment has no place in business, Charles. Just look at what I've made of the mess that was left me." He turned around in his chair and stared out again at the factory.

"But what happened to him?"

"What do you mean?"

"Where is he? Where did he go, what did he do?"

"He did what he'd always done. He wasted his time and money trying to make candies no one wanted to buy and paid no attention at all to money. If he'd been smart, he would have moved on to something else. Something different. That's what he was supposed to do." He took a puff on his cigar and stared up at the ceiling. "I start to feel badly about it sometimes, but then I remember: You can give a fellow a chance, but you can't make him take it. "

"But—if you took his candy?"

"I didn't take it. Is that what has you so gape-mouthed? You think I stole it from him?"

It certainly seemed that way.

"I got it fair and square. Had him sign an agreement every time he borrowed money."

"But he couldn't have understood . . . ."

My father shrugged. "Doesn't matter. It was all done legally."

"And this is your rival? The man you want to put out of business? Again?"

"That's the one. The favor I told you about."

"Did you ever consider he might not take it well? Seeing as how this will be twice you've taken his business away?"

"There's more to it than I can tell you, but trust me when I say it's for his own good."

The whole thing didn't sit well with me. It didn't seem right.

"That's why I'm counting on you. We need to shut him down as soon as possible."

My new shirt was pinching my neck. I slid a finger down the back and tried to loosen the collar. I didn't care what old Mr. Dreffs said; rubber collars were definitely better.

"The sooner people forget there was ever a Francis Kendall, the better. For him and for us. Come January, I don't want anyone to be able to remember that his business ever existed."

I couldn't help but feel sorry for the man.

My father pressed a button on his desk. "I want you to sit in on this meeting I'm going to have and then . . . take tomorrow off! In fact . . . why don't we both take tomorrow off? Go to the air meet out at the airfield? Enjoy ourselves? What do you say?"

Mr. Mundt appeared at the door.

My father nodded at him. "I'll need you to take notes."

The secretary came in and sat on a chair in the corner.

"Now, then. The first thing to do is to get City Confectionery candy out of the city's stores."

I decided to do a little scouting. That's what I'd done back in Chicago when business was slow and I needed to drum up customers; I'd called on the competition. I asked Nelson to take me to City Confectionery.

"Been a long time since I had some Fancy Crunch," Nelson noted.

"What's that?"

"Fancy Crunch? Well . . . it's nuts, covered with a fancy coating. Pink, green, yellow. That coating crunches when you bite into it, and then those nuts crunch some more."

"So they're good?"

"They're fine."

Fine? Fine never sold anything to anyone. At least not for any length of time.

"Real fine. But they're fancy."

I asked Nelson to stop at the end of the block. Pulling my tie from my collar, I shrugged my coat off and then left them both on the back seat. I walked past the building, rolling up my sleeves as I went, and then turned the corner into an alley.

There was a wide door at the back of the building with boxes stacked in front of it. I picked up a box, then put a shoulder to the door and pushed. It swung open, sending out a puff of warm, sugar-scented air as I stepped into a large kitchen. Everything was white: the floors, the walls, the clothes and caps the workers wore. The only color came from the nuts that were being thrown around in large metal pans. The clatter was loud, but it was hardly on the scale of the Standard factory. And in spite of the din, the employees carried on conversations, laughing and talking as they worked.

If my father's factory was hell, this was clearly some kind of paradise.

"Where should I put this?"

One of the men put down his pan and stepped toward me. "What is it?"

I tried to hold the box away so I could read the label, but I couldn't catch a glimpse of it. I tried to shrug. "Got me."

The man took it from me and walked from the room.

I followed him. "So what are you making? Some kind of candy?"

He smiled. "If you want a package of Fancy Crunch, just go on up front and ask."

"They'll give me one?"

"Sure. Help yourself. We all do."

"All of you?" There had been at least a dozen people back there in the kitchen.

He shrugged. "Sure. We take what we want."

They did? Gillespie never let the workers take any Royal Taffy from the factory, although I'm sure some got smuggled out in coat pockets now and then. "They don't worry about the money that's lost?"

"If a man's gotta eat, might as well eat Fancy Crunch. That's what Mr. Kendall says."

I could see why they weren't doing well. "Nice guy, that Mr. Kendall?"

"He's the best!"

"Been working here long?"

"Five years now. But that's nothing. Most everybody else has been here longer than me. Could you hold on to this for a minute?" He held out the box toward me.

I took it while he cleared a place on a shelf in a closet. "There's a lot more boxes where this one came from."

"I'll find somewhere for them to go." He was looking around the shelves as he said it, and I'm sure he came to the same conclusion I did. He'd have to go find a different closet. Because it looked like he needed a hand, I brought in the rest of the boxes and then helped him pile them in a hallway. By the time I left, I'd found out everything I needed to know about City Confectionery.

After listening in on the meeting and after having visited City Confectionery, I went back to my father's house feeling more dirtied and more shamed than I had ever felt back when I'd worked for Manny. Mr. Kendall may not have a head for business, but his employees clearly loved him. There was something ruthless and much too bloodless about plotting to destroy a man's business. It felt more honest somehow to beat him up in an alley or break his legs. At least then he could see what was coming and have a chance to defend himself.

Augusta was waiting to go somewhere when Nelson dropped me off, so I decided to do some exploring. To think that we'd had to huddle together in a shack up in Chicago while he'd been living it up down here in one of the biggest houses in the city!

The entry hall downstairs was carpeted with all kinds of red rugs laid end to end. The paneled wooden walls and staircase smelled of the polish the maids were always rubbing into it. The dining room walls were paneled in white with a gold design painted around the top edges.

Out to the back of the house was a room I'd never even seen before. It was topped with a dome of stained glass. I guessed the room to be Augusta's, since it was decorated like a jungle with trees and flowers and a parrot that squawked as I stepped out onto the tiled floor. My father had an office on the main floor that looked like a library, and Augusta had what she called a sitting room. There was also a parlor done up with furniture that made what Dreffs had called my "posterior" hurt to even look at.

Up above, on one side of the second floor, were six bedrooms, mine among them. There was a ballroom on the other side with a shiny patterned wood floor and a row of chandeliers hanging down its center. The house was bigger than the whole block where I'd lived on the South Side. And I still hadn't finished exploring.

The Queen of Love and Beauty must have lived in a house like this one her whole life. And I bet she was surrounded by men who'd done the same. She probably hadn't given me a second thought after she'd disappeared into the crowd that night.

So I shouldn't think about her either. Shouldn't *keep* thinking about her. Why couldn't I stop thinking about her?

Because she'd looked at me.

Usually girls like her looked right through me. And if they bothered to see me at all, they backed away in fear. As if I might pick their purses . . . which I rarely ever did, and never had I taken something from someone who didn't deserve it. A girl like her had never thrown herself into my arms before as if she trusted me to help her, to take care of her. Not like that girl had.

I shook my head to clear my thoughts, telling myself to stop thinking and start looking. There now—there was a door set into the wall at the back of the second-floor hall that I'd never noticed before. Another closet? I opened it.

Another set of stairs.

But it didn't have a carved banister like the others, and it hadn't been polished to a shine. At the top I had to bend forward to keep my head from bumping against the low ceiling of the third floor. It was darker up here, the windows much smaller.

I looked into the first room. The walls were white-washed and so was the furniture. Just a narrow iron-framed bed and a small wooden table with a white basin and pitcher on top of it. The second bedroom was like it. And so was the third. When I looked into the fourth, though, I got a surprise.

"Mr. Clarke!" Jennie had been sitting on a bed, twisting something between her hands. She leapt to her feet when she saw me. The other rooms had been what my mother had always called "serviceable," but this one was filled with color. The bed covers had been embroidered. There was a garland of red and white, green and yellow draped around the window, and there was a tin can filled with what looked like flowers on her small bedside table. In fact, Jennie, in her black-and-white uniform, was the only plain thing in that room.

"What are you doing?"

She'd shoved whatever she'd been working on into her apron's pocket. "I just came up to change out my shoelace. I only meant to be gone for a minute."

"What was it you were making?"

She put a hand into her pocket and then, with a sigh, brought it out. "Just a bit of foolishness." She held it out to me.

It was a Royal Taffy candy wrapper that she'd folded and wrapped into the shape of a flower.

"That's nifty." I looked around the room. "Is this how you made that?" I nodded toward the garland.

"Oh—not that. That's much easier. You just take the wrappers and twist them a little at the edges . . ." Jennie smoothed out her flower and demonstrated. "Like that. The red is Royal Taffy. The green is Fancy Crunch."

"That's not going to be around for very much longer."

I hadn't realized I'd said the words out loud until her eyebrows had risen in alarm. "Why not?"

"I, uh . . . just heard . . . they're going out of business."

As she pushed to standing, the wrapper fell from her lap. "Out of business!"

"But—not just yet." I shouldn't have said anything. To make her forget my words, I pointed at the garland. "What others do you use?"

"Others?"

"Wrappers. For the different colors."

Her brow hadn't cleared, but at least she wasn't staring at me anymore in that awful, wounded way. "Switzers and Tootsie Roll wrappers, all joined together with a length of thread."

It was something my baby sister might have done. She'd always seemed to find a way to use whatever scraps of this and that someone had left lying around.

"You won't tell, will you? About my being here? All the others think it's a waste of time."

I spied a wooden figure of a little bird. He was a colorful fellow, propped up against the tin can. It looked like . . . was it a whistle?

"I never do it when I'm supposed to be working. Except . . . well . . . for now. But I was about to go back downstairs."

Her words drew my attention back to her. "Why would I tell?"

She sent a timid look up at me.

It caused me to remember something I'd forgotten. I wasn't Charlie anymore. I was Charles. "Er . . . no. Of course not. Sorry. Just didn't know . . ." I backed toward the door. "Sorry. I don't belong here."

Truth was, I didn't really belong anywhere.

15  *Lucy*

"Lucy?" My mother walked right past the parlor and continued on toward the kitchen. "Lucy!" The house had been a noisy place this morning, with visitors keeping the maid busy opening and closing the front door.

I placed my book on the divan and went to the front hall. I hadn't really been reading anyway. I'd been daydreaming about *him*. That man from the ball with his delicious chocolate-colored eyes. "Mother?"

She whirled around, hand at her heart. "My stars, but you gave me a fright! That messenger was a man from the mayor's office. They need you over at the air meet right away."

"But . . . I was just there." I'd opened the air meet for the city just three days before.

"I know it, but—" She threw her hands up in the air. "They've an automobile waiting for you outside. You need to change. *Now*."

With the maid's help, I put on my new canard blue crepe de

Chine dress with the hobbled skirt that my aunt had insisted on buying for me in Paris. Its scooped neck had fasteners in the Russian style on both the bodice and the drapery of the skirt. I'd seen hobbled skirts on some of the women in the city, but none of theirs could rival mine. I could hardly walk, it was draped so tightly. Fingering the satin *Queen of Love and Beauty* sash that I'd slipped on over my dress, I debated whether to coil up my hair and secure it in psyche puffs at the back, but I decided there wasn't time. Instead, I gathered it up and wound it into a pompadour, sticking a few pins into it and jamming my hat down on top. There! Now no one would ever know what my hair looked like underneath.

Mother was waiting for me at the bottom of the stairs, but she was still in her green percale housedress.

"Aren't you coming?"

"The doctor said he would stop by. I thought I should stay."

"Then—"

I heard the screen door slap shut and the tread of heavy footsteps. "Where's Lucy?" Sam's voice.

"I have no idea," answered Mrs. Hughes.

Mother was wringing her hands. "I sent the coachman down to the confectionery and asked him to bring back Samuel Blakely to escort you."

I felt my brow lift.

Her mouth folded. "There was no time to ask anyone else."

The service door swung open and Sam appeared a moment later. He'd slicked his hair back and was wearing a tweed suit coat over a white shirt and necktie. I couldn't help but smile. If my life this year was going to be one long string of events, at least I had a friend by my side.

"Hello, Mrs. Kendall."

Mother nodded before passing by me on her way to the stairs.

As she put a hand to the banister, she paused. "There will be newspaper reporters there. I don't have to tell you . . ."

She didn't. I knew all of her hopes depended upon me. And now, since my candy had failed, I was ready to accept that responsibility. If marrying well would save our family, then that's what I was going to do. Unless it required encouraging the attention of Walter Minard. In that case, I was prepared to fail.

Sam helped me into the carriage, then took the seat opposite me.

"You look very nice today, Sam."

A flush rode his cheeks, and he pulled at his tie. "Thought I ought to wear this. You being the queen and all."

It suited him. As he sat there, idly thwacking his thumb against his knee, I considered Sam as I might have done a suitor. He'd become handsome while I'd been away. He'd grown into his nose, and maturity had filled out the lean hollows in his cheeks. Imagine that! Sam Blakely. A girl could do worse. A vision of horsey yellow teeth passed through my thoughts. A girl could do much worse, indeed.

Which reminded me.

I pulled his handkerchief from my handbag and gave it to him.

He snatched it from me, with Fancy Crunch-colored fingertips. Seeing my look, he held them up. "We were panning nuts today. Pink candy coating . . ." He held the other hand up. "And green." Folding the handkerchief, he tucked it into his suit pocket.

"Someone went to an awful lot of trouble to embroider that for you."

He gave me a keen glance before looking away.

"She did very nice work." Better than I could have done.

He said nothing.

"What does the 'H' stand for?"

"Howell."

Samuel Howell Blakely. "Are you sweet on someone, Sam?"

"No!" A deep flush appeared at his collar and washed up toward his ears.

"Is it anyone I know?"

He refused to answer. But Sam was sweet on someone. I knew he was. It was the only explanation for his odd behavior. And the embroidery. Who could it possibly be? And was he . . . was he courting her? I couldn't imagine Sam married. He was hardly . . . well . . . I supposed he *was* twenty now. That was a marrying age. If I could marry, then he certainly could.

As I thought about the sons of St. Louis, my stomach began to sour. I knew them all; I'd grown up with them. We'd taken dancing lessons together at Mr. Mahler's. And attended fortnightly dances together as well. But while I'd been in Europe, they'd been . . . here.

I wanted someone different, someone . . . new. Someone like that man at the ball. Who was he? And which family did he belong to?

Sam leaned into the cushion and stretched an arm along the back of the seat. "Did you ever see one of those flying machines, Lucy? While you were over there in Europe?"

Flying machines? "No." And I hadn't been able to stay for the first day of the air meet, earlier in the week, either. I still couldn't quite bring myself to believe that a man could fly.

When we got to the airfield the machines were lined up, one behind the other, like a row of overgrown mosquitoes. How on earth did they mount up into the sky? People said they soared through the air as if they were birds, but I remained a skeptic. I'd always held a secret affection for Doubting Thomas. Why *should* he have believed an impossible thing just because others said it was true? What was wrong with having to see in order to believe?

"Miss Kendall?" The mayor's secretary approached us, wiping at the sweat that had formed on his brow. "If you'll follow me." He gestured toward the grandstand. "We've had word the president might be on his way."

President?

Sam sent me a quizzical look.

I shook my head, not wanting to seem ill-informed. I'd ask the secretary later, in private.

The secretary escorted me to the stage, then held my hand as I sidestepped my way up onto it. On a table that had been set up by the podium, a large medallion had been displayed next to a bouquet of red roses. "These were meant for the winner of today's race, but if the president decides to come, you'll hand him the flowers and then the medallion. After that, I'll step forward and ask if he'd like to address the crowd."

Sam poked me in the side.

"Ouch!" I muttered it under my breath.

"Ask him!" He mouthed the words.

"You said the president? The president of what?"

"President Roosevelt. He's here for the Republican Party's election campaign."

Beside me, Sam's jaw dropped open. "President—!" His eyes looked like they might pop from his head.

"He's—but—he's coming *here*?" Suddenly I found it awfully difficult to speak. My heart had doubled its beat. President Roosevelt! No one had warned me that there would be a president here. I might have . . . I might have . . . done a dozen things differently if I'd known! I couldn't have worn anything better than I was wearing. But I might have taken the time to properly pin up my hair. And actually wash behind my ears that morning. To meet the former president! Everyone knew he was much better than the current one. "I don't know if I—I don't—"

"We're not certain he'll come, mind you, but if he does, at least we'll be prepared." The secretary showed us to a seat at the front and center of the stage before bringing the president of the Chamber of Commerce over. "Mr. Foster will introduce you. The mayor's with President Roosevelt at the moment."

"But—but how do I know if he's coming? And what do I say?" No one had warned me. A simple "Welcome to St. Louis" speech couldn't be very difficult. But what did one say to a president?

"On behalf of the city of St. Louis, I welcome you to . . . to . . ." There were so many people standing out there watching me. So very many people. Is this what the rest of the year was going to be like? Welcoming complete strangers to this event or that banquet? I looked back toward the grandstand. Toward the mayor's secretary.

He shrugged.

Did that mean the president wasn't coming? If he wasn't coming, then what was I supposed to say? I smiled, took a deep breath, and rolled my shoulders back the way I'd learned in elocution class. "I welcome you to our fair city." There. I'd done it. I stepped back from the podium only to realize I hadn't actually opened the day's meet. "And I officially pronounce—"

I heard a cough and turned to see the mayor's secretary gesturing frantically at me to move aside. As I stepped back, the crowds before me drifted away as people began to line the airstrip and hawkers stepped forward to sell postal cards and candies.

State policemen, using megaphones, warned us all to keep our distance from the air machines. As the crowds stepped back, I could see a parade of cars come bouncing toward us across the field. A shout went up. Immediately echoed, it was accompanied by a fluttering of handkerchiefs.

Sam rose and came to stand beside me. He put a hand to his eyes. "I think—"

"What is it?"

"I think it's—well . . . it's the mayor. And . . . and the president! I'll just . . . I'll go see . . ." Without a backward glance, he hopped down from the stage and loped off toward the fast-approaching cars. But he wasn't the only one to abandon me. As I stood there, the people sitting in the grandstand did the same. Soon I was the only one left.

Well!

What good was being the Queen of Love and Beauty if I was going to be stranded, alone, on a stage?

No one was watching me anymore, so I lifted my skirts just as high as I could, which wasn't very high considering how narrow the skirt was, and tried to figure out how I was going to get down.

Charlie

I'd watched as that same man the Queen of Love and Beauty had talked to at the ball ran off toward the air machines. I'd watched as everyone else followed suit. But I wasn't prepared to watch as she shuffled around, trying to get down off that stage.

What was the point of wearing a skirt that couldn't be walked in?

I'd have thought at least one of those fancy fellows would have stopped for just one minute to help her, but none of them did. They all jumped off the grandstand like tramps from a railcar. As my father went off toward the airfield, I moved in the opposite direction.

I couldn't take my eyes off her, even though I knew I should. She looked even more beautiful in the daylight than she had at the ball. Back in Chicago, I might have whistled my appreciation, but I had the feeling she wouldn't take it the way I meant it. When I got there, I took off my hat, held it to my chest, and bowed. "My Queen of Love and Beauty!" I reached up and offered her my hand.

Her eyes widened, and she smiled down at me. "Will you forever be my champion? I was wondering how I'd make it down off these steps."

I held her hand firmly as she descended. And though I probably shouldn't have, I kept hold of it once she'd made it to the ground.

"I'm afraid I can't remember your name."

I winked. "It's because I didn't tell it to you."

She arched a brow and drew her hand from mine. "Then you have me at a disadvantage, because you must know mine."

In fact, I didn't. I only knew my father didn't like her. But then I didn't like my father much either. Maybe that meant she and I could be friends. "What would you like my name to be, then?"

"I'd like it to be what it is."

Enjoying the blush that colored her cheeks, I held out my arm. "Want to go take a look?" I nodded in the direction of the airfield.

Though I'd hoped she'd link her arm with mine, she didn't.

"I can't go anywhere with a man I don't know, and there's no one here to introduce us. Surely you agree it wouldn't be proper."

"The name is Charlie."

She seemed to smile in relief. "And mine is Lucy. I've been wanting to apologize for walking into you on the street that day . . . and to thank you for looking after me at the ball. I don't normally require the assistance of complete strangers. You must think me terribly foolish."

My only clear memories of the ball were of her tear-stained cheeks and the caramel scent of her hair. I didn't think she was foolish at all. "No. I don't."

When she looked up at me from beneath the brim of her

hat, I was the one to blush. I ushered her ahead of me and was reminded of just how tight her skirt was at the bottom when she could only hobble forward. But why go anywhere? The person I most wanted to be with was right beside me. I hailed a hawker who was selling Royal Taffy. I bought two of them, before I realized she probably wouldn't want one. As a candymaker, she must be used to fancier sweets than taffy. But I handed it to her anyway. It would have been rude to eat both of them in front of her. "Would you like one?"

She paused so long that I thought she would refuse. But then she smiled once more. "I probably shouldn't, but they're my favorite."

"They're my favorite too." They always had been. Long before I'd found out my father owned the company.

"Then we have something else in common."

In common? Me with her?

"Something besides being wont to lurk in dark balconies during important balls."

I shoved mine into my pocket as she pulled at the red wrapping. "Here." I took the stick from her, ripped open the top, and then handed it back.

She smiled what looked like an apology. "I don't have the chance to eat these very often. But there's something about them. Something . . . I could just never . . ." Her words trailed away as she put it to her mouth and then her eyes closed as she took a bite.

I could fall in love with a girl like this. I could fall in love with *this* girl . . . if I weren't the kind of man I was. I might have planted a kiss on that pretty mouth of hers, but thankfully, Charles reminded me a gentleman would never do that. No wonder they looked so annoyed and irritated most of the time.

Her eyes opened.

"Have you ever tried to make one of these? Like you tried with that other candy?"

She colored. "Oh! No. No. I never have." But she took another bite and a look of pure pleasure crossed her face.

I crooked my elbow for her. "Let's go see the air machines."

She slid her arm through mine. "Do you think it's . . . safe?"

"The president must think it is." I pointed toward an air machine that Roosevelt seemed to be inspecting.

"He's not going to go flying in it?" There was a catch in her voice.

"I don't think . . ." The pilot had come to stand beside him. He spoke to the president for a moment, then gestured toward the seat.

She grabbed at my forearm. "He wouldn't!" She sounded frightened. "It looks like it's only held together with string and India rubber bands!"

I placed my hand atop hers and gave it a squeeze.

The president smiled and clapped the pilot on the back.

Then the aviator shrugged and put a foot to the machine. But someone yelled from the crowd, "Go on, Mr. President!"

"Do! Go for a ride!" The cry was caught up and repeated, and a few more cheers were given before the policemen began to enforce the perimeter again.

Beside me, Lucy nibbled at the rest of her Royal Taffy.

I wondered what would happen if I told her who I was? Maybe . . . if she knew who my father was . . . wouldn't that be something else we had in common? That we both came from candy families? But how could I say it without seeming to brag? And why say it at all? When I wasn't quite sure what I thought of my father, it seemed dishonest to try to use him for my gain. Besides, there couldn't be that many candymakers in the city. She probably already knew him. And if she did, then how was I supposed to explain myself? As a long-lost son? I sent a sideways glance at her. Probably better not to mention my connection to Standard at all.

She stiffened. "Look!"

The president, hand on his hat, was climbing into the air machine. Was he actually going to do it?

Lucy had gone pale. "He's going to fly."

A man jogged up to the machine and started the propeller as the pilot strapped the president into the seat. A second man pulled blocks away from the wheels.

With a wave from the president and a salute from the pilot, the air machine began bumping down the airfield.

Lucy clutched the empty taffy wrapper to her chest.

We leaned forward with the rest of the crowd as the air machine rolled past us down a grassy strip of airfield. In spite of the policemen's shouts to stay back, the crowd surged toward the machine to watch as it raced toward the end of the runway.

"It's not going to make it." Lucy's voice was low and her face was white.

It was reaching the end of the airstrip.

"Sure it will." It had to, didn't it?

"I can't look!" True to her word, she clutched at my lapel and buried her face in my coat.

I put an arm around her, urging her to turn with a nudge from my shoulder. "You have to look. It's going to be all right. Trust me."

When she looked up at me, her blue eyes had darkened with fear.

I couldn't help laughing. "It's going to be fine." I pulled her close and kissed her on the cheek, beneath the feathery hat she wore.

She looked up at me, hand on her hat. Her glance focused on my eyes. My lips.

As I bent toward her, she lifted her face toward me.

I put a hand to her cheek. "They'll make it. I promise."

Somewhere behind us, a band broke into a song.

Her eyes widened, then she dropped her gaze and pulled away to stand beside me. Together we watched as the machine took a short hop and then vaulted up into the air.

Her hands flew to her mouth. "They're flying. They're flying!"

A cheer went up around us.

The crowd pivoted as the air machine made a wide turn and came back around to swoop over us. I lifted a hand to wave, glancing over at her. She was doing the same. It flew past us and then out so far away it was no larger than a speck. Then it turned and came toward us again before plummeting toward the ground.

The crowd gasped, and Lucy's hand seized mine.

I would have told her again that everything was fine, but I wasn't at all sure that was true. A shriek rang out before the machine suddenly turned its front end up and began climbing once more.

Lucy's hand went limp.

I looked down at her, but she didn't see me. Her eyes were fixed on the air machine, a look of wonder on her face. We watched the rest of the president's ride, hand in hand, until the machine came skipping back down the airfield. She turned to me and opened her mouth to speak as I bent to drop a kiss on her pretty little mouth. But that man who'd abandoned her on the stage returned and interrupted us both.

"Did you see it, Lucy? Did you—?" His eyes dropped to our hands.

She pulled hers from mine with a start. And a blush. Her gaze crept up toward my face, then veered toward his. "Yes, Sam. Of course I saw it. Everyone saw it."

Ignoring her, he addressed himself to me. "I don't think I know you."

What would a gentleman do?

Who cared? I'd been acting like Charlie all day. I stepped forward. "No. I don't think you do."

"Sam, this is Charlie. Charlie, this is my . . . Sam. Sam Blakely."

Her Sam. I felt like someone had just kicked me in the gut.

My father hailed me from the crowd. "Ah! There you are."

Lucy stared at him a moment before turning to look at me. Her brows drew together, then sprang apart.

I put a hand on her arm. "What is it? What's wrong?"

My father nodded at her and then spoke to me. "I see you've met Miss Kendall. Again. Lovely to see you, Lucy, my dear."

Kendall? Had he said *Kendall*? But . . . she couldn't be a . . . a Kendall? Could she? A City Confectionery Kendall?

Lucy turned to me, a smile as brittle as toffee fixed to her face. "It was very kind of you to attend to me. Thank you for your assistance, but I won't be needing it any longer." She turned her back on me and joined Her Sam.

"Please. Don't—don't go." I reached for her hand.

"I have someone I'd like you to meet, Charles." I could tell my father was getting impatient.

"*Charles?*" She said the name as if she didn't know me. "Charles *Clarke?*"

I stepped toward her.

She retreated.

"Charlie. It's *Charlie*."

"So you said. You just forgot to mention that your last name is *Clarke*."

"It's not like—I mean—when I met you—Lucy, you have to believe me! I didn't know who you were. I don't—" I stepped close so I didn't have to speak so loudly. "*He's* not me!" I glanced over my shoulder at my father. "I'm new to town. From Chicago." Why did she keep looking at me like that?

"I thought—I'd hoped." She took another step away from me. "You seemed so different from all the others."

"I *am* different." She didn't know how true those words were. "Please, believe me: I didn't know who you were, back then, at the ball."

"So you Clarkes only try to ruin the companies of people you *don't* know? Is that supposed to be some sort of recommendation? Are you trying to make me feel better?"

"If you would listen for just a minute—"

"Why?" She raised her skirt with such force that I heard the fabric tear. And then she stepped forward so quickly that I almost stumbled trying to move from her path. She pressed a fist to my chest. "So *you* can steal from us too? Is that what you were trying to do at the ball? Find out what kind of new candy I was making?" When she removed her fist, a Royal Taffy wrapper fluttered to the ground between us.

"No—no! I didn't even know your father was in candy. As a profession. Believe me, if I had—"

"If you had known, you would have stopped trying to push us out of the business? Or given back the recipe your father stole from mine?"

"Now, wait just a minute!"

"I thought you were a gentleman."

"I was. I am." I wanted to be. "I'm your friend." That last bit I hissed because I didn't want my father to hear.

"I will *never* be your friend, Charlie Clarke. And you can tell your father that we're not giving up. We have just as much right to make candy as he does."

My father shook his head as we watched Lucy lurch away

into the crowd. That skirt she was wearing tried to trip her with every step.

"You didn't mention your rival had a daughter."

"That's her. She used to be such a charming little girl."

"It's *her* father's business you're trying to destroy?"

"That's the one. City Confectionery."

It was the worst news I'd ever heard.

17  Lucy

"Are you all right, Lucy?"

I was not.

"I meant to tell you."

I was trying to put as much distance as I could between Charlie Clarke and myself. It wasn't easy in a hobbled skirt, even if I had ripped the seams, so it took a moment for me to comprehend Sam's words. "Tell me what?"

"That . . . well, I mean . . . that the man you were talking to was Mr. Clarke's son."

I stopped dead in my steps and turned to face him. "You knew?"

He shrugged.

"You *knew* who he was?"

"I . . . might have."

"And you didn't tell me? Were you *going* to tell me?"

"I figured you knew. He met practically everybody at the

ball. And everyone's been going on about it. Mr. Clarke's son come to town and all."

Nobody had been going on about it in front of me. Except for Winnie. And I hadn't once imagined that my man in the balcony was *him*. "I can't believe I . . ." Trusted him. Had been talking to him. Had let him hold my hand. Had almost kissed him. Twice! I couldn't believe I had genuinely liked him. And the whole time he'd been a *Clarke*!

"Lucy?"

"What!"

"The carriage is over there." Sam put a hand to my elbow to steer me in the opposite direction. "And you don't look much like you're the queen of anything right now. Just so you know."

I fixed a smile to my face and greeted the city's citizens as Sam escorted me to the carriage. Once inside, I bit my cheek so that I wouldn't shed the tears of humiliation that were building behind my eyes. Had Mr. Clarke's son been laughing at me the whole time? The whole time he was standing beside me, holding my hand, pretending as if he wanted to kiss me? "He is going to *rue the day*."

Sam shifted forward. "What's that?"

"Mr. Clarke's son." Charlie. May that name never pass my lips again. I'd changed my mind: I was *not* going to allow Mother to sell the company. I was going to put Standard Manufacturing out of business instead. "That man is going to rue the day he ever met me."

Instead of dropping us at the house, I had Sam ask the coachman to take us to the confectionery. I meant to ask for Mr. Blakely, but I hadn't seen any of the employees since my return. And even though I was more than mad at Charlie, I wanted to know how Edna's mother was doing and whether Hazel's sister had married the man who'd been courting her when I left. And then Velma told me her daughter was back with a new grand-daughter in tow and Morris asked me to taste a new coating he was experimenting with for Fancy Crunch. And that was before I'd even made it past the roasting ovens. By that time, Sam had disappeared. When I finally found him, I asked if I could speak to his father.

Sam scratched at his ear. "He's probably back in the packing area."

Mr. Blakely hadn't been brought up from the kitchen to work in the office without protest. He'd been the only one to leave Standard Manufacturing with my father. And like my father and me, he preferred candy making to bookkeeping. He still snuck back into the confectionery whenever he could. "I really need to see him. Do you think you might be able to find him? I could wait in the office."

Sam went off to get him while I walked over to the office and turned the lamp on. I went around to the desk and tried to make sense out of a teetering stack of papers.

As I was dusting off the desk, Mr. Blakely walked into the office, Sam trailing behind.

"Miss Lucy—welcome back! You wanted to see me?"

I went over and returned the embrace he offered. "I wanted to ask you a question. When was the last time we had advertising posters printed?"

He tugged at his ear as he consulted the ceiling. "I think . . . it must have been . . ." He sighed. "To tell you the honest truth, I don't know exactly."

"So we haven't put up any new advertising since the Royal Taffy posters covered all of ours up?"

"I don't think so."

"Why not?"

"I hadn't realized . . ." Mr. Blakely tugged at his ear again. "They covered *all* of ours?"

"Yes! There's not one Fancy Crunch poster remaining in the city." If there was, I hadn't seen it.

"Well, that doesn't . . . that's not right!"

"It's not right. And it needs to be rectified."

He folded his arms across his chest. "I agree."

"Good. So . . . who does all that?" I couldn't recall whose job it was.

"Your father." Sam and Mr. Blakely both said it at the same time.

I sighed. If it was my father who had been supposed to do those things, then for certain it had actually been my mother. She was the only one who had ever done anything that wasn't related to the actual candy making. And I couldn't consult her about this because she wanted so badly to sell the company. And all the money in it was hers to begin with. "We need new posters."

Mr. Blakely nodded vigorously. "Yes, we sure do."

"So I'll need you to order them."

He shook his head just as vigorously. "I don't mind ordering the sugars or the nuts and all of that, but I don't know anything about posters."

I looked at Sam, but he refused to meet my eyes.

"We're going to let Standard run us out of business for want of a few posters?"

Sam shifted his feet. "And for the fact that they have Royal Taffy."

"There is *nothing wrong* with Fancy Crunch!"

He and Mr. Blakely looked at me glumly.

"Is there?"

Sam lifted a shoulder and let it fall back into place. "It'd be better if . . ."

It would be better if people would buy it. It would be better if it wasn't so expensive to make. And it would definitely be better if Charlie Clarke hadn't gone out and covered up all of our advertising posters, as I suspected he'd done. If I ever saw him again, it would be too soon! "Sam?"

He flinched. "Yes, Lucy."

"I'm going to need your help with something."

We headed back home, Sam and I. I asked him to distract Mother so that I could sneak into her sitting room and rummage through her chest of drawers. She had insisted upon looking after the company's correspondence and ledgers herself. As many times as I had headed for the kitchen with my father, she had called me to come look over the accounts with her.

"It's all well and good to make candy, but someday I hope you'll marry someone who can make money." She would fix me with her keen-eyed stare. *"Never marry a dreamer. They haven't a care in their head for dollars and cents."*

She would complain about this thing or that thing. She would deplore the convention that kept her running the business from a distance instead of being present at the confectionery.

I would tally the figures and the columns just as quickly as I could and slip out while her back was turned. For all that he was a dreamer, I much preferred caramelizing sugar with my father to writing out receipts with my mother.

But now I needed information. I needed to look at the accounts in order to find out how much money there was to spend. But I had forgotten that her plans included not only selling the confectionery, but also securing a good marriage for me.

"Lucille." She stepped into the front hall as we came in the front door. "I was just telling Mr. Arthur about your voyage to the Continent."

Mr. Arthur. My hopes withered.

Curse my fashionable skirt. I hadn't been able to sneak by fast enough! "I'm rather busy right now." I whispered the words to her as I tried to shuffle past.

"Not too busy to gallivant about town with Samuel Blakely." She hissed the words at me. "The air meet must have ended hours ago."

"It only—"

"Mr. Arthur was there." She seized my hat from me and pushed me toward the parlor. "I don't need to remind you of his prominence in this city. And it's no secret that he's in need of a wife."

I caught Sam's eye as I went and gestured with my chin toward Mother's sitting room. If I was to be stuck in conversation, at least Sam could do the sneaking for me. I was certain Mother would join me in the parlor.

But she didn't.

"I would like to have a word with you, Samuel Blakely."

He sent a terrified glance in my direction.

I bit back a sigh, fixed a smile to my face, and reminded myself that I was, indeed, the Queen of Love and Beauty. And then I went into the parlor and resigned myself to entertaining Mr. Alfred.

Mr. Arthur.

Mr. Alfred Arthur.

Oh dear.

18 —————— *Charlie* —

I decided to get to the bottom of my father's dispute with Lucy's father. I might have asked Augusta, but I didn't quite trust her to tell me the whole truth. So I did what I'd done in Chicago when I needed to find something out. I went to the streets. On Grand Avenue I bought a newspaper off a newsie, tucking it under an arm. And then I reached into my pocket and brought out a Royal Taffy. "I'm looking for some information."

The boy eyed the candy. "Could be I have some."

"It would need to be the truthful sort."

"That might cost extra."

My opinion of St. Louis improved as I added another Royal Taffy to the first.

The boy looked up the street and down. Then he snatched the candy from my hand, hiding it in a pocket of his grimy, moth-eaten coat. "What do you want to know?"

"Everything about Standard Manufacturing. And City Confectionery."

A look of suspicion crossed his face. "Is that it?"

"Why? Don't you know anything about them?" I held out a hand. I wasn't going to give away two perfectly good Royal Taffies for nothing.

"I know everything about them! And so does everyone else. You're not from around here, are you, mister?"

"Tell me."

"They were partners, some years back." The boy could only have been eight or nine years old, but he said it with the straightest of faces.

"That part, I know."

He shrugged. "That's it. You know it all, then."

"But what happened? Why aren't they partners anymore?"

"Mr. Clarke was hired by Mr. Kendall to help with the factory and before Mr. Kendall could even blink, Clarke stole the company from him and kicked him out the door."

"Stole? I don't think he actually *stole* the factory."

"All those rich people got some fancy way of explaining it, but in the end, Mr. Clarke had everything and Mr. Kendall had nothing. Not even the candy he used to make. What would you call it?"

"I heard it was all done legally."

"Legal?" He sneered. "Might have been legal, but that doesn't mean it was right."

Put that way, it did sound an awful lot like stealing. "But . . . doesn't Mr. Kendall still make candy?"

"He vowed he'd come up with something better than Royal Taffy, but he never has." He patted his pocket as he spoke.

"And what about . . ." What about Lucy? What about me? "What about their families?"

"There's a Mrs. Clarke, but she's never had children. They say Mr. Clarke used to have a family somewhere up north. There's

154

some son come to live with them. They say he's going to take over the factory when Mr. Clarke dies."

"They do, do they? A handsome fellow, is he?"

He looked at me in a squinty-eyed way. "Not to my way of thinking."

I handed him another Royal Taffy.

"On second thought, I seem to recall people saying he's real handsome."

That was better. "Tell me about the others. The Kendall family."

"The mother's got the money, and she waves it under Mr. Kendall's nose every now and then just to remind him that it's all hers. Only the old man had a heart attack, and he's laid up at home trying to die."

"Wait—what?"

"Word is Mr. Kendall's bound to die soon."

Lucy's father? The one she said she'd made candy with?

"And there's a daughter. Went away to Europe for a while. Just got back."

"What's she like?"

He shrugged. "She's the VP Queen. Her mother's decided to marry her off. That's what they say, anyway."

"To anyone in particular?"

He shrugged again. "The Minard kid is going to make a play for her, but the smart money is on the Arthur son."

"Arthur son . . . ?"

"You know: the electricity company Arthurs. But he's so old he could practically be her father." The newsie had begun to walk away.

"Is there anyone else?"

"Why don't you find out for yourself? Go to all those fancy parties. You're the Clarke son, after all, aren't you?"

Scamp.

I left the newsie and walked on down to the factory. I had to find some way to let Lucy know that I hadn't meant any harm. That I was only trying to . . . destroy her father's company.

As I walked along, I passed a wall I had covered with Royal Taffy posters. Not seeing the Fancy Crunch posters beneath them didn't mean I couldn't feel badly about having covered them all up. I cursed myself. Things were supposed to have gotten less complicated in St. Louis, not more.

The dinging of a streetcar bell warned me to get off the tracks. I stepped onto the sidewalk and read an advertisement as it passed: *Give the Queen of Your Heart a Royal Taffy.*

The queen of my heart would probably throw it back into my face.

I had to at least talk to Lucy. Let her know that . . . what? Why would she want to hear any more from me than she already had?

I stepped off the sidewalk and tipped my hat at two ladies who were walking by. Continuing on my way, I saw a box of Royal Taffy on display in a five-and-ten-cent store window. The city was one big advertisement for my betrayal. What could I possibly say that could change her mind about me?

You're the prettiest girl I've ever seen?

I want you to know you're the perfect VP Queen?

When I found out about your father, I felt pretty mean?

Listen to me! I was thinking in poetry. But I had a feeling Lucy Kendall wouldn't want to hear any of it. The only thing she'd want from me is a promise that her father's company was safe. And that would require betraying my own father, just when I'd finally found him again. Just when I'd been offered a second chance at life. Which would just about serve him right. Except that . . . I couldn't. Lucy seemed to want the one thing I couldn't give her.

Mr. Mundt pointed to my father's office door when I arrived. I went in and sat in the chair across from him.

"I've seen your posters, Charles. A fine job you've done."

I found myself straightening. "Thank you." Had he really stolen the company or had he done it like he'd said? Did it really matter if the result was the same? And how did I feel about calling myself the son of a man who prided himself on taking advantage of others?

"But I've been told it's time now for more aggressive measures. We need to do something more immediate."

More aggressive? Than plastering over all the Fancy Crunch posters in the city?

"City Confectionery is still making candies. I'm working on getting their candy off the shelves, but in the meantime, we need to get them to stop production."

"Why?" Why did Lucy have to be a Kendall? Why couldn't she be a Miller or a Jones or a—a Smith? And why did my father have to be so set on shutting down her father's company? "What did he do to you?"

"Who?"

"Mr. Kendall."

"It really has nothing at all to do with him. I wish I could tell you more, but I can't. It was part of the agreement. Just know that my hands are tied."

His hands were tied? Then how was it that he was making plans, having me put up posters, and talking about taking immediate and aggressive action?

"I owe someone a favor, and there's really nothing more to say about it."

"Are you sure this person you owe the favor to is . . . above-board?"

157

He chuckled. "You're just going to have to trust me."

"Frankly, that's the one thing that's never been easy for me to do." No. That was wrong. I'd trusted him without question as a child. But I didn't know if I'd ever be able to do it again.

"You can't believe I would ever do anything illegal!"

No. Just dishonorable and spineless and cowardly.

"I'm your father, Charles. And I would never ask you to do something I wouldn't do myself."

What was it that I wanted from him? He'd given me a job, he'd welcomed me into his home, he'd said he was sorry . . . but somehow, it wasn't enough. "I just don't think anybody's going to thank us for destroying a dying man's company. A dying man's *candy* company."

"You've got to learn to think with your head, Charles, not your heart. I can't tell you it didn't make me a little queasy to agree to do this. But in the end I think, like me, you'll see that it's the right thing to do."

19 —————————————— *Lucy* —

"I was quite disappointed in the president. I would have thought he would refuse the ride." Mr. Arthur was all but wagging his finger like some old spinster maid.

I nearly laughed. He expected President Roosevelt to decline a ride on an air machine? When had the former president not taken a risk? Or a dare?

"Now every young boy will want to be just like him. If God had meant for man to fly, He would have given us wings."

"But . . . didn't you at least find it rather exhilarating?" I had a difficult time not smiling when I thought of those men soaring through the air like birds.

"No. But why should we speak of it? I'm sure you were only there because of your duties." He looked at me expectantly.

I had been, hadn't I? But something willful and perverse within me wanted to insist that I had not. Probably due to the influence of Charlie Clarke. I ought to have scratched his eyes out instead of held his hand. "Of course I was."

He nodded to himself as if he had checked off an important point on some list. "Please don't think me a boor if I say that St. Louis could not have picked a better Queen of Love and Beauty."

"That's very kind of you, Mr. Arthur."

"No more kind than you have been to me. And I insist that you call me Alfred."

Mother beamed from the corner where she had joined us some while before.

"That's very kind . . . Alfred." I felt as if I had stepped into a pot of taffy. As if my feet were stuck and I couldn't free myself. I'd become accustomed to that feeling during my travels in Europe. It seemed every young man my aunt and uncle introduced me to had wanted to attach himself to my side, while all I wanted to do was look at the cathedrals and tour the museums. And visit the candy shops. In Europe I had always avoided those situations by pretending an endless fascination with our guides. Here, I had no such distraction. I smiled at Mr. Arthur as I clenched my folded hands.

"Tell me, Mr. Arthur, about the electricity business."

His brows peaked beneath the near perfect wave of his honey-colored hair. "That would be far too tedious a topic for a girl like you, Miss Kendall."

If I couldn't talk about his work, then what else was there to talk about? Politics were forbidden. Religion was impolite. I hadn't read the newspaper that morning, and he didn't look like the sort of man who read novels. "Do you have any . . . any plans for . . . for . . ."

His brow lifted.

"For Christmas?"

"*Christmas?*" He colored, moving his neck as if his collar had suddenly become uncomfortably tight. "That's more than two months away, but I don't mind saying that I hope so."

Was there nothing he would speak of? "We generally pass a quiet day at home."

Mother spoke up from her corner. "But of course we are happy to partake in new traditions."

We were?

She was looking at me, a smile frozen on her lips.

"Um . . . yes!" I looked toward Mother, and she nodded. "We are always happy to partake in new traditions. In fact, in Italy fifers herald the Christmas season, and in many places children set out their shoes for St. Nicholas to fill instead of their stockings."

He blinked.

"In some regions of France, there's a man who's believed to come around and give spankings to the naughty children. A sort of . . . opposite of Santa Claus."

Mr. Arthur's face had gone slack in horror. "I hardly think that sort of thing to be proper! Do you, Miss Kendall?"

I had thought it rather quaint and quite charming, but apparently I had misjudged his capacity for new traditions. "I suppose it must seem very different."

"Indeed." He ought to have clucked like an old hen. Instead, he rose. Bowing first at Mother and then at me, he said his good-byes and left.

Sam had gone before Mr. Arthur had taken his leave.

Drat!

Mother found me in the front hall, examining my sagging pompadour in the hallstand mirror. She stood behind me and poked at the place where my hair had begun to slide, pulling out a pin and then pushing it back in. "Nobody wants to hear about Europe, Lucy."

Then why did she keep bringing it up? "I didn't know what else

161

to say! Mr. Arthur didn't provide much scope for conversation, and generally, we celebrate Christmas the same way every year."

"I want you to know that I had a word with Mr. Blakely's son."

"With Sam?"

"Do you insist upon using his Christian name just to spite me?"

I looked at her from the mirror. "No. I insist upon using it because I grew up with him." What was it she wanted me to call him?

"It isn't decent that you address him so familiarly. He'll scare away your suitors; they'll think you've let him take advantage."

"Of what?"

"Of your affections."

"Sam?"

"Mr. Blakely."

I turned around to face her. "What did you say to him?"

"I simply told him that his presence was doing you more harm than good, and if he cared at all about you, he would do what he knew was best."

Which meant he probably hadn't had the chance to snoop at all. "So he left?"

"He did." Mother raised her chin as if daring me to protest.

"You're the one who asked him to escort me to the airfield. I hardly think it's fair to summon him one moment, then banish him the next." Though she wouldn't worry at all if she'd known about that handkerchief he kept in his pocket.

She simply continued staring at me until her gaze faltered as she sighed. I remembered then why it was she had stayed behind.

"What did the doctor say?"

Her mouth stretched tight. "There's very little change."

"So he hasn't gotten any worse." I felt my spirits lift.

Mother shook her head sadly. "He hasn't gotten any better either."

"Can I go see him?"

She looked at me for a long moment, then sighed. "What could be the harm?" She watched me as I walked up the stairs.

I tapped on my father's door.

"Come in."

He smiled when he saw me. "Sit down. Tell me what you've been doing. The doctor still won't let me get up. I feel like the world's gone on without me."

"I went to the air meet today."

"Did you see one of those flying machines?"

I nodded. "I saw the president too. President Roosevelt. He flew in one of them."

"He didn't!"

I told him all about it. Most of it. Everything except Charlie and holding his hand. And my inane hope that he would kiss me.

"And what happened after?"

"After . . . ?"

"The air meet. I'm not deaf. You spent a good hour down in the parlor talking with someone."

Trying to talk to someone. "It was Mr. Arthur. He was waiting for me here when I got home."

"Arthur . . . ?"

"Of the electricity company. Mr. Alfred Arthur. Mother's determined that I marry. Soon."

Papa patted my hand. "You can't be upset with her for that. She has only your best interests in mind."

I smiled. "I'm not upset." At least not about that.

"So what is he like?"

"Who?"

"The Arthur heir."

"He's pleasant." Not at all like Charlie Clarke. I kissed Papa on the cheek. "But I'm to let you sleep."

"I don't understand how I can be so tired when I spend all my time doing nothing at all." He smothered a yawn with his hand as he spoke.

"The doctor says we're not to tax you."

He smiled, but said nothing in protest. By the time I had reached the door, his breathing had deepened and his head had rolled to his chest.

Mother met me out in the hall. "We've an hour before supper. I'd like you to come help me with the accounts."

I was about to protest when I realized it would suit my purposes exactly. I followed her down to her sitting room. I read her the bills as she noted them in her account book. She spent a minute adding up the figures, then turned the book around and passed it across the table to me. "See if I haven't made a mistake."

I checked her figures and then checked them again. Looking up, I saw her biting at her lip as she stared out the window. "This can't be right." I went through the bills again and verified that she had written them correctly. I added the column up once again.

Two hundred dollars.

That's all that was left us.

I turned the book around and passed it to her. "You were right. There was no error." A coil of fear was twisting in my stomach.

She looked up at me as if what I'd said was of no importance. "Do you see now why I have to sell the confectionery?"

"No." I didn't. "I think now is the time to try harder. To figure out how to sell more." To beat that Charlie Clarke and his awful father at their own games.

Mother glanced down at the book and closed it with a firm hand. "No. Now is the time to face the truth and put an end to all of this while we still have the chance to do it."

"But why? Why can't you just believe, keep fighting like the rest of us?"

"Because I'm tired, Lucy! I'm tired of living from dream to dream. I'm tired of having to scrape and save. But most of all, it's because I want to see you do better for yourself than I have. And I can only do that if we sell the company now."

"You sound as if you hate this."

"I don't hate it. I despise it. I despise it for what it took from me. I gave this business all of my money, all of my dreams. And it's returned to me nothing of value. It's taken far more than it's ever given in return . . . even when we still had Standard."

"Nothing? You can't say it's given us nothing! Why—"

"You've seen the books. The machines themselves are worth more than the money that's in our account. The sooner we sell, the better the wedding we can give you. If we wait too much longer, you'll have nothing. That's why I sent you to Europe. I saved for years to be able to do that, hiding the money from your father."

"But I thought—I thought Aunt and Uncle paid—"

"They offered to, but I wouldn't let them because I'd wanted to take you myself. I wanted us all to go on the same trip your grandfather had planned for me when I was your age."

"Planned? What happened?"

"I met your father, that's what happened! I was so blinded by his charm and that ready smile, so taken with his dreams that I gave up my own. And I've been giving them up ever since!" She took my hand in hers as tears shimmered in her eyes. "You see, *I* wanted to be the one to show you Paris and introduce you to the Alps. I wanted to visit Pompeii and Vienna. And if we still had Standard, then maybe I would have. And maybe I would have been able to find you a husband worthy of the Clary name. That's the real reason I sent you. And that's why you came home with a trousseau."

My mouth fell open as I remembered all the young men my aunt had introduced me to. All the gowns I'd brought home in my trunks. I had traipsed across the Continent admiring churches and paintings, devouring candies, and never once had I given any real thought to why I had been allowed to go. I pulled my hand from hers. "I see."

"You hate me now too."

"I just wish . . . did you *ever* like candy?"

Something close to a sob came from her mouth. "You've always been so single-minded, Lucy. Not everything is about candy. I wish you could see beyond yourself." She clapped a hand over her mouth, pushed away from the table, and walked from the room.

Charlie

Another Thursday evening, another concert. We passed all the grand houses in Portland Place on our way into the city. I wished I could be in one of those brightly lit drawing rooms instead of trapped inside the car, pushed up against the door, sitting beside my father.

"Who is it this evening, Augusta? The orchestra?" My father asked as if it didn't really matter.

She gave him a sidelong glance as she drew the fur collar of her coat tighter about her neck. "The symphony."

He chewed on his cigar for a moment. "Don't see what the difference is. They both use the same instruments."

"A symphony orchestra plays symphonies."

"Hmph." He bit down hard enough on his cigar to bite off the end. He spit it into his hand and looked around as if for some place to hide it.

I offered up my hand.

He dropped it into my palm without hardly moving. Maybe he was hoping that if he didn't look at Augusta as he did it, she wouldn't see him.

She did.

He was fumbling with his lighter. "So what are they playing?"

"Tonight's is not a symphony concert."

"Ah! So they're *pretending* to be an orchestra."

"They will be playing popular music." She didn't sound like she approved.

"So why don't they call themselves an orchestra? Just for tonight?" He winked at me as he said it.

She was staring straight ahead. "Because they're the *symphony* orchestra."

"Don't see why it makes such a difference."

"Because it does."

"Isn't she something? She keeps track of all these things." Father took the cigar out of his mouth and smacked a kiss onto her cheek.

She pushed him away, but in the glow of the streetlights, I saw a blush creep up her cheeks.

I tried to imagine my mother knowing about things like that, but I failed. Recognizing when a sock could be re-darned and when it should be thrown away; judging when meat could still be boiled and eaten or when it was too far gone; knowing when the rent could safely be put off another month or two. Those were the kind of skills required of a mother trying to raise three children on her own.

Maybe my father had needed a wife like Augusta in order to become successful at his candy factory. But couldn't my mother have become that sort of woman if he'd given her half a chance? I snuck a peek at Augusta. I had to admit that she wasn't a bad sort. Not really. It's just that she wasn't my mother.

The concert was like all the others I'd attended since I'd come to town.

Long.

And very loud.

The first part ended with those big booming drums. I hid a yawn behind my hand and then escorted Augusta to the refreshment area. My father went to the smoking room. I bought Augusta a glass of lemonade and stood by her side as she greeted the people I'd already come to know too well. After a while, I excused myself and wandered over to the concession where candy was being sold.

I bought two packages of Royal Taffy, since I hadn't thought far enough ahead to bring my own. I was planning to eat them both, but then I saw Lucy Kendall.

She was standing at the far side of the lobby, that shiny sash looped over a shoulder. The Queen of Love and Beauty was holding court. And chief among her suitors was that blond man who had covered for my mistake about golf. I owed him a favor. What was his name? Alfred something. Or was it Arthur?

I walked by the group and caught his eye, giving him a look at the second Royal Taffy I'd bought, raising my brow.

He nodded at Lucy, excusing himself, and then he came over toward me.

I handed him the treat.

"I don't usually eat candy, but it's been such a long time. . . ." He tore the wrapper off and bit into it. Chewed for a moment before swallowing. "Thanks. You're the Clarke son, aren't you?"

"That's me. Charles Clarke."

"Alfred Arthur." He held out his hand and I shook it. "I'd been meaning to catch you again. Say—why don't you join me at the club next Thursday night for the candidates' reception?"

Candidates . . . for what? I had no idea what he was talking about, but if it meant I could skip a concert, I guessed I should be delighted. That's what all these rich fellows said. *I'd be delighted.* "Sure. Thanks."

"Splendid. I'll see you there, then. Around seven?" He tipped the Royal Taffy toward me by way of leaving.

I tipped my own right back.

"What were you saying to him?" The words came in a hiss from behind me.

I couldn't help smiling as I turned. "Miss Kendall. What a pleasure." I bowed. I was starting to get the hang of all this fancy talk and polite manners.

She didn't smile back. In fact her eyes were shooting sparks at me. And her attention seemed to be caught by my hand, which still held the Royal Taffy. "I meant it, what I said at the air meet. I had no idea who you were. And I never planned to take anything from you." Except for a kiss. I had wanted one of those.

"It doesn't matter what you intended. What matters is . . . what is. You are a Clarke, and I am a Kendall."

What matters is what is. She was probably right. Greater than the difference between Clarkes and Kendalls was the difference between her upbringing and mine. If she were angry with me now, she'd never speak to me again if she ever found out the kind of man I'd been in Chicago. "I just wanted to say that I'm sorry. For everything." For every hope, for every wish, for every dream I'd dreamed at night. Why did she have to be so pretty? And why did she have to be so easy to talk to . . . back before she knew who I was?

She looked pointedly at the candy I held in my hand. "Taffy is for children."

Hadn't I been trying to be nice? That was just plain mean.

"I seem to remember that you liked it well enough. You said it was your favorite."

"I've changed my mind. And I've come to tell you to leave Mr. Alfred alone."

I raised a brow. "Mr. *Alfred*? Don't you mean Mr. *Arthur*?"

"I meant Alfred. Mr. Arthur. He asked me to call him Alfred. I was quite flattered."

"If you say so. But isn't he a little old for you?"

"I've always considered age an advantage. It brings maturity of both body and mind. Which are things I doubt you'll ever possess."

Behind her shoulder, I saw the woman I assumed to be her mother looking around the lobby. "You'd better . . ." I inclined my head in that direction.

"Just stop talking to him. And stay away from me."

"I would, if you weren't so set on finding me."

She sent me an icy glare before sailing off in the other direction. I couldn't help smiling as I finished off my Royal Taffy. She sure had spirit. And I couldn't much blame her for being mad at me. She was right, in a way. Though I had nothing against her family's company, my father sure seemed to. And she was more right than she knew when she'd warned me to stay away. But I wished . . . I wished that we could talk again. The way we had back at the ball. But a man like me wouldn't be good for her. And besides, a fellow couldn't hope to keep any secrets hidden when a girl like her looked at him as if she could see down into his soul. But Mr. Arthur . . . Alfred . . . Lucy might be just the girl for him. Maybe she could loosen him up a little.

"I've changed my mind." My father made the pronouncement as we were walking up the front steps into the house later that evening. He drew me off into the parlor. "I've just had a—" he ran a hand through his hair— "a brilliant idea! About City Confectionery."

"You've changed your mind?" Maybe I could tell Lucy she didn't have to hate me after all.

"Well . . . not completely. I've decided that City Confectionery would be just the thing for you. Something manageable, something small for you to start off with."

"I—? I don't understand."

"We'll stick with what we planned. I'll buy them out and we can be a father-and-son company. How do you like the sound of that?"

"I don't know if—"

"I'll give it to you." He took a big puff on his cigar. "It'll be all yours. What do you think?"

"You're going to give it to me?" He was going to give me *Lucy's* company?

"Why not? To make up for all those birthdays I missed. And besides, Christmas will be here soon, won't it?" He patted me on the arm as he walked out of the room.

I followed in a daze. Father and son. In spite of how much I'd always sworn I hated him, he'd just offered me the gift I'd always longed for. He'd offered me even *more* than I had hoped for: He actually seemed to want to make up for lost time. He was ready to buy me the company just as soon as I could destroy it. Maybe I should have been grateful, but the only thing I could think of was Lucy. How I was being offered her dream . . . and how she'd murder me if she ever found out.

21 ———————————— *Lucy*

"We need more money." As much as I'd thought about the company in the past few weeks, that's what I couldn't get around and always had to come back to. We didn't have enough money.

Mother looked up from her table with a sigh. "That's what I've been trying to tell you. That's why we need to sell the company."

"I wonder . . . could we just borrow some?"

"Your father tried that very thing. That's how we came to be in this position in the first place. He didn't seem to understand that eventually you have to pay it all back. Now we have no Royal Taffy *and* we're burdened with a pile of debt. If only he'd had some sense. I'll never understand why he couldn't just leave the business!"

"But have you tried borrowing any money *lately*?"

"Of course I have. Last year, just after you left for the Continent."

"Where?"

"Where what?"

"Where did you try? Which bank?"

"Our bank. And they won't consider extending a loan without your father's consent. And he won't admit to having failed again."

"But it's your money."

"Yes, Lucy. I know that!" Exasperation had made her voice testy. "It's *my* money, but according to them, it's *his* company. You've had your chance. I've given you the time you requested. Now it's my turn."

"What about Aunt Margaret and Uncle Fred?"

"Absolutely not! I will not have my own sister throw our failure up in my face."

I couldn't imagine my aunt or uncle ever doing that. "You mean you haven't even asked them?"

"No. And I never will."

"But they wouldn't mind. I know they wouldn't. I could—"

"I *forbid you* to do it."

"But I don't see why—"

"Because she has everything she's ever wanted. She has everything *I* ever wanted! I would rather move down to South St. Louis than let her know how destitute we've become. It was bad enough that she was the one to take you to the Continent . . ."

"But what if I could find some money?"

"Find some? As if it's hiding somewhere?" Mother sounded incredulous. "I'll tell you where it all is. It's tied up in the building and all the pots and the kettles and those huge piles of ingredients that your father only used once before discarding. It's in the pockets of the people who aren't buying Fancy Crunch because they're buying Royal Taffy. That's where you can find it."

"But what if I could?"

"What if you could." She threw up her arms. "If you can . . . if you can, then I suppose you can consider yourself the savior of the company." She folded her hands atop the ledger book. "I know you don't want to hear this, but I've run out of alternatives. If we don't sell soon, we may lose everything. As it stands now, I might still be able to preserve something. Waiting isn't delaying the inevitable. It's costing us. At the moment, I still have something to bargain with. The more we delay, the worse our position becomes."

What she hadn't said in all that was *no*. We needed money. Who did I know that had some?

Mr. Arthur.

Mr. Alfred Arthur with his big house on Westmoreland Place.

At some point I would have to marry someone, and Mother had already said that she wanted me to marry well. If someone had to marry Mr. Arthur and all his money, why shouldn't it be me?

I didn't really know him.

But I could get to know him.

I couldn't really talk to him.

Perhaps I would learn to . . . given enough time.

I didn't really like him.

But I didn't *dis*like him. And besides, that had never stopped anyone I knew from marrying. Just look at Father and Mother.

Deep inside a worm of doubt began to squirm in my stomach and a little voice suggested that perhaps the better place to look for an example was to my aunt and uncle. Wouldn't I rather have a marriage like theirs?

"In any case, finding money is neither here nor there."

I jumped at Mother's words, startled from my thoughts.

"The candidates' reception is down at the club this evening. I don't want us to be late."

Me. She didn't want *me* to be late. I didn't see why I'd been invited at all. Sighing, I went upstairs to change into something suitable. Something proper. I found my new dove-gray dress with its gored bodice and French lining. I liked the plaited flounce that flowed from the bottom of my hips toward the floor. The lacing at the yoke and sleeves was so singular that I hadn't yet seen anything like it in the city. I drew it on and fastened it up. Then I repinned my hair, teasing some of the waves from the pins so they would curl around my face.

I took my new silk hat from its box and set it on my head as I smiled at myself in the mirror. I looked eminently respectable, completely proper, and wholly suited to be the wife of someone like Mr. Arthur.

But it still didn't quiet that voice. And as hard as I tried, I couldn't quite squash that worm.

As we entered the dining room of the club, Mother inclined her head toward the back of the room. Through the jostling of the crowd I could see Mr. Arthur. "Why don't you go over and greet him? I'll be along in a moment."

My heart sunk straight to my toes. That meant that I would have to talk to him by myself, and I'd already used up the topic of Christmas, which ought to have been good for at least an evening's worth of conversation. It wasn't that he was so terrible a person. Really, he was terribly nice. It's just that he was so . . . serious. And stolid. There wasn't anything indecent or disreputable about him. I doubted he had ever once contemplated doing anything scandalous. I hadn't either, of course, but it would nice to think he had the capacity to.

I girded up my courage as I approached and smiled at him as if he were the most fascinating man I'd ever had the pleasure to meet. "Good evening, Mr. . . . Arthur." Had I chosen the right name? I cursed my schoolgirl games.

"Miss Kendall!" He shook the hand of the man he'd been

talking to and then he turned to me. "Good evening. But please, do call me Alfred."

I might if I could remember it. As I stood there beside him, Mother came toward us and smiled at Mr. Arthur in greeting.

"I hope you won't think me rude, dear ladies, but I invited someone to join us."

Thank goodness! Maybe it would be someone I could talk to.

"He's new to the city. Seems like a lively fellow."

Even better.

"How kind you are, Mr. Arthur, to think of him."

"There he is! Perhaps you know him." He hailed someone with a salute. I fixed a Queen of Love and Beauty smile on my face in preparation of a greeting. I was determined this friend of Mr. Arthur's would be my savior.

And then Charlie Clarke sauntered into view.

Mr. Arthur pumped his hand enthusiastically. "Good to see you, Charles. Thanks for coming."

"I wouldn't have missed it."

"Have you met the Kendalls, then?"

He smiled as he looked at me quizzically.

I gave my head the slightest of shakes.

"No. I haven't had the pleasure of an introduction."

"Well, then, Mrs. Kendall, Miss Kendall, may I present Mr. Charles Clarke."

I glared at him. "Are you associated with the Standard Candy Manufacturing Clarkes?"

"I am, Miss Kendall. However did you guess?" He flashed a set of dimples as he smiled.

I'd dimple *him*, given half the chance!

"That's right!" Mr. Arthur was beaming as if he had done us all a favor. "You're both in the candy business. Must have a lot in common."

Mother looked at Charlie in an apprising sort of way. "Mr. Clarke." She held out a hand to him.

Traitor.

Charlie took it up and kissed it. He spouted some sort of nonsense that had Mother blushing and then turned his attention to me. "Are you enjoying yourself, Miss Kendall?"

I'd enjoy myself more if I could hit him over the head with one of those brass spittoons that sat in the corner of the room.

Mother patted me on the hand. "I think I'll go find some punch."

Mr. Arthur stood. "I'll join you." He bowed. "Would you care for some, Miss Kendall?"

"Yes. Thank you." I waited until they were gone before I let my smile slide from my face.

Charlie had turned toward me. "I've been hoping for a chance to talk to you again."

"Why? So you can tell me more lies?"

His brows crumpled. "It's not like that, Lucy. I never intended to mislead you. It's just that I never had the chance to really introduce myself. I was going to at the airfield, but by then it was too late."

"And if you'd known then what you know now . . . ?"

He took up my hand. "Then I would have told you that you're right not to trust my father for a second. I don't. And I never have."

I pulled my hand from his and wrapped it firmly around my handbag. "A lot of good that does us now! How would you feel if our positions were reversed?"

"Desperate. Angry. Frightened."

He was so . . . so *right* that tears threatened to spill from my eyes.

"Do you think . . . is there any way we could still be friends?

You were the one person in this city I felt like I could really . . . talk to."

And he was the one person in the city who had really seemed to understand how I felt about candy. The one person who didn't try to talk me out of my ideas or try to convince me that girls shouldn't be meddling in business. He looked so lonely and so hopeful standing there that I almost said yes. "I wish . . . I wish we could but . . ."

He closed his eyes for a moment and took in a deep breath. When he opened them and looked at me, it was with the profoundest regret in his eyes. "Don't say any more. I know. I knew it when I first met you, that day you ran into me on Olive Street. Some things just don't belong together." He bowed and turned away and I had the oddest sensation. As if I'd lost something, something important, that I didn't know how to get back.

"Wait!"

He stopped.

"I—" Couldn't let him leave. Not like that. He was right in a way: Why should our fathers ruin what had been a blossoming friendship? I'd enjoyed his company. I would have enjoyed it still if I hadn't known who he was. "I want you to know that if your father hadn't stolen our company, then—"

He swung to face me. "He *didn't* steal it."

"He did."

"He didn't."

Charlie seemed very certain about something of which he had no knowledge! "He stole the company and our candy."

"No. He didn't. There was an agreement between my father and yours."

An agreement! "If there was an agreement, then why has my father always told me your father stole it from us?"

"I don't know. Why don't you ask him?"

"He's always told me that because it's the truth!"

"My father might not be the most trustworthy man in the world—"

I gave a most unladylike snort.

"And he might not have been exactly aboveboard in the things he's done, but I don't think he'd lie about this."

"Apparently he has."

There was a hesitation of indecision and a confusion in his eyes, but then it was replaced by a narrow-eyed stare. "I don't think so. I think he's telling the truth."

"What are you saying?"

"I'm saying you're wrong."

Wrong! I grabbed at my handbag with both hands to keep from reaching out to strangle him. "I almost felt sorry for you a moment ago, but I've changed my mind. I hate you."

His brows peaked, then dimples flickered in his cheeks as if he couldn't decide whether to laugh. "Now you've gone and hurt my feelings."

"No, I haven't. You don't have any."

"That's not—"

"Stop talking to me."

"You can't—"

"Stop it!" Unfortunately, the words came out right as the band ended their song with a flourish. I feigned a spasm of coughing as Mr. Arthur returned with a glass of punch, which I didn't want and didn't need, but somehow had to manage to drink.

The candidates for office at the city and state level spoke for much longer than was necessary on issues like street paving and telephone taxes. Things that were extremely important and truly tedious. No wonder we were the only women in attendance, though none of the candidates failed to have his photograph taken while clasping my hand.

Afterward, Mr. Arthur collected our coats and helped us on with them. Then he escorted us to our waiting carriage. Charlie came along. Though I refused to speak to him, Mother stopped to thank him for his attentions that evening.

Charlie bowed.

"I think—" Mr. Arthur paused. "I think this was a most enjoyable occasion. I was going to ask Mrs. Kendall and her daughter to accompany me to a lecture next week. Perhaps you'd like to come as well, Charles."

Charlie's eyes rested on me for just a moment. "I think . . ." His lips twitched. "I think I'd like that."

22

Charlie

"So what do people do around here for Christmas?" I asked Nelson the question as I helped him wax Louise on Sunday afternoon. It was the end of October, but a stiff wind had blown in from the north that made me think of Christmas rather than Thanksgiving.

"Oh . . . this and that."

"Isn't there any big event?" There had to be something, somewhere that would be the perfect place to sell Royal Taffy. Since the candidates' night at the club, I found myself, surprisingly, agreeing with my father. The sooner we could put City Confectionery out of business, the better. Better for us, but more than that, better for Lucy. I'd come to believe that my father was telling the truth. It wasn't a matter of whether we'd buy the company, it was a matter of when. And with Lucy's father dying, it seemed kinder to put an end to her misery—and her hopes—than to prolong them. "Isn't there something everyone in the city looks forward to? In Chicago we had Marshall Field's."

"Who?"

"Marshall Field's. One of those big department stores. They always did the windows up for Christmas."

"We got one of those, too. Only it's called Stix. Stix, Baer and Fuller. December first, every year, they have a big to-do when they unveil the display."

A big to-do. That's what I'd been hoping for.

As soon as I got to the factory, I asked Mr. Mundt to telephone the store manager and arrange a meeting.

"For what purpose, Mr. Clarke?" he asked as he picked up the telephone.

"Money, Mr. Mundt. I'd like us both to make a whole lot of money."

⁂

I met with the store manager the next day and asked how they planned to decorate their window for Christmas.

"Windows, Mr. Clarke! We have several of them. And we're quite proud of our decorations."

"Have you planned the display yet?"

"Planned it? We designed it back in May! We're already building it. It's the end of October, after all. We've really only a month left!"

As I sat there feeling foolish, I pushed my hands into my pockets. My fingers closed around something. I brought it out. A taffy wrapper. "I was hoping Standard Manufacturing could be a part of your display."

"Standard? As in . . . candy?"

"Every kid dreams of candy, don't they? Think of all those . . . sugar plums dancing in their heads." I didn't even know what a sugar plum was. "I know Santa is usually thought to bring big gifts, but sometimes a Royal Taffy is all a child really wants."

His brow folded in doubt.

"I'm not saying that Royal Taffy should be the only thing in the display."

"Certainly not! Our customers expect a certain sophistication. If they want Royal Taffy, they can find it in the confectionery department."

This wasn't going as well as I'd hoped. "I know they can, but Christmas is about wishes, isn't it? Children wish for candy. And . . . besides . . ." I looked down at the Royal Taffy wrapper in my hand. "They're *red*!"

"They're . . . red?"

"Royal Taffy wrappers. They're the color of Christmas."

Now he was looking at me as if I were crazy.

"Can't you can find some way to use some of these?" I pushed the wrapper toward him.

"I suppose . . . maybe . . . ?"

"What is the display this year?"

"It's a parlor, filled with gifts. With an electric fire in the fireplace."

Gifts. That was good. "Why couldn't Royal Taffy be one of the gifts?"

"It's just . . . candy."

"It might only be candy to you, but to the newsie on the street corner, it's a symbol of . . . luxury and everything that's good in the world. He might not be able to afford a . . . train set or a . . . a sled. But a Royal Taffy is something he might just be able to hope for."

"Maybe . . ." He fiddled with the wrapper I'd pushed toward him, crumpling it into a ball in his hand.

"Stix, Bauer and Fuller should be about Christmas for everyone, not just for the few who can afford to do it up big. What if . . . what if I gave you some Royal Taffy?"

"And . . . ?" He was looking at me as if he wanted more.

"And . . ." What? What else could I do? "You could . . . make . . ."

He twisted the wrapper and looped it around his finger.

"You could make—what are those things you hang on the wall? You know . . . those big circles that have holes in the middle?"

"Wreaths?"

"Yes! You could make wreaths with these wrappers. See, if you twist them just so . . ." I tried to make a flower the way Jennie had, but I failed in the doing of it. "If I brought you enough of them, could you do that? And you could make . . . garlands. Garlands out of the Royal Taffy wrappers too. It would be like a . . . a child's best fantasy come to life! A real candyland."

He pursed his lips as he seemed to consider my words.

"And we could make you a poster. Special. Just for the store display that would say *Santa's Sweetest Gift*."

"It's unorthodox."

"But then, Stix isn't any old store."

"No . . ."

"And just think, you'll have children staring at your windows all day long. And when their parents ask them what they want for Christmas, they'll say. . . ."

"They'll say they want what they saw at Stix."

"You want to give away how many?" My father frowned as he thumped on the desk with his fingers.

"Several hundred. And some empty wrappers." Lots of empty wrappers.

"For what?" He leaned forward in his chair.

"For the Stix Christmas window. Just think how many people

will see Royal Taffy at the display. They'll see it along with all those toys and presents they're wishing for. With a big sign saying *Santa's Sweetest Gift*. Even the newsies who can't afford to buy any of those things will see the poster. We couldn't pay for that kind of advertisement."

"Apparently, we can." He leaned back as he rolled his cigar between his fingers.

I forced myself not to beg. It hadn't gotten me anything when I was a child. It wouldn't do anything for me now.

"'Santa's Sweetest Gift,' eh?"

I nodded.

"I like it. We'll give it try. Just this once."

"Just this once."

I had Mr. Mundt call the store manager and arrange for another meeting the next day. I was driven over to Stix by Nelson. We were followed by a delivery truck carrying cases of Royal Taffy and rolls of wrapping. I met with the display supervisor, and we talked through the ideas.

"When can you have that sign to us?"

I had to figure out how to have it made first. "I think . . . well, when do you need it?"

"Sooner would be better."

"Then you'll have it soon."

Soon was easier said than done. The company that usually did our printing didn't have the time. "We're booked through Christmas. Busiest time of year." The supervisor shoved a pencil behind his ear as he shouted the words over the rattle and bang of the presses.

"But I really need—"

"Can't do it."

"It's only one poster."

"Then I really can't do it."

I returned to the car and climbed into the back seat, slouching into the corner.

"Something wrong, Mr. Charlie?" Nelson shot me a glance over his shoulder before pulling the car out into the street.

"I told my father I could have a poster done up for the Stix display and I don't think I can do it." I didn't want to see his face, didn't want to see the disappointment when I told him. I'd seen enough disappointment on my parents' faces to last a lifetime. I really thought I'd had a great idea when I'd come up with the display. A way to increase our sales without directly harming City Confectionery. I didn't mind outselling them, I just didn't want to know that I'd hurt Lucy and her company directly.

"You'll think of something."

I wished I felt as confident as he sounded.

I was still worried Wednesday evening while at the opera. It was some story about a man and a woman who were madly in love but couldn't be together. Truth be told, it seemed to me that's what they were all about—at least the three operas I'd seen. Only this one was set in Persia. The stage background was a palace painted in gold and blue and green. Last week's had been some kind of workshop decorated with orange and red and brown. From where I sat, the background almost looked real. I wondered how it was they managed that.

During intermission, I went down front to take a look.

No one was really watching, so I walked up onto the stage and ducked behind the curtains. If the theater was empty behind me, it was a madhouse there on the other side of the curtains, with people running here and there, carrying things on and off the stage.

"Hey, you! Get out of here." A man with a surly look to him

picked up a candlestick and pointed it out toward the theater beyond me.

"I just . . . I was only taking a look."

"Not allowed."

I pointed to the background scenes. "I was hoping to talk to the person who painted these . . . these things." Whatever it was that they were.

"The backdrops? That's me. What do you want?"

"I wanted to tell you how swell they are."

He crossed his arms. "Are they now?"

"*I* think they are. They're the best I've ever seen." They were the only ones I'd ever seen. At least up close.

His stance relaxed. "I like to think I do good work."

"The best. A man of your talents shouldn't be so modest. You do the *best* of work."

"I went to school to study."

I blinked. Isn't that what people usually did at school? Study?

"For art."

"Ah." He went to school for art. That meant . . . he was an artist! "Say. You wouldn't be interested in doing a little something for me on the side, would you?"

"What? You mean, like a commission?"

"Exactly. A commission. I want to hang your work in a place where everyone in the city can see it."

23

Lucy

November swept by in a whirlwind of conventions and banquets and balls. Needing a reprieve from my duties, I'd found comfort in the kitchen, where Mrs. Hughes was bustling about.

I was quickly losing hope that we could save the company. I wished I had the time to develop a premium line of sweets, the way I had hoped to when I'd come back from Europe, but my failure with the hazelnut chews made me reluctant to try again. Besides, any new recipe required experimentation, and experiments took money.

I looked down at the colorful nuts I held in my hand.

If only we could sell something fancier than Fancy Crunch. Although . . . Fancy Crunch was fancy. At least . . . it was supposed to be. All those brightly colored candy-coated dragées. Father had created them from an old French recipe. I'd seen dragées by the jarful in Europe.

Maybe . . . was there any way to make them even fancier? What if I could turn *them* into my premium line of confections?

If we didn't mix the colors . . . and if we put them into a different sort of package and tied them up with a ribbon . . . Maybe, just maybe, we could charge more for them.

The next morning, I mentioned the idea to Mother.

The Women's Society at church was having a rare Saturday meeting to sort through donations for the missionaries. I found her in front of the hall mirror adjusting the position of the feathers in her hat. She pulled one of her hat pins out and then stuck it back in with a vengeance that made me wince. Then she stopped and sighed as she listened to me speak.

"Do you realize this is the first time I've left the house since that candidates' meeting last month? I was hoping to be able to go somewhere I wouldn't have to think about heart attacks or candy or money. For one blessed hour I would like to pretend that everything is all right. Is that too much to ask?"

As she turned I realized dark circles had gathered in the hollows beneath her eyes. And lines had been pressed into her cheeks. When had she gotten so old? And why hadn't I noticed before?

She clamped her handbag beneath her arm as she pulled on her gloves. Then she turned and walked toward the door.

I followed her outside, down the front walk to the carriage. "I'm sorry. I didn't realize. Never mind."

The coachman offered his hand, but she stopped and squared her shoulders as she faced me. "No. Tell me again. You were talking about different packaging for Fancy Crunch. What are you proposing?"

"Well . . ." I hadn't thought that far ahead. And I hadn't realized the toll that Father's illness had taken . . . now I wished I'd never opened my mouth. But she was standing there looking at me, waiting for me to continue. "What about clear cellophane instead of that green wrapper? So that the color of the candies could be seen?"

"There would still need to be a label."

"And there would be one. We'd paste it on the front, just like we do now."

"I don't see what difference any of this makes. I've already told you, Lucy, the company is going to be sold."

"I just thought maybe—"

"All of these thoughts about candy are a waste of your time. Especially since you have more important things to think of. Like suitors."

"But if it didn't cost any money . . . ? Please?"

"It serves no useful purpose. The company will be sold whether the packaging stays the same or changes."

"Please."

"In fact, it's not a bad idea, and if I say yes, it's not because you're changing my mind about anything. It's because if we don't finish this conversation, I'm going to be late." She put her hand into the coachman's.

He helped her up into the carriage.

"So you're saying . . ."

"I'm saying *yes*." She pinned me with her look. "But I don't mean anything by it except to hope that you'll finally stop all this foolishness. I have plans, Lucy, and I won't be dissuaded from them."

"I know." I was hardly able to refrain from clapping, but I did let a smile slip. I couldn't wait to try my idea.

On Monday morning, I went down to the confectionery to talk with Mr. Blakely. The staff was panning Fancy Crunch, layering on the candy coating, so I had to shout over the din of a thousand nuts tumbling back and forth across the metal trays.

"You want to what?" He squinted as he leaned closer.

"I want to change the packaging."

He blinked. "Why?"

"So we can charge more."

"So we can . . . ? How?"

"If we can separate them by color, and sell them in clear cellophane and tie it all up with a ribbon, then we can say they're fancy."

"They already are. They're Fancy Crunch."

"Fancier."

"Fancier." He looked up at the ceiling for a moment and then began to nod. "All right. If we don't have to mix the colors, then we can save some time. That might help. Only . . . what do you want to charge?"

"Seven cents? Instead of a nickel?"

He shrugged. "Why not?"

"And do you think we could get some boxes out by the end of next week? So they can go on sale those first few days in December?"

"We'll try."

Thanksgiving was on Thursday and then Christmas was coming. With a new year on its way and Fancy Crunch becoming even fancier, the Kendall family's luck was about to change. I could just feel it.

 *Charlie*

My father was pacing in front of his desk when I went in to see him on Tuesday morning. He greeted me with a smile as he took the cigar from his mouth. "Charles! I've been inspired. What if we could make Royal Taffy fancier?"

Fancier? It was taffy. There wasn't anything fancy about it. "Fancy how?"

"Packaging."

"Then . . . you'd make more money. Maybe." At least that's the way I saw it.

"Right!"

"As long as the packaging didn't cost more and you could raise the price."

"Can't raise the price, but we need to be fancier. That's your new job. Figure out a way to do it without costing us more."

I felt my brow lift. "That might be asking for the impossible." Again.

I worked the next day on the problem, keeping Mr. Mundt busy making telephone calls to our packaging suppliers. By the end of the afternoon, we'd figured out how to do it. I told my father about it later that evening.

"So it can be done?"

"It can, but the question is whether you really want to."

"Why wouldn't I?"

"It won't be easy. We'll have to change the whole packaging process. Cellophane instead of waxed paper, although I got in our Royal Taffy red on a separate label. Looks like the old one, only it's white with red lettering. We can twist and tie, with ribbon, instead of using glue for sealing."

"Not a problem as long as we can change it all back."

Change it back? "You mean . . . you don't plan on—"

"It's only a temporary measure. Few weeks . . . just through Christmas. Then we can go back to the way things were."

"But it's going to require the girls learning a new way to do things. The process is going to get slower before it can get any faster. And slower means we won't make as much money. At least not right away."

"We don't have to."

"But I thought—!"

"Leave the thinking to me. Just tell me how we're going to do it. And fast. Tomorrow's Thanksgiving, but I still want the fancier taffy in the stores by early next week. Before the first of the month."

It nearly killed me and Mr. Gillespie, but we did it. On Monday, boxes of the fancier taffy left the factory on the morning trains. That was two whole days before December first. By then, people across the nation would be able to celebrate Christmas with fancier-looking taffy.

It was a shame there was a symphony that evening. I would have preferred polishing Louise to hearing more screechy fiddles and banging drums. I was coming to hate my swallowtail coat. But it couldn't be helped.

And neither, apparently, could talking to most of St. Louis's unmarried daughters. It was funny how many of their mothers pushed them toward me; I wasn't used to being considered a catch. They'd all run away screaming if they knew the kinds of things I'd done, the sort of business I'd been involved in. But I tried to treat it all as seriously as they did. If only to have someone to talk to, even if it was just Winnie Compton. She'd turned her smile on me when she saw me, and when Augusta went over to talk to her mother, she came to stand beside me.

"You should go talk to Lucy. She looks lonely."

"I'm the last person she'd want to talk to." The last person she should be talking to.

She sent me a frank glance. "I think you're about the first person she'd like to be talking to."

I laughed. "Then you must not have heard how much she hates me."

"It doesn't matter what she says, what matters is what she believes."

I knew that what Lucy thought and what she believed were the same things, but Winnie wasn't the worst of the bunch of girls I was supposed to talk to, and I wasn't ready to go back into the auditorium, so I played along. "Then why doesn't she say what she believes?"

"Most people don't, you know. I think you're one of the most handsome men I've ever seen, and one of the nicest, but I would never actually say that because you might take it the wrong way."

"How could anyone take that the wrong way?"

"You might think I'm sweet on you."

"And you aren't?"

"I don't think it would make much difference whether I was or I wasn't, do you?"

How was I supposed to answer that?

"I think you like Lucy just as much as she likes you."

"Lucy?" I did, in fact, like her. But there wasn't much point in admitting it. "I think she's one of the meanest girls I've ever met."

She swatted me on the arm. "You're just saying that. It's not really what you believe." She considered Lucy again, tilting her head first this way and then that.

"Then what *do* I believe?"

"I just told you what you believe. But I wish someone would ask me what I believe."

"What do you believe?"

"I believe it would be a lot less trying and much more pleasant if you both just stopped saying things about each other and started talking to each other."

"I . . . can't. As much as I'd like to. I'm not the person she thinks I am."

Winnie put a hand to my back and pushed me forward. "So you need to go over there and tell her that. Don't listen to what she says. Remember what's important is what she believes deep down inside."

"You don't understand, Winnie. I'm really not who she thinks I am. I'm much worse. There are some things in my past that I'm not very proud of."

A frown pinched her pretty eyes at the corners. "It doesn't matter what she says or what she believes she believes. What matters is what she really believes. So go over there and tell her what you believe."

"I believe . . . if she knew what I believed . . ."

196

She raised a brow. "Yes . . . ?"

"If she knew what I believed . . . you know what? It doesn't matter what I believe, what matters is what is. And there's no way to get around that."

She was shaking her head. "But you're not talking about what *is*. You're talking about what *was*. Those are two different things. You're not the same person anymore."

"How would you know?"

"Haven't I seen you at church, Charles Clarke?"

"Every Sunday." Whether I wanted to be there or not.

"Don't you listen?"

" . . . No."

She threw up her hands. "Well, why on earth do you go?"

Winnie was looking at me for an answer, but I didn't have one. "Because my father expected me to" sounded pitiful, even to me.

"If you did ever happen to listen, then you would hear what I just told you: You don't have to be who you used to be."

"You're talking about sin. And sinners."

She fixed me with a look that made me think she might just be a Sunday School teacher in disguise. "We're all sinners, Charles Clarke."

"Let's just say for a minute that I agree with you."

Winnie smiled. "But that's not really what you believe, is it?"

"Let's pretend I do. But what if . . . what if I watched someone get murdered?"

"Watching isn't the same as doing."

"No. But say I knew what was likely to happen, and I didn't do anything to stop it."

"Why not?"

"Why not?"

She nodded. "Why not?"

"Because . . . because I . . . wasn't brave enough. I was afraid the same thing might happen to me."

"So the other man died because you were afraid."

That was about the way of it. "Yes. So I stood there and watched. It's probably the worst thing I've ever done."

She stood there looking at me, but it wasn't judgment that shone from her eyes. It was concern. The same concern that used to shine from my mother's eyes. And I couldn't stand it from her any more than I could from Winnie. So I tried to distract her. "What's the worst thing you've ever done?"

"Me? Well . . . I broke a plate once, in the kitchen, as I was trying to get a cookie."

"That's it?"

"I wasn't supposed to have one. And I lied about breaking the plate. And then the stable boy got in trouble for it. And I felt really bad about it all and—"

"Fine. So we have me, who caused another man to die. And we have you, who . . . stole a cookie. Compared to me, you're an angel."

"You might say that, but really, you have to go with what God believes. And He believes we both did the wrong thing. We're all sinners."

"But that's just it! How can people say that I just have to . . . what is it people have to do?" I was trying to remember what it was that Honest Andy always said. "Pray? Ask God to forgive me? When that's all you have to do too? It doesn't seem fair."

"Fair to whom? I'd say it's more than fair to you. Why are you complaining?"

"Because there should be more."

"More what?"

"More required."

"Why?"

"Because I'm worse than you are."

She was shaking her head before I'd even finished talking. "Not to God. To Him we're both the same."

"But that's just it! How can I believe in a God who believes that you're just as bad as me?"

"Well . . . actually, He probably believes that you're just as bad as I am."

"It doesn't matter! The point is, it's nonsense."

I should have kept my opinions to myself. She was looking at me, brows furrowed, eyes clouded with confusion. But then they cleared. "You're saying it's nonsense because you feel like you should have to do more than I should in order to feel forgiven."

That was one way of saying it. "Exactly."

She was smiling now. "But that's just it!"

"What's . . . it?"

"That's where you're wrong."

I waited for her to explain, but she didn't, she was watching the people in the lobby, lips curled into a smile. I'd just told her religion was foolish and she was smiling? "*What* am I wrong about?"

She glanced up at me, startled. "Why . . . the whole thing!"

I watched the crowd for a while too, but I couldn't keep myself from wondering what, in particular, I was wrong about. "Could you be more specific? What exactly am I wrong about?"

"The part about you. And the part about God."

Which was just about all of it . . . which was what she'd said in the first place. For pete's sake! I was starting to think just like Winnie. "Could you . . . explain?"

"About . . . ?"

"About God."

"Well, it's just that you're looking at it wrong, that's all."

"*How!*"

She blinked as she took a step back.

"I'm sorry. I didn't mean to yell. I just . . . want to know how."

"I'm not sure *how* exactly. I mean, I don't know who told you the wrong thing to begin with. But the truth is, it's not about what *you* have to do to at all."

"Then what is it about?"

She shrugged. "God. It's about God."

"How?" If I had to say that word one more time, I was going to wring her pale little neck. And then I really would be a murderer.

She sighed a deep, long sigh. "It's about God, Charles Clarke, and what He's done. It's not about you. It's never been about you. Because you're not good enough and you never will be."

So much for flattery.

"And neither will I ever be. God is the one who says how, and He says the same thing to you as well as to me. So neither of us have to do anything at all but say we're sorry and ask for His forgiveness."

Which brought me back to the same thought I'd always had. "That just doesn't seem right."

"Well, it doesn't matter what you believe, does it?"

"Doesn't it?"

"No. That's what I've been trying to tell you. It's not about you and how you believe you have to make things right. It's about God."

"That's it? Just let Him . . . take care of it? That's all?"

"Mostly." She frowned. "I wish you'd listen in church once in a while. There's more. But mostly, that's it."

"Just leave it up to Him . . ."

"It can't be worse than what you've been trying. You haven't been able to make things any better by yourself, have you?"

I wasn't able to spend very long thinking about it. As Winnie walked away, Lucy took her place.

"I don't know how you found out about this!" She was waving a package of Fancy Crunch in my face.

I grabbed her by the hand and took it from her. The package looked different than I was used to seeing. The nuts were wrapped in clear cellophane and there were ribbons tied around the ends. "I have no idea what you're talking about."

"My idea. We're talking about *my* idea. My idea to make a fancier package so we could charge more. Only you did it first and now Fancy Crunch is overpriced and we're—humiliated! Thanks to you."

"You're not the only one who can come up with ideas. City Confectionery isn't the only company that can tie candy up in ribbons."

"No—but we're not the ones who sell candy to the entire nation. We're the ones who have to count every penny in order to survive. I hope you're happy, Charlie Clarke!"

I wasn't, in fact. In spite of what she thought, I wasn't happy that we'd beat them at their own game because my instincts were telling me that more was going on than either of us knew. And that there is no such thing as coincidence.

25

Lucy

The Queen of Love and Beauty was wanted everywhere by everyone for everything. Mr. Arthur had somehow become my constant companion at these functions, although Sam filled in when he wasn't available. Sam came again the morning of December first to deliver me to Stix so I could open their Christmas window display. As he helped me up into the carriage, he offered me a package of Fancy Crunch. "Just in case you get hungry."

I smiled my thanks, putting it into my handbag as he settled onto the seat across from me.

Once at Stix, the manager met us on the sidewalk. He led us through the people who had gathered to witness the unveiling of the window and then escorted us inside. As we approached the furrier's department, he gestured to the employees who had lined the aisles and said, "Behold: our Queen of Love and Beauty!"

The employees clapped and smiled.

He gave me over to the furrier who separated me from Sam, drawing me off into a corner. After taking a quick measure of my dimensions, he scurried behind a curtain, then soon returned, arms filled with what turned out to be a gleaming ankle-length, double-breasted boulevard coat.

"Coast seal trimmed with Alaskan bear."

I'd never seen anything so beautiful. Even its puffed sleeves were elegant.

The furrier's assistant removed my sash, handing it to the manager, and helped me into the fur. The furrier himself adjusted the collar and the shoulders. I could gladly have worn it for the rest of my life.

A second assistant presented a hat box to him.

The furrier drew from it a Cossack-styled hat. "Russian pony and white fox fur." He pronounced the words with much satisfaction as he set it gently atop my head. It was wrapped with a black satin ribbon that was secured by a round buckle sparkling with rhinestones.

"Quite, quite nice." The manager was admiring the furs. "And all for you to keep after the window display opening. It will be good for advertising."

For me? To keep!

"Oh, but you mustn't forget—" The manager held my sash out.

The furrier frowned, but the assistants helped me draw it down over the enormous hat and settle it over my shoulder.

The furrier was still frowning, but as I looked at him, his face brightened. He summoned an assistant with the crook of his finger, then whispered into his ear for a moment. The man nodded and bent to pull out a drawer. When he straightened, he was holding a mass of white fur. As he stepped forward, I gasped as a tail and paws seemed to lunge toward me. Stepping forward, the furrier took it from his assistant and held it up. "White fox fur in the new style." He poked at the tail, sending it swaying.

Oh! It was a *muff* from which all those limbs dangled. I hoped I would be able to keep from laughing while I wore it.

After they had dressed me, I was led toward the corner of the store where the display window awaited. Though we stood off to the side of the raised platform, I could tell the crowd outside had swelled. I could hear the chatter of voices and the shuffle of footsteps along the sidewalk, and I imagined I could feel their anticipation. Every Christmas, except the last one, I had been out there among them.

The manager was beaming. "I hope you're good at playacting, Miss Kendall."

"I don't think . . ." I didn't think that I was.

"You're going to be Santa's helper. There's a parlor set up out there, and you're going to help him put presents around the tree. It's important that the folks gathered outside see the furs you're wearing. And important, as well, that they see each present."

"So you want me to . . . ?"

"Exclaim over each one. Hold it up! Make sure everyone sees what it is!"

That didn't seem too difficult.

"And then, when the last present is placed, you'll be giving your own gift to Santa." He held out a Royal Taffy to me.

"Oh. No. No, thank you." I'd vowed never to touch one again.

"This is the gift." He took my hand and pressed the Royal Taffy into it. "This is what you're going to give Santa."

"A Royal Taffy!" He couldn't be serious.

"Yes. The entire window has been decorated with Royal Taffy wrappers."

I leaned forward to take a look and felt my mouth fall open. Those Royal Taffy wrappers were everywhere. Some clever person had fashioned wreaths and Christmas ornaments out of them. Pieces had been strung together and fastened with bows to make garlands for the Christmas tree. And above the parlor's hearth, a large advertisement proclaimed that they were *Santa's Sweetest Gift*.

"You do know that my father owns City Confectionery?"

"Yes. Of course I know that. Everyone knows that. And I do hope he's feeling better . . . ?"

"Then how can you ask me to—"

The manager clamped his hand around my arm. "The Queen of Love and Beauty belongs to the entire city of St. Louis." He smiled at the employees who stood watching us before whispering into my ear, "Try not to take it personally, Miss Kendall."

Try not—!

"So you'll hand Santa his Royal Taffy, then you'll both need to sing along with the band."

Wait. "Pardon me?" They wanted me to *sing*?

"You should be able to hear the band quite clearly through the window."

"What song is it?"

"Adeste Fideles."

"*All* the verses?" I really only knew the chorus. Some families gathered around their pianos every night at Christmastime and sang carols, but my family had never been one of them. We'd never, all of us, gathered around anything at all.

Eventually, about ten minutes past the hour, Santa ambled down the central aisle of the store, stuffing a pillow into his red coat as he walked. "Sorry. Couldn't escape from the jail."

Jail?

The manager put a hand to my shoulder. "It's Mr. Slater. Superintendent of the city jail."

Mr. Slater? Santa was Mr. Slater? Had he always been Mr. Slater?

"Are you ready?" The store manager was looking at him anxiously.

"Just give me a minute."

He put a hand on his belly and tried out a *Ho, ho, ho*. It ended in a violent, wracking cough. He cleared his throat, and then looked around wildly for a spittoon.

An assistant was dispatched to find one. When he finally returned, Santa had gone red in the face. Once he spit, he fluffed up his beard.

The manager handed him a pair of spectacles, which Mr. Slater set atop his nose. He hitched his belt up over his pillowy girth and drew on a pair of gloves as he stepped up onto the platform.

Sam offered me a hand and helped me up onto the stage. I stepped out in front of the curtain and paused. There were an awful lot of people out there.

"Wave!" I turned around to see the manager gesturing me forward. "Smile!"

I waved and smiled.

"Ho, ho, ho!" Santa turned toward the street and waved.

A gaggle of children, faces pressed to the window, waved back.

He pushed his spectacles farther up his nose. "Where did they say that pack was supposed to be?"

"I . . . don't know." I tried to speak the words through my smile.

"Ah! There it is." As he walked across the stage, past the Christmas tree, he tripped on the edge of a rug. "Blasted, blistering bobtails!"

I felt my brow rise and tugged it down. Thankfully the children couldn't hear through the glass. I waved again.

A little girl with saucered eyes waved back.

"Well . . . let's get this over with. I've a murderer waiting for me back at the jail." He tugged loose the tie at the top of the bag and peered inside. "What've we got? Let's see . . ." He pulled a doll from his pack and handed it to me.

Pulling a hand from the muff, I nestled her in the crook of my arm and smoothed her hair as I turned to face the window, smiling once more as I held it up.

A little girl on the other side of the glass stretched an arm out as if she wanted to hold it.

"Lift her skirts up." The direction came from the manager who was still standing at the side of the platform.

"What?"

"The skirts! Lift them. It's got a petticoat beneath."

I did as requested.

"Pull on one of her curls."

Still smiling, I grasped one of the curls that had been tied up in a bow, stretching it out and then letting it bounce back into place. I kissed her on the cheek and then set her down beneath the tree.

Santa handed me a drum.

I took it from him.

He followed it with a set of gilded sticks.

"I don't . . . I can't." How was I supposed to help Santa if I had to hold onto the muff as well? I took it off and clamped it beneath my forearm, but the legs and the tail kept swishing up into my way.

"Oh, just give me that foolish thing!" Santa took the muff from me and tossed it into the corner.

I beat on the drum with the sticks for a moment, then deposited them both under the tree. "I was wondering, just because I'm curious, what sort of sentence would a person be given if they covered up a company's advertising signs?"

"Ten to twenty, depending."

"Months?" Maybe something good could come from Standard's poster campaign after all. Maybe I could have Charlie locked up in the city jail.

"Days."

Oh. "But . . . what if they were truly meanspirited about it? And covered up every single one?"

"Doesn't matter. Advertising is free. You're talking about putting playbills and such up on lampposts and in alleys?"

I nodded.

"Smile!"

I wished the manager would stop ordering me around! I smiled.

"Isn't no law against it. It's if they put those posters up on public property. That's what could get them twenty days for defacement. Here." He shoved a toy train at me.

I took it from him and held it up.

"Show them the wheels! Spin them around!" The words came in a hiss from the other side of the curtain.

I spun the wheels and smiled. "So even if this person covered up *all* of some other company's signs, it wouldn't be a crime?"

"'Course not. All you'd have to do is cover up that company's signs with signs of your own." He passed me a phonograph.

"How am I supposed to—"

"Keep smiling!" That manager was truly beginning to bother me. "Bend your ear to it and dance!"

How was I supposed to dance *and* bend toward it when I could barely keep from dropping it?

"You're scowling." Santa was peering over the tops of his spectacles at me.

I smiled. Then I staggered over to the tree and dropped the phonograph on the platform.

I heard a gasp from behind the curtain. "Careful—that goes for thirty dollars!"

When I turned, Santa was pulling a tricycle from his pack. He mouthed *Ho, ho, ho* over his shoulder.

I wrestled the tricycle away from him. The pedal got stuck in the folds of the boulevard coat as I turned. I smiled anyway as I tried to free myself. "Haven't you got anything smaller in there?"

"Nothing that I'd want to give anyone." He pulled out a pipe and handed it to me. "Can't stand the stuff myself."

Neither could I. But I held it up to my face. The scent of tobacco tickled my nose and I nearly burst in the effort to keep from coughing.

"Twirl!"

"What?" If that manager said one thing more, I was going to leave and let him do all the holding and demonstrating and smiling.

"Twirl! So people can see the coat."

"The . . . ?"

"The *one you're wearing*."

I twirled. And then I set the pipe down atop the drum.

"Can't you look any happier?"

"No, I can't!" I hissed the words through my smile.

Santa pulled a pair of beautifully embroidered slippers from his pack.

I took them from him, looking inside and on the soles to see if I could tell what size they were. Belatedly, I held them up for everyone to see and then made a show of looking down at my feet as if I wanted to keep them. One of the little girls standing at the window giggled.

"Last gift." Santa was holding out a long telescope.

I took it from him. "Thank goodness." After holding it up and striding the length of the window, as Santa set up the stand for it, I put it down on the tripod and then bent and pretended to scan the crowd.

The little girls and boys at the front window jumped up and down, waving their arms. As I straightened, I slipped a hand inside my bag.

A cough came from behind the curtain. "Don't forget the Royal Taffy."

I wasn't about to. Taking the taffy from my pocket, I held it out for everyone to see. Gasping in pretended shock, I clapped my hand to my cheek and then, in apparent horror, cast it away from me toward the curtain.

"Ouch!"

I hoped I'd hit the manager.

"What is she doing?"

Taking the packet of Fancy Crunch from my handbag, I smiled at the crowd and mouthed the words *Fancy Crunch*. Then I handed it to Santa. Raising one foot, I leaned toward him and kissed him on the cheek.

"That's enough foolishness for today," he muttered. Then he pantomimed another *Ho, ho, ho*.

Hiding my face with the muff, I attempted to sing "Adeste Fideles" along with the band. I lowered it whenever the chorus came along. When the song finished, I bid the crowd farewell with what I hoped was an exuberant wave.

Several of the children remained at the window for so long, I thought my hand would come right off my arm. But eventually they left. And then there was only one man left standing on the sidewalk in front of the window.

It was Charlie Clarke.

And he was glowering at me.

26

Charlie

"Did you see the *Post-Dispatch*?" My father tossed it down the table toward me.

I caught it, then unfolded the newspaper to see a photograph of Lucy Kendall, foot kicked up, kissing Santa Claus. The headline proclaimed, *Father Christmas Prefers Fancy Crunch*.

"How did that happen?"

I wished I could tell him that I didn't know. "It was Lucy."

"What?"

"The Queen of Love and Beauty. Lucy Kendall. She didn't do what she was supposed to."

"The Kendall girl?"

"Yes. It was all arranged. She was supposed to hand Santa a Royal Taffy. Only she didn't."

"Figures. Kendalls are like that. They don't do what they're supposed to." The thought didn't seem to please him. "I may owe a favor, but that doesn't mean I have to be taken advantage of! You need to find some way to fix this."

Curse Lucy Kendall!

All that hard work. No thanks from my father. No "Well done." Just a command to fix what she'd messed up. If I'd known, at the Veiled Prophet Ball, that she'd cause me so much trouble, I would have tossed her over the rail of that balcony instead of handing her a handkerchief.

Fix it.

How could I possibly fix this? Every kid, every person in St. Louis knew that Santa preferred Fancy Crunch to Royal Taffy. If I didn't want so much to strangle her, I might have admired her for it. For a girl she was doing pretty well at the underhanded side of business.

Fix it.

Who could give a better endorsement than Santa Claus?

I jammed my hat on my head and walked out of the bedroom only to realize, halfway down the stairs, that I was wearing one of those rolled-neck sweaters . . . with a pair of worsted wool trousers and my suit coat. I paused in my steps. Old Dreffs would definitely not have approved. But who was really going to notice?

Everyone.

Everyone who mattered in St. Louis would realize I wasn't the man I was supposed to be. Did I care? Truly? Not enough to change. I kept going, walking down the front steps to the waiting car, wishing I was wearing a cap that I could pull down around my ears as I went.

"What's wrong, Mr. Charlie?" Nelson scrambled to open the door at my approach.

Only everything. "My father just asked me to do the impossible."

"Isn't nothing impossible for God, Mr. Charlie. Surely you know that by now."

I smiled. I couldn't help it. It was something my mother would have said. It was nice to know that somewhere, someone still believed that. "Thanks, Nelson."

"I mean it, Mr. Charlie. Nothing means nothing."

Nothing? I was betting even God couldn't solve this problem.

The first few weeks of December went by in a blur of taffy-scented activity. Orders were up, and not just in St. Louis. The rest of the country was demanding more Royal Taffy too.

My father was happy.

Mr. Gillespie was at his wits' end. He couldn't seem to get supplies into the factory fast enough, and one day a spark from a machine started a fire. That morning, as he saw me approach, he pointed out toward the floor, toward the workers that were swarming the place like ants. "They just won't work fast enough."

"They're not machines. They're people." Boys and girls, mostly. He was pushing the workers to make more Royal Taffy, ordering them to work through breaks, so they could have Christmas Day off. I didn't like the way some of the girls looked so peaked, though, and I mentioned it to him.

He sent a sharp-eyed glance in the direction of the wrapping station. "They look fine to me."

"They look like they're falling asleep on their feet. And what about the Boys' Brigade?" That's what I called that long line of boys who wheeled pails of syrup to the mixer. As we watched, one of them fell out of line and was nearly hit by a cart that was carrying crates from the wrapping table to the loading platform.

"Happens all the time. Don't worry. If he can't keep up, then I'll find someone else who can."

"We can't keep expecting them to work like this. Christmas is still a month away."

He shrugged. "Less than. So they have to. Or we'll end up like City Confectionery."

"What do you mean?"

"Mr. Kendall always used to treat everyone like family. Insisted on it. Little good it did him. That's why he got into trouble. Always trying to make things better for everybody. Sentiment doesn't pay. That's what your father says."

No wonder Santa Claus preferred Fancy Crunch. City Confectionery sounded like his kind of place.

First Presbyterian Church was having their nativity the evening of the seventeenth, a whole weekend before Christmas Eve. Even though it wasn't our normal church, Augusta insisted that we all go, since my father had promised to provide a donation to their missionary fund.

"I don't know why I can't just have it delivered." He was peering at his piece of duck over dinner as if he didn't know what to do with it.

"Because it's Christmas." Augusta signaled for more wine.

"Not for another week."

She gave a sigh as if this were just one more battle in a long-running conversation. "What's the use in giving a donation if no one knows that you've done it?"

He put down the knife he'd been trying to cut the duck with and picked up the meat with his fingers instead.

"Warren!"

"Don't know why we keep being served things that can't be eaten. It's too small to cut. I wouldn't do this if we were having some fancy party, but it's just two of us." His gaze caught mine and he winked. "The three of us."

"Yes. And Charles needs the benefit of your good example."

"He's a smart boy. He knows he should do as you say and not as I do." He kept gnawing on the bone. Finally, he laid it on his plate and then wiped at his lips with his napkin. "I suppose you should choose what I'm to wear this evening so I don't embarrass you again."

"I already did."

"Good. That's good." He took another drink of wine before rising from his chair. "I'll just have a cigar and then I'll dress."

Augusta frowned as he left, then gave her napkin a good twist before she set it on the table and followed him.

At the church, I paused behind my father and Augusta as they walked up the steps. I didn't like churches. Not the one I'd been going to since I got here and not this one either. I always felt like everyone was watching me. Left over, I suppose, from my boyhood when the preacher always guarded the offering plate. I'd never done anything bad, but that hadn't stopped me from feeling like other people expected I might.

Not that I could have blamed them.

But mostly, I didn't want to have anything to do with a God who'd just sat and watched as a seven-year-old boy had taken charge of his family. It hadn't seemed fair. And if I were being honest, I'd always resented Him for it.

And I resented Him even more now, knowing that my father had been getting rich while we'd been living on the South Side. Where was the justice in that?

I'd taken up the habit, in Chicago, of staying at a saloon so long on Saturday nights that it was late on Sunday mornings before I got home. If church got to be too bad, maybe I'd start doing the same thing here.

Unfortunately, I'd delayed too long and now the entry had

filled with shepherds and wise men and a child-sized Mary and Joseph. They were ringed by a real goat and several sheep, one of which began to nuzzle my overcoat.

A boy dressed up in a bedsheet with a pillowcase tied around his head pulled at the sheep's lead.

A little girl with feathered wings strapped to her back knelt beside the sheep and offered it her bouquet of ivy, which the sheep wasted no time in eating. She burst into tears. "I only wanted him to smell it."

The boy sneered. "It's a girl sheep. And besides, those aren't flowers. They're just leaves."

"Well, he wasn't supposed to eat them!" Tears poured down her cheeks.

"It's a *she* sheep."

"I don't care. He's dumb."

"He is not." The little boy stepped closer and glared down at her. "Take that back!"

"He is. Everyone knows you shouldn't eat ivy."

"Stop being mean." He reached down and shoved the little girl, who toppled onto her bottom and began to wail.

"He pushed me!"

One of the wise men came to her defense. He was holding one of those fancy carpets around his shoulders and a feather duster was tied to his head. He stalked over and placed the vase he was carrying down on the floor. "Who did, Bessie? Who pushed you?"

"He did." She pointed a pudgy, dimpled finger at the shepherd.

"I didn't mean to. It's not my fault she—"

The wise man had already leaped on him.

"Hold on, now." I waded in and tried to separate them. One of them kicked me in the shin; the other stepped on my foot. And before I could pry them apart, the other two wise men had put down their own vases and joined in the fight.

"Wait just a second here!" I managed to grab the shepherd and pushed him behind me to try and keep him safe. "Three on one isn't a fair fight."

"He said Bessie was dumb." The first wise man stood with his arms crossed. The feather duster had fallen down around his ear.

The little boy I was trying to hide peered out around my side. "No, I didn't! She said *my sheep* was dumb."

I put my arm out to keep the others from advancing.

"I did not." The little girl had stopped crying and was now petting the sheep.

"You did too!"

"Well, he is."

"See! She *did* say it."

"Children!" One of the sourest-looking women I had ever seen clapped her hands and then formed the kids into lines. "Matilda! Mary would never hold Jesus that way."

An older girl was holding a live baby straight out from her chest, letting its feet dangle in the air as she flexed her knees, bouncing up and down like a jack-in-the-box. "But this is the way my mother holds him."

"Mary would hold baby Jesus like this." She took the child and cradled him in her arms as if he were some sort of China doll.

"He'll start crying."

"Hold him *like this*." The lady pushed the baby into position in the girl's arms, even though the kid had already started crying.

During the fight, the wise men's vases had shattered. They were standing beside me now looking at the pieces. "What're we supposed to give Jesus?" Bessie's protector was casting a worried glance in the direction of the teacher. "Miss Pirkle's going to yell at us."

I knew all about the Miss Pirkles of the world. The South Side had been lousy with them, all those prune-skinned spinsters trying to do the world some good . . . and making it hell on earth for little boys in the process. "Here." I pulled some Royal Taffies from my pocket. I'd taken some with the old red wrappers from Mr. Mundt's box; the new packaging just wasn't the same. I handed one to each of the boys. "Just . . . pretend you're carrying your gifts beneath your robes. And when you get up there, give Jesus one of these instead."

"Thanks, mister!"

I would have warned them about not eating the candy beforehand, but the teacher was already pulling the wise men into the line. I slipped into the sanctuary down the side aisle as they all went down the middle. By the time the wise men had reached the manger, I was in my seat.

Augusta smiled at me, though her eyes were shooting daggers.

"I was helping the children."

Her fury faded. I could tell she'd settled for mercy when she leaned close. "The mayor's grandchild is Baby Jesus."

That probably explained why there was a photographer standing just to the side of the manger scene.

The wise men did me proud. They held those rugs around their necks with the tightest of grips. And then they crowded so tightly around the manger that I doubted anyone caught a glimpse of the Royal Taffies they gave the baby.

"Is that . . . ?" Augusta looked at me with a frown.

I shrugged.

I was ready to breathe a sigh of relief as they moved away and the choir broke into a chorus of "Hark! The Herald Angels Sing." But the baby chose that instant to wave his arms. And clasped in one of those tiny fists, for all the world to see, was the bright red wrapper of a Royal Taffy.

"Well done, Charles. I knew you could do it."

My father slid the paper down the table toward me at break-fast. When I unfolded it, I saw a picture of the previous evening's nativity. Across the top the headline blared *Santa Might Like Fancies; Jesus Prefers Royals.*

"Genius. Pure genius." He raised his cup of coffee in Augusta's direction. "What did I tell you? Like father, like son!"

27

Lucy

"I would like to invite you, Miss Kendall, to a Chamber of Commerce banquet on Tuesday, next." Mr. Arthur was looking at me expectantly.

My spirits sunk to my toes. Courting a suitor was difficult work. It had been bad enough that evening to endure a hard wooden chair as I sat through a lecture by a boy genius from Harvard on something he kept calling a fourth dimension. He'd had the irritating habit of interrupting himself to scribble mathematical equations on a blackboard, which had swayed alarmingly with every jot and dash of the chalk. When his lecture had moved into the importance of Euclidean something or others, I had closed my eyes, taken deep breaths, and imagined myself back in Crete. At least the reception afterward at the university's faculty dining room had the benefit of refreshments.

If truth be told, I rather thought I'd earned the right to *not* be escorted anywhere by Mr. Arthur on Tuesday, after having been escorted by him all over the city for several months. And it irked that he kept calling me Miss Kendall. But whenever I opened my mouth to tell him to call me Lucy, the words just wouldn't come out. He was a very nice man, but all that niceness had a way of annoying me. Rather like anise flavoring. It was the one thing I couldn't stand in candy. Or, apparently, in men.

I smiled. "I think . . . we had already agreed to an invitation elsewhere that evening." I saw Charlie Clarke skulking around by the door. If I hadn't cheated with Fancy Crunch at the Stix, Bauer and Fuller window display, then I would have been fuming about the *Post-Dispatch*'s photo of Jesus grasping a Royal Taffy. What sort of trickery had he undertaken in order to accomplish that? Whoever said turnabout was fair play must not have been acquainted with the Clarkes.

"What's that?" Mother smiled as she came to stand beside me.

Mr. Arthur nodded at Mother. "I had asked Miss Kendall to accompany me to a Chamber of Commerce banquet on Tuesday."

"Of course she will." She turned her eyes on me. "Won't you, my dear?"

I tried to keep my shoulders from sagging; it wasn't easy. "I must have been mistaken about the other engagement. It would be an honor to go with you. Thank you, Mr. Arthur." I wondered . . . maybe if I asked him, Mr. Arthur would loan me some money.

He gave me a very reserved, very proper smile.

No.

I had the feeling that he was very much like my father. He would never approve of a girl conducting business. And I couldn't imagine him ever tying on an apron and helping me make candy. He probably shared my mother's view that ladies didn't belong in the kitchen.

So . . . how would a marriage to him make things any different from the way they were now?

Panic fluttered through my stomach as I considered a future that was every bit as bleak as my present. I couldn't imagine Mr. Arthur giving me a loan, and I couldn't imagine him approving of my helping in the confectionery. Perhaps I should have turned my efforts to helping my mother find a buyer for the company, but with Charlie Clarke in town, the whole thing had become a matter of principle.

I couldn't just let Standard run us out of business.

If only Father would get better. If Father were well, then maybe *he* could ask Mr. Arthur for a loan. And if we were married by then, if we were family, then how could Mr. Arthur refuse?

Married to Mr. Arthur, my life wouldn't be much different than it was now, but I could have the satisfaction of seeing Standard's efforts to ruin us blocked. Would that not be worth it? If I had to sacrifice my welfare for my father's honor, maybe it was a sacrifice worth making.

Besides, Mr. Arthur wasn't unhandsome. He was attentive to Mother. He was completely respectable in every single way. And I had to get married at some point, didn't I? All my other school friends already had. Why shouldn't I have some say in who I married? Why couldn't I do the picking instead of being picked?

But then . . . shouldn't I be happy about it? About him?

"It looks like old Alfred's getting ready to propose."

I jumped as a voice spoke from my side, and I turned to see Charlie Clarke. I didn't see why he had to say it with such amazement. Did he think me unfit for marriage? I'd traveled the Continent, I knew three languages, and I was a distinguished graduate of both Mary Institute and Mr. Mahler's dance academy. "I hope he does, because I mean to accept."

If I had wanted to see jealousy in his eyes—which I was quite sure I did not—I might have been disappointed. What I did see was a stiffening in his jaw and a flash of . . . something . . . in his eyes. "Are you sure?"

I lifted my chin. "Why wouldn't I be? It would be cruel to encourage hope in a man only to nip it once it started to flower."

"You don't really like him. I'd thought you might do him some good, but now, I'm not so sure."

He'd said it so confidently, so matter-of-factly, that it made my blood boil. "Are you saying—what are you saying?" Was he saying I wasn't good enough for Mr. Arthur?

He grasped me by the elbow and leaned so close I could see the prickles of whiskers on his chin. "I'm just saying that you might want to think this through."

"Who are you to say whom I ought to marry? And what do you want me to do, Charlie? Wait for the 'right man'? Bide my time and just—just—make candy in my kitchen until my father's company's been run into the ground? The right man is the one who can save it."

"So . . . this has nothing to do with him? It's about *candy*?"

"Who are you to talk? Everything you do is about Royal Taffy!" I wrenched my elbow from him and took a deep breath in an effort to calm myself. "Thank you for your concern, Mr. Clarke, but I'll marry whom I choose."

"Don't you think you should marry someone you want to be with? Someone you want to come home to? Someone you can't wait to talk to at the end of the day?"

Yes, I did. What I wanted was a marriage like my aunt and uncle's. But sometimes you couldn't have what you wanted. "Mr. Arthur is a fine man. I will admit that I haven't known him long, but I'm sure, in time—"

"In time! If you don't like him now, then you never will."

I shrugged my shoulders. "Why wish for lemon meringues when you can only find lemon drops?"

"Are they really all that's available?"

Mr. Arthur was the most eligible bachelor in town. And the only one I didn't mind spending time with. I didn't have the advantage of marriageable third cousins like Annie Farrell had or old school friends. "I wish you would tell me where to find an alternative!"

His pupils seemed to shrink, and for a moment I thought I'd caused him pain. But then I remembered who his father was, and I pushed away the thought.

"There could be a man right here, right now, who would love you with all of his heart if you would only give him a chance." His voice was quiet, but intense.

"Here? At a university lecture?"

"A man who would speak up if he thought you might accept him."

"And why wouldn't I?"

"What if . . . what if he had a past? What if he weren't quite what he seemed? If he'd . . . spent some time in jail?"

"You mean . . . you mean he's a criminal?"

He said nothing.

"I'd like to see him try to talk to me!"

The corners of his mouth twisted in a sardonic smile.

"In any case, Mr. Arthur is the only man who's presented himself. I'm already nearly twenty years old, Charlie, and soon my family will lose its business. Who will want to marry me then?" My goodness but my future was bleak . . . bleaker than I'd realized. And I didn't thank Charlie Clarke for pointing it out to me.

"Any man with any kind of sense would want to marry you."

He said it with such sincerity, such vehemence, that it nearly took my breath away. I could see how some girl might be deceived by his cool self-assurance. By those eyes that seemed to peer deep down into the soul. He'd probably had women back in Chicago swooning over his dark good looks and those tantalizing dimples. Longing to touch that jagged-looking scar on his jaw and basking in the familiar way in which he addressed himself to complete and total strangers.

"But why shouldn't you marry someone you *want* to marry?" It was the question I'd been asking myself. And I still didn't have an answer. "Because . . . because there is no such man." Tears choked my throat. Tears of despair. Of wishes squandered and dreams lost. "And if there is . . . I don't know where to find him." I turned from him then. I didn't want him to see me cry. And I didn't want him to come to my rescue. Not ever again.

I found an empty table far from Charlie Clarke. As I lifted my skirt to sit in a chair, I saw Mr. Arthur approaching. He waited until I sat before taking the seat beside me. "Surely you know why I've been so keen on getting to know you." He handed me a cup of punch as he spoke.

He *was* going to propose! Panic rose and beat its wings against my stomach. He was going to propose, I was going to say yes, and we were going to be married.

He set his own cup on the table. Taking out his pocket watch, he sprang the cover and, after glancing at it, snapped it shut with a click. He looked at me, face placid, eyes serene. "I wish to propose that you marry me."

I wasn't looking for romance. I'd never been looking for romance. And in spite of what Charlie Clarke had said, I still wasn't. Not exactly. But in that moment I realized I had been expecting something that sounded a bit less like a business arrangement and more like a romantic attachment. Or at least . . . a warm friendship. And though I didn't have anything against learning in general, a lecture about impossible theories seemed an odd place to speak of marriage. "And why do you propose that I marry you, Mr. Arthur?"

He blinked and sat back in his chair. "I believe there are many good reasons."

"Could you do me the favor of telling me what they are?" Maybe that would help me forget my conversation with Charlie and make me feel better about the prospect.

His brows drew together. "I find this highly unusual."

I smiled what I hoped was an endearing smile. "Please, won't you indulge me?"

A flush began at his neck and climbed up his face. "Of course. I wouldn't want you to think me indifferent." He leaned forward and drew my hand from the cup of punch, enclosing it in his own. I might have expected to feel some heat through my glove, but I felt nothing. "I'm an Arthur." He looked at me, brow raised, as if hoping, I suppose, that might be enough.

"Yes. I've known that for quite some time now." And really, that's all that mattered, wasn't it? His being an Arthur could help our family save City Confectionery.

"I'm of an age, Miss Kendall. It's time for me to settle down."

"Is there anything about your plans or your dreams, Mr. Arthur, that has to do with me in particular?"

"You're a very nice girl!" He said it as if I might protest that I was not.

He might be surprised to find out that I wasn't, considering that I had once held hands with Charlie Clarke at the airfield and had almost kissed him. "But don't you think that if we're to be married, there ought to be some sort of attachment between us?" Or . . . attraction?

"Do you?"

I hadn't used to think so. I'd thought that I could marry any old person just like I might be able to make candy with any copper pot.

He released my hand. "I think that we could have quite a good marriage. I'm very agreeable. I've always been told so."

He was. There was nothing at all wrong with him. But . . . that didn't mean he was necessarily right . . . did it? Oh! Charlie Clarke ruined everything. Even my marriage proposals. But now that I'd broached the topic, there was nothing to be done but continue. "I think you'll find that a girl would like to believe that she's more than just a . . . just a girl . . ."

He blinked. "But . . . you are one."

I was. Whatever point I had been trying to make seemed lost and rather silly now. "It's just that . . . a girl wants something more."

"Like what?" He was looking at me with interest, as if he really wanted to know.

"A girl would like to know that . . . she mattered." I doubted that Mr. Arthur would ever look at me with anything other than that calm, serious, levelheaded look he had in his eyes. And I didn't think him capable of ever raising his voice at me. Not like Charlie. Could I even . . . ? I wondered if I might be able to make him mad. To make him feel anything at all.

"A girl." He took my hand. "You mean, you?" He was looking at me with a surprisingly keen glance.

I blushed. "Yes. I think I would." Why shouldn't I matter?

"Then put your fears to rest. I can't think of a more suitable companion, and in time I'm quite certain that we'll come to care very much for each other. Love has the best chance of growing when it has a foundation of mutual respect." His ears had gone pink. "And I would consider it my duty as your husband to support your family as if it were my own. I know you must be concerned about your mother, considering your father's illness."

I felt a flush of shame sweep over me. I guess I'd just assumed that Mother could take care of herself. Mr. Arthur was a much better person than I would ever be. And he'd said what I had wanted to hear. So why didn't I feel better about his proposal? I should be happy. I *would* be happy. I'm sure I just . . . needed . . . some time to get used to the idea. "Then I accept your kind proposal, Mr. Arthur."

After Lucy and her mother had gone, Alfred joined me at my table in the corner. Apparently lectures by child geniuses were not to be missed. I was trying to hide from all the girls Augusta kept sending my direction. And I was trying to plug the hole that Lucy had opened up inside me. I don't know why I'd been surprised at her words. What had I expected? That she'd welcome a man like me with open arms?

Alfred downed the rest of his punch and then set the cup on the table with a satisfied sigh. "That's done, then."

"What's that?"

"I proposed to Lucy Kendall."

Something inside my stomach clenched into a tight little ball. "And?"

"She accepted."

Of course she had. Why shouldn't she? As she'd said herself, who was I to say whom she should marry? "Congratulations." I'd tried to hate the man, but there was nothing about him to dislike. I'd tried hard to find something, but he was so polite, so nice, that his worst enemy would have been forced to admire him.

"Thank you." He was looking very calm for just having gotten engaged to the best girl in the whole city. He should have been whooping or cheering or clapping himself on the back.

"You should celebrate."

"Hmm?" He was looking at the bottom of his cup as though he were wishing there were more punch in there.

I took it from him. "We should go celebrate your engagement. In style." That's what a man did for a friend, wasn't it? Helped him celebrate?

I should have kept my big mouth shut back there. If Lucy was going to marry anyone, then it *should* be a man like Alfred. He was almost perfect. Irritatingly perfect. And the most irritating part was that there wasn't anything wrong with him! They were perfect for each other.

I took his hat from his hand and put it on his head, then pulled him up from his chair and pushed him toward the door.

Nelson dropped us in Chestnut Valley. I picked a saloon that had the "Maple Leaf Rag" drifting from its door and walked into it.

Alfred stood in the doorway, looking uncertain. "I've never been in this place before."

I waved him in. "It's just like the rest of them."

"I mean . . . I've never been in any of them before." He took a hesitant step forward.

"Ever?"

"Never." He looked as though he wished he could still say that.

"Where's your spirit of adventure?"

"I don't have one."

Two mistakes in the same night: thinking Lucy might accept me for who I was and assuming Alfred was just a regular fellow who'd want to have a drink with me. I'd been wrong about them both. "Just . . . sit there for a minute while I order a drink." I pointed to a table in a shadow by the corner. "Then we'll go."

He glanced toward the stage as he sat.

I ordered up a whiskey for myself and a sarsaparilla for him. When they came, I wasted no time in taking a drink, enjoying the satisfying burn as it went down my throat. Alfred was sitting at the table, straight as a ruler, hat perched on a knee. So much for celebrating. I swallowed a sigh as I joined him, vowing I wouldn't let him hurry me along. A man ought to be able to appreciate his whiskey. As I set my glass down on the table, I admired its golden color.

The ditty the piano man was playing tinkled to an end.

I stomped on the floor along with the rest of the crowd.

Alfred refrained, sipping his sarsaparilla instead.

A girl pushed through a lopsided curtain and planted an elbow on the piano. She was dressed in a blue ruffly skirt and a blouse that was short on fabric and small in size. She reminded me of the Tribley Twins back in Chicago. Though she looked almost respectable, she had the same large round eyes and the same dark hair that she'd spun into a roll up on top of her head. Her mouth was a perfect red bow. "Let's stay for this song. She might be good." She had that look about her. And even if she wasn't, she'd take my mind off Lucy.

Alfred eyed the door again.

"Just one song. I promise. Then we'll leave."

The piano man took a run up and down the keys with his

fingers while the girl twirled the red rose she held in her hand. Then they launched into a song.

> *I am dreaming dear of you, day by day*
> *Dreaming when the skies are blue, when they're gray . . .*

She'd turned to sing directly to us. Rather . . . directly to Alfred. No, that wasn't quite right. She wasn't singing; she was crooning.

That was two girls who couldn't seem to get enough of him. What did he have that I didn't? I took another swallow of whiskey.

> *Let me call you "Sweetheart," I'm in love with you.*
> *Let me hear you whisper that you love me too . . .*

As the song drew to an end, the girl tossed her rose at Alfred.

He caught it, stared at it for a moment, then looked up at her. A silly grin was plastered across his face. "I'd . . . I'd better give this back to her."

"She didn't lose it. She threw it at you. *On purpose.*" The old throw-a-bone-to-a-wealthy-dog trick. I tried to take it from him, but he held on to it. I think he might have even growled at me. He strode toward the curtain and swept it aside, hat in one hand, rose in the other. I didn't see him for another half an hour. And then, when he appeared, that girl was draped on his arm.

He was smiling down at her as if she were the best thing he'd ever laid eyes on. "This is Evelyn."

I threw a glance at up her. I'd been wrong. She wasn't like the Tribley Twins at all. She was old. She had to have been at least thirty.

Alfred was scowling, making gestures toward her with his chin.

Good grief. I stood. "Pleasure."

"She's going to come to dinner with us."

"We're going to dinner?" Hadn't he eaten back at the university?

He scowled again. Even-tempered Alfred Arthur was getting testy.

"Oh. Oh! Yes. To dinner." I linked my arm through his. "We were going out to celebrate. Did you know Alfred, here, has just got himself engaged?"

She drew her arm from his and took a step away from him. "Congratulations."

Alfred mumbled something.

"Congratulations is what I told him too. We came here to celebrate."

"Then celebrate you should. I won't keep you."

"No. Don't—" Alfred had caught her by the hand as she tried to leave. "Please, come."

She looked at him for a long moment. Looked at me. "On one condition. You'll have to tell me all about your new fiancée."

She was a sly and sneaky one. I could tell.

I suffered through poached egg soup, broiled fish, and boiled beef at the Planters Hotel. And then I suffered some more as Nelson drove us all back to Chestnut Valley. When we dropped Evelyn at the saloon, Alfred got out of the car too.

I stuck my head out the door. "You don't want to walk back to your place from here."

He turned, walking backward. "It's a bit early to be going home."

Early? It was nearly midnight. Evelyn had already disappeared into the saloon. He was glancing over his shoulder at the door as if he'd like to follow her through it. The very same door he hadn't wanted to enter just a few hours before. "Alfred: Go home."

He saluted. "I'll be fine."

I had a bad feeling about this. A man engaged to a girl like Lucy shouldn't be flirting with a saloon singer. But he wouldn't be the first engaged man to do so. And who was I to try and defend someone's honor? Alfred Arthur was a grown man. I just had to trust that he could look after himself. And that he'd come to his senses. Soon. Before Lucy found out about anything.

"I'm getting married, Papa." I had only just been proposed to, so the words sounded strange. It was like being back in my Italian language class in Florence and learning to say "I love you." Though I'd repeated the words after my tutor, they'd held no real meaning.

My father reached out his hand toward me.

I knelt by the side of the bed and offered him mine. What little color he'd regained since I'd returned to St. Louis had disappeared. His breathing had become shallow and labored. I was more worried now than I had been back in September.

He squeezed my hand. "I only wish I could walk you down the aisle."

"Maybe by then you'll be able to. It's only going to be a small wedding." At least . . . I hoped it would be.

"Who is it? Or did you tell me and I've forgotten?" He laid his head back down on the pillow.

"Alfred Arthur."

"Alfred . . . oh." The smile left his face.

"What? You don't like him?"

"He's just so . . . sensible. Though I suppose there's nothing wrong with that. It's just that I had hoped for someone with a little more . . . spirit. Someone more like a cinnamon drop than a butter mint."

"He's very agreeable."

"I know he is . . . but . . . don't you ever wish he'd be disagreeable? Just so you could . . . I don't know . . ." He sighed. "Never mind." He ran a hand across his eyes. "I haven't been thinking clearly, lately. Of course you should marry him, Sugar Plum."

"He's a very good catch."

He smiled. "You sound more like your mother every day." He sighed. "That's good. You should listen to your mother. I should have listened to your mother."

"Papa—"

"I should have. She's smart. Smarter than I ever was. If I hadn't spent all our money . . . if I'd never signed . . ." His eyelids drooped and his chin dipped toward his chest, but then he blinked his eyes wide.

Signed what? "What did you sign?"

"What?"

"You were talking about signing something."

He sighed. "What's done is done. Don't worry your pretty head about it." He tried to hide a yawn in his shoulder, but I saw it and rose.

"You don't have to leave."

"I should let you sleep."

He yawned again and this time he didn't bother to hide it. "Maybe I should."

Mr. Arthur came over the next afternoon. Alfred. I ought to think of him as Alfred. But Alfred sounded so . . . familiar. More familiar than I wanted to be. We sat, the three of us, in the parlor. Mr. Arthur—*Alfred*—presented me with a ring. It was a large square-cut diamond that glittered as he pushed it up onto my finger.

Did it have to be so big?

He and Mother discussed wedding plans as I sat there and stared at the ring on my finger. It seemed so permanent. And the way it sparkled—as if it couldn't stop announcing the fact that I'd become engaged—was truly horrid. I wondered if people would treat me any differently. I wouldn't be Lucy Kendall for much longer. Soon I would Mr. Arthur's wife. I tried to stop the twisting of dread in my stomach, but I couldn't. And then a thought occurred to me. "Won't—won't the Veiled Prophet people be upset if I get married? I've only just been crowned."

Mother patted my hand. "I've already thought of that. And I'll meet with them this week. Considering your father's condition, I'm sure they'll understand."

My father's condition. Of course they'd understand that I'd want to get married soon . . . before he died. A chill crept up my spine.

"Anyone would understand that." Mr. Arthur smiled at me.

"Thank you . . . Alfred." I said his name just to try it out. To see what it would be like. I supposed I would have to say it on a regular basis. At least I would once we married. Alfred. Alfred. Alfred. I might as well begin practicing now.

Mother's voice interrupted my thoughts. "I think the twenty-second would be fine. What do you think, Lucy?"

I blinked to find both Mother and Mr. Arthur staring at me. "About . . . ?"

"About the date of the wedding. What do you think of February twenty-second?"

"*February?*" That seemed awfully soon.

"Weren't you listening?" Mother didn't quite frown as she spoke, but worry furrowed her forehead just the same.

"I had hoped it could be small."

"Absolutely not." Now Mother was frowning. "What could we expect people to say if you were married so quickly and so quietly? And besides, I've been dreaming of your wedding for years now. I want you to have everything that I didn't."

Mr. Arthur's ears had gone pink. "I think . . . perhaps your mother is right."

She consulted the tablet upon which she'd been writing. "I'll reserve the church for the wedding on the twenty-second. We'll have the reception at the Planters Hotel afterward." She looked up at me. "I had always hoped to have it here, of course, but we need to spare your father the fatigue of all the noise and activity." She turned her attentions to Mr. Arthur. "We'll see the printer this week about invitations, and I'll write up an announcement for the newspapers. Unless you would rather do so, Mr. Arthur?"

"Ah . . . no. No. I don't think so. Well, I . . . had better . . . I should go." He'd taken a handkerchief from his pocket and was swabbing his face as if he were sweltering. As if it were July instead of December.

Mother looked at me, brow raised, and gestured toward the front hall.

I rose and escorted him toward the door. "Thank you, Mr. Arthur. Mr. . . . . Alfred. Thank you. For coming by."

"It was my pleasure, Miss Kendall." He put his hat on and tipped it at me before walking out the door. I wondered if he'd still tip his hat once we were married. I wondered if he'd ever call me Lucy. And I wondered, too, how it would feel to be introduced as Mrs. Alfred Arthur. If anyone would make fun of my new name the way I had once made fun of his.

The next morning Mother took me back to Vandervoort's to consult with the dressmaker about my wedding and reception gowns. We lunched at a tea room, then went on to Planters Hotel to discuss plans for the reception. Twelfth Avenue was decorated for Christmas, with pine trees lining the walkways and an enormous tree set up in the middle of the intersection with Washington Avenue. I ought to have been in good cheer.

The manager invited us into the dining room, where we all sat down to go over the arrangements. He and Mother talked about when the reception would start and how long it would last. Whether the ladies' dining room or the Moorish room should be reserved and what to use for decorations. They talked about hothouse orchids and Boston ferns. Smilax and red roses.

"You'll want the cake table in the middle, of course."

Mother nodded.

"And the cake done in the new way? With pillars separating the two layers?"

Mother agreed.

"Can the cake be chocolate?" I didn't like to make it, but I didn't mind eating it.

She looked at me, brows tilted in exasperation. "A chocolate wedding cake? Chocolate is for children." Mother turned to the manager. "We'll have a normal wedding cake, two layers, with pillars."

"Fine." He noted something in his notebook. "That's fine. We'll decorate with orange flowers and ivy." The manager tapped his pencil on the menu he had set before us. "Shall we discuss the rest of the food?"

I let them decide how many courses there would be and what would be served. Then the manager cleared his throat. "We can deliver upstairs whatever remains. Unless you prefer a different arrangement . . . ?"

Mother looked toward me before glancing away. "I . . . am not sure what Mr. Arthur has planned. I had assumed they would be leaving that afternoon by train—"

"He's already arranged for a room that night."

That seemed odd. "For what?"

They both turned toward me.

The manager's face had colored. "He's reserved a suite for the night of the wedding."

"Oh." I had forgotten that I wouldn't be going home afterward. "Oh!" And I hadn't realized that I would be staying here. With him. "I . . . need . . ." I made some sort of excuse before I fled from the room.

⁂

I couldn't breathe. Could a person die from not breathing? Just as the world began to turn white around the edges, my lungs opened up and I swallowed a mouthful of air with a great *whoosh.* I sat in the nearest chair, concentrating on breathing in and breathing out.

In, out. In, out.

Everything would be fine.

In, out. In, out.

All I had to do was get married.

In, out. In, out.

Even Julia Shaw had gone and eloped while I'd been away. How hard could getting married be?

In, out.

It wasn't easy trying to save the company by myself. I wished there were some other way to do it.

In, out.

I wished there were no Charlie Clarke.

In, out.

But if wishes were candy, then I would be eating all the Royal Taffy I wanted.

In.

Wishes were for children.

Out.

And I wasn't a child anymore.

30  *Charlie*

I was out for the third night in a row with Alfred. And Evelyn. I should have been at a Christmas concert, but I couldn't stand to think of leaving the two of them alone. The way he kept looking at her made me afraid he would do something stupid.

Or *ungallant,* as he was so fond of saying.

He excused himself to go get Evelyn a drink.

She put an elbow to the table and leaned her head against her hand as she watched him. "You know he shouldn't be marrying that girl."

"I know." I knew! That's what I'd told Lucy.

"He doesn't love her."

And she didn't love him. "It's not about love." At least that's what Lucy had said. "It's about candy."

"What?"

I shook my head. "Nothing."

She'd turned her big green eyes on me. "Why do you hate me so much?"

Who knew? I should be thanking her. If she could get Alfred to leave Lucy alone, she'd be doing me a favor. I once thought Lucy might be able to loosen him up a little, but he was so loose now he was in danger of leaping onto a stage and crooning a song himself. He didn't deserve Lucy. With the best girl in the world on his arm, he seemed set on taking up with a saloon singer.

But I had a feeling that Alfred Arthur was one of those fellows who would never go back on a handshake. Or a marriage proposal.

Back in Chicago, I would have been cheering for a working girl like Evelyn. I would have wanted to see her snag a rich man. But now I knew the rich man. And Alfred was too nice—too good—to be waylaid by a girl with those intentions. Except that he wasn't being so nice right now, was he?

And then again, his money was the reason Lucy wanted him too.

So which of them was worse?

And why did I even care?! Lucy wanted nothing to do with me anyway.

One thing was sure: Alfred couldn't keep seeing Evelyn without consequences. Someone was going to notice soon. And once word got out, he'd be ruined. It wouldn't matter that he was an Arthur, and no one would care that he was usually so dull and grim.

But most of all I was worried about what it would do to Lucy. She'd have no one but me to thank for the humiliation of having lost her fiancé to a saloon girl. And it would give her one more reason to hate me.

Evelyn laid a hand on my arm. "I'm not a bad person."

She wasn't. I'd revised my opinion over the past two nights. She was nice in the very same way that Alfred was nice. They'd be a perfect match if she weren't a saloon singer. Though she'd been blessed with an angel's voice, she'd been cursed with the inability to use it anywhere but in a place like Chestnut Valley.

"Is it so terrible to want to have someone to talk to? Someone who really seems to understand me? Someone who could look after me?"

When it came down to it, she only wanted the same thing that Lucy did. And I hated them both. Girls were nothing but trouble.

"We've become quite fond of each other. What's so wrong with that?"

There were all kinds of everything wrong with that, that's what was wrong with it! I was going to have to have a good long talk with the fellow.

⁂

"Isn't she wonderful?" We were watching Evelyn sing from our table in the corner. Alfred, who hadn't been in the habit of drinking anything stronger than lemonade, had just that evening decided he liked beer.

"She's a saloon singer." May Evelyn forgive me! But even she would say there was no point in denying the obvious. And she'd never tried to . . . which only made the whole thing worse.

"She doesn't have to be. Not forever."

I grabbed him by the collar, dragged him past the bar, through the kitchen, and then threw him out into the alley. "Get ahold of yourself!"

He stood there blinking at me as he swayed in the moonlight. "I think I'm—" He bent over, hands to his knees, and vomited. "Sorry. That was uncalled for." He took a handkerchief from his pocket and dabbed at his mouth. Then he looked around as if wondering what to do with it.

Why was it that rich people couldn't seem to figure out what to do with their messes? I tore it from his hand and threw it into a garbage can.

"But—that's mine!"

"Do you want it back?"

He gave the garbage can a leery look. " . . . No."

"Listen to me. If you don't stop this right now, you're going to ruin everything."

"I hardly think that—"

I held up a hand. "Just listen. You're engaged to Lucy Kendall. How could you even think . . . whatever it is that you're thinking?"

"I'm not . . . I mean . . . I never intended—but what I feel for Evelyn—"

"What would Lucy say, seeing you standing here, declaring your feelings for some saloon girl?" Why was I defending Lucy Kendall? Why was I out here in the alley with Alfred trying to make him stay faithful to the girl I wanted? Curse Lucy Kendall. This was all her fault!

I put a hand to his shoulder. "You're a reasonable fellow. What do you suppose all those folks at the symphony and opera and . . . and *church* would think of you spending your nights down here?"

He looked toward the saloon. Grimaced. "Right. You're right. I don't know what I've been doing. This is completely unlike me. Of course, you're right. I can't imagine . . ."

I could. I could imagine all sorts of terrible things happening.

"I should break things off with Lucy right now."

Wait. "What?"

"It's the only honorable thing to do."

I caught him by his collar as he tried to walk past. "Wait just a minute. Are you telling me . . . ?"

"I'm an honorable man who's been going about all this in a completely dishonorable way."

That was better. "That's what I've been trying to tell you. You can't be engaged to Lucy and go around spending so much time with Evelyn. It isn't right."

"Which is what *I've* been trying to say. The only honorable thing to do is to break the engagement."

"You mean . . . you're choosing *Evelyn*?"

He straightened his tie, swiped a hand across his mouth, and squared his shoulders. "Yes. That's exactly what I'm going to do."

Apparently my mouth had fallen open because I found myself closing it back up. "Just how many of those drinks did you have?"

He squinted up at the night sky. "One . . . two . . . three. I had three."

"What you need is time. In a few hours the beer will wear off, and you'll start thinking like yourself again."

"I *am* thinking like myself. I'm more myself than I've ever been."

"It's the beer talking. Believe me."

He put a hand to his chest. "It's not the beer. It's my heart."

"Hogwash! Now, are you coming or not?" I started down the alleyway toward the street.

He screwed up his jaw and raised his chin. "Not."

"I'm warning you, Alfred!"

"I'm not coming. Besides . . . I left my hat inside."

"You left your *hat*?"

He nodded. "Inside. I'll just go get it. If you'll pardon me . . ."

I hoped he would pardon what *I* was about to do. He hadn't left me any choice. I did what I'd done back on the South Side when a fellow wouldn't listen to reason. I hauled back my fist and then I popped him in the nose.

At least, that's what I meant to do. But he ducked. Then he started bobbing and weaving like the best of prizefighters.

"Stop it, Alfred! Stand still."

"Can't. Boxing Team, Columbia University. Class of '01. I was their best pugilist."

I took a second swing at him.

He ducked again.

"Alfred Arthur! You ought to be ashamed of yourself!" Evelyn called out from the saloon's back door.

Though Alfred didn't put his hands down, he stepped back, away from me, and shot a glance at her over his shoulder. "He said I shouldn't be spending time with you."

Evelyn put a fist to her hip. "And he's perfectly right!"

I—I was?

"You mean . . . you don't want me?" Arthur put his fists down. And then he stumbled toward her.

I was tempted to belt him one, but that wouldn't have been polite. Not when his back was turned.

"Not like this. It isn't right." She pulled her lips into a firm, straight line that all the Miss Pirkles in the world would have been proud of. "Now." She handed him his hat. "I want you to go home and think about what it is that you want."

"But, Evelyn!"

"And when you've figured it out, then we can talk."

31

Lucy

"I can't do it anymore, Lucy. It doesn't seem right." Sam was pacing on the back porch Friday evening as I stood watching, clasping my arms around my chest to keep warm. The sun was lingering in the darkening sky as though dreading the plunge into the cold, dark oblivion beyond the horizon.

I peered at him through the gloom. "It's not as if we're the first to ever do it. What's the harm?"

"The harm is, what if somebody sees me? And the other harm is, I have actual work to do. Down at the confectionery! My father's counting on me."

And so was mine! . . . Even if he didn't quite know it. "Think of it as a . . . a chance for more people to try Fancy Crunch. The reason it hasn't been selling is that people have forgotten they can buy it. We don't have the money to put up new posters, and Standard has been taking all of our business."

He paused and sent me a dubious look.

"Really, Sam. You're doing everyone in St. Louis a favor.

You're giving them the chance to remember how much they like Fancy Crunch." And if everything went like I planned, then sales would go up and we'd have enough money to stay in business . . . though I'd still have to marry Mr. Arthur. I put that thought aside for the moment. I'd been doing quite a bit of putting that thought aside recently.

"I guess . . ."

"It's not like you're taking their candy from the shelves. You're just putting ours in front of theirs. You're *rearranging* things."

"I suppose . . ."

"You know they'd do the same if they'd thought of it." In fact, they probably already had. I wouldn't put it past that Charlie Clarke! "Just one more day. Please?"

His face was tense with indecision but finally he nodded, patted his hat down around his ears, and headed toward the porch's screen door.

"Can't you stay? I was thinking of making some fudge. I know how much you like it."

"Can't. I have plans."

Plans that were better than fudge? He'd never turned down fudge before. What was wrong with him?

It was hard to sleep that night. It wasn't because I'd eaten too much fudge and it definitely wasn't because I was feeling guilty. The Clarkes deserved whatever they got. It's just that hiding their taffy behind our Fancy Crunch was only a temporary solution. What City Confectionery needed was a permanent way to make more money.

We could sell more candy. That would bring in more money.

We could spend less to make the candy. That would bring in more money too.

Or . . . we could charge more for the candy. But we'd already tried that and it had just caused more people to buy Royal Taffy.

There had to be a way! I had to think harder. I had to think smarter. But first I had to suffer through Christmas Eve. And Christmas Day.

Christmas Eve wasn't too terrible. I had to share the church with Charlie Clarke, but the Clarkes always sat behind us, so most of the time I was able to pretend he wasn't there. When I walked past their pew after service ended, I looked the other direction. Mother wanted to hurry home to make sure we could have supper while Father was still awake, so we didn't even linger in the foyer.

The maid delivered the food upstairs on Chinese lacquer trays so we could all eat together, but Father quit halfway through. He said all the chewing tired him.

Mother nodded toward the bed, and I went to cut the rest of his meat up for him, but he waved it away, so I put the tray aside. We finished soon after, Mother and I, but before leaving, I gave him the last of my Mozartkugels as a present. His eyes gleamed, and for a moment it seemed like old times. But he only set it on the nightstand before lying back on his pillow and saying good-night.

Father had always been the chief enthusiast of holidays, so without him, Christmas Eve was simply another frigid winter's night. And Christmas morning was just another case of the sun rising, tardy and pale, to survey a bleak winter morning.

I gave Mother the tablecloth I bought her in Brussels, and she gave me a set of monogrammed napkins. Large A's had been embroidered upon them in satin stitch with shiny white silk thread. I put them in my hope chest, laying them on top of the

251

newspaper-wrapped pillow tops, lace doilies, linens, and my rapidly dwindling collection of uneaten candy. As I closed the lid I thought about the dreams and wishes I had placed inside that chest over the years. How simple they now seemed. How happy I had once imagined I would be. But life hadn't turned out the way I'd expected.

I hadn't planned on Mr. Arthur, and I hadn't known there would be a Charlie Clarke.

It felt as if I'd wasted all my dreams. It seemed as if I ought to have hoped for other things. But I didn't know what they were. And, for better or worse, it was too late now.

32

Charlie

My father did nothing by halves. Even Christmas was celebrated with a lot of fuss. There was a big scramble by the staff the week before to get everything decorated, along with a continual mouthwatering mixture of smells drifting out from the kitchen. It all led up to a big dinner on Christmas Day, after church. We probably could have fed the whole orphanage downtown with all the food that was set in front of us.

My father gave Augusta a sparkling necklace and matching earrings. She gave him a cigar cutter decorated with diamonds. And then my father handed me a large envelope.

"Open it, open it!" I could hear echoes of my sisters in my father's impatience and excitement.

I drew out a sheaf of papers, turning them over so I could read them.

But my father couldn't wait any longer. "It's a deed!"

"A deed." What was a deed?

"So you can build a house."

"A . . . what?"

"A house! I bought you a lot across the street."

"A lot . . ." A lot of what?

"I set up a meeting with our architect on Tuesday afternoon. You can start building just as soon as you want."

"You bought me . . . you want me to build a house? Right here? Next to you?"

"Can't live with us forever. I doubt you'd even want to." He sat back in his chair, his smile as large as any I'd ever seen. "So what do you think?"

I didn't know what I thought. I didn't know what to say. It was hard to hate a man who wasn't doing anything hateful. Who wasn't doing anything at all but trying to make up for the past. Trying to make me happy. I could feel my anger slipping away.

And the problem was, I didn't know what to do without it.

*

If my father celebrated with enthusiasm, he also worked with enthusiasm. The day after Christmas, he went right back to the factory. And me along with him; I'd recently been given an office down at the end of the top floor. I started the morning by reviewing the sales figures for the first two weeks of the month, but had hardly finished reading the report when Mr. Mundt summoned me to my father's office.

My father waved me in. "I've had word from our customers that their stock has disappeared. And though I would like to believe it's due entirely to strong Christmas sales, I'm being told their receipts don't match their inventory."

"Their stock has disappeared? You mean . . . their candy?"

"Yes. From the shelves." He was staring at me as if I understood what he was talking about, but I didn't.

"Shelves? You mean the ones in the stores?"

"The very ones."

Candy disappearing from shelves? "That's impossible."

"Possible or not, it's happening. And I want you to put a stop to it."

⁊〇᷎

If someone was stealing, it wasn't our fault, was it? Wouldn't that be the stores' responsibility? I figured someone was swiping the candy as it was delivered and then claiming they'd never seen it. Happened all the time in Chicago. One of the clerks was probably smuggling it out of the store and then reselling it to someone and pocketing all the money. Could be these St. Louis people weren't as wise to goings-on as folks up in Chicago.

I started out at Vandervoort's, asking to see the manager.

He appeared, tall and spiffy, though he kept having to push his glasses back up his nose. I introduced myself and got directly to the point. "I wanted to speak to you about the Royal Taffy disappearing from your shelves."

Blinking rapidly, he pulled his chin in toward his neck as if he weren't quite sure what to think of me. "They haven't been disappearing from the shelves."

Exactly as I'd thought.

He pushed his glasses back up his nose. "I assume you've fixed the problem, then?"

It was my turn to blink. "I only just started investigating. It's been happening all over the city, but your store is the first I've visited."

"We've been waiting for you to come." He was looking at me as if I should say something.

"Haven't you done any investigating yourself?" It wasn't my fault they'd employed a thief.

"I hardly think that's my place!"

"If Royal Taffy has been disappearing, I'd think you'd want to find out why."

"I wouldn't call it disappearing, but I already know why."

"You do?"

"Don't you?" Now he was glaring at me.

"I have my suspicions."

"Suspicions! I hope you have more than suspicions. Just how long am I supposed to wait?"

I didn't quite understand. "Wait for . . . for what?"

"For you to take the extra taffy off our hands."

"Extra? But . . . I thought taffy was being stolen from your stock room, and if that's the case—"

"No one stole any."

Nothing he was saying made any sense. "But if no one's stolen any and it's disappeared from your shelves, then . . . what's going on?"

"That's what I want to know!"

I felt my brow crumple as I tried to figure out what he was saying. "I don't—I can't—"

"Someone pushed all the Royal Taffy to the back of our shelves and then put packages of Fancy Crunch up in their place."

"They . . . what?"

"Which made us think that we'd sold out of it. So we placed another order. And then we discovered the taffy at the back of the shelves and now we have twice as much taffy as we can possibly sell." He said it as if it were all my fault.

"Now, wait just a minute! Are you accusing us of—"

"I'm not accusing you of anything. I'm simply saying that the only person who profits from us buying twice as much taffy as normal is you."

"But—!"

"I don't mind telling you that I'm grieved, Mr. Clarke. I'm

a long-standing customer of your father's, and this is the way I'm treated?"

"We don't—we haven't—it wasn't us!"

The same story played out all across the city.

The week before, someone had spent a lot of time pushing Royal Taffy to the backs of store shelves and placing Fancy Crunch in front of it.

Most of the stock clerks just assumed they'd sold out of taffy and had placed orders for more. And now they were all raising Cain about it.

As soon as I returned to the factory, I went to have a talk with Mr. Gillespie.

"They're saying what?" His eyes had gone wide, and he was swallowing as if he had something stuck in his throat.

"They're all saying they double ordered and that it's our fault."

"But why?"

I shrugged. "Because who else profits, besides us, if they buy more than they need?"

"Uh . . . ?" He was looking around the factory as if desperately searching for someone else to blame.

"Do we do things like that?"

"No!"

I hadn't thought so—I had hoped not—but it did me good to hear him say it all the same. "So you *didn't* send a man out to hide our taffy."

He threw up his hands. "We don't do things like that! For goodness' sake! I'll tell you what it sounds like: It sounds like Mr. Kendall, the way he used to spread rumors about Mr. Clarke and such. But I promise you: We've never done anything like that."

Maybe *we* hadn't, but someone else had.

Who would benefit the most from the disappearance of Royal Taffy? I didn't have to think very hard to come up with an answer.

It was easy to know where to find Lucy. Her activities were published in the newspaper. Queen of Love and Beauty to open this event and Queen of Love and Beauty to preside over this gathering or that banquet. And so when I found out she was going to be at the new zoological club's meeting the next day, I made sure I was there. And when she glared at me, I smiled right back.

"I didn't know you had an interest in zoology, Mr. Clarke."

"I have a keen interest in females, Miss Kendall. And they all seem to adore animals." I shrugged. "So I figured this was as good a place as any to meet some."

Her eyes seemed to spit fire.

"You know, a funny thing happened this week. All the Royal Taffy in the city disappeared."

"Did it?"

"Yes. And when I went to investigate, guess what I discovered?"

That pretty mouth of hers clamped right up. "I wouldn't know."

"I think you might."

"Are you calling me a liar, Mr. Clarke?"

"No. I'm calling you a cheat."

Her cheeks burned red.

"Maybe not *you*, exactly, but that man you always seem to be with. '*Your Sam*' I believe you once called him. I'm trying to decide whether or not to ask the police to make out an arrest warrant." I wasn't. Not really. I'd spent enough time already at police stations.

She went pale. "He didn't! I mean—"

"The good news is that all those stores thought they'd sold out of Royal Taffy, so they all re-ordered. Our sales in St. Louis doubled last week."

Her eyes narrowed to slits. "You just have to ruin everything, don't you?"

"*I* ruin everything? I really don't think that's fair!"

"Oh? And was it fair to cover up all our advertising in the city? And then to take over all the streetcars too?"

She had me there. But I hadn't known her back then. "Business is no place for a lady."

"And apparently it's no place for a gentleman either."

Somewhere deep inside, her arrow hit its mark. "You should stop playing with candy and start working on growing up. Alfred Arthur wouldn't marry you if he knew you were just a common criminal."

"Are you threatening me?"

"I haven't decided yet."

She lifted her chin, though her gaze had dropped to the floor. "I should go."

"Listen. You're involving yourself in things you shouldn't. You don't know what you're doing. If you keep on like this, someone's going to get hurt."

She lifted her foot and brought her sharp-heeled shoe down on my instep. "I agree. And it's not going to be me!"

I managed not to react until she passed me and walked out the door. And then I sat down, cradling my foot in my hands.

33

Lucy

The day after the zoological club meeting, I helped deliver food to the city's orphanage on behalf of the butchers' association. And afterward, I stopped in at Winnie's. It seemed like the polite thing to do, since she'd come to call on me on Tuesday afternoon. And besides, there was no one else to talk to about Charlie Clarke. Sam was avoiding me, Mother wouldn't understand, and how could I even mention to Father that I had talked to a Clarke?

There was no one else visiting, but when I took a seat on her sofa, far away from her parakeet, she sat down right next to me, nattering on about the weather and the Christmas holiday and all the other pleasantries that one expects to hear on at-home days.

But I wasn't feeling very pleasant. "I can't stand that Charlie Clarke!"

She handed me a cup of tea. "Why not? I always thought him very agreeable . . . although I have to say that he doesn't seem to listen very well."

Listen well? He didn't do anything well! He was always messing everything up. "He's very *dis*agreeable, Winnie. He's the height of—of—*disagreeableness*! He even had the nerve to call me a common criminal!"

"Why?" She took the lid off the sugar bowl and held it out to me.

I dumped two spoonfuls into my cup and then chased the sugar around with a teaspoon. "Because . . . because he's a Clarke, that's why!"

She blinked. "The Clarkes aren't common criminals."

"They ought to be! I arranged for Fancy Crunch to be reshelved in front of Royal Taffy in some of the stores in the city . . ." In most of the stores in the city. "And he accused me of—of—*that*."

"It sounds like . . . maybe you *are* a common criminal."

"Are you taking his side in this?"

"I'm not taking anyone's side." She passed me a plate of ginger snaps.

I took one and bit down on it. Hard.

"I'm just saying that it seems like he might be right. About this one thing. And maybe not about anything else. Although he could be. Maybe." She shrugged. "It's possible. He seems nice."

"He is *not nice*!"

"He is to me."

Then she was the only one. "He's pretending. Trying to make a good impression in order to hide his true self from everyone. Besides, he started it."

"He reshelved Royal Taffy to hide Fancy Crunch?"

"No. But he got that picture in the newspaper with Baby Jesus holding a Royal Taffy."

"That was so sweet." She clasped a hand to her bosom. "That chubby little fist holding on to the—"

I didn't need to be reminded. "And before that, he covered up all of our advertising posters in the city and—"

"I was just remarking the other day how everywhere I go I see those posters. It really makes a person want to go right out and buy one. Just thinking of it now . . ." She picked up a cookie and began to nibble on it.

"Which is why I had to do *something*. Don't you agree?"

She considered my question for a moment, head cocked. "I'm not sure, really."

"About what?"

"I'm not sure I agree. Anyone can put up posters, but sneaking into a store and putting your candy in front of theirs—"

"It wasn't sneaking. Anyone can go into a store. It's a free country."

She frowned. "It feels like sneaking."

"It's not sneaking. I didn't sneak."

"Who did?"

"Who did what?"

Her eyes blinked wide. "The sneaking."

"Nobody. Nobody snuck anywhere."

"So then are you saying you *didn't* reshelf their candy?"

"I did. I mean, *I* didn't. I had someone else do it. But the point is—"

"Then they're the common criminal." She started in on another cookie as if we weren't talking about anything important.

"What?"

"That was the point, wasn't it? Who the common criminal is?" Winnie smiled as if she'd won some prize. "It's the person who switched out the candies."

"That's beside the point."

"But you're right—you aren't a common criminal. Only . . . I can't figure out who is. If it wasn't you, then who was it?"

"No one!"

"Then no one switched out the candy?" Winnie seemed genuinely puzzled.

"Just forget about the candy. We were talking about the Clarkes."

"That's right! I'd forgotten. We were talking about the Clarkes and how nice they are."

"How mean they are."

She put her cookie down on a plate. " . . . How mean are they?"

"Very. Very mean."

She looked at me quizzically for a moment, then shook her head. "No they aren't."

"Yes. They are!"

"Maybe . . . in your experience they could be, and in my experience they couldn't be." She said it as if she'd decided the matter once and for all.

"A person can't be nice and mean."

"Of course they can be. You are. You've never been nice. At least, not until this year. Not since I've known you and that was in first grade. But maybe . . . were you nice before that?"

I didn't know how to begin to answer.

"In first grade you told Minnie her hair was the wrong color to be an angel in the Christmas pageant. And in second grade you told Alice that Miss Shipman didn't like her. And then in third grade you wrote that note to Ella that said Rose didn't want to be her friend, do you remember?"

I remembered. I'd wanted to be the angel in the pageant. I'd wanted Miss Shipman to like me more than she liked Alice, and I'd wanted Ella's friendship all to myself.

"And in fourth grade you—"

"I get your point."

"And you've always been mean to me too. Do you remember telling me that it might be better if I just pretended to sing during choral society?"

I'd always wished I could sing the way Winnie did. I'd wished I could laugh the way she did too. I'd even practiced when I was younger. "But . . . then why do you even like me?"

She cocked her head as she looked at me. "I'm not sure really. Except that since you've gotten back from your trip you've been less mean than you used to be. And we're practically the only two girls who aren't married. And . . ." She shrugged. "That's probably why."

"So . . . you don't like being my friend?"

"*I* like being your friend. I'm just not so sure you ever liked being mine."

"I'm sure that's . . ." It was probably the truth. A great wave of shame and humiliation washed over me. I set down my teacup. "I'm sorry, Winnie."

"Don't be sorry. I figured you *could* be nice. It wasn't a matter of your not being able to. I thought maybe you just hadn't had enough chances to be. And if you were ever downright rude, then I just wouldn't invite you to my at-homes anymore. And besides, I can be mean too."

If she could, she'd never, not once in all the years I'd known her, shown it.

"It's just like I was telling Charles." She picked up her cookie and took a bite. Then she took a sip of tea.

"What?"

She blinked her eyes wide again. "What?"

"*What* were you telling Charlie?"

I waited while she finished her cookie and wiped the crumbs off into her teacup. "It was about how we've all done bad things. And how you don't have to be who you used to be. And . . ."

She frowned as she looked at me. "You don't listen at church either, do you?"

"I don't try to *not* listen . . ."

"You and Charles are just same, then. And really, that's the point, isn't it?"

I was the same as Charlie? The man who'd dared to call *me* a criminal? "I find that hard to believe." And in fact, I didn't. I couldn't. We weren't the same at all.

"That's what he said!" Winnie shook her head as she poured herself more tea. "Would you like some?"

"No. Thank you. But . . . how did you mean we were both the same?"

"You're both the same at believing you're not the same and being wrong because you are."

"Are what?"

"The same."

"But that's what I've been trying to tell you since I got here. We're not the same at all!"

She clucked. "We're all the same, Lucy."

"No—we're not! You're—you're ten times as good as I am, and he's a least a hundred times worse."

"That might be what you believe, but that's not what God believes. He believes we're all the same. We're all as bad as each other."

She couldn't be right, but that didn't stop me from feeling bad about how I'd treated her. "I'm sorry I did all those things . . . I hadn't realized." But I had, hadn't I? I'd known exactly what it was I'd done. She was right. I was mean and bossy and selfish. "I wish I could do something . . . to make it up to you somehow."

Winnie turned the full force of her smile upon me. "Just stop being that way and I'm sure everything will be fine. You don't have to be the same person you were."

I said something to her that I never thought I'd say. "Thank you, Winnie, for being my friend."

She beamed. "You're welcome."

It came to me as I left her house that I might never really have had one before.

"Tell me what it is you're doing again?" Sam was standing in the doorway of the confectionery office, on Wednesday morning, glancing down the hall. "My father doesn't really believe in using the telephone."

I had my hand on the transmitter, rehearsing once more what I planned to say. "I'm not making *him* use the telephone. I'm going to place the telephone call myself."

"I don't know if that's such a good idea."

I didn't either. But I had to do something. I couldn't just stand by and watch as the confectionery went out of business. What would Edna and Morris do if they lost their jobs? And what about Velma and Hazel? Let alone Sam and Mr. Blakely! The confectionery was a family. That's what my father had always said. So if I had to be sneaky in order to save it, then . . . that's what I had to do. At least, that's what I'd been telling myself.

The line hummed, and then the operator answered the call.

"Standard Candy Manufacturing, please."

The line hummed for a moment more before someone picked up on the other end.

"The receiving clerk, please."

"One moment." The line went silent before there came a rustling as someone else took the line. "Yes?"

I crossed my fingers behind my back. "I'm the sugar supplier calling about your order."

"Which supplier?"

"Sugar." Lying wasn't as difficult as I thought it would be!

"You're calling about what?"

"Your order."

"Why?"

This wasn't going the way that I'd hoped. My elation had been premature. "I wanted . . . to verify it."

"The order? Or the shipment?"

"The . . . order."

"That would be the purchasing clerk, then." The line went silent before it was picked up again. "Hello? Purchasing clerk."

"I'm calling about your sugar order. I wanted to verify it."

"Which order?"

"The most recent one." I hoped I sounded more confident about all of this than I felt . . . and a lot less guilty.

"I mailed it out to you just last week."

"We haven't received it yet, and I didn't want to presume how much sugar you might need. That's why I wanted to verify it."

"Oh! Just one moment." I heard the sound of the telephone being set down. He came back after a minute and read his order to me.

"It seems very odd that we haven't yet received it. To what address did you mail it?"

"Why, to yours, of course!"

That wasn't very helpful. In order to cancel the sugar shipment to Standard, I needed to know who their supplier was! "But to what address in particular? Perhaps it got misdelivered."

"I used the address I always do."

"Could you just tell me what it is?"

"Don't you know?"

I wondered if he would be able to hear it if I gnashed my teeth. "Of course I do. I just want to make certain that you do."

"Why wouldn't I?"

"I'm not saying that you don't. I'm hoping, in fact, that you do."

"I find this very unusual."

"And so do I." I tried to sound officious. "Normally orders don't go missing. Maybe it got misplaced somewhere between you and us due to the weather. In any case, if you want to get that sugar, I'm going to have to try to find that order." My goodness! Was it always this way? Did one lie always lead to two or three? I'd left Winnie's house with such good intentions, and here I was, being mean again. Worse than mean. I was being truly horrid.

"Just one moment." I heard a shuffling of papers and then the voice came back. "It was sent to you at Main Street."

"To me?"

"Well . . . to Colonial Sugars."

Success! "That certainly sounds like the correct address."

"Can I give you the order over the phone, then? That way you'll be certain to have it." The voice gave me the details, which I failed to write down.

"I'll hand your order in today." I crossed my fingers extra hard, ignoring the guilt that was insisting I abandon my plan.

"I hope it won't be delayed. Mr. Clarke wouldn't like that."

I was quite sure that he wouldn't.

After ringing off with Standard and telling myself the end justified the means, I placed a few more calls.

Sam sighed as he slouched against the wall. "Are you done yet?"

"Yes, Sam. I'm quite done." I pulled on my gloves, took up my handbag, and looped it over my wrist.

"Good!" He stalked into the office and then pulled me out by the arm. "I don't mind telling you that I don't think it's right, what you just did."

The truth was, neither did I. But it couldn't really be helped.

Saturday evening was a night off from being the Queen of Love and Beauty, but my presence was still required at the club. A benefit for the city library was being hosted there by the ladies' auxiliary, and I had been enlisted to pour coffee.

As we entered the dining room, Mr. Arthur waved his hat at us.

Mother waved her program back at him. "Go ahead and sit by him. Your shift at the coffeepot doesn't start for a little while. I'll join you in a bit."

I clutched at her hand. "Come with me." Please! I never quite knew what to say to him.

"Don't be foolish. I'm sure you must appreciate the chance to be alone with your fiancé for a few moments." She practically shooed me in his direction.

He looked rather glum as I approached. Though he stood to greet me the way he normally did and nodded his head at me just the same as always, there was something not quite normal in the way he refused to meet my eye.

Perhaps . . . "Are you not feeling well, Mr. Arthur?" I gave him another glance as I sat down.

"No. I'm not."

Poor man. He sounded so miserable as he said it. "Please, don't feel you have to stay here for my benefit. Wouldn't you rather go home?"

"No. Yes." He closed his eyes for a moment as he pinched the bridge of his nose.

"If you're ill . . . ?"

He opened them. "I'm not ill. Not exactly. It's just that I want very much to do the right thing."

"I'm sure no one would mind if you left. In fact, they probably won't even notice." The dining room had been filled to bursting when we'd walked in and there had been others behind us waiting to enter.

"You don't think so?" He sounded rather queer.

I hoped it wasn't the influenza. "I wouldn't give it a second thought if I were you. Truly."

He leaned over to kiss me on the cheek. "You're a treasure, Lucy Kendall." It was one of the most heartfelt statements he'd ever made to me. I smiled at him as he left.

Being Lucy Arthur might not be so bad after all.

34

Charlie

"There's something going on down in the factory." Mr. Mundt whispered the words to me on Monday as he shot worried glances toward my father's closed office door.

"What?"

"I don't know."

He didn't know? He usually knew everything. "If you don't know, then . . . how do you know?"

He held up a finger. "Listen."

I turned my ear toward the office door. "I don't hear anything."

"Exactly!"

He was such a strange man. I began to ask him to explain himself when I realized what he meant. There was nothing to be heard. There was no sound, no noise. Nothing at all. I started for the factory at a run.

When I reached the factory floor, the only machine working was the mixer. I approached some of the workers who stood in a cluster talking, as absolutely nothing took place around them. "What's happened? What's wrong?"

One of them shrugged. "Don't know. There's no sugar for the melting pots."

No sugar? I ran to the men who stood staring at the giant kettles. "Why aren't you working?"

"There's no sugar to melt."

I grabbed one of the bucket boys. "Why don't you have any syrup?"

"Isn't none." He was standing there looking at the bottom of his bucket as if hoping some might appear. "Hey, mister." Another of them tugged at my coattails. "We still going to get paid?"

"Yes." It wasn't their fault they didn't have any work to do.

If the problem wasn't with the mixer, and if they didn't have any sugar to melt, something must have happened to the supplies. I talked to a receiving clerk and was told that no sugar had been delivered.

Mr. Gillespie was standing there arguing with one of the other clerks. "What do you mean there aren't any shipments?"

The clerk shrugged. "There aren't any shipments. Nothing's come in today."

I walked over to the bay and peered down the tracks that were normally packed with trains.

Mr. Gillespie threw his hands up. "Then—you'll just have to use the reserves while I place some calls."

"We have."

"You've already called our suppliers?"

"We've already used up the reserves."

"Why didn't you tell me? I should have been told!"

The man shoved his hands into his pockets. "We figured there was more coming along."

We looked down the tracks in unison as if we were doing one of those tango dances, but there were no trains. It was clear that nothing was coming down those tracks today.

"I guess . . ." Mr. Gillespie turned to look at me.

What was there to say? "Finish up that last batch of Royal Taffy, then send everyone home." There was nothing else to be done.

❧

Back with Mr. Mundt up in the office, I took over the telephone. I called our suppliers, one by one. Their response to my inquiries was the same. They insisted that we had called and canceled all of the week's deliveries. And they were all planning to charge us extra for their trouble.

"Can I just ask you when it was that we called to cancel our order?"

"It was . . . on Wednesday."

"Can you tell me whom you spoke to?"

"It was someone from your . . . it was . . . it had to have been . . . your purchasing clerk?" There was a long pause. "Yes. I think so. It would have been the purchasing clerk."

"Just a moment, please." I waved Mr. Mundt over and covered the transmitter with my hand. "Who is the purchasing clerk?"

"Mr. Davis. Dennis Davis."

I held the transmitter back up to my mouth. "Then it must have been to Mr. Davis that you spoke."

"No, sir."

"No?"

"No."

Mr. Mundt had been so certain. "Then . . . who was it?"

"Couldn't tell you. Only that it was a lady."

"A lady? There's no—" A *lady*! I highly doubted that. There was only one person it could possibly have been, and she was no lady at all. I knew as sure I was standing there that Lucy Kendall had called all of our suppliers and told them not to

273

ship the week's orders. No candy was being made thanks to her. And now I had to go explain it all to my father.

"But why would she do such a thing?" My father asked as if he were fascinated by the possibilities. "I don't understand."

Didn't understand? I would have thought it was clear as day. We were trying to get rid of her father's company.

"It's at cross-purposes with the plan, and the longer we wait, the worse my position gets, but . . ." He shrugged. "I don't see that there's anything more to do right now. Until those supplies get here, we'll have to shut our doors."

That's about what I'd figured. "I'll let all the workers go home. Although . . . I did tell them that they'd be paid."

He raised a brow. "You told them wrong, then."

"It wasn't their fault we didn't have the supplies."

"Of course it wasn't. But I can't pay them if I don't make any money."

I thought of the Boys' Brigade and how thin some of them were. "If they don't get paid, then some of them might not eat this week."

"That's not my problem."

"Some of the men will probably lose their homes."

"Again: Not my problem. My problem is keeping my customers happy. The customer is the person who matters."

"Do you even know who that customer is?"

"Of course! It's the variety stores and Stix and Vandervoort's and places like that."

"The real customers are people just like those workers down there. They're the newsies who earn a few cents a day and spend some of it on a Royal Taffy. Do you—do you even *realize* what you're selling? It's not candy. It's a—a dream. It's not sugar and oil and flavoring. It's a blessed five minutes when they don't have to think about anything else but how *perfect* a Royal Taffy tastes. You're selling a vision of all that's right in the world. *That's* your product. And that's your customer. And you won't have any of them if we can't keep the workers."

He dismissed all of my outrage with a wave of his cigar. "I've never had a problem keeping workers. The minute one walks out of the factory, there are ten more willing to take his place. Why should you care what happens to them?"

"Because I used to be one of them! I scraped together every penny I could so that we could pay the grocer's bill. And I never had any left over for candy."

At least he had the grace to looked shamed. "I . . . didn't know."

"Because you didn't care to." I couldn't stop the words from coming out of my mouth. "What did you think happened to us once you left?"

"Your mother's the one who sued for divorce."

"You left us. She only made official what you'd already done. You left us in a house that was falling apart with no food in the cupboards and no wood for the fire. Do you even know what happened to Tillie? Do you want to?"

For a moment he looked just as weary as my mother always had. "Of course I know. How could you think I would forget about all of you? Just because I wasn't there didn't mean I didn't care, that I didn't know."

"You knew? About the consumption?"

"Your mother wrote to me."

"You never . . . said . . ." He'd never said anything about it. Never showed his face at all in the fifteen years since he'd left.

"I'd made such a mess of things, I figured the best I could do for all of you was just to stay away."

"The best you could do. So . . . you knew and you didn't do anything about it."

"I did do something. I sent your mother money so she could take Tillie to a special doctor. In fact, I started sending your mother money the moment I got established here. And I kept sending money. But she wouldn't take any of it. She always sent it back . . . until Tillie."

I remembered that. I remembered taking my mother and my sister to a doctor. Remembered thinking that at last all my work had been good for something. That I'd finally earned enough money to do my family some good. Only I hadn't. It was my father's money that had paid for it. And Tillie had grown too ill by then. "But you never came. Not when she was sick. And not to the funeral."

"Son. I'd given up that right."

"Did you know about Ruthie? How she got married at sixteen to a lout who isn't worth ten dimes?"

"Your mother didn't—"

"Because he had a car. She married him because he had a *car*. They don't have a house and they hardly have anything to eat, but he has a car." I felt like hitting something.

"You can't blame me for her poor judgment."

"I could blame you for her lack of any model to judge *by*, but as I look at you I realize that's not fair."

He fumbled with his lighter.

"Even if you'd been there, you couldn't have given her an example good enough to measure anyone by."

He set the lighter down. "That is not fair, Charles. I run a business, not a charity."

"You've made that more than clear to everyone who works here!"

"I didn't get where I am by worrying about my workers. Or their pay."

"No. You got where you are by stealing someone's recipe and then taking care of yourself."

"That's not what happened. I was given that recipe, fair and square."

"You can't just—just steal someone else's life because you don't like yours. You don't get to throw people away and start over!"

"I never threw you away."

"You might as well have."

He sighed. "I'm sorry you feel that way."

"I don't even know why I'm standing here listening to you. I don't even know why I came."

He put his cigar down and came around his desk to put a hand to my shoulder. "Because I want to make it up to you. I want to help you. I want to give you the success that I spent years working for."

He wanted to give me something. Well. It was about time. It was past time. He was offering me everything I'd always wanted as a boy. The chance to work with him. The chance to be with him. The chance to know him. He finally wanted me to be his son. But I no longer knew what I wanted. And I didn't know who I was.

I had Nelson drive me back to the house. I pulled my mother's old satchel out from under the bed and put one of the worsted suits into it, followed by three of my new shirts. The rest of the clothes weren't worth the space. I'd come to St. Louis wearing a suit that Mr. Dreffs had thrown away and an old derby hat. If the only thing I took with me was a change of clothes, then I would leave a better man.

There was no one in the city to say good-bye to, except for

Winnie, maybe. But she'd probably only ask me questions about church and accuse me of not listening to anything. And there was Lucy. But I didn't want to see her gloat. She'd figure out soon enough that I'd gone. And it wouldn't take her much longer to realize that my leaving changed nothing. My father was bent on the Kendall family's destruction. If I could say nothing else about him, he always seemed to get what he wanted.

I went down the service stairs and out to the garage.

Nelson was bent over Louise, a rag in his hand. He straightened as he saw me. "Going somewhere, Mr. Clarke?"

"I was hoping you'd take me over to Chestnut Valley."

"Gonna do some dancing tonight?"

Or play some cards. I'd sent most of last week's pay check to my mother in Chicago, just like the week before. At least she hadn't sent any of it back. But if I wanted to leave the city with a train ticket in my pocket, then I needed some way to buy it.

I didn't take my satchel with me; I left it in the garage. Only a fool brings everything he owns with him to the gambling table. I was down to my last Royal Taffy when I finally won enough money to make it worth going to the train station.

"Sure would have liked to have won that candy."

I looked over at the man who was staring at the taffy with true regret. Tossing it to him, I gave a nod and a wink to the others.

"Tell us we have a chance at winning back our money tomorrow night."

"Sorry to disappoint." By the next evening, I hoped to be in Colorado.

I walked back to the house. The wind was brisker than when I'd left. I turned up the collar of my overcoat against it, but the cooler air did me some good, helped to clear my head. Once home, I grabbed my satchel, pushed my hat farther down on my head, and set off for the train station.

Or I would have if I hadn't nearly run my father down in the process.

He stepped back from the walk onto the winter-hardened grass, looking pointedly at my satchel. "Where are you going?"

I shrugged. "San Francisco."

He took the cigar from his mouth and motioned back into the house. "Don't. I hadn't realized . . . I thought . . ." He sighed. "I might not have been the man I should have back then, but I'm worth knowing now. Now I'm a man you can be proud to call your father."

"It was never about you." It was about me. And my sisters. And my mother.

"I understand I did a lot of things wrong. But I want you to stay."

He wanted me to stay. "And what about me? I wanted a lot of things back when you left, and I never got one of them." My throat had gone tight, and there was a lump in it that I couldn't quite swallow. Cold air always did that to me.

"I've missed you."

"And you think *that* can make up for the past fifteen years?" Somehow I managed to get the words out.

"I hope so."

I swallowed. And then I swallowed once more. "I'll take that into consideration."

He moved to embrace me, but I put a hand out to stop him. And then, because I couldn't speak, I turned and went back into the house.

He wanted me to stay. Though his words had done me good to hear, I would have said no if I'd known what was waiting for me down at the factory. Getting the machines back to work was more of a headache than anyone expected. The different sugars came quickly, but there was a delay in getting the flavoring. And additional butter couldn't be delivered until the beginning of the next week. It took sugar, vinegar, flavorings, water, *and* butter to make Royal Taffy. We couldn't start production until all the ingredients arrived.

Dwindling numbers of workers showed up at the gates each morning. And each morning we turned them away. When my father asked me to sit in on his meeting with the company's lawyer, I was more than happy to.

It was with a bad temper and a growing headache that I attended a concert Thursday evening. Every beat of that big drum drove the pain further into my skull. By intermission, all I wanted was to leave. Knowing that I couldn't, I decided a stiff drink would have to do. I angled my way to the bar and ordered a whiskey for myself and a lemonade for Augusta. As I turned to leave, I saw Lucy Kendall. Everyone else seemed to be deceived by her bright blue eyes and caramel-colored hair. Everyone else was taken in by the way she smiled as if you were her favorite person in the world. By the way she looked you in the eyes when you were talking as if what you had to say was important.

But I knew the truth.

I handed Augusta her drink, downed my own, then made my way through the crowds to Lucy. There were a few things I wanted to tell her.

When she saw me, alarm flared in her eyes. She stepped behind Alfred as if she hoped he would protect her.

I pushed him aside, grabbed her by the arm, and pulled her

along with me toward the far wall. "It was you, wasn't it? You're the one to blame."

Alfred trotted along beside us. "Here, now! Watch yourself, Clarke! You're going to tear her sash."

Her sash. The ever-present reminder that she was the Queen of Love and Beauty. I almost laughed in his face. I would have if my head hadn't been hurting so badly. "She's no queen! And there's not one ounce of love in her cold, black heart!"

Lucy put a hand on her fiancé's arm. "I'm fine. If Mr. Clarke has something to say, then we might as well let him say it." Her chin tipped up as her eyes glinted.

I stepped toward her.

She stood her ground.

One more step, one more inch, and I could have devoured her. Or murdered her.

"You'd better just—just—*watch out!*" I'd never wanted to strangle or kiss a girl so badly in all my life. It must have been the headache. Or the whiskey.

She smirked.

That decided me. "It's all a game to you, isn't it? Standard will survive, and we'll start making Royal Taffy again by the end of next week. You haven't hurt us at all. But you'd better explain yourself to all those boys and girls who aren't working. They aren't getting paid for yesterday or today or tomorrow. And while you're explaining, you might want to figure out where their families are going to sleep once they get turned out of whatever shack it is they've been using. That's the problem with you rich people, you have no idea how people really live!"

The smirk had fallen off her face, and she took a step back as if she were afraid I might hit her. "I didn't mean—"

"Don't tell me what it is you meant to do! Just figure out how to fix what you did."

35   *Lucy*

As I stood in front of my dresser after the concert on Thursday night, I tried to unfasten my pearl necklace, but my trembling fingers kept slipping from the clasp. I hated pearls! They were just so—so *round* and perfect. I choked back a sob.

"Just figure out how to fix what you did."

Every boom of the drum in the symphony's fourth movement had driven a stake into my heart. It was only due to the greatest of efforts that I hadn't dissolved into tears during the carriage ride home.

I put the necklace back into its case, then drew a kimono on over my corset and drawers.

I hadn't really given a first or second thought to the consequences of canceling Standard's deliveries. As much as it grieved me to say it, Charlie was right. The people I'd hurt weren't him and his father; it was the workers who labored at the factory. I'd hurt people like Sam and Mr. Blakely, Morris and Edna . . .

the very kind of people I'd thought I was protecting. My father would be so ashamed of me.

I sat down on my bed, covered my face with my hands, and wept.

How had everything gone so wrong?

All I'd wanted was to save the confectionery for my father. To make him see that I was worthy of helping him. The only thing I'd ever wanted to do was make candy. And now, even that talent had deserted me. The Veiled Prophet candy had made it plain that I had no taste.

I might as well be Walter Minard.

Father was right. Girls shouldn't meddle in business.

And Winnie was right: I was mean.

But Charlie was the right-est of them all: Maybe I really did have a cold, black heart.

I pushed away from the bed and took a deep, steadying breath. Then I gave myself a long, hard stare in the mirror. In the morning I would tell Mother to sell the company. I would still be engaged to marry Mr. Arthur, but that wasn't the worst of things. He was the most eligible bachelor in the city. Making a good marriage was what I was supposed to do. Maybe that's the best that I *could* do. Maybe I'd expected too much from life and from myself.

I couldn't be unhappy with my engagement; it was a brilliant match. Mr. Arthur was every girl's dream. I may have encouraged him for the wrong reasons, but in the end it had turned out right, hadn't it? It was the only smart thing I'd done these past few months.

As I stood there sniffling, I pulled the pins from my hair, letting it tumble down over my shoulders. Then I picked up a hairbrush and started counting strokes. *One, two, three . . .* I would put an end to all this foolishness and I would concentrate on becoming Mrs. Alfred Arthur. I sighed as I watched myself in the mirror. *Twenty-two, twenty-three, twenty-four . . .* I would do what I was meant to do because what I wanted to do wasn't possible. I brushed my hair for a while longer before bending at the waist to let my hair fall toward the floor. Then I started brushing it out from underneath. *Forty-seven, forty-eight, forty-nine . . .* I couldn't create a candy worth eating, and I couldn't keep Standard from destroying City Confectionery. I hadn't been able to do anything at all since Charlie Clarke had come to the city. *Eighty-one, eighty-two, eighty-three.*

Ouch!

I took some extra care untangling a knot at the nape of my neck before I started counting again. *Ninety-eight, ninety-nine, one hundred.*

I swept away the last of my tears, put my brush away, and turned the light off. In the past, tears had always made me feel better. They'd always made room for more comforting thoughts. But tonight I discovered that nothing had come to replace them. No hope and no peace. I felt even more empty than I had before.

I had just broached the topic of the sale with Mother over breakfast when Sam banged through the kitchen and into the dining room.

Mother greeted him with a look of exasperation. "May we help you, Mr. Blakely?"

"I just needed to know what to do with the extra Fancies."

"Extra?" Mother said the word slowly as if she didn't quite know what it meant. Today was delivery day, and he usually only took enough in the wagon to cover what had been ordered.

"Stix, Bauer and Fuller wouldn't take theirs."

"They wouldn't take their own order?"

"Nope. Said something about a contract with Standard."

I had a bad feeling in the depths of my stomach where my hate for Charlie Clarke normally dwelled. "What exactly did they say?"

"Said they wouldn't take it."

"Besides that."

"On account of the contract."

"What contract?" Mother and I echoed the same question.

"With Stix—"

Mother was going to wring his neck if he wasn't careful. "Yes, but did they say what the contract was about?"

He shrugged. "Candy, probably."

"I'm going to go and straighten this out." I put my napkin on the table and rose from my chair.

Mother covered my hand with her own. "That's what we have Mr. Blakely for."

"He doesn't—"

Mother indicated Sam with a gesture of her chin.

I lowered my voice to a hiss. "You know he won't do anything about it."

Sam didn't even pretend not to be listening. "He did. He said he'd put the Fancies back into inventory, but I should check with you first to make sure." Mrs. Hughes had served him a plate filled with eggs, and he was shoveling them into his mouth with relish.

"See?" I gestured toward Sam with an open palm. I was still going to have to straighten things out.

"I don't care about Stix or Mr. Blakely or boxes, Lucy. You were about to say something about the proposed sale—"

"Sam, can you take me down to Stix?"

"Lucy—if you would just listen!" Now Mother had stood as well.

When she grabbed for me I ducked and moved toward the kitchen. "We can talk when I get back."

I waited for an hour before the manager became available. He smiled as he greeted me. "The Queen of Love and Beauty, herself! What can I do for you this fine morning?"

It was cold and dreary and it was very nearly noon, but I hadn't come to quibble. "I was told that you wouldn't take your delivery of Fancy Crunch this morning."

"Ah." He dropped my hand as his smile slid from his face. "Isn't there someone else to whom I should be speaking?" His gaze was darting in every direction but my own.

Father was ill, Mr. Blakely unsuited to business, and Mother would just as soon sell the company as figure out what had happened. "Perhaps we could speak in your office."

"I don't—"

I stepped through his door before he could say anything more. "We had to take your order back to the confectionery. May I ask you why you refused it?"

He was lingering in the doorway as if he hoped I might rejoin him in the hall.

I turned my back to him and sat in the chair positioned in front of his desk.

"I—just—" I heard him heave a sigh. He came around to sit behind the desk. "I really don't feel comfortable—"

"You must understand City Confectionery's situation . . . considering my father's illness . . . ?"

"Of course, of course!"

"So I'm certain you'll also understand why we were concerned when our deliveryman came back without having fulfilled your order."

He sighed again as he fiddled with a pen. He looked up at me. "If you must know, it's our new contract with Standard Candy."

"Fancy Crunch isn't a Standard candy."

"That's where the problem lies. Is there not someone else from your company I can speak to, Miss Kendall? Someone from the business office, perhaps?"

"Mr. Blakely is the superintendent charged with production, but today he happens to be . . . supervising. He couldn't come himself, but I assure you that he has complete confidence in me."

"There's really nothing to discuss. Standard's new contract doesn't allow us to sell City Confectionery products."

"When you say, 'doesn't allow . . . '?"

"The contract forbids it."

"How can Standard forbid you from selling our candies?"

He gave me a look that was fraught with pity. "If we sell your candies, then they won't allow us to sell theirs."

"Why that's—that's—not fair!"

"Fairness is something I find overrated. Surely you can agree with me that sentiment has no place in business. Our arrangement with Standard is purely contractual and has nothing at all to do with you."

It had everything to do with me! "But as a man of business, can't you see how this would damage our company?"

"It's not within my power to control."

"So you're going to choose Standard over us?"

His brow peaked in disbelief. "I have to choose Standard. I sell two Royal Taffies to every packet of Fancy Crunch that I sell. You must see that I have no choice. My hands are tied."

"But I—can't you—!"

He rose, walked around his desk, and took me by the elbow.

Then he led me to the door. "If I can make a suggestion, Miss Kendall? You'll be much more successful as a Queen of Love and Beauty than you will be in business. Fancy Crunch will always be a personal favorite, but I have to be able to sell my customers the things they want."

36

Charlie

Lucy came at me on Tuesday evening in the club dining room, eyes blazing, finger wagging. "I'll admit that what I did was wrong, but what you did was completely and absolutely underhanded, sneaky, and patently unfair!"

"I really don't—" She wouldn't stop coming, so I took a step backward and then another. And still she kept at it. People at the club were starting to stare at us.

"Don't tell me you didn't know about the contract with Stix."

What could I say? I tried the obvious. "What contract with Stix?"

She poked me in the chest with her finger. "You despicable, loathsome liar!"

"What do you want me to say? You caught us red-handed."

That shut her up. The eyebrows that had slanted with suspicion now gathered with hurt. "You . . . you knew about it?"

"We're not playing a game, Lucy. My father means to run your father out of business. I could tell you it's not right or it isn't fair, but it doesn't make any difference. And if delaying only means you'll keep playing dirty tricks, then can you blame us?"

"How could you?" The words came out in a whisper that ripped into my heart.

"Lucy, I'm sorry."

"But—you can't do that!"

"I think . . . in fact, that we did." All legal and proper. That's what the lawyer had been for.

Her chin trembled for just a moment. And then she lifted it, nostrils flaring.

"But I agree with you. It *was* dirty and underhanded." It didn't hurt to admit to what was true, did it? I stepped closer. "And if Stix signed the contract, I wonder how many others did too?"

"No one else but Stix refused their deliveries."

"*This* week."

Her brow furrowed for a moment; then she looked at me through narrowed eyes. "Why are you telling me all this? Why are you being nice to me?"

"There's more to life than winning. And I don't want to win anything this way." It was bad enough that City Confectionery would be given to me once my father had bought it. And it was bad enough that Alfred was sneaking around with Evelyn behind Lucy's back. How much worse could things get? I nodded and then stepped around her.

She touched my arm with her hand. "Thank you."

I couldn't even bring myself to look at her. "Please, don't thank me." I didn't deserve it.

I stayed with the car until after Nelson had parked it in the garage, and then I helped him pull the cover up over it. As I walked back to the house, I caught sight of Jennie as she went in the back door.

Wondering why she was out so late, I followed her inside and then up the back stairs. A nice girl like her shouldn't be out alone after dark. I caught up with her as she opened the door to her room.

"Mr. Clarke!" As she put one hand to her chest, the other shoved something into her pocket. "You gave me a fright. Do you . . . do you need something?"

No. Yes. "I just . . ."

She took her hand from the doorknob and stood before me, hands folded in front of her.

"I'm sorry. Never mind." She reminded me of my baby sister, and I'd just wanted to make sure she was all right. And to be honest, I'd wanted someone to talk to. A regular person. Someone who didn't have to worry about dinners and balls and what people might say about her. But I'd forgotten that she hadn't known me as Charlie; she only knew me as Charles. "Never mind. Enjoy the rest of your night. And be careful out there after dark."

She bobbed her head before turning and slipping through her door. But not before I had a glimpse once more of what was inside: an iron bed and a dresser with a pitcher and basin. A small, threadbare rug on the floor. And all those fanciful flowers and wreaths she'd made of candy wrappers. Royal Taffy's red mixed with Fancy Crunch's green. There was more furniture and more warmth, more hope in that small room than there had been in the house where I'd grown up.

How was it right that a maid in my father's house could look forward to a better future than either of my sisters would ever have? That she could hope for things from him—food, a bed, and board—that my sisters had never received.

Why was I so bent on staying here? Why didn't I leave? I stood there at the top of the stairs and thought of doing just that. Why should I stay and help a man so bent on destroying others . . . even though he insisted he was just returning a favor?

Because he left.

I had to stay because he had gone. I had to prove to myself that I was worthy of his having stayed. If I could just—just be the son he'd needed. If I had been that son back then, maybe he would have stayed. That's what I had always thought. That it was some fault in me that had driven him to leave.

But . . . that wasn't what he'd said, was it? He said he'd thought I could do a better job than he had.

I hadn't understood it when he'd said it, and I didn't understand it now. The only way I could make sense of it was if I stayed. No matter what he asked, no matter what he planned. I'd just have to trust that he was telling the truth about returning that favor. But could I? Especially when it was hurting Lucy? Could I trust that he was telling me the truth?

37

Lucy

I passed a quiet Wednesday morning reading to my father. When I went downstairs for lunch, Sam was in the kitchen talking to Mrs. Hughes. He was leaning against the counter as he ate. "It's the strangest thing!" He was shaking his head as he bit into an apple.

"What is?" There was a terrible feeling of doom in my stomach and an insistent prickling at the back of my neck.

He glanced over his shoulder at me and then straightened, setting the apple down on his plate. "Everyone's returning their Fancy Crunch orders."

"Returning . . . ?"

"Pa says they keep insisting that we're using spoiled ingredients."

What? "But . . . we aren't! We never did. Not even back before the law changed when we could have." It was something Father would never do.

Sam shrugged and went back to eating his apple. "Of course not. But that's what everyone's saying."

"Did you ask why?"

"Why what?"

"Why they're all saying that."

"No." He took another bite, breaking the skin with a crunch. He chewed for a moment, then swallowed. "They must have heard it from someone, though."

Someone? I knew exactly who that someone was. Desolation swirled through my chest, stealing the wind from my lungs. What was there to hope for now? If everyone thought our candy was spoiled, then it was just a matter of time before they stopped placing orders altogether.

Of all the dirty, no-good tricks! Hell was too good for Charlie Clarke. I hoped there was someplace even darker and hotter and more miserable for his soul to go and rot. If he thought that this was going to make me stop fighting, then he was sorely mistaken!

By the time Mr. Arthur picked Mother and me up for the electricity company's annual ball, I was furious . . . though not so furious that I failed to note there was something different about Mr. Arthur. He seemed . . . *more* . . . somehow. More interesting, more vital. Even . . . was he more handsome? I took a long look at him. Definitely more handsome. As he escorted us up the walkway, his step was almost jaunty.

Unfortunately, he left me little time to admire him in close proximity, his attention being devoted to the details of the evening. There was to be an electrical light demonstration interspersed with the dances. But even his neglect was benign. And he was ever the gentleman. He'd invited Charlie to the ball in order for me to have some company. And no matter how much I protested, Mr. Arthur insisted that Charlie and I dance.

When Charlie offered me his arm, I must admit that I might have taken hold of it with a bit of unladylike violence. Once on the dance floor, he looked down at me as if the whole world was coming down on his head instead of mine.

How dare he look more miserable than I felt!

I felt like pinching him, but I rapped a gloved fist against his chest instead.

He glanced down at me as if startled.

"How can you be so—so—*mean*?" I'd wanted another word, a better word, but there was just no other description for the way that he was being. And once I said it, tears began to leak from my eyes.

He'd stepped away from me, and the hand that had held mine was now cupping my elbow. "Oh . . . Come on, don't—!" He looked around the room wildly as if he didn't know what to do with me.

"I am *not crying*!" I swiped at my tears with a crooked finger. How could my tears betray me at a time like this! "I'm not like you, Charlie Clarke. The company is all that we have. It's all *I* have. You father has piles of money, and he's earned it all from *our candy*. Can't you just leave us alone? How much more do you have to take from us?"

"I don't—"

One of those colored searching lights of Mr. Arthur's electrical demonstration found us. In that sudden bright clarity, Charlie's features were frozen in relief. As soon as it moved on, he grabbed me and tried to pull me off the ballroom floor. But I had tired of being pulled around by him. "Will you stop!" I wrested my arm away.

But he seized me and dragged from the dance floor anyway.

And then he pulled me to his chest and kissed me, stealing my breath just as surely as his father had stolen Royal Taffy.

I broke away, my thoughts in a whirl. What had we been talking about? I'd completely forgotten. "Wh-why did you do that?" And why were my hands clenching his lapels?

"Because I wanted you to stop talking for just one minute." There was a look of astonishment and wonder in his eyes. He put a hand to my face and caressed my cheek.

Something had gone wrong with my ears. I couldn't quite understand what he was saying. "I didn't—I mean—"

"Hush. Just . . . stop." He bent once more, and this time I stood on my toes to meet him halfway.

I'd never imagined that a kiss could be so delectable. So sweet. I forced my hands to let go of his coat, but instead of returning to my side, they wandered up to his hair. And then around to the back of his neck. Oh my! "Charlie . . . ?"

He stopped, pressing his forehead against mine for a moment, looking into my eyes. "If it's all the same to you, I think it's better if we just don't talk."

"I . . . I couldn't agree more." I was still having trouble breathing. But for once, a Clarke had stolen something from me that I didn't care if I ever got back.

"Maybe if you just—" We both spoke the words at the same time. And we both had the same air of desperation. And regret.

He gathered me fiercely into a tight embrace, and when he released me he took a step back, holding up a hand to stop me when I would have followed. "I'm trying to do the right thing."

I was too. There was his father to think of. And my father. And—oh my goodness!—Mr. Arthur. My hands flew to my cheeks as I considered what it was that we'd just done. What I'd just done.

There was agony and misery mixing in his eyes. "I just wish that our fathers—that you—that I—"

I dared to look at him again, and in doing so I discovered that whatever had just happened was something I desperately wanted to happen again. I closed the distance between us and pressed a kiss to his cheek. How could it be that I had finally discovered what it was that I wanted? And that this, too, was an impossible wish? "We can't do this, Charlie. There are too many things between us."

He smiled then, but it was sad and somber. As if he were saying good-bye. "Don't worry. I hardly think a man with a past like mine has a chance with a girl like you."

He flinched as I laid a hand on his arm, and then he backed away. When his eyes met mine again, the window to his soul had been curtained.

38

I settled myself into one of the plump, upholstered chairs at the club while I waited for Alfred on Thursday, but it wasn't very comfortable. Nothing had been comfortable since I'd kissed Lucy Kendall at the ball. Alfred Arthur might be kind of stuffy, and I suspected he might be spending too much time with Evelyn, but he was the one engaged to Lucy. Not me. And no matter how I felt about her, I had no right to even *think* about kissing her. Even back when I'd worked for Manny, I'd never been good at stealing things. And I wasn't about to start now.

But really, there were some things a man just couldn't bear. Was it my fault I thought of caramel every time I saw her? Or that she had lips that just begged to be kissed?

I got up and grabbed at a newspaper someone had left lying around, and there was Lucy's picture on the inside page. Why did she have to be so pretty? And so pigheaded? And why did she keep clinging to her company? Couldn't she see that City Confectionery could never succeed? Standard was too big, and my father was too stubborn. The only move left for her was to admit defeat. If she'd just give in, then maybe we could be friends again.

Friends—and *nothing more*!

No meetings, no dances, and definitely no more kisses.

Her picture in the newspaper seemed to turn and glare at me. I closed the paper, folded it, and tossed it onto the table bedside the chair.

"Ah! I thought that was you."

I glanced up to find Alfred heading toward me.

"I need you to come with me."

"Sure." I got to my feet. We were supposed to have lunch together. And from now on, I was determined to be a better friend. The best friend a man could have. Even though he didn't deserve the girl he was going to marry. Not with the way he'd been seeing Evelyn. But then, he hadn't been the money boy for a man like Manny White. And he hadn't stood by and watched while a man got murdered. He deserved Lucy more than I did.

Alfred nodded over toward the entrance.

I headed out at a fast pace. I was more than ready to leave.

Alfred caught up with me. "I have something to tell you." There was a set to his jaw that I didn't much like.

I stopped. "Do I have to beat you up again?"

His eyes twinkled as a corner of his mouth turned up. "You never beat me up in the first place, if I remember correctly."

I should have. I would have if he hadn't jumped around like one of those circus kangaroos. I sighed as I followed him out the door and into his car.

He directed the driver to Forest Park. "I wanted you to know that I've come to a decision about Lucy."

So had I. She was probably going to be the death of me. "And?"

"I'm going to tell Evelyn good-bye. It's the wise thing to do."

I should have felt relieved, but all I felt was guilt. I'd kissed his best girl at his own company's party.

"I just . . . wanted you to know."

I nodded.

"Because Lucy ought never to know."

"Well, I'm not going to tell her!" In fact, I'd planned never to speak to her again.

Alfred knocked on the glass that separated us from the driver. The car stopped and the driver got out and came around to open my door.

I looked at Alfred. "That's it?"

He nodded. "That's it. I hope you won't mind . . ." He inclined his head toward the clubhouse, back in the distance. "I don't quite feel up to lunch today."

I gave him a nod as I got out, then watched the car drive away. And I couldn't help but feel like he was taking a piece of my heart with him as he went.

I skipped lunch; I wasn't hungry anyway. Word must have got around that I was back at the office, because Mr. Mundt came to get me for a meeting. I tried to concentrate on what my father was saying, but I kept seeing Lucy's eyes. Those big blue eyes that had gone soft and starry when I'd kissed her.

And I kept thinking about her mouth.

I must have kissed at least a dozen girls, but none of them had ever had lips as sweet as hers. If I closed my eyes and thought back to that night, like I'd done a hundred times since, I could still taste them. And smell her. And remember what it felt like to hold her in my arms.

But I shouldn't have done it.

Not when she was engaged to Alfred. There were some things a fellow just shouldn't do.

But it was something I could always remember. A thought to get me through the long, dark nights. I used to imagine a table filled with food when I was a boy. And a warm, crackling fire. Now I could imagine Lucy with her beautiful hair and her glittering blue eyes. And I could think of pulling her into my arms and kissing her as if I had a right to.

I fiddled with the pencil that sat in front of me, picking it up and balancing it atop my hand. But why was I wasting so much time thinking about her? I'd never had a chance with her anyway.

If only we could go back to the way it was before, at that first ball. And at the air meet. Before she'd known I was a Clarke and I'd found out she was a Kendall. But why regret what could never have been? I couldn't have hidden my past from her forever. And once she found out, I'd be sitting here, just the same.

I slammed a fist down on the pencil, making it cartwheel over my hand.

"Charles!" At the sound of my father's voice, my vision of Lucy vanished.

"What?"

"Is this not important to you?"

I blinked, trying to clear thoughts of Lucy from my mind. "I'm sorry. Of course, it's important."

"So what are your thoughts?"

My thoughts? He wanted to know my thoughts? "Well . . . I . . ." I grabbed hold of the pencil and tapped it a couple times against the desk. "I . . . agree."

"About which?"

"Both . . . ?"

He stared at me for a long moment. Then he grunted. "Maybe you're right."

"I am?" I wondered exactly what it was that I was right about. Did it really matter? "I am. Of course, I am."

"You're thinking the end justifies the means? Is that what you're saying?"

Was I? Had I? I nodded.

"We'll just have to keep in mind that I'm doing this as a favor. It might seem underhanded. It's a bit sneakier than I'm used to. I would prefer, of course, to just have this business all over and done with. It's costing me every day this drags on! But you and I both know the truth. Even if it looks like . . . well, it's not *il*legal. People are free to make their own choices, aren't they?"

"I'm sure—"

"It isn't our fault if their choices make life easier for us."

"I don't think—"

"The company fell into my lap to begin with, so we'll just call this whole thing good luck and make the most of it, then."

Make the most of what?

"It's a good idea, I think. No reason why we shouldn't do it ourselves. For a limited time. Wouldn't want to do it forever. We'd run ourselves right out of business."

"Can I ask . . . what exactly is it that we're going to do?"

"We're going to do what you suggested."

Had I suggested something? "I don't quite—"

"We're going to lower the price of Royal Taffy, just like City Confectionery is going to do with Fancy Crunch."

"But if they're already going to do it . . . ?" What was the point?

"Exactly. That's why your idea was so clever. They're going to lower their price to four cents. We lower ours to three and we undercut them. Don't know if I would have been brave enough to do it myself. I hate to do business that way, but when you're right, you're right. No use in prolonging the inevitable. Let's get this done and over with. And then you can have City Confectionery for yourself."

I knew my mouth was hanging open, but I couldn't seem to close it. I'd never suggested that. I couldn't have! "You mean—"

He winked at me. "It's a winning strategy, son. With your plan, we'll finally be able to put this rivalry to rest."

39

Lucy

The idea of marrying Mr. Arthur was becoming untenable. Especially when I dreamed of Charlie's kisses at night. During the daylight hours, I fantasized of running away from the city. At night . . . at night I imagined a world where Charlie Clarke wasn't my enemy. Where he was just some stranger with entrancing dimples and dreamy eyes who could take my breath away.

What had I done!

Nothing. That's what I told myself. I'd done nothing at all. Charlie had kissed me first. I could never have kissed him back if he hadn't started it. The whole thing was his fault. And if I ever saw him again, I was going to avoid him. I just . . . wouldn't talk to him anymore. And I definitely wouldn't think of kissing him.

It's not as if I'd ever be kissing him again in any case.

Even if I wanted to.

Which I didn't. I couldn't. I was engaged to Mr. Arthur, for goodness' sake! What kind of woman engaged herself to one man and then went around all moony-eyed dreaming about another?

Someone very wicked. And mean and bossy and selfish.

It wouldn't be so bad if I could picture Mr. Arthur reaching for my hand, gazing into my eyes, seeking me out the way my uncle always sought my aunt. Always waiting for her, always watching for her. Always wanting her. If I could imagine my marriage would be like that . . . I sighed and looked out the other side of the carriage as I admitted to myself that even that might not be enough. Mr. Arthur's regard for me would mean nothing at all if I didn't return it. If I didn't also reach for him. Long for him. If I didn't want him the way my aunt always seemed to want my uncle.

They were a pair. Like eggs and sugar, butter and cream, I couldn't conceive of one without the other. Yet I could imagine living quite happily apart from Mr. Arthur for the rest of my life.

I'd done it so far, hadn't I?

It was possible I could come to have feelings for him. In time. But what if I didn't? What was the point in being a peanut if there was no brittle to go along?

What if . . . what if I was making the biggest mistake of my life in marrying him?

What if I was? What was the alternative? Charlie Clarke? I nearly laughed. There was no way that would ever work out. I was stuck with the man I'd agreed to marry.

I couldn't back out now . . . could I?

I slid a glance toward Mother. I couldn't. She would never forgive me. Mr. Arthur would never talk to me, and St. Louis would never let me forget it. Better to live in a respectable marriage than to be forever linked to scandal.

Wasn't it?

Was it?

I allowed myself to slump before I remembered ladies didn't do that. A small voice inside my head whispered that ladies also didn't kiss the friends of their fiancés or the destroyers of their family's businesses or their avowed enemies either. Ignoring the voice, I straightened and dug into the tufting of the bench with a finger as I thought about what else there was to do.

"Stop fidgeting." Mother's voice only added to my anxiety. We were on our way to a benefit for the Confederate Soldiers' Home. And I wouldn't be fidgeting if could get Charlie out of my head.

Mother pulled my hand away from the tufting of the bench and held it between her own. "You need to bring all your efforts to bear on this tonight. People are already looking at you as the new Mrs. Arthur. And you will be, in less than a month."

"I'll be as charming as I can be."

"I had hoped you would be more charming still." Mother said it with a smile, but I could tell that she meant it.

The benefit began with a speech by the mayor, which was followed by speeches from several of the Home's residents. My, but they were getting old! And so feeble. It was difficult even to hear them. Afterward, someone passed me an old lidless army coffee boiler and told me to solicit donations for a raffle. It wasn't until after the band had struck up an old reel that I had the chance to look for Mr. Arthur.

I was hoping that I might somehow stumble upon him. I'd determined to let my first reaction upon seeing him be my guide. If it was pleasant, then perhaps there was hope for us after all.

But he wasn't there.

I felt a surprising wave of disappointment wash up from the tips of my toes to the tops of my ears.

"Are you quite all right?" Mother whispered the words into my ear as we sat listening to the band.

"I'm fine."

"Why don't you go get some air?"

Some air. Exactly what I needed. Some space, some quiet, to think. I stepped out into the hall, pushed past the drivers who were waiting in the entrance, and walked down the steps to the sidewalk. The melody of the reel and the sound of stomping feet drifted out behind me. Exchanging the warmth of the building for January's chill air, I left all of the conviviality behind me.

I wandered along the sidewalk, wishing I'd thought to bring my coat. As I headed toward the shadow of the building, craving the loneliness of solitude, the glow of a cigarette caught my eye.

Someone else had gotten there first.

Continuing past, I might have gone all the way to the corner if I hadn't heard someone call my name.

I squinted into the dark. "Mr. Arthur? Is that you?"

He stepped from the shadow into the glow cast by the street-lights, letting the cigarette drop as he came.

"I didn't know you smoked." And I didn't know why it should bother me, but it did. In a peevish sort of way.

"I don't. Not normally." He shrugged. "Sorry."

"It's fine."

"It's not fine. It's a shameful, dirty, detestable habit."

At least we were agreed on that.

He glanced up at the building behind him. "I meant to go in, but I just . . . I couldn't. Do you ever feel . . . if you went to one more dinner or one more ball or did one more thing you were supposed to that you might just . . . explode?"

Explode? "Not exactly. Although, I've often felt that I might someday just . . . dissolve. Into a puddle, rather like molasses, and run out into the gutter and just disappear."

He'd been nodding along until I got to the molasses part. Then he'd stopped and started staring. I didn't know what else to add, or how to explain myself any better, so I didn't say anything.

And he didn't say anything.

We stood there for quite some time saying nothing, listening to the music coming out of the entrance.

Then he sighed and let his head fall back, looking up at the smoke-smudged sky. "It's just that I find myself wondering whether I'm meant to go on like this forever, doing all the things I'm supposed to, when I feel so unaccountably lonely most of the time. It defies explanation. Here I am, surrounded by people, and . . ." He straightened and glanced my way. "How rude that sounds. I apologize. Again. Please forgive me. I don't know what I'm saying. It's just that I'd hoped . . . with you . . . do you think . . ." He fished around in his pocket and when his hand came out, it was grasping a cigarette case. "I was hoping that with you I wouldn't be so alone." He took a cigarette from the case and lit it. "Not an auspicious beginning, perhaps, admitting I'm going into this for purely selfish reasons." He took a draw, then expelled the air with tremendous force. "You could do worse, I suppose. But it's up to you now . . . if you want the chance to do better . . . Please don't misunderstand, I'm not trying to break our engagement. Unless you want to. I'm the one who proposed, after all. I'm only wondering if . . . if you actually want to be engaged."

He was offering me a way out. And yet, though I opened my mouth to respond, the words wouldn't come out. I couldn't give voice to my feelings. He'd bared his soul to me. He'd been so honest, so genuine, that I knew I couldn't break his heart. Not tonight and not ever. And I vowed that he would never know what had happened between Charlie Clarke and me. As I'd said that night at the ball, there were too many things between us.

Taking the cigarette from Mr. Arthur, I let it fall to the sidewalk and then I linked my arm through his. "If we're bound to have to do all these things anyway, then why not do them together?"

40 — *Charlie*

Alfred came up to me at the theater on Friday evening as intermission was ending and everyone was filing back into the auditorium. He held out his hand.

I gave it a shake.

"I need to ask you a favor. Could you meet me tomorrow down at Cleve's? About ten?"

"Who's Cleve?"

A smile split his face as he gave my hand another shake and clapped me on the forearm. "I keep forgetting you're new to the city. It's a what, not a he. A jewelry store down on Grand."

I nodded, standing on my toes, searching for my father and Augusta. "See you there at ten."

As Nelson opened the car door for me, I saw Alfred pacing in front of the window.

He wasted no time in opening up the door to the store and

shoving me through it. "I have to choose a wedding present for Lucy, and I need some advice. I've no idea what she likes."

She liked air machines and adventure and candy. She liked waltzes and skirts she couldn't walk in and the color blue. Though I should have excused myself from the job, I let him push me into the store anyway.

Alfred explained what he was after, and the clerk behind the counter moved toward a display case filled with pearls. He took out a necklace and laid it across a piece of velvet.

There were five strands to the necklace, each longer than the next, the pearls alternating with gold beads.

"No. Lucy doesn't like pearls." The words came out of my mouth before I could stop them.

Alfred looked at me, surprise in his eyes. "She doesn't?"

I shook my head. I didn't know for sure, but it just seemed like pearls were too . . . proper.

"What about some opals?" The clerk had already moved on to the next case. He pulled a large ring from the display and held it out to Alfred. The band had flowers and swirls carved into it.

I told the clerk to put it back.

Alfred blinked. "I rather liked that."

"It's not right." Lucy wasn't some sentimental girl. She was a woman.

The clerk put it back into the case and pulled out a different ring. One with a sparkling green stone surrounded by—

"Are those diamonds?" Alfred had taken it from the clerk and was looking at it with interest.

"Five carats' worth, sir."

"I don't think Lucy would like a ring." I tried to give it back to the clerk, but Alfred wouldn't let go of it.

"*I* like this ring."

"But you don't make candy, do you?"

311

He snapped his gaze to me. "Lucy doesn't make candy. The confectionery makes candy."

"She makes candy all the time." Or she used to. Isn't that what she'd said that night at the ball?

"Why? Don't the Kendalls have a cook?"

I plucked it from his hand and gave it back to the clerk. "Trust me. She'd never wear this."

"The point isn't whether she'd wear it. The point is that I'm thinking of her. And I need to get her a wedding gift."

"But you're thinking of you, not her."

"I wouldn't buy myself a woman's emerald ring!"

"You've got the wrong ring. Or the wrong woman."

His glance was sharp. "Then what *would* she like? A bracelet?"

"You can't just—"

"No rings, no necklaces, no bracelets. You're not being very helpful, Charles." He was frowning as he pulled out his pocket watch and flipped the cover open. "I've wasted enough time." He surveyed the case of rings again. "I'll take that emerald."

The clerk nodded and pulled it from the case, box and all.

"But I don't think—"

"I've spent enough time as it is. Besides, I don't think she'll complain. There are five carats of diamonds in that ring."

What could I say? It was nice. And expensive. But was as unlike Lucy as Evelyn was.

I walked around the store, looking into the cases, as Alfred paid for the ring. Lucy wasn't going to wear it. She wouldn't even like it. Shouldn't he know that about her by now?

What if—what if I told her *I* loved her?

This wasn't a contest. And if it were, then Alfred would win. Would win? He'd already won! They were getting married. And anyway, why would she want to marry a man like me? Because I knew her. I knew her in a way Alfred Arthur never had and never would. And I would never see another woman the way he'd been seeing Evelyn. I nearly laughed. Since when had I become such a choir boy? It's true I wasn't the man I used to be. Since coming to St. Louis, I'd become downright respectable.

I'd never be able to make up to Micky Callahan for what I'd done. There was no one I could tell I was sorry. No matter how hard I tried, I'd never be able to make it better.

Winnie's words came back to me. *"You're not good enough and you never will be."*

That was the truth.

But what else was it she'd said?

"It's about God. So it doesn't matter what you believe, does it? It's not about you and how you believe you have to make things right."

I wish I'd listened to the preacher the past few weeks. Then maybe I'd understand what Winnie'd been trying to say.

So what was it about?

God. That's what she'd kept saying. It was about God and what He'd done for me, not about what I was trying to do for myself.

I was a coward and a rotten friend. I stood by and watched while a man was killed. I was doing it to save myself, but it turned out the joke was on me. All I'd done was realize I wasn't worth saving.

But what if Winnie was right? What if the problem wasn't God? What if the problem was me? If that were true, then that was good news. I couldn't hope to change the way the world worked, but maybe I could hope that He could change me.

"You ready?"

I jumped as Alfred clapped me on the shoulder. "Sure."

"You thinking of getting married yourself?"

"What?"

He pointed to the display case in front of me. It was filled with engagement rings. "I can tell you it's a trying business."

"Don't you like Lucy?"

"I like her fine."

Fine? "If I were marrying a girl like her, I think I'd be feeling more than fine."

He shrugged as he stepped past me toward the door. "I proposed. I can't back out now."

I hadn't suggest that he should. But . . . "What if you could?"

He paused and gave me a long searching look. And then he sighed. "I can't. It's not done. And even if it were . . . it wouldn't be right . . . would it?"

Confound loyalty and honor! But how could I tell him to do something that would only end up hurting her? "No. It wouldn't."

He patted the box he'd put into his pocket. "Then the best thing to do is get it over and done with."

41  Lucy

It was the first of February, three weeks to the day of our wedding. I was trying hard not to think about it, but the note I held in my hand made it difficult. I couldn't quite make sense of it.

The maid who had handed it to me had already gone back to sweeping the front hall, but she straightened and paused for a moment. "Did you . . . want anything else, miss?"

"Hmm? Oh. No. Nothing. Thank you."

The note was written on electricity company letterhead in a bold but regular hand.

Meet me at Union Station. Leaving town on the 11:15 train for Memphis.

                                                    AA

Mr. Arthur had never sent me a note before. I hadn't thought him the type of man to write love letters, but I hadn't ever expected to receive anything like this either. He wanted me to meet him at the train station?

Why?

Did he want to . . . elope? Mother's comments about Julia Shaw echoed in my head. I could only imagine what people would say about me, the Queen of Love and Beauty, running off to get married. My cheeks burned. Maybe . . . he just wanted a small wedding. Nothing wrong with that. It's what I wanted too. But wouldn't it be better just to go to the courthouse? Surely people wouldn't be half so scandalized about that.

Leaving town on the 11:15 train.

Eloping was supposed to be . . . well . . . it was shameful, but it was also supposed to be romantic, wasn't it? It had to mean that he couldn't wait one day more to make me his bride. Why else would he be in such a hurry? And didn't that imply something about me? I should be flattered, really. I was quite sure that I wasn't supposed to feel trapped and panicked and . . . and shamed.

It was probably due to the shock of it all. If I had woken knowing that today was to be my wedding day, I would be feeling differently. I would feel excited and happy. Perfectly blissful. I folded the note and put it into my pocket, sliding my hand along the banister as I walked up the stairs.

I was to be married. Today.

I had known I was *going* to be married. That's what it meant to be engaged to be married. But somehow I'd never actually thought of becoming married. Of the actual being married to Mr. Arthur.

Alfred.

I'd have to call him Alfred now. I felt my chin start to pucker as I walked into my room. I shut the door behind me. I would *not* cry. There was absolutely nothing to cry about.

316

Meet me at Union Station.

I knelt beside my hope chest and pulled a package of caramels from its depths, peeled the cellophane wrapper from one of them, and thought about it all as I sucked on it. I couldn't back out. Not now. He'd given me the chance, and I'd refused. I couldn't change my mind.

Could I?

I trembled as I thought about it.

No. I couldn't. Breaking the engagement at this point would be even worse than eloping. So that meant I was going to be married *now*. I swallowed the rest of the caramel, then looked around the room that had been my own for nineteen years. I had no idea what to do. There was a difference between thinking about getting married and going to get married, and I hadn't understood that until right this minute.

I wished Sam were here.

But what could he do? Except tell me not to go?

In spite of all reason, I had a peculiar longing for Charlie Clarke. For a person who would, even for a moment, hide me from the world and hold me in his arms as if he treasured me. As if he cared for me. Understood me.

But that was foolish.

If he knew about Mr. Arthur's note, he'd probably offer to drive me to Union Station himself.

I was caught between ruining my reputation or breaking an engagement . . . which would in turn ruin my reputation. I unwrapped another caramel. Really, they were some of the best caramels I'd ever had. They didn't stick to my teeth, and once they had warmed in my mouth, they melted into a delectable cream. I plucked another from the package and popped it into my mouth as well.

If I wanted to slip away unnoticed, I couldn't take too much with me. I tiptoed down the hall and up the back stairs to the attic. There I wrestled an old Oxford bag from a heap of luggage in the corner. Back in my room, as I opened it, the handle slipped its fittings. I pushed it back into place while I contemplated what to pack.

I didn't have much time.

A second dress, surely, for the wedding. I wouldn't want to wear the one I'd traveled in. I'd wear my coat, but I'd need a pair of fresh stockings and extra shoes. Another pair of gloves. And something to sleep in. I grabbed my favorite nightgown, but then thought the better of it. Hadn't I ought to take something better? If Mr. Arthur were going to see it?

Mr. Arthur *was* going to see it.

Alfred.

Alfred, Alfred, Alfred. I needed to call him Alfred now.

The thought made me want to hide in the closet.

Married people had to do . . . what they did . . . once in a while. A cold sweat prickled at the backs of my ears. I hoped it wouldn't be too often. But how bad could it be? Rapturous embraces, passionate kisses, and that sort of thing. It must be pleasant or people wouldn't do it, would they? Although . . . I could think of quite a few things people did that weren't pleasant at all. They just did them because they had to.

My knees began to shake.

I stuffed another pair of stockings into the bag. It wouldn't do any good to think about things too much. There would be time for all of that later. I fastened the bag, took one last glance around the room, and then tiptoed down the hall.

I paused as I passed Papa's room. Should I . . . ? No. I'd only start to cry. I was going to be married. I was supposed to happy. And I would be . . . just as soon as I could. Once I got on the train, probably. Hopefully. Soon.

When I got to the platform, Mr. Arthur was already there. He was pacing in front of one of the cars. I faltered in my step for just a moment. Every girl should be happy on her wedding day, so I put a smile on my face, clasped the bag in front of me with both hands, and continued on toward him.

A look of relief crossed his face when he saw me. "Thank goodness! I didn't think you'd make it." He glanced back over his shoulder at the train. "There's not much time."

"I'm ready."

An odd look crossed his face. "Well . . . that's . . . good. That's good." He cocked his head as a frown creased his forehead. "Ready for what? Exactly?"

I raised my satchel. "For the train. The 11:15 for Memphis. That's what you said."

"Oh. Oh! You thought you . . . and I . . . ?"

What else had I been meant to think?

"The thing of it is . . ." He paused and licked his bottom lip. "The thing of it is, I can't marry you."

"What?"

"I can't marry you because I've decided to marry someone else. We're eloping. Today. Right now, as a matter of fact."

"You can't marry me." I tried to make sense of what he was saying.

"I . . . don't think it would be appropriate. Considering."

He'd had me worry about extra stockings and nightgowns and then come all the way down to Union Station just to tell me he didn't want me? "You couldn't have written me a note?"

"I did."

"Or stopped by the house on your way here?"

"I . . . couldn't . . ."

"I thought we had an arrangement!"

"I know. I just—I didn't know—I really have to go. The train's about to leave."

"You're *leaving* me?"

"I'm sorry to be so rude about it all. That's why I've put it out that it's all my fault. I hope you'll forgive me. I'm sure you'll find plenty of shoulders to cry on once everyone hears how I've jilted you."

I was being jilted?! "But I don't—what am I supposed to do?" How was I supposed to marry the most eligible bachelor in town if he was eloping with someone else? "What happened to being agreeable? And thinking that we would come to care for each other? That love might grow with time?"

"I found that love, Lucy. Only . . . it wasn't with you. I'm sorry. I would have sworn to you that it didn't matter—but I've found, in fact, that it does. And it wouldn't be fair to marry you if my heart belonged to someone else. Someday, I know you'll understand."

Understand!

"I hope you'll forgive my leaving. I can't stay, not after breaking our engagement. Society wouldn't be very accepting."

"But—but—" What was wrong with me? That's what I really wanted to ask him. I didn't like him, not in that way, but I wanted him to like me. So what was it about me that wasn't worth jumping on a train to elope with? What couldn't he bring himself to love?

He glanced over his shoulder at the train. "Don't worry. I had a word with Charles. He'll see that your prospects aren't tarnished. He's good at getting the word out."

"Charlie *Clarke*?" Did he want me to thank him for that?

The train hissed a cloud of steam as the conductor walked the platform, shooing passengers onto the train.

"I really have to go. You've been wonderful about all this. Thanks." He gave me a salute and then hopped onto the train. And not once did he look back.

42   *Charlie*

"Lucy!"

She turned away from me, dropping her head, causing her hat to shield her face.

"Lucy Kendall!" I stood on the running board of the car as I hailed her outside Union Station. I couldn't keep the dimples out of my smile. Alfred was out of the picture. Now was my big chance.

She stalked on, as if she was determined to ignore me.

I told Nelson to follow her.

Cupping a hand to my mouth, I shouted toward her. "Don't worry. Alfred told me everything."

As she came to a halt, her bag swung back to whack her in the knees. She staggered. "What exactly did he tell you?" Her face flushed an angry red.

I sprung down off the running board and took her by the hand. If she'd get into the car, then I wouldn't have to shout at her. "He told me how he'd decided to elope with Evelyn. And how he was going to break the engagement." She wasn't looking at me quite the way I'd hoped she would. "I was . . . I was thinking you might not want to walk home alone."

As she stood there, glaring at me, her mouth fell open. She gasped. And then her eyes narrowed. "Who is Evelyn?"

I winced.

A shout went up from the steps of the station. "Yoo-hoo! Lucy Kendall—is that you?" Winnie Compton was waving a handkerchief in our direction.

Lucy started and lunged toward the car before I even had the chance to move. She threw the bag at me, ducked beneath my arm, and burrowed into the bench.

I told Nelson to drive on up to Vandeventer. As I put the bag on the floor and settled in next to her, she glared at me.

"You knew about this? About *her*?"

"I . . ." didn't know what I should say.

She gasped and put a gloved hand to her mouth. "You've met her, haven't you?"

"Really, I don't think—"

She pierced me with a look. "This is all your fault."

I put up a hand. "Now, wait just a minute—"

"Before he met you, Mr. Arthur was a nice man! He would never have snuck around with some—some other woman."

"I'm not . . . *not* nice!"

"It's not bad enough that you people steal our candy? You have to steal my fiancé too?"

"It's not like that, Lucy. In fact, I thought it was good of him to warn me about this."

"You would!" She sat there for a minute, mumbling to herself beneath that huge feathery hat of hers. "So tell me: Why did he tell *you*?"

I shrugged. "He saw the work I'd done with Royal Taffy, and

322

he knew if anyone could advertise it around the city that he was the one to blame, I was the man for it."

"So you're going to *advertise* me? As if I were . . . some piece of candy?"

"Don't worry. It shouldn't be too hard. You're much sweeter than a piece of Royal Taffy." I tried out a wink on her.

Her mouth clamped into a scowl as she clasped her hands around the handle of her bag.

"Listen. I'm really sorry, Lucy."

She threw a look toward me. "You . . . you are?"

"Of course I am." Though I was happy about the way things were turning out, that didn't mean Alfred hadn't done a bad thing by running off the way he had. Although her question seemed odd. "Why? Is there a reason I shouldn't be?"

"I just thought . . ." Her glance grazed my lips, then shot away. "Never mind. Just . . . don't talk to me." She made a point of staring out the window.

"We should be friends, you and I." We should be more than friends. "Especially since Alfred's not here anymore." I took her hand in mine.

Nelson pulled up to her house. For a moment her hand went limp in mine, but then she pulled it away. And her lips collapsed into a firm, thin line.

I put a hand to her cheek. "Tell me . . . can I hope there's a chance for me? Now that he's gone?"

She didn't pull away from me, but I didn't like the gleam in her eyes either. "Are you willing to stop trying to put us out of business?"

Business. For one blessed minute, I'd forgotten about all of that. Why did she always have to hold it over our heads? "I have to be honest with you, Lucy. There's nothing you can do or I can say that will stop our fathers' rivalry. At this point, don't you think the best thing to do is just . . . get out of the candy business? While you still can?" There was nothing to be gained by holding out anymore. I'd seen the figures. I'd read the reports. I'd walked the streets. There was hardly a packet of Fancy Crunch to be found in the city.

"So you think that just because my father's dying you can—"

"No! It's not like that."

"Then you think the only way your father will be proud of you is if you destroy a dying man's dream?"

"You're not listening!" I only wanted to help her. I only wanted to have her. And I couldn't do either of those things as long as she kept being so muleheaded.

"I'm trying to." Her shoulders dropped as the corners of her eyes drooped.

I reached out to cup a hand to her face.

She put a hand to my chest as she looked up into my eyes. When she spoke next, it was in a whisper. "I want to know how a man who makes me feel the way you do can treat my dreams so poorly." She closed her eyes. "But the only thing I understand is that your father matters more than mine does and that your wishes are more important than my dreams."

She was going to be stubborn, then. I dropped my hand. "If you could just be reasonable, when this is all over—"

Her eyes flew open. "When this is all over, it may well have killed my father, Charlie Clarke. Why can't you just—be somebody else!" She pushed open the door and yanked on her bag, only to wrench the handle off. It tipped onto its side, the mouth yawning open, spilling all of its contents.

I bent to collect them. "Let me help—"

"No. Please! I don't want your help." She stuffed a dress back into it. Stockings. Gloves.

I held out a dress to her.

She snatched it from me. "I would thank you to keep your hands off my—my—"

Of all the irksome, unbearable, irritating women! "Your nightgown?" I felt my eyes flash as I threw it at her.

She caught it. As she shoved it into her bag, she glanced up at my face. And then her mouth dropped into an O. She dropped the bag entirely, backing away from me, up the walk toward her house.

I bent and picked it up, offering it to her.

She didn't move to get it. In fact, all she did was retreat farther up the walk.

"Lucy?"

"Don't—" All the color had drained from her face. "Don't . . . don't touch me."

"I just wanted . . ." I offered the bag to her again.

She wrenched it from my hand. "It's you."

I'd always imagined her saying those words, but in all my imaginings, she'd never said them with quite that note and horror and fear.

"Are you all right?"

"You—you—" Her teeth were chattering so hard I could hardly hear what she was saying.

"I what?"

"You killed that man. That poor man. The one who—"

As I reached for her, she took one last, long look, clasped the bag to her chest, and fled toward her house.

I pulled on her doorbell, I pounded on the door, I yelled her name, but the door never opened. If only she'd give me the chance to explain.

But she didn't. And she probably never would.

How had she found out about Micky Callahan? And how was it that I'd imagined I would never have to tell her? That I could ever hope to hide something so terrible from a woman I had come to . . . to love.

Love.

What would Lucy do with the information? Would she tell anyone else? It didn't matter. If Lucy had found out, then it was only a matter of time before everyone else did too. And what could I say? I might as well have killed him.

Nelson drove me back home, and I stayed around to help him wax and polish Louise. It was an afternoon's worth of work, and it gave me something useful to do.

Things hadn't gone at all the way I'd hoped. I was supposed to pick Lucy up at the train station, let her cry on my shoulder, and then help her get over her broken heart.

Dreams were for children.

"Careful there, Mr. Charlie. You're going to rub the shine right off the brass."

"Sorry. I'll just . . ."

"Why don't you give that rag to me and go on up to the house?"

I walked up the drive as the sun was setting and saw a shadow flit around the corner of the house. It was short and small. One of the street scamps? Leaving the drive, I followed it around the back of the house. As I did, I discovered something I hadn't counted on. The scamp was a she. I caught up to her as she was reaching for the back door and grabbed her about the arm.

"Ow!" She tried to pull her arm from my grasp.

"I'd like to know what you think you're doing!"

As she looked up at me, the porch light fell across her face. She had that same look of fear and terror that Lucy had.

I released her and stepped back. "Jennie?"

She blinked. "Mr. Clarke!"

"What are—why are you prowling around out here?"

"I . . . was . . . it was my afternoon off."

"And you're just now coming back?"

Her gaze dropped toward the ground as she lifted her chin. "What I do with my time is my own business."

Of course it was, but the way she refused to meet my eyes made me want to make it my business. She wrenched the door open and disappeared up the servants' stairs. I retraced my steps back to the front walk, wondering whether I should be concerned.

Charlie Clarke: a murderer.

Somewhere, something deep inside me had cracked and then crumbled when I'd realized exactly where I'd seen him before. It felt very much like dreams disappearing and hope dissolving.

No wonder I'd always had the feeling that I knew him.

I opened my hope chest and reached down to the bottom, to the layer of souvenirs that I had wrapped in newspaper when I'd come home from my travels. It didn't take long to find what I'd been looking for: that page from the *Chicago Tribune* I'd read in the carriage on the way home from Union Station.

Spreading it out on the floorboards, I smoothed it with my hand.

A twenty-two-year-old member of one of the South Side's notorious athletic clubs was arrested for the murder of Micky Callahan.

Arrested for murder.

A tear dotted the newssheet. And then another and another. I gathered it up and clutched it to my bosom as I sobbed into the page. I don't know how long I sat there, clinging to that newspaper, weeping into its folds. But then suddenly, I began to laugh. The one person I had convinced myself was exactly like me had turned out to be a murderer. The one person I had been able to talk to. The only person who had ever looked at me as if I really could be a candymaker.

Even when the worst thing he'd been was a Clarke, Charlie had never tried to destroy my dream . . . just my father's company.

I looked again at the face that, despite all my intentions and reason, had become so dear. And then I rolled over onto the floor, pulled my knees to my chest, and started crying all over again.

"Lucy?" My mother's voice. A gentle touch on my shoulder.

I opened my eyes, but it seemed so dark.

"Lucy?"

As I scrambled to sitting, the newspaper dropped from my eyes and I found myself on the floor in my bedroom, my mother kneeling at my side.

I squinted against the glare of sunlight from the windows.

"What on earth . . . ?"

"I . . ." I balled the newspaper up and stashed it behind me, trying to hide the evidence of a tiny infant hope I hadn't even known I'd possessed. Then I swept a hand across my eyes to rid them of the grit of dried tears. "I fell asleep."

"Evidently." She gave my face a searching glance. "I was coming to get you for our afternoon calls, but I think you might want to freshen up first." She helped me up, but when I would have gone to the bathroom, she placed a hand on my arm. "I know the wedding is quickly approaching. It's perfectly natural to feel a bit—"

"There's not going to be a wedding."

Her brows drew together. "Second thoughts aren't unheard of—"

"Mr. Arthur broke our engagement."

"Mr. Arthur? But—"

I felt a tear slide down my cheek.

"Oh, Lucy . . ."

I moved away as she tried to embrace me. "If you don't mind, I'd like to be alone."

After she left, I crammed the newspaper down to the bottom of the chest and banged the lid down on top of it. Then I went into the bathroom to wash away the evidence of my tears.

How foolish I was being!

The best thing to do, the safest course of action, was to forget that Charlie Clarke had ever existed. That he had ever been the man at the ball or the friend at the air meet. To stay as far away from him as I possibly could. But as I'd slept, the article had imprinted itself on my tearstained cheeks. And as I looked into the mirror, Charlie Clarke's eyes stared back at me.

We visited Mrs. John Dunnert, Mrs. Edward Dunnert, and Mrs. Hiram Dunnert—who, for reasons of family quarrels and pure spite, had their at-homes on the same afternoon. Talking to one was exhausting. Trying to carry on polite conversation with all three in succession was grueling. Especially with Charlie Clarke attempting to invade my thoughts. As we drove back up Olive Street, I asked Mother if I could walk the last few blocks home.

"From here?"

"It's not very far."

"By yourself?"

"I'll be fine."

Concern etched lines in her forehead as she reached out and touched my hand. "Are you sure?"

"I'm sure."

I hadn't gone ten steps when a dark green automobile swerved from its lane and screeched to a stop beside me. Charlie Clarke leaped out.

I took a step back and held my muff out, legs and tail dangling, between us. "Don't touch me!"

He continued toward me, hands up, palms out. "I need to talk to you."

I turned and kept walking.

It didn't take him long to catch up. Curse fashion and its hobbled skirts! If only a streetcar would come. I'd take it all the way to Forest Park if I had to. I glanced over my shoulder, but there were none in sight.

"I just . . . I need you to understand."

"Understand what? That you killed some poor man? I read the newspaper article, Charlie. Stay away from me." Why had I insisted on walking home by myself?

"I didn't kill anyone."

"If you'll excuse me, I need to be getting home. I'm expected. My mother's waiting for me."

"Lucy—" He put a hand to my arm.

I pulled away. "You can't . . . you can't be a liar and a murderer and a—and a *Clarke* and just talk your way into people's hearts. And dreams. You can't just pretend to be so kind. And caring. And . . . a perfect gentleman." Why was I crying again? Charlie Clarke wasn't worth my tears.

"I never killed anyone. They arrested me on the *suspicion* of having killed someone and—" He yanked his hat from his head and twisted it between his hands. "The truth of it is, I might as well have killed that man. His name was Micky Callahan, and he'd been my friend for . . . forever. I didn't kill him, but I was there when he died. I watched it. I watched it all, and I did nothing."

"Why?" Why did I want so much to believe him? And when had I started to care so much?

"Why? Because it seemed like there was no other choice. I was seven years old when my father walked away one day without even saying good-bye. I tied myself to a two-penny thug because that's the only way I knew how to make a living. I never did anything really wrong. I just . . . made it easier, I guess, for other people to."

I didn't know what to believe anymore. "What do you want me to say, Charlie?"

"I . . ." He gave his hat another squeeze as he shot me a doleful, searching glance. "I don't know."

"You want me to say that everything's going to be fine? That— that I don't care about what happened in Chicago? Is that what you want?" I couldn't believe I'd thought, for one brief moment after Mr. Arthur had left, that Charlie Clarke might be . . . everything I'd ever hoped for!

"I—"

"How can any of this work out?" How could anything be fine ever again?

"I only . . . I guess I was hoping you'd understand. But now I can see I was expecting too much." He smoothed the brim of his hat and set it on his head. "I'm sorry I wasted your time."

When I walked away, he didn't try to stop me.

I needed to make something. Something to take the sting out of Mr. Arthur's elopement and the revelation of Charlie's true nature.

I'd so badly misjudged them. *Both* of them. In the same way I'd misjudged my hazelnut chews.

And that hadn't been the worst of it. The worst of it had been telling Mother about the broken engagement. I'd failed at making candy, and now I'd failed at making a good marriage too.

I tied on an apron and got out a pot. I wavered as I stood in front of the icebox. Caramel or fudge?

Neither.

It needed to be something chewy. Something I could sink my teeth into.

A butterscotch chew.

I took some butter from the icebox and some vanilla essence from the cupboard. I found some sugars, vinegar, and corn syrup in the pantry, and I pulled the salt cellar closer to the stove. Putting the sugars, vinegar, corn syrup, and salt in the pot along with some water, I stirred them together.

Was that—?

I paused, spoon over the pot as I glanced toward the back door. I thought I'd heard something. But . . . no. I went back to my cooking, watching the mixture bubble as I stirred, anticipating the way the ingredients would blend together. Soon there was no white sugar and no brown sugar left. There was only a soft, silky, glistening syrup. It never ceased to amaze me how they could combine with all the other ingredients to create something so different still. I added the butter and stirred for a while.

Then I measured in some vanilla and poured the candy out into a pan.

But—there it was again. A creak from the back porch.

Standing by the side of the door to keep myself from view, I drew the hem of the curtain aside and peered through the window.

There was nothing to see.

I let the curtain drop and went back to my pan, smoothing the candy out to the edges. Perhaps I'd only been imagining things. I'd probably been imagining things.

But then it came again.

I grabbed the rolling pin from a drawer and went to the door, rattling the handle. "I hear you, out there! And I'm coming out if you don't leave."

I wasn't, of course, but whatever was out there didn't have to know that.

Silence.

I stood by the door, waiting. Hearing nothing, I pushed aside the curtain once more. And then I screamed as a face pressed against the window and a hand turned the doorknob.

"It's just me, Lucy."

"Sam!"

"Let me in. It's freezing out here."

"Sam Blakely—!" I couldn't unlock the door for the shaking of my hands.

"Just open the door, Lucy."

"I—I can't." I burst into tears. I couldn't move the bolt.

"I didn't mean to frighten you." He was talking through the window at me.

"Well, you did!"

"I really didn't mean to."

"You never mean to do anything! You've always been so nice, so helpful, and so . . . so . . . here! And now, when I really need you, you're not!" I swiped at the tears that were leaking onto my cheeks.

"Lucy. Open the door."

"I wish I could."

"Just . . . here." He pulled the door toward him, pressing it against the frame. "Now try."

I gave the bolt a shove and it slid through the casing.

He pulled the door open and stepped through.

"What were you doing out there?" I was still clutching the rolling pin.

"I didn't realize how late it was . . . I just had to think. Away from the house." He looked up at me, then over at the candy. "Can I?"

"It hasn't set."

"Doesn't matter."

He dipped a spoon into the pan. It came away trailing long caramel-colored strings. He scraped the candy off the spoon with his teeth and then licked at the remnants that clung to the silver. "You know, things are changing Lucy. I'm not really yours. I mean, I'm happy to help you out and everything, but I don't belong to you."

He couldn't have offended me more if he'd slapped me. "I know you don't belong to me."

"And I don't mean to disappoint you."

"How could you disappoint me?"

"I just . . . came here to think. I wanted to be alone. I have some things to figure out."

"Maybe . . . maybe I could help you."

A flush lit his cheeks. "No. I don't think—I mean—it's nice of you to offer and everything, but I don't think you'd under-stand."

Why didn't anybody think I could understand anything?

"I have to go." He retreated to the porch, pulling the door shut behind him.

I pushed aside the curtain and watched him walk off into the night. "What on earth . . . ?"

Mother was in her sitting room when I left the kitchen for bed. She gestured from her table as I stepped into the front hall.

"Would you like to talk about Mr. Arthur?"

"No."

She came to me and took my hand from the banister. Clasping it in her own, she pulled me into the parlor. "I'm so sorry, Lucy."

At least she hadn't turned on the light. I couldn't really make out her face and could only pray that she could not see mine.

"The things of the heart hurt so terribly."

Things of the heart?

"You might think that you'll never love again, but you will."

"Love again?"

"I know it's too soon to speak of it, but just know that things will get better. You're so young. There's time enough for love."

"I'm not . . . I don't care . . . I didn't love him, Mother. I didn't want him for . . . for . . . *that*. I wanted him for what he could do for us. How he could help us."

She withdrew from me, looking at me as if she'd never seen me before. "You never loved him?"

"Why did you think I agreed to his proposal?"

"I thought . . . I mean . . ."

"Isn't that what you wanted? Didn't you want me to marry well?"

"Yes! Of course I wanted you to marry well. But I wanted you to marry well for your own benefit, not for ours. The company is finished. There's no hope of saving it. I never wanted—" She seemed to swallow her words. Then she sighed.

"You've never even tried to save the company, Mother. All you want to do is sell it!"

"I know the success of the company is all you and your father ever wanted, but I've given up. I gave up a long time ago. Don't make the same mistake I did. It's not worth your soul. It's not even worth your dreams. Candy isn't everything, Lucy."

"But it's *something*. Candy is something. I was going to be the girl who made candy and saved her family. And then I was going to be the girl who married Mr. Arthur and saved her family. But now I don't have Fancy Crunch, and I don't have a fiancé. And now I don't even know how to save myself!"

44   Charlie

In spite of Lucy's feelings toward me, I was good as my word. I put it around the club that Alfred had broken her heart. And then I talked about it again at the country club on Saturday night, just to make sure the point had been made.

Lucy Kendall was ready and waiting to be swept off her feet.

Although she'd made it quite clear she didn't want me—and how could I blame her?—I didn't mind trying to help her out. Her opinions about me stung, but I ignored them. What else had I expected her to say? Besides, I'd been the one to introduce Alfred to Evelyn, so I figured I owed her something.

Although . . . she didn't exactly look very grateful.

She didn't really even look at me at all. Not until I was finished talking to some judge's son. Then she marched up to me and poked me in the chest with her fan. "Were you talking to Mr. Whitley about me?"

I resisted the urge to take that fan from her and snap it in two. "I told him you're looking for a chance to mend your broken heart."

"I'll thank you to keep yourself out of this."

I would if I weren't already so much a part of it. If I didn't want so much to erase that look of hurt and betrayal in her eyes. "Alfred made me promise to help you."

"But he didn't really know what you're like. So I'll thank you to leave me alone."

She couldn't have hit a truer mark if she'd tried. "What? With all of them?" I tipped my head toward the refreshment table, where several of the city's most eligible bachelors were lounging.

"With any of them!"

As she stood there glaring at me, I realized something was wrong. Things didn't sound right. The conversation wasn't as loud as normal. There was more hiss and less hum.

I'd gotten used to people sizing me up at these places, looking me over, sliding me glances. But it wasn't me they were looking at tonight. Tonight those glances and smiles and whispers were directed toward Lucy.

The job Alfred had given me might be harder than I'd thought.

I slid a glance toward Lucy.

A flush had risen on her cheeks. And underneath her proud and noble brow was a glimmer of hurt.

I offered her my arm.

She looked at it for one long moment and then she took it. And as we stood there together staring back at all those whispering people, Winnie Compton came and joined us.

On Monday morning, my father called me down to the factory for another meeting. "We need to talk about that strategy of yours. We're already sending out orders for this week, so our new pricing is going to have to wait until next week."

"New pricing . . ." I vaguely remembered him mentioning that.

"Right. The new pricing: three cents instead of five. That should beat Fancy Crunch when they go to four cents next week."

Fancy Crunch was changing their pricing? "But if they haven't already done it . . . how do you know they're going to?"

He smiled. "Let's just say I have a person on the inside."

"Lucy!" I'd finally caught up to her. I'd had to push aside half the attendees at the Chamber of Commerce luncheon in order to follow her outside.

She didn't even turn to look at me. "I thanked you for your support on Saturday night and I meant it. But I don't really wish to speak to you."

"You don't have to. Just listen."

"I don't wish to listen to you either."

I pulled her arm through mine and hustled her off down the street. "Fine. I'll talk and you'll not listen."

She stumbled as she tried to keep up with me. "Will you—"

"There's a spy in your company."

She stopped so suddenly that I nearly swung right around her on the slippery soles of my new shoes. "A what?"

"A spy. There's somebody giving information to my father about your plans."

Her eyes grew wide and then they narrowed with suspicion. "And why would you tell me?"

"I've let a lot of people down, let a lot of people get hurt. But I don't want you to be one of them. If somebody's telling my father your secrets, then it has to be someone close to you. I don't think . . . that doesn't seem . . . well . . . it's dangerous."

"What secrets?"

"The change you're going to make next week in your pricing."

She pulled her arm from mine and then took a step back from me. "That's very clever of you."

"To work out the connection?" I thought so.

"No! To try to trick me into telling you our plans."

"I'm not trying to trick you! I'm trying to protect you."

"I don't need your protection. I'm quite capable of looking after myself."

Why did she have to be so stubborn? "No, you're not. Because someone close to you is a traitor."

"Even if that's so, why should you care? If you think I've forgotten what you truly want, then you're mistaken. Why should you take the trouble to warn me?"

"Because—"

She lifted a brow.

"Because I . . . I like you, Lucy. Don't you know that?"

For a fraction of a second, her eyes softened. But then she blinked. When she opened them, they'd gone a steely blue. "I will admit that I was fond of you once too."

"Fond? I'm not talking about fondness! I love you!"

"How could love exist between us, Charlie? What does it have to grow on? Your duplicity or my dirty tricks? Beyond the fact that you're not the person you represented yourself to be—"

"I never—"

"—*even if* I did love you, how could I admit to it? Do you know how much it would cost me? It would be a betrayal of—of myself and everything I've ever wanted. You're asking me to give up everything that's important to me, to pretend as if none of it mattered. And I can't do it!"

45

"Lucy! Wait—"

I walked on, ignoring Charlie's cries and the burning of my cheeks.

A spy. I ought to have laughed, it was that ludicrous. But something about the idea made the skin at the nape of my neck crawl.

As I walked away, I promised myself that I would not look back. I *would not* give Charlie the satisfaction. Did he think that by making professions of love he could hide his true intentions?

The viper.

The absolute snake!

Love! He had a very funny way of showing it, using his supposed affections to hide some ulterior plan. Only . . . Standard had come out with new packaging right as we had. And how had they known that we were planning to lower our prices?

I walked on for a moment, considering.

He'd probably talked to one of our workers, that's how. That's what he had to have done. It's the only way he could have known. Because if there truly were a spy, he ought never to have told me. If there were a spy, then the advantage was all his. Besides . . . Mr. Blakely was a talkative sort. He could easily have spoken in the wrong company.

But still . . . why would Charlie have bothered to tell me? Nothing made any sense. Unless there really was a spy.

There wasn't a spy.

There couldn't be.

Curse Charlie Clarke for putting such thoughts into my head!

As I continued down the street, I caught a glimpse of Sam. Now, there was a person I could talk to, a person who'd understand! I sped my walk to catch up with him.

He turned the corner.

I slipped past a group of women who had gathered around a shop window and hurried to follow him. As I turned the corner, someone caught my arm.

"Pardon me!" I pulled it, only to find it was Charlie's hand that had caught me.

"Look." He nodded past me toward Sam.

Sam had taken a note and a bag from a girl's hand. He opened the paper. Read it. Cupped a hand to her chin and then shoved it into his pocket. He looked as if—

"You there!"

Both Sam and the girl turned at Charlie's cry. A blush swept both their faces as Charlie strode toward them. "Let me see that!"

Sam stepped forward, placing himself between Charlie and the girl.

"Let me see it." Charlie held his hand out. "We saw you shove something into your pocket, Blakely. Out with it."

Sam frowned. "It's no business of yours what my girl has to say to me in a note."

"It is if you're corresponding with my maid about company secrets."

Company secrets? "Sam?" How did he know the Clarkes' maid?

"That's what you're doing, isn't it? Selling City Confectionery information to Standard?" Charlie scuffled with Sam for a moment before stepping back with the note between his hands. He unfolded it with a flourish and began to read it aloud. "'My dearest Samuel . . .'" His ears went pink at the tips as he refolded it and handed it back to Sam. "Sorry."

Sam shrugged as he put it back into his pocket, but his cheeks were flushed, and his eyes were shooting sparks.

"If you weren't passing secrets and you weren't spying . . . then what's in that bag of yours?"

Sam leaned around Charlie and offered it up to me.

The Clarkes' maid linked her arm through Sam's. "It's some pieces of Royal Taffy mixed with some Fancy Crunch."

I dipped a hand into the bag and then I passed it over to Charlie. I placed the mix of candies into my mouth, closing my eyes as a symphony of flavors and textures exploded and blended in my mouth.

Charlie was staring at the mixture in his palm as if he didn't know quite what to do with it.

I poked him with my elbow. "Try it."

He picked out a piece of Royal Taffy and put it into his mouth.

"No. You have to try them both together." The girl demonstrated as she said it.

He put a piece of Fancy Crunch into his mouth, too. His brow lifted as he began to chew.

"See?" Sam offered some to the girl.

"So that's what all this was about?" Charlie gestured toward the bag.

Sam nodded. "The way Lucy's been carrying on about you—"

"I haven't been *carrying on*." Honestly!

Sam sent me a look beneath gathered brows.

"Much."

"The way she's been carrying on, I didn't think she'd look too kindly on my eating Royal Taffy."

"And the way you've been scheming against City Confectionery . . ." The girl had slipped her hand into Sam's as she talked to Charlie.

Was this the girl who had embroidered Sam's handkerchief? I wasn't quite sure I approved. "So neither of you are spies, then?" If they weren't passing secrets, then who was?

"Spies?" The girl's eyes widened, and she began to laugh. "A spy? Me?"

"You thought—?" Sam's voice had gone high. "You actually thought that I would betray you, Lucy?"

"No. No! I never thought that. Charlie did."

As he turned toward Charlie, the hurt in his eyes seemed to demand some sort of answer.

Charlie put a hand up. "You were acting suspiciously . . . and Jennie was sneaking around."

"Miss Harrison." Sam had put an arm about the girl's shoulders.

"Miss what?"

"Miss *Harrison*. She should be Miss Harrison to you."

"Oh. Right. Miss Harrison, then."

All this was fine and good, but there was still a question to be answered! "If it wasn't you, Sam . . . then who is it?"

"Who is what? What are you talking about?" Sam's appeal was made to me.

"Someone at the confectionery has been giving information about our packaging and pricing to Standard."

"Are you sure?"

Charlie answered for me. "Yes."

I didn't want to believe a friend had betrayed me, but who else could it have been? "Sam? Are you sure you didn't speak to anyone about our plans?"

"No. I didn't. I promise."

Charlie handed the bag back to Sam. "Not even to Jen—Miss Harrison?"

The girl looked at me, worry clouding her eyes. "I never heard anything about them. Not until just now."

But if Miss Harrison hadn't said anything and Sam hadn't said anything, then who had?

My encounter with Sam and Jennie had done nothing to soothe my worries or Charlie's fears. I believed him now. There had to be a spy at work. I was certainly glad it wasn't Sam, but if it wasn't him, then who was it?

His father?

Mrs. Hughes?

The coachman?

It made me fear to be alone with those I had always trusted. That week, I spent less time in the company of others and more time with my father. And whenever Mother wanted another eye to go over the books, she found a willing volunteer.

46

"What is it?" Lucy whispered the words as she stood in the hotel lobby on Valentine's Day evening, waiting for Mr. Byers to bring her a glass of lemonade.

Had I been staring at her again? I blinked. "I've come up with a plan."

"Well? What is it?" She was searching the crowd as she nibbled on a fingernail. "We probably shouldn't be seen speaking."

"Here's what I want you to do: You need to tell everyone you can think of that you're planning on doing something completely different with the company. Something so different that it will cause whoever the spy is to run straight to my father."

"Like what?"

"Like . . ." Like what? "Your mother is trying to sell the company . . ."

"And I've been trying to save it. That covers everything that's happened since I got back in September. And almost everyone who counts knows it."

"Then it can't be about selling or saving the company. Maybe . . ." What? "Maybe . . . you could say you think the company should produce something else entirely."

"All right . . ." She settled her gaze on me.

"Something like . . . I don't know . . . tires!"

"Tires?!"

"For cars. Or air machines. Or bicycles."

"Tires?"

"Well, candy hasn't been very successful for you . . ."

For a minute I was afraid she'd thump me with that sharp, pointy fan she always carried, but then she gave a weary-sounding sigh. "Fine."

"And that's the way you'll tell it. A tire for a different purpose to each person. And as soon as I hear anything about tires from my father, I'll let you know."

"And . . . ?"

"And then we can figure out who the spy is, based on who you told what to."

"But . . . I don't know who it is. So who should I tell?"

That was a good point. "How many people could it be?"

"It's not Sam."

"No." At least we were clear now on that.

"It could be his father."

That was one.

"Or . . . the coachman?"

"Sure. That's two."

"Maybe . . . Mrs. Hughes? Our cook? She knows everything. She always has."

"Fine."

She glanced off over my shoulder as she nibbled on her lip.

"Is that it?"

She shrugged. "I don't know. It could be any of them. Or

none of them!" Fear rippled in the depths of her eyes. "I hope it's none of them."

"So tell each of them something different. And then . . . you have to be sure, Lucy. Is there *anyone* else? It has to be someone close to you. Someone who's heard you talking about the company."

"They all are. And they all have."

Then it had to be one of them. Byers was returning with Lucy's lemonade. "Once my father tells me what he's heard, we'll know who it is."

＊（◯〜

"They're going to what?" I wasn't quite sure I'd heard my father correctly. After a week's worth of concerts and plays and dances, going in and out of the cold winter weather, I'd come down with a head cold.

He leaned close. "City Confectionery is courting a German buyer. I've no idea what's going on! I thought everything had been decided. And now, after all this time and all our effort, they want to sell to a European."

"Why?"

"How should I know? I was the one who was doing them a favor. And now we have to come up with a better offer!"

"Germans? Are you sure?"

"Why wouldn't I be?"

A German buyer? Lucy hadn't said anything about Germans. Wouldn't she have told me if there were Germans? What had happened to the tires? And why couldn't Kendalls just do what they were supposed to?!

I sent a message to her anyway, asking her to meet me at the soda fountain on Locust Street the next afternoon. And just in case the spy intercepted my message, I waited outside the door

349

for her. When the carriage dropped her off, I linked my arm through hers and walked her off down the street.

"I thought you said to meet you at the soda fountain."

"I did."

"You said it was important."

"It is."

"Then why are we walking away?"

"Because you suspected the coachman, didn't you?"

Her eyes went round as she nodded. "What did you hear?"

"My father says you're hoping for a German buyer . . . ?"

Her brow collapsed for a moment, then cleared as all the color drained from her face.

"I thought we'd agreed on tires, but it sounded strange. So I thought I'd tell you what I'd heard."

She nodded. Then followed it with a shake of her head. "It's true that I said it, but it's not true that we have a German buyer."

"Then . . . ? Who is it? Who's our spy?"

"I don't . . . know. I'm not sure. I only told one person about the Germans." Her brow furrowed as if she were trying to work something out. "It wasn't true, not when I said it, and it's not true now. I just wanted to . . . I wanted some time, Charlie. I really don't want to have to sell."

"I know you don't. But you have to tell me who the spy is."

"I only wanted to—"

"That's fine, Lucy. It doesn't matter. The important thing is that we know now."

"I wanted, I was hoping—"

"Who is it!"

"My mother."

Her . . . ? Her mother? "Are you sure?"

She nodded.

How could it be her mother? "Wasn't there anyone else you told?"

"No. Who else would there have been? But if it's my mother . . . how could it be, Charlie? How could it be my mother? And what should we do now?"

⁂

What should we do?

I told Lucy I'd figure something out. It wouldn't do any good to ask my father directly. I was afraid he'd only deny it. Besides, I had a feeling Lucy needed to hear it from both my father and her mother. And the only way to do that was to get them to meet.

I convinced my father to have lunch with me at the club the next day, and I asked Lucy to arrange the same with her mother. We met, the two of us, a quarter of an hour before.

She was trembling.

"Are you all right?"

"I'm fine."

"No. You're not."

"If you're nice to me right now, Charlie, I'm going to burst into tears. The best thing you can do for me is say something mean." She was looking at me expectantly.

"I . . . can't."

Her features seemed to sag. "Please."

The whispered word tore at my heart. "You're the most ornery, most cantankerous woman I've ever known."

Her mouth turned up at a corner.

"And the most beautiful."

"Charlie." Her lips curved into a wobbly smile as she stretched out a gloved hand toward me.

"If you weren't a Kendall . . ." I leaned toward her as I took her hand in my own.

351

Her mother walked into the dining room and Lucy stiffened, pulling her hand from mine.

I gave her hand a squeeze before I released it.

When my father appeared, five minutes later, I led him toward the table where the Kendalls were seated. As we approached, Mrs. Kendall nodded. Lucy glared. If I didn't know how frightened she was, how betrayed she felt, I never would have known it.

"I believe you all have met." I smiled for the benefit of Lucy's mother.

Father took the cigar from his mouth. "It's been a while."

Lucy tried to smile, but the warmth didn't reach her eyes. "Why don't you both sit with us?"

I pulled out a chair and sat before anyone could protest, leaving my father standing. He looked away from us toward a table in the corner. "I don't think—"

I looked up at him. "You and Mrs. Kendall must have a lot to talk about. With those Germans intending to make an offer for City Confectionery."

Mrs. Kendall's mouth dropped open, but she quickly shut it up.

My father cleared his throat. "I don't think you ought to be talking business in front of the ladies, Charles."

"Please don't worry yourself, Mr. Clarke." Lucy's look was withering. "My mother certainly has no qualms about talking business in front of you."

"Lucy . . . ?" Mrs. Kendall sounded as if she were pleading.

"It was you, wasn't it? We knew there was a spy in the company, and it was you." Lucy's eyes were begging her mother to deny it.

Mrs. Kendall only sighed. "It was."

"But why?!"

47

Lucy

There was only one way any of this made sense. "Are you . . . trying to sell us to *Standard*?"

Mother did nothing to avoid the accusation. In fact, she seemed to welcome it, her eyes flashing. "Who else did you think would want to buy us?"

"But—*Standard*?"

She raised her chin. "Yes. Standard Candy Manufacturing!"

"You would have sold *our company* to Mr. Clarke?"

"I already gave it to him once. I thought that would be the end of it. But then your father started the confectionery—"

"Wait a minute." Charlie was pointing a finger at his father. "Just one minute. This favor you've always talked about owing . . ."

His father had pulled a cigar from his coat pocket and was rolling it between his fingers. "Well, you see . . ."

"There's no point in denying it, Warren."

Warren? My mother had called him Warren? As if they were . . . friends?

"We made a deal, back ten years ago." Mr. Clarke was looking at my mother from the corner of his eyes as he spoke.

Mother was nodding. "I arranged it so he could have the company."

Arranged it? "You stole it!"

"Stole it?" Mr. Clarke laughed. "Edith had the contracts written up for me. All I had to do was sign them."

Lies! Why wouldn't they tell the truth? "Stop being friends!" I must have said it too loudly, for the members at the other tables turned to look at ours. I lowered my voice. "Stop it."

Mr. Clarke blinked. "But your mother did me the favor of a lifetime."

"And so this past summer, after I realized your father wasn't getting better, I asked for his help in return. The company would already have been sold if you hadn't come back from Europe so set against it."

"But—"

"And if you hadn't contacted the Germans."

"I didn't!" At least I gained some satisfaction from the confusion that clouded her eyes. "I made that up."

Her mouth crimped down. "Then all you've done is delay the inevitable. I've already accepted Warren's offer. All you've done by delaying is to leave the company in worse shape for him." She looked over at him. "I'm sorry. I meant to offer you a company worth your money and now . . ."

Mr. Clarke looked at me. "At the time of my offer, back in the summer, it was a fair price. But then you threatened to tell your father and you insisted on keeping things going . . ." He stared at his cigar. "I don't mind telling you what I agreed to is now an overpayment. The longer I had to wait, the more I wanted to have it all over and done with. So your mother agreed to help things along by telling me your plans."

My mother reached for my hand. "All I've ever wanted is to be rid of the candy business. Your father could have had a perfectly decent job down at your grandfather's bank, and he would still have his health. He could have been the chairman by now. We could have moved from Vandeventer Place. And . . . and *I* could have been the one to take you to Europe! You could have loved me."

I looked over at the man who had once loomed so large in my life. He no longer seemed especially fearsome. I turned back and spoke softly. "I didn't ever not love you, Mama."

She began to cry. "That's the first time you've called me that since you've been back. Did you know that? I sent you to Europe with my sister knowing that it could only take you further away from me. Only put more distance between us. But how could I not have allowed you to go? How could I not let you improve yourself?"

Why hadn't I ever been good enough for her the way I was?

"Truly, Lucy. What I've done, I've always done for you."

I pushed away from the table. "But you've betrayed us. Both of us."

"Betrayed you! All I've ever done is try to look after you and your father. You haven't an ounce of sense between you. Candy won't keep you in clothes or in food."

"You've never understood us."

She threw up her hands in apparent exasperation. "No, I guess I never have. I've never understood what it's all about."

"It's about money." Charlie's father pronounced those words quite firmly.

Both Charlie and I turned on him. "No, it's not!"

"It's about . . . it's about dreams." Charlie spoke to his father almost viciously. "And the world being perfect for just one moment."

Mr. Clarke shook his head as he looked at me. "Things have a way of working out for the best. Once I buy City Confectionery, I'm going to give it to Charles to manage. I can see you have some hold on his affections. Maybe he'll even keep the name."

It would have been kinder to have struck me. I closed my eyes against the greatest betrayal I had ever experienced. I'd known Charlie was my enemy. I had fought against him knowing that we only wanted what our fathers did, but I could never look at him again knowing he'd wanted to take what was mine. "Charlie?" I was hoping that he would tell me it wasn't true. That his father was mistaken.

"It wasn't my idea."

"So you're really going to . . ."

"That was never what I wanted. It was his idea. Lucy, you have to believe—"

I walked from the room, trying my best not to give voice to the sob that was strangling my throat.

Once home, I fled to father's room. I couldn't help it. Mine seemed so desolate and lonely. "It's over. Mother's sold the company." There was no point in keeping it from him any longer. Tears cascaded down my cheeks. I pulled off my gloves and swiped at them with one of the leather fingers.

"She told me."

"I tried, Papa. I tried to save the company."

"I don't see how you could have done much about it."

"I tried to make a new candy, and I tried to make people buy more Fancies. And then, I tried to marry Alfred Arthur. But none of it worked!" Nothing I'd tried had made the slightest bit of difference.

"I know, Sugar Plum." He opened his arms to me, and I knelt beside the bed and took refuge in them.

"I wanted to save the company for you."

"I know you did. But now it's time to let it go."

"I tried. I tried to do it, but you were right about me." That's what hurt the most. "I'm not any good at making candy. I'm not good at any of it."

"Not good at it? You're better than I ever was."

"But . . . but you always said . . . you said you didn't want me making candy."

He leaned forward and brushed my tear-drenched hair from my cheek. "I always said I didn't want you in the confectionery because I knew what it would do to you, not because you weren't good at it. You're too much like me. I didn't want you to make a mess of things the way I had. You have all the talent in the world, but even talent won't keep sugar from burning if you keep it on the stove too long."

Lines of fatigue had set in around his mouth. I'd overtaxed him with my worries. I kept forgetting he wasn't well. "I just wanted you to be proud of me."

"I've always been proud of you."

Now I was crying in earnest. "It's not fair."

"Life's not fair, Lucy. It's not fair that a moment's inattention can turn taffy into toffee. But they both have their uses."

"What are we going to do?"

"We're selling the company, just like last time, and we're letting someone else worry about it."

" . . . last time?"

"Just like when we sold it to Clarke the first time. We've done this before, we can do it again."

"But you always said that he stole it. Did . . . did he not steal it?" Had Charlie really been telling the truth the whole time?

He put a hand atop mine. "That's what it felt like, Sugar Plum. Imagine walking into work, into my own company even, and being told I didn't have the right to be there anymore. That I couldn't even make my own candy. It felt . . . it felt like . . . it felt like watching sugar burn. There's nothing you can do to stop it or make it better. It's too late to do anything at all."

"Then he didn't steal it from you?"

"That's sure what it felt like." He was staring off into the space beyond my left shoulder, and what color had been in his face had drained away.

"You should get some rest, Papa."

He started. "What?"

"Rest. You should get some rest."

"I've had a lot of time to think in the past few months. Your mother has always been right about me. And you can say anything you want about Warren Clarke, but he's done better with that taffy than I ever did. Can't fault him for profiting from my mistakes. He deserved the company."

I tried to smile, but I just couldn't. How could he say a Clarke deserved anything? I left him and went down the hall to my room, sat down on the floor in the corner where my silk chair used to be, and wept. If father had actually made an agreement, then the loss of Royal Taffy wasn't Mr. Clarke's fault. It was my father's fault.

Everything I'd believed to be true was a lie.

That night I woke with a fright. I sat, hand at my heart, listening for whatever had jolted me from sleep. As I waited there came a thunderous explosion. It rattled the windows in their casements and it lightened the curtains drawn over them, sending light streaking across the bedroom.

I jumped from bed and drew the curtains back. The sky glowed above the rooftops of the houses across the street.

As I stood there, I heard another explosion and saw flames flash against the night sky. I put a hand to my eyes to block the brightness. It looked to be happening down south. At just about the place where I used to see the Standard Manufacturing smokestack pierce the sky.

Only . . . it wasn't there anymore.

Apprehension squeezed my heart as I slipped away from the house the next morning. I had tried, all night, to convince myself that the explosion had nothing to do with Standard.

It hadn't worked.

I took the streetcar to Grand Avenue and then walked south, hat pulled low across my forehead, fur coat drawn tight about me. Curls of smoke drifted across a pale sky. The farther I went, the more an acrid odor permeated the air. It was interlaced with the smell of burnt sugar. When I finally reached the corner of Magnolia and Nebraska, I saw my fears had been well-founded. Standard Candy lay blackened and broken, the ribs of its factory steaming in the morning's light. Though I had thought to get there before anyone else had risen, and in spite of the fact it was a Sunday, I joined a crowd of dozens who had gathered to view the sight.

Firemen were about, rushing here and there, when flames flared from the charred ruins.

Charlie was there. He was standing beside his father, staring silently at the scorched and twisted mess. As I watched, a creaking groan spread through the building. A fireman shouted. The crowd shifted backward as the last of the supports crumbled and fell into the smoldering ruins.

A heady kind of elation soared in my heart until the words of Winnie Compton came back to me: *"You're mean and bossy and selfish."* She'd been absolutely right. I was.

I hurried from that place, stumbling back north. I nearly ran the first four blocks, but I had to pause, lungs heaving, to collect my breath.

I returned to the house just as Mrs. Hughes was stirring up the fire.

"You're up early. Did you hear that excitement last night? Sounded like the Fourth of July!"

"I heard it." I walked past her toward the front hall.

"Don't you want any breakfast?"

I wasn't hungry.

"You're mean and bossy and selfish. . . . You've never been nice."

Winnie was right. I'd been all those things. I still was. What I'd felt as I saw the smoldering ruins was triumph, not pity. Only it wasn't a victory. The Clarkes weren't the villains in all of this. My father was.

And so was I.

We were two candies pressed in the same mold who wanted to blame others for their failings. I took after my father in more ways than I had ever wanted to. But now, I could finally see the truth. My mother was the hero of my family. She's the only one of the three of us who had always maintained a firm grip of the possible, who had never stooped to lying, cheating, or sabotage . . . until I'd forced her to.

I begged off going to church that morning, saying I wasn't feeling well. But the fire was all anyone wanted to talk about. Mother mentioned it in passing when she came up to see me after church. And that's all Sam could speak of later that afternoon when he came over with his father to have dinner with us. By then, nerves had driven me from my room down to the parlor. I couldn't stand to be alone with my thoughts any longer.

"It burned all the way to the ground. You should see it, Lucy!" He whispered the words as we ate dessert.

I had.

"I doubt they'll be able to rebuild."

That's what I'd wanted, wasn't it? I'd wanted Standard to be destroyed.

"It's uncanny, isn't it?"

"What is?"

"That fire. It's like God heard your prayers or something."

After Sam and his father left, I wrapped the fur coat around me and headed out the door. I needed . . . something.

I needed not to be myself anymore. I needed to change.

Though I had no place to go, I struck off down the street and out of Vandeventer Place. Before I knew where I was going, I was walking up the steps of the church.

It's not that I wanted to talk to God.

That's what I'd been trying hard not to do ever since I'd left for the Continent. In all of the churches that I'd visited in Europe, in all the cathedrals that I'd seen, I'd made a point of ignoring the divine. If God had given me such a passion and talent for something I wasn't allowed to do, I'd decided He deserved it. But it turned out my passion was misguided, and I didn't have all that much talent for making candy anyway.

Everything I'd thought His fault was actually mine.

I paused at the top of the steps. When I couldn't think of anywhere better to go, I opened the door and went inside. And then I slid into the back pew; I didn't have any right to sit up closer. Not until I set a few things straight.

48

Charlie

I'd thought the church a safe bet for some peace and quiet. Things were glum back at the house. The fire summed up my life to this point. All my hopes, all my dreams, all my hard work come to nothing.

Mrs. Kendall and my father. Who would have thought it?

Maybe I should have put my efforts into helping Lucy and her company instead of trying to destroy them. At least I would have been helping an honorable cause.

Father had vowed to catch whoever had set fire to the factory, but having seen the factory from the floor, I knew there were a thousand ways a fire could have started that had nothing to do with criminals or arson.

I heard the door to the church scrape open and was surprised, a moment later, to see Lucy slide into the pew opposite mine. I was going to say something, but then I saw tears making a trail down her cheek.

I'd dried those tears once, but I had no right to anymore.

Not when she had looked at me with such shock and betrayal before she'd run from the club.

She folded her arms atop the pew in front of her and rested her head on them with a sob. "I give up!"

"So do I."

She gave a cry as she jumped. "Charlie Clarke." Her protest wasn't very loud, and it wasn't very heated. In fact, she seemed kind of tired. And worn.

"Sorry."

"Are you . . . are you following me?"

That made me smile. "No. Can't a person talk to God in private? Not that it will do any good. Talking to Him, that is."

Those tears kept snaking down her cheeks.

I dug a handkerchief from my pocket and slid down the pew, passing it across the aisle toward her. "It looks like you've won after all. We're through."

The news didn't seem to cheer her. "What are you going to do?"

I shrugged. "Something different. Head out west." Go somewhere no one knew me. Find someplace to start over . . . again.

"Do you know what happened?"

I shook my head. "My father thinks someone set the fire, but my bet's on a spark from one of the machines." I left my pew and went to sit beside her. "What's wrong?"

She turned her head from me. "*You're* asking *me* what's wrong? When it's your company—your whole future—that's been burned to the ground?"

I reached out and turned her chin toward me.

"Can't you even be mean when you have the right to be?" A tear slid down her cheek. "I accused you of such terrible things. But I've done worse—I've been worse—than you ever have. You only watched while someone died. I actually wanted to see you destroyed. I did! You were only suspected of being a criminal;

I would have turned myself into one given half the chance. I've been so selfish and mean and . . . just plain awful. And I'm so sorry. You didn't deserve any of it. And neither did your father. Ten years I've spent hating him for stealing our candy, and all for no good reason."

"Same here. I thought, after he left that day, that my father didn't care about me. I thought he didn't love me. But he did. I've spent so many years hating him . . . and I just . . . can't anymore."

She wiped at her nose with the handkerchief. "But now you have him . . . and everything else."

"I did. But the taffy's gone. It's over."

"It's not that difficult to make."

I shook my head. "It was made in such big batches. And now, without the machines . . ."

"Can't he buy new ones?"

"Well, sure. And he will. Insurance should cover it, but the old machines were . . . old."

"Just ask them to be re-made. Shouldn't the company that made them before be able to do it again?"

"The company's gone out of business. So new machines would have to be found. Different ones." At least that's what my father had said. "Different kinds, different sizes."

"They'd still make fine taffy," she insisted.

"But how would we know much of the ingredients to use? If the drums and vats are different sizes . . ."

"Just use the recipe."

"Nobody knows where it is. And besides, when your father created it, he wasn't using any machines. He was working with pots and ovens and people."

Lucy straightened, brows bent. "Then how were you making it?"

"I don't know." I'd never gotten involved with the actual process. "Everybody just did what they'd always been doing, I guess . . . and now, with everything ruined . . . Say! You don't think your father still has—"

She shook her head. "He wouldn't have the recipe. And besides, he said he'd never make it again. And now he can't."

"But maybe he could remember. Maybe he could tell you and—"

"He can't even get up from bed. How could he make a batch of taffy? Or the five or six he'd need to recreate it?"

"I just wish . . . if we could figure out how to make the taffy—"

Lucy suddenly rose from the bench and pushed past me, handkerchief to her face. "I'm sorry, Charlie. For everything."

I'd had Nelson drive me to the church, but I told him to go on home. I wanted to walk. Halfway home, an idea came to me. It was a long shot, but I hoped it might just work. When I reached Vandeventer Place, I turned onto it. I needed to talk to Lucy.

The maid answered my knock and invited me in. It didn't take long for Lucy to appear at the top of the stairs. As she came down, I could see she wasn't crying anymore, though her eyes were still red. When I explained to her what I wanted, she only blinked as if she didn't understand what I was asking. "You want me to what?"

"I want you to figure out the recipe for Royal Taffy. I know you can do it. Please? You once told me you could make anything. And make it even better than it had been before."

"I don't know, Charlie. . . ."

"Don't you know how to make taffy?"

Her shoulders dropped. "You tasted the result of my last attempt to create a candy."

366

I took her hand in mine. "Please, Lucy. I know you can do it. I need you to do it. I'm begging you. Regardless of your personal feelings for me and for Standard . . . you're our only hope. You could save it all. You could save *me*."

Those last words seemed to reach her. "I'll try." She squared her shoulders as her chin tipped up. "I'll do my best. For you."

I wanted to reach out and kiss her, but she had already agreed to do me one favor. I couldn't bring myself to press her for two.

49

Lucy

My heart stuttered at Charlie's words and then it started once more at a gallop. Make a taffy? I'd always longed to make a taffy, but it was the one thing that had been forbidden when my father lost the company.

After Charlie left, I sent the coachman down to the confectionery for Sam. While I was waiting for him, I gathered all the ingredients that I would need. By the time he appeared I was ready.

"I need your help, Sam."

"Now, Lucy, Jennie's made me promise not to do anything else underhanded. I won't—"

"I'm not going to ask you to steal anything. I don't want you to break any laws. I just. . . ." I wanted it to be like old times again. "Would you help me make some candy?"

His face brightened. "Caramels?"

"No. Taffy."

"Taffy?" He spoke the word slowly, sounding it out, as if it were a trap. "You mean . . . like . . ."

"Yes. Like *Royal* Taffy."

Father's recipe had been a cross between butter taffy and pulled taffy. It had the mouthwatering, creamy taste of the former and the chewy texture of the latter, but the combination meant I might have to do a lot of experimenting. I mixed sugars, water, and vinegar in a big pot. Once it had started to boil, I added some butter. When it was done, I poured it onto a buttered pan and sprinkled some vanilla flavoring on top. Once it cooled enough to handle, I buttered my hands and then gathered it up and gave it to Sam.

He stared at it for a moment before he tried to hand it back. "This doesn't look like Royal Taffy."

"You have to pull it first. Don't you remember?" I pointed to some hooks that had been fastened to the wall years before.

He threw it over one of them, pulled to stretch it, then swung the long ribbon up to re-loop over the hook—looping and pulling and looping and pulling until it stiffened and lightened in color. And by then it was cool enough to taste.

Crossing my fingers behind my back for luck, I lifted a piece to my mouth, closed my eyes, and took a bite.

It was nothing like a Royal Taffy. Wrong taste, wrong texture. "Throw it away."

"Throw—? What! Why?" He was already chewing on a big hunk of it as he wiped sweat from his brow with the sleeve of his shirt.

"Throw it away. It's not right."

I made five batches of taffy that afternoon, varying the amounts of white and brown sugar, adding more butter to some, using less in others. But they were all wrong. I'd finally gotten the texture, but I hadn't yet discovered how to match the taste.

There was something distinctive about Royal Taffy that my own taffy lacked. There was a sweetness to it that I couldn't seem to duplicate. It wasn't about sugar. I'd tried adding even more, but it had only made everything worse.

The next morning, I woke determined to fix my recipe. The texture was perfect. More than perfect. If I couldn't taste anything, I would swear I was making Royal Taffy. But the proof was in the taste, and I hadn't yet mastered it.

It looked right, it felt right, it even smelled right.

But something was off, and I had to figure out why. Duplicating Royal Taffy was the only way I knew to show Charlie how truly sorry I was about everything.

The kitchen door slammed as I was eating breakfast.

Sam!

I excused myself from Mother and went back into the kitchen to catch him before he disappeared.

He took one look at me and went right back outside.

I went after him. "Sam—I need your help this morning. I want to make more—"

"No. No more taffy!"

"I really need you, Sam. I can't pull it by myself."

He took his hat from his head. "I've more work to do than candy making. I'm paid to get things done around here."

"Please, Sam. I'm desperate."

"My arms won't work anymore! And I still have to muck out the stables; I was supposed to do it yesterday. I'm not some machine, Lucy, I'm a man." With that, he clapped his hat back on his head and stalked out toward the stable.

I went back into the kitchen. He'd have to come into the house sooner or later. And when he did, I'd ask him again to help me.

I peeled some potatoes and chopped some carrots for Mrs.

Hughes. But after that, I gathered the ingredients for taffy again and started once more from the beginning.

I'm not a machine.

That much was true. Only a machine would never tire of pulling taffy. I'd always quickly wearied of it as a child, back when my father still made the candy.

It had been magical back then, seeing those batches turned out of the copper kettles and the workers pulling it out into ropes. Even though I always buttered my hands before working with the taffy, I used to lick my palms afterward, enjoying the mix of my salty sweat and the sweet candy.

As I thought about my candy making days, back when my father had been well, I felt a smile lift the corners of my mouth. I closed my eyes, and I could almost taste the product of our time together.

My eyes flew open. That was it! Sam was right. He was a man, not a machine. That was the whole problem. I stepped out onto the back porch. "Sam!"

This time there came no footsteps in response to my call. No answer to my plea.

I stepped from the back porch and out into the yard. "Sam?"

"I'm not coming, Lucy." His cry drifted out from the corner of the house.

"Sam—I figured it out! You have to help me."

"Jennie's waiting for me. I told her I'd take her out for a soda. I'll be back later. I can help you then."

"But—this is more important! I need you now."

He peered at me from the corner. "There's nothing more important than my Jennie."

His Jennie? "What am I supposed to do?"

"You got along just fine without me on that long trip you

took. I expect you'll get along just fine without me now." He disappeared.

Frustrated and determined, I turned on my heel and hurried inside. I needed help, and I needed it now. Running upstairs, I grabbed my hat.

"Lucy?" Mother called as I ran out the front door. "Your father! Be quiet."

"I have to do something. I'll be back." I shoved the door closed with my foot as I pulled on my gloves.

I followed Sam to the Clarke house. While he went around to the back, I walked up the steps to the front. A butler opened the door at my knock. I put my card into the silver tray he held out, then stepped into the front hall.

"Mr. Clarke, please. Mr. *Charlie* Clarke."

His brows quirked, but he showed me to a parlor, bowing as he took his leave. I sat on a chair and passed the time looking at the room around me. I had always thought Vandeventer Place the ultimate in addresses, but I realized as I sat there that time and progress had conspired to surpass it. The homes here at Portland Place had doubled in both size and elegance.

Fifteen minutes passed before Charlie appeared. I marked each minute by the mantel clock.

"Lucy?"

Thank goodness! I was beginning to think he might not be home. "I need your help."

"Then I'm at your service."

"Come with me. And please don't wear anything you don't want dirtied."

"So now you want me to . . . ?"

"Here." I handed him two sheets of cellophane that I'd rubbed with sweet butter. "Wrap them around your hands and then pull the taffy from those two hooks." I gestured toward them with a lift of my chin. I was measuring out ingredients to boil up another batch.

"I don't know how." He was just standing there looking at me as if I'd asked him to leap over the moon.

"Then you have no business selling candy, Charlie Clarke!" I took the cellophane from him and picked up the lump of taffy, looping it over one of the hooks. Then I pulled, hard. It stretched out into a long rope. I swung it around like a jump rope to loop it over the hook again. "Like that. You'll have to do it until the color lightens." I left the taffy hanging there and handed him the cellophane.

"Doesn't look that hard."

Ten minutes later, he was puffing and panting, wiping the sweat from his brow with a swipe of his forearm. "Tell me it's almost done."

"It's almost done."

"Are you telling me the truth?"

"No."

"I can see why we had machines to do this. How much longer?"

"A couple more pulls."

He pulled once. Twice.

"Now three more."

"If you weren't doing me such a big favor, I'd have left by now."

I let him pull for a few more minutes and then stopped him mid-pull. "It's done." I stood on tiptoe and took it down from the hooks. Putting in on the table, I patted and smoothed it. And then I cut it, forming it into Royal Taffy-shaped pieces. I wanted so much for it to be right! I handed him one. "Try it."

"Don't you want to go first?"

I shook my head. I was too afraid that I would taste what I wanted to taste instead of what was.

He bit into it and then pulled. The taffy trailed long thread-like strings as he pulled it from his mouth. He closed his eyes as he chewed. A look of triumph flashed across his face and then relief relaxed his features. He opened his eyes. "You did it!" He passed the rest of the piece to me.

I took a bite.

It felt right.

I chewed. Swallowed.

It tasted right too!

"I did it!"

With a whoop, he embraced me. For just a moment, I enjoyed the feel of his arms around me, but then I pushed him away. I didn't deserve his thanks or admiration. I didn't deserve anything.

I sent Charlie home with the promise that I would transcribe the recipe. After checking and re-checking the amounts that I'd used, I wrote it down using proportional measures. That way, no matter the size or capacity of the machines, it would always taste the same.

I went to see Father before dinner.

He smiled when he saw me and put aside the book he had been reading. "I never had much time for books before." His smile was apologetic.

"It's the third one I've seen you with this week."

He held it up so I could view the cover. *Tom Swift and His Airship*. "It's difficult to stop." He placed it on the table next to a pitcher of water. "You seem distracted lately, Sugar Plum." His glance was fixed to my cuff.

I looked down and saw a splotch of taffy clinging to it.

"I've done something, Papa. Said some things. And now I don't know how to fix them."

"A candy coating covers a multitude of sins."

I wished it were that easy. "But what if . . . I've gone too far? What if I've done something . . . bad? Denied forgiveness and understanding to people who truly deserved it?"

"Well . . . if you've reached the hard-crack stage, there's no point in trying to get back to firm-ball."

No. Nothing could be the same between Charlie and me, or between my mother and me, as it had been before. "Do you think a person can do something bad enough that they can't ever be forgiven?"

He sighed. "Well, now . . . I don't know. God, for instance— He can forgive anything."

"Do you really think so? Truly?"

"He's supposed to love us. Forgiving comes with the loving, to my way of thinking."

"I've never . . . I mean . . . how can you *know* that He does? What if things don't make any sense? What if there's no way to make a happy ending out of how I've acted? Or what I've done?"

"A good candymaker can use almost anything, can't he? Just because you've got sugar and butter doesn't mean you have to make a caramel. Why can't you make something else? And besides, who's to say a caramel is better than a brittle?"

But I liked caramels. I leaned over and kissed him on the forehead. My dear, sweet Papa. It used to be that candy could solve all my problems.

"You're frowning."

"Not everything has to do with candy." I'd spent a lot of time wishing Charlie weren't a Clarke. For the first time, I could remember, I wished I weren't a Kendall.

I made another batch of taffy that night, after everyone had gone to bed. I owed the Clarkes something more than a recipe. The recipe was theirs by right. If I wanted to make a true apology, I owed them something more. Something true. Something of myself. And like Father always said, a candy coating covered a multitude of sins.

For the second day in a row, Lucy showed up on my doorstep. She thrust two cellophane-wrapped packets into my hand. "I want you try one of each of those and tell me which is better."

"One of . . . ?" I looked down at the packages.

"They're candies."

When I glanced up from the packets, she was nibbling on her lip. "Now?"

"Please."

I led her into the parlor, then put the packets down on the tea table and opened them. Both sets looked like Royal Taffy. "We already tried these yesterday. And they're fine. They're perfect."

"Just try one of each." Her hands wound around each other, and she looked for all the world as if she wanted to be anywhere but there.

I chose a piece from the first packet and took a bite. It tasted like a Royal Taffy. "It's fine. If you're worried whether you got it right—"

"I'm not. It's right. But . . . could you try the other?"

I picked up a piece from the second batch and tried it. "It's . . ." There was something crunchy inside.

She was looking at me with such fear. And such hope.

I liked it. I liked it a lot. "It's better. It's even better than the first one."

Triumph flared for one brief instant in her eyes. And then it died. "You're just saying that." She whispered the words as if she couldn't bear not to believe me.

"I'm not. It is." It was. There was something new, and fresh, and crunchy about it. It made my father's Royal Taffy seem old and tired.

"What's this?" My father walked into the parlor. His gaze came to rest on Lucy.

She took a deep breath as she faced him. "I've made a candy, and I think it's even better than Royal Taffy."

He grunted. But when she held out a piece toward him, he took it. As he bit into it, his brows flared, and then he nodded. "You must have your father's talent. But how are you going to produce something like this in that kitchen of yours? Times have changed. People want more, faster."

"I'm not planning to produce it. I'm giving it to you to make once the factory's been rebuilt." She took a piece of paper from her pocket and laid it on the table next to the packet.

My father was stretching for the paper. "Let me see that."

I blocked his hand. "Don't you dare give it to him, Lucy!"

She blinked, but she took it up once more. "But . . . it's his. You asked me to make it for you."

"It's *yours*. You're the one who recreated Royal Taffy. If it weren't for you, we'd have nothing at all."

My father was pointing to the recipe she held. "It is mine. By rights, it's mine. I signed a contract for that candy."

I took the recipe from her. "But you changed the recipe, Lucy. You made it better. You could have great success with this. This candy is what you've been hoping for."

My father scoffed. "It might be different, but I don't know that it's *better*."

I lifted a hand toward Jennie, who'd been passing in the front hall. "Come over here for a minute, Miss Harrison. I'd like to ask you a question."

She eyed me for a moment and I thought she'd refuse, but then she stepped into the room.

"Tell me which of these you like better." I gave her one of each piece of candy. The original recipe and Lucy's new one.

She tried them both.

"I liked the second one."

I smiled. "Thank you, Miss Harrison." I included Father in my smile. "That piece was Lucy's."

"It doesn't mean anything. It's still a Royal Taffy."

Jennie looked at him oddly. "No, sir, it's not."

"Yes, it is. Now, then." He addressed himself to Lucy. "Give that recipe to me."

"Don't do it!" City Confectionery was already ours, but with this new recipe, Lucy could start another company.

"She owes it to me."

I turned on my father. "She owes you nothing. You walked away from one life and had the good luck to just walk into another. You never did the hard work needed to make anything. But Lucy has. If you want this recipe, then you're going to have to pay for it. You're going to have to give something up in order to get what you want this time."

Lucy stepped away from both of us. "I do owe it to him." She looked at me. "And to you, Charlie. So here." She stepped past me and handed the recipe to my father on her way to the door.

My father shoved the recipe into his pocket and strode through the parlor toward the front hall. "Now, Charles. Let's get to work. We have a factory to rebuild. And a new candy to produce. Are you coming?"

"I . . . don't know." The butler was opening the door for Lucy.

My father stopped. Turned around. "I could stand here and offer apologies forever, but it's not going to change what happened, and it's not going to fix anything. I can never give you back the time we were apart; I'll regret that until I die. And you can think of me what you will, but that's not going to change anything either. Can we agree that I took a coward's way out when I gave you my responsibilities? And can I tell you that I'm proud of the way you took care of the family and proud of the man you've become?"

"You're . . . proud of me?"

"I always have been. And I'm too old to be starting over again. I need you, son." He extended his hand.

"You know, we never wanted you to be something you weren't. We just . . . we just wanted you. To be there with us."

"I'm sorry." He said it with tears glistening in his eyes. "You'll never know how sorry I am."

Because I couldn't bear to look at him anymore, I threw an arm around him. And then, at last, he gave me the one thing I'd always really wanted: an embrace. I couldn't see my father through the tears in my eyes, but there was something I needed to say to him. "If it's all right with you, then, I think I will stay. And I'll help you. With everything."

For the next few days, I followed Father and Mr. Gillespie around the factory site, planning for the rebuilding. I made it clear that what had happened before should not be allowed to happen again.

"All the machines in the process need to be located next to each other. In the order they're used."

"Standard practice." Father waved off my concerns.

"No. It wasn't. It was never standard practice."

He stopped and looked at me. "What do you mean?"

"I mean that children were carrying the syrup in wheelbarrows from one side of the building to the other and then back again."

His brows spiked. "Not very efficient."

"No. And we're not going to employ children anymore."

"Why not? They worked well before."

"They're not very efficient. And besides that, it's just not right. When we order the new machines, we'll make sure that small hands aren't needed to work them."

"But they minimize costs. We don't have to pay them as much as an adult."

"We shouldn't be employing them at all. If you want me to stay, then you'll have to agree. And we shouldn't just have employees. We're making candy, for pete's sake! We should be more like . . . like family."

"Family!"

"Or at least we should treat them that way." Mr. Kendall might have run his company into the ground, but the people at City Confectionery still thought he walked on cotton candy. If there was anything he'd done right, it was the way he'd treated his workers. "There are lots of factory jobs in this city. People should choose to work here because they want to, not because they have to."

Father chewed on his cigar for a while, but eventually he agreed with me. "You seem to have it all figured out."

"I do." I did. All except for one thing. I couldn't figure out what to do about Lucy.

Lucy

"There's someone to see you, miss. In the parlor." The maid's voice at my bedroom door interrupted my packing.

"Tell them I'm indisposed." It wasn't far from the truth. I was helping Mother pack up the house. I'd long since made my peace with her. In a way, she'd been right all along: Candy hadn't been good for any of us. So we were leaving it, and St. Louis, behind, preparing for a move to Denver. The doctor thought the dry air would be better for my father.

The confectionery was being inventoried for the sale to Mr. Clarke, and the papers were to be brought over at the end of the week for signing. Though it was already the first of March, with the convenience of trains and frequent stops along the way, we hoped to have Father settled into a new house by Easter.

The maid's footsteps retreated back down the hall as I grabbed at my Queen of Love and Beauty sash and spun it into a ball. Fall had started out with such promise, but if I'd ever done anything to earn that title, I was certain I didn't deserve it now. I jammed it into a trunk and piled some pairs of gloves on top of it.

I opened my hope chest and paused to survey my souvenirs from Europe. My sketchbook from the Alps and the viewing disks from Florence. The lace doilies I'd bought in Brussels. How long ago all of that seemed. How young I had been back then. I started to place some handkerchiefs atop them, then thought the better of it, and put one of the doilies aside for Winnie. The friend I'd never appreciated and never respected—who'd proven to be the truest friend I'd ever had.

Those footsteps returned. They paused in front of my door. "The gentleman says you'd want to see him."

"Really, I don't think that I do."

"But, Miss Lucy—"

"Please, send him away."

The maid looked at me for a long moment. She opened her mouth to speak, but then twisted it shut and turned on her heel. She did not return for quite some time, and when she did it was with another missive. "Your mother would like to see you downstairs, miss."

Sighing, I pushed up from the floor. My hair was slipping its pins, but what did it matter? As I walked down the stairs, I picked pieces of lint from my skirts. When I was done packing, I vowed to find a mop and chase all the dust from my room.

"Yes, Mama?"

I rounded the corner to find Charlie Clarke sitting across the table from her. She was smiling at him.

He scrambled to his feet. His hair was oiled back, his collar was tall, his shoes were gleaming. His suit was . . . immaculate. He looked the perfect gentleman.

I looked the perfect housemaid. I wished I'd had time to pluck all of the lint from my skirts.

"Miss Kendall." Charlie turned his dimpled smile on me.

I struggled to keep it from affecting me. "Mr. Clarke."

"Come, Lucy. Sit." Mother gestured to an open chair, next to Charlie's. "Mr. Clarke has come to us with a proposition."

Charlie turned toward me as I sat. "Rebuilding is underway, and we've begun to order up supplies. But as I was looking at your recipe, I realized there was one thing in it we'd never bought before."

I resisted an urge to bite at my nails. I didn't want to think about sugar, and I didn't want to think about taffy. Candy making was behind me now.

"Your recipe has Fancy Crunch as one of its ingredients."

"I put all of my favorite things into it." I had figured it would be the last chance I'd have to create a recipe, so I'd wanted to make the best candy I could.

"It so happens we never owned a machine that could pan nuts."

No. And at the confectionery we'd always done everything by hand. I glanced over at Mama. She was still smiling. "I suppose . . . are you here to buy our panning trays?" Is that the proposition he had come to make? "I don't think we'd have enough for you—and I'd assumed that they'd go along with the sale, but—"

"No."

I looked up at him. "No? Then—?"

"I'm here to contract with City Confectionery to pan the nuts for us."

" . . . What?"

"I want City Confectionery to make Fancy Crunch for us. Exclusively. We'd need all you have in order to produce our new candy in the amounts that we'll need. It's going to be our new bestseller, so we're willing to pay you a thousand dollars for it."

A thousand! I grabbed Mama's ledger book and quickly did a calculation in the margin. I looked up at her.

She was still smiling.

"A week."

"A week!"

I recalculated and then recalculated again. It couldn't be right. "Are you . . . sure?"

"Yes. At least, that's what I was *hoping* to pay."

"That can't be right."

"Sure it can."

"But the confectionery is yours. You bought it from us. We've all but signed the final papers."

He shrugged. "If you insist." He drew a packet of paper from his coat pocket with a flourish and laid it on the table in front of Mama.

"What is that?" I reached for the papers, but my mother pulled them away and started flipping through them.

"Royal Crunch is going to be produced just as soon as we can start making it, according to your recipe, using candy-coated nuts."

"*City Confectionery's* Fancy Crunch. That's what you'll need to put on the wrapper. If you're using our nuts, then you're going to have to say so." Mama's voice was quite firm. "And you must know that we're planning a move to Denver."

"But . . . but . . ." I didn't understand. I looked over at my mother. "You said you were finished with candy! You said it had been nothing but trouble. And I agree with you."

She looked up from the papers. "I'm finished with scrimping and scraping to get by. I'm finished with being ignored by my husband and my own daughter. But I also realize that I did neither of you any favors by trying to sell your dream out from under you."

Charlie laid a hand on my arm. "I'm aware of your move, although I was hoping . . ." He gave me a look that made me blush. He cleared his throat. "Among other things, I was hoping that instead of selling your company outright, you might consider leasing it to me."

My mother was reading the contract, making notations in the margin. "I'll have to consult our lawyer about this."

Charlie was nodding. "I hope you will."

I was almost afraid to speak. And most definitely afraid to hope. "Leasing . . . you mean we'd be . . ."

"We'd be partners."

Partners!

"If my past doesn't offend you. I'm not proud of the person I was, back in Chicago."

"And I'm not proud of the things that I've done and said since you came to the city. Can we forget about the past and just . . . keep going?"

He looked over at me with regret pooling in his eyes. "No."

"We can't?"

Charlie shook his head. "How can we?"

All of my hopes, all of my delight at seeing him again, died.

"I don't think we should try to forget the past since that's what's brought us here. But maybe . . . ?" As he paused, his dimples flashed.

"Yes?"

"Maybe we can remember and move forward."

"But . . . are you sure, Charlie? *My* candy? You want to sell my candy?" I could hardly dare to believe it.

"Across the nation. It's the best candy that anyone who's tried it has ever tasted."

"But I tried to destroy your company, Charlie. And I tried to hurt you."

"You did hurt me."

"I'm so sorry."

He smiled a smile that made everything inside me turn to syrup. "I'm sorry, too."

"I just wanted . . ."

"To win. I know. So did I. But I discovered there's something even sweeter than winning." Charlie took my hand and pulled me up from the chair.

"What's that?"

"You." He bent to kiss me, cupping his hands to my face.

There was a time when I never would have admitted it, but he was right. There was something sweeter than winning. I put my hands to his wrists, trying to find some anchor against the sensations that had made my head spin.

"Surely Mr. Clarke can do better than this!" Mama was clucking over the contract, crossing out something in the text.

"Yes, I'm sure he can." Charlie winked at me.

I smothered a laugh, and then I rose up on my toes and closed my eyes as he bent to kiss me again.

A Note
from the Author

Candy is a surprisingly serious business. On occasion, it's even been a ruthless one. Recipes cannot be patented or copyrighted, so the industry has been subject to corporate espionage since its beginnings. The hijacking of delivery trucks, stealing of recipes, and other acts of mischief were not uncommon.

The turn of the last century saw an evolution in the industry from the anonymous penny candy made in private kitchens to marketed and branded candy made by gigantic factories. It also saw the interplay between the practices of the nineteenth century's big-business tycoons and twentieth-century progressives, between sweat-shop labor and laws that promoted workers' rights. In 1914 Arkansas became the first state to enact a child labor law. It took a while, but the nation finally followed suit in 1938.

Candy was the great leveler of American society, one of the first conspicuous luxuries that became available to the lower classes. Candy wasn't just a treat back then, it was an arriving.

389

In an era where consumption by the masses was growing, to buy a piece of candy was, in a very literal sense, to buy a piece of the American dream.

Though the candy industry has always offered a diverse array of treats, Americans have a long tradition of scorning anything having to do with hazelnuts, just as Europeans have generally disdained everything having to do with peanuts.

Flying machines were sights to behold when they first took to the skies. By 1910, nearly anyone who'd read a newspaper knew air machines truly flew, but, like the doubting apostle Thomas, they didn't actually believe it until they saw it for themselves. What a wonder that must have been! On October 11, 1910, at Kinloch Field in St. Louis, Teddy Roosevelt became the first president to fly in an airplane.

When I was planning this story, I wasn't quite sure where to set it. Something inside me whispered *St. Louis*, even though I wasn't familiar with the city. But as I began to research, I realized my subconscious was smarter than I was. At one time St. Louis represented everything that was big and wonderful and full of promise in America. It was a perfect location for this story. Those readers familiar with St. Louis will know that I did not make up the Veiled Prophet Ball. A Queen of Love and Beauty has been crowned at that ball for over one hundred and thirty years. Although the event was originally planned to coincide with harvest, in recent times it has been moved to the month of December. In 1910, Lucy Norvell was crowned the Queen of Love and Beauty. In the interest of disclosure, I should mention here that I chose my Lucy's name long before I discovered this fact.

Mr. Jacob Mahler of the black velvet ballet slippers ruled the ballrooms of St. Louis well into the 1920s. His dance studio provided the required social training for several generations of the city's elite. Over thirty Queens of Love and Beauty grew up under his watchful eye.

The independent woman and the single mother are not inventions of modern society. History is filled with stories of women who were discarded by their husbands or had to learn how to make do when their spouses weren't able to function due to disease or disposition. We like to think people in the past did things the right way, but that's never been true. The very first family in recorded history was dysfunctional.

Great injustices and many prejudices are produced the moment we decide we're better than everyone else. Most of the time, in a paraphrase of Winnie Compton: *We're all the same at believing we're not the same and being wrong because we are. It's about God . . . and what He's done. It's not about us. It's never been about us. Because we're not good enough, and we never will be.*

— *Acknowledgments* —

To my agent, Natasha Kern, and to my editors, Dave and Sarah Long, who were excited about this book from the word candy. To the wise person who suggested the perfect solution to my biggest character problem . . . and inadvertently discovered one of the themes of this novel. To Maureen Lang, first reader and friend, who encouraged me during a frenetic writing schedule. To Erin Fryman who graciously answered my questions about candy making. And to my husband, Tony, whose love is sweeter even than candy.

More Historical Romance From Siri Mitchell

For more on Siri and her books, visit sirimitchell.com

Hannah has never questioned her Quaker beliefs. But as lives hang in the balance, will she be forced to choose between forsaking the man she loves and abandoning the bedrock of her faith?

The Messenger

Three seamstresses at an opulent dress shop dream of a better life. But will the secrets they harbor cost them the love they desire?

A Heart Most Worthy

She lives in a world where wealth and image are everything—and she is loved by all. But at what cost?

She Walks in Beauty